KING CITY GANGSTERS

The Snowdon Massacre

Raymond G Dennis

Forgetful Farm Press
Susquehanna, PA

Dedication

For my son Aaron, who asked me to write short stories
to accompany his board game. King City Gangsters, to
which I wrote a novel instead.

____

Acknowledgement

Thank you, Nanc (my loving wife), for your patience,
proofreading, and supporting my crazy ideas.

TABLE OF CONTENTS

EPISODE 1

THE SNOWDON MASSACRE

"Well, if it ain't Danny O'Shea, the only honest copper in King City." The voice of Desk Seargent Murphy, with its deep Irish brogue, reminded me of my fault-finding father. It echoed around the lobby of the Carvonshire Station House.

"Come to pick up your pay?" The Sarge, a hefty man, looked down on me from behind his equally hefty oak desk.

"Yeah, Sarge, every Friday afternoon, like clockwork." I was real sure I was the only honest cop in the Carvonshire District, not sure about the whole of King City.

"Don't you feel guilty about tak'en the money? Your sheet is pretty slim."

Big talk for a bum who spends his time pushing papers around, making like he's doing something.

But then, he had a point; my arrest record hadn't been stellar of late. The way I see it though, fighting crime is more about protecting King City citizens rather than boosting your stats or fixing things up for appearances after the fact. Besides, I'm the go-to guy when serious crimes need solving.

"Nah, don't bother me at all, Sarge. Least I'm not just sitt'en on my fat ass all day."

"Punk."

With that, I left Murphy hanging and strolled down the hall to the cash room, where Officer Dulley was issuing weekly pay in stacks of greenbacks. I only got what was coming to me, my detective salary, not anything more. I had no claim on that side pile of dough supplied by the Jones Gang, the mob that ran the Carvonshire District. But I have to admit, the payola kept things running smooth in Carvonshire, but I wanted no part of it.

Before prohibition, we had crime to deal with. But since then, King City has been lousy with opportunities for criminal enterprise, while citywide corruption was a foregone conclusion. Bootlegging was at the center of it all. I tried my best to navigate it.

"How's it going, Dulley?" I said, as I settled in front of the barred cash window.

"Ducky, O'Shea. How about you?"

"Same." I leaned one elbow on the counter as Dulley counted out my pay.

"Are you plann'en on dispose'n of all this moola tonight?"

That wasn't a fair assessment. I'm a responsible guy: pay my rent and my bills. I spread my money around; don't spend it all Friday night. Not all of it, maybe most of it.

What's a single fella in King City supposed to do, anyway; live like a monk, give to charity, support his mother and her slacker boyfriend?

"Go'en to Lizzy's tonight. There's a band in from Chicago."

"Oh yeah, I heard of them, Big Agnes and her jazz trio. My wife would love to see them. Do you think you could get us in?" Dulley's hand rested on my stack of greenbacks. I'm also the go-to guy in the precinct for access to the nightlife venues. I got my connections.

"Sure thing, Dulley. I plan on head'en over early. I'll leave word with the doorman. Say O'Shea sent ya."

"Nifty. Thanks O'Shea." He passed the cash across the counter and under the bars.

Lizzy's ain't my regular hang-out. I prefer the speakeasy on Griffin Street over a clip joint (*) like Lizzy's. Griffin's is nice and quiet, no ruckus, and has decent local bands, mostly playing ballad-style jazz, real smooth. But Lizzy's brings in the out-of-town entertainment, big names. But then, Griffin Street has got the prettiest dames; it's a toss-up most Fridays.

Another downside to Lizzy's is that it's owned by Maxine Snowden, the crime boss of the Jones Gang. She uses the place as her headquarters.

Max and I aren't on the best of terms. Meaning, she doesn't have anything on me (I don't take bribes), and I don't have anything on her, unfortunately. I can't write her off, though. I do owe her a favor that goes way back. For now, we keep our distance. The manager of Lizzy's, Johnny Preece, on the other hand, we got history. I scratch his back; he scratches mine.

Back out on the street, the sun was shining for a change, and everything (for the moment) was right with the world. I headed over to Tony's to get my ears lowered. I spent the rest of the afternoon jawing with the boys, which is my usual on Fridays.

It's not like I'm goofing off on Friday afternoons. I take care of business while I'm there. I got an arrangement with Owen, Owen O'Carroll, the shop's proprietor. He bought the shop from an Italian fella when the Italians moved out of the neighborhood, the south end of Carvonshire, when the Irish started moving in. He kept the name Tony's Barbershop. Said it would make his place distinctive, a business decision.

In any case, Tony's is where I make my connections. All my informants know where I'll be on Friday afternoons. That makes it real convenient for them to find me when they got some dirt to share. They don't have to hustle all over town trying to track me down. Try to look out for others; that's my motto.

After a quick stop for supper, I was at the Walgreens Building early. The Walgreens Drug Co. occupied the ground floor.

Old Man Walgreens from Chicago had expanded to King City, opening up a store a few years ago. Thanks to prohibition, he was raking in the dough, selling prescription alcohol at a premium. If a fella could afford it, whiskey was available legally at a steep price for a pint at the pharmacy and the doctor's fee to prescribe it.

My destination, Lizzy's, sat atop the four-story building.

I was puffing a little from climbing the three flights of stairs. Avoiding elevators is a passion of mine; don't trust the contraptions. The squeaking and clanking give me the heebie-jeebies.

Lizzy's is situated at the penthouse level of multiple downtown Carvonshire buildings that create a particularly unique feature of the district that the locals call the Roofs. It is, in effect, a world of its own, and totally controlled by the criminal element.

Along with the building elevators and the stairwells, the Roofs can be reached by staircases that extend up from the elevated train platforms. The El train runs above the city streets, a story and a half above ground. Many of the buildings are also interconnected at the roof level. Once you're up on the Roofs, you can move around from building to building on pedestrian bridges at the roof level, skywalks.

The climb up a stairwell to the Roofs for the entertainment, especially jazz, is worth it for me. A variety of other tastes can be accommodated on the Roofs with its assortment of clip joints, creep joints, gambling dens, and speakeasies. All kinds of nefarious activities are in the works that a copper, such as myself, has to turn a blind eye to in order to spend time taking in a night of jazz and a couple of bourbons (two is my limit).

Besides that, for the most part, those who frequent the Roofs aren't innocent. They're taking the risk and should suffer the consequences for their actions, most of the time just hangovers and regrets.

From the stairwell's penthouse, I crossed the roof to a garden atrium that shields the entry to Lizzy's. At the entrance door, I announced myself with three sharp raps.

I was early. I enjoy spending a little time in peace with my bourbon before the joint erupts. Me and my bourbon have a special relationship.

The peep slot slid back. A couple of shifty eyes looked me up and down. The peep slot closed, and the door swung open.

As promised, I left word with the doorman about Dulley and his wife, who wouldn't arrive until much later.

I made my way to a table near the back hallway door. I skid a chair around and sat down with my back to the wall.

Surveying the place (cops do that), everything had the feel of a typical evening at a clip joint. Two bartenders behind the bar were washing up glasses, a couple of barmaids stood around puffing on their ciggys, and the bouncers at the door stood like statues, arms crossed, hoping for a dull night. Several couples, also early, hoping to get the best seats, were occupying tables near the stage.

Behind me, at the back of the house, was a door flanked by two goons in black suits with sizable bulges under their jackets. They were guarding the door to Max's office, her headquarters. I didn't expect to see her this evening; she seldom appears in public, not even in her own joint, which was fine with me. All I wanted to do was listen to music;

no encounters with unsavory characters, especially the one who controlled the entire Carvonshire District and could snuff people out with a bat of her eyelashes.

The band members passed by me as they entered from the back hallway and headed toward the stage. In place, they started checking for tune. The pianist was tapping the keys. The fella with a trumpet dangling at the end of his arm chatted with the sax guy in between riffs. And the singer, Big Agnes Black, eyes closed, was sipping a drink along with the rhythmic swaying of her generous body from side to side.

This quartet was the reason I came here tonight, a band from the big city with an excellent reputation for pouring out real smooth jazz, my kind of music. Lizzy's is a major hot spot for jazz, not only in the Carvonshire District but all of King City.

A barmaid came round and took my order, two bourbons, straight. I unrolled my wad of Jack (*) and laid a few greenbacks on the table.

There I was sitting, unknown to me at the time, in the calm before the storm. I raised a glass of bourbon to my lips but stopped halfway. The hair on the back of my neck bristled.

Something was wrong; too quiet. I scanned the room real quick. The band members on the stage were huddled up, chatting. From their station at the front door, the two bouncers were moving slow toward the back exit, too slow.

I jumped off my barstool and headed in the direction of the stage, not slow. By the time the first shot rang out, I was running. I leaped onto the stage and gathered up Big Agnes and her band in my arms like a brood of chicks, pushing them back toward the hallway that led to the dressing rooms in the back of the joint.

They got the idea real quick. We ducked into the hallway as a full-fledged gunfight broke out.

"This way." I pointed and hustled the four of them to the back of the hall, to the staircase. Taking up the rear, I checked back, my heater drawn.

We plunged into the darkened stairwell, three flights of steps, noisy but not as noisy as the gunfire up above.

On the ground floor, our gang burst out into another narrow hall. I needed to get to the front. A hand-painted exit sign hung at an angle over the outside door to the alley. "No, no, no!" I yelled.

I grabbed Agnes by the arm and brought her to a halt. "Not that way," with as loud and commanding a voice as I could manage. Up ahead, the sax and piano players, unheeding, pushed the door open, and out they went. The trumpeter stopped and looked back at me. My expression must have spoken to him, finally.

Rat-a-tat-tat erupted outside as the door swung closed behind the two unfortunates. A tommy (*). Whoever was behind this action had stationed a Chopper Squad (*) in the alley. No one was supposed to leave this joint alive.

"This way!" In the lead now, I darted into a side hallway. I shouldered my piece.

The hallway led us to another stairwell. I took Agnes's hand and guided her down three flights of steps; the trumpeter followed up real close.

At the bottom, through a doorway, we stumbled down another flight of stairs into the building's cellar, where the stink of stale beer and rancid wine assaulted us.

At the foot of the steps, my charges gravitated to the only light in the cellar, a single dusty bulb hanging from a cord. It didn't cast enough light for anyone to grasp the size or scope of the room. The best you could say for the place was that it was cool and absent a hail of bullets.

"Trapped like rats," the trumpeter whispered, his trumpet dangling from his right arm. Must be a matter of life itself, that trumpet.

It only took a few moments for the eyes to adjust to the dark. I moved past the circle of light to a far wall. A section of the wall was occupied by a shelving unit stacked with wine barrels, tops facing out. Moving to the left side of the shelving unit, I put my shoulder against it and shoved, but it didn't move.

"Give me a hand, pal," I called.

In a flash, the trumpeter was at my side, helping with the shove.

The fake shelves and barrels, a narrow facade, slid open, revealing the dark mouth of a tunnel.

The trumpeter was eye-balling me. "You one surprise after another, man."

I ducked into the opening and motioned the other two into the new darkness. A large wall-mounted lever switch snapped when I flipped it, illuminating a black-walled mine shaft.

"Get er back in place." I tapped the trumpeter on the shoulder.

We moved the fake wall back in place, concealing us, at least from those who weren't aware of this secret passageway.

"Stay close," I commanded as we started down a steep incline that led into the bowels of a subterranean labyrinth. "Careful now." I was worried that Agnes might lose her footing; the floor of our escape route was a little rough and wet.

Far as I know, I'm the only copper with knowledge of this secret Underground.

About 50 paces in, I stopped and toggled another wall switch. To our left, another long passage suddenly appeared, lit by light bulbs hanging every 30 feet or so.

"Let's git a move on." I led the way into the tunnel: the city above was held up by a structure of timber posts and beams. Water dripped from the ceiling here and there, adding damp to the coolness.

Hustling along at near a jog, I glanced back. The lanky trumpeter was a step behind, but Agnes labored ten paces back, panting, her chest heaving. Her body wasn't built for speed. Her lungs were more than adequate for propelling a melody, but not her body on those wobbly legs.

I brought my packages to a halt under one of the hanging bulbs that dotted the tunnel.

Agnes caught up, entering the dim circle of light. Her bosom heaved for air.

I gave them a minute to catch their breath.

"Shouldn't we keep mov'en?" the trumpeter said.

"We're safe here."

"Don't feel all that safe." The trumpeter said. "What if we bump into someone down here?"

"You're good as long as you know the password, and I know the password."

"And if you didn't?"

"You don't make it out."

"Who are you man?" The trumpeter asked.

"O'Shea, Detective Danny O'Shea, King City Police."

"What's a copper do'en hanging out in a clip joint like Lizzy's?"

"It's the copper who usually runs the line of questioning."

"Don't pay him no mind, Detective; can't help hisself." Agnes had pulled in enough air to puff that announcement out.

"How'd you know about this tunnel?"

"See, can't help hisself."

"I got my connections."

The tunnel was part of a dark labyrinth of mining tunnels, shafts, and chambers that lay underground well below the street level.

In the old days, way back, King City had a booming coal mining operation. But eventually, the veins of black gold petered out; coal wasn't paying its way. Around the same time, King City started growing, on the railroad line, new industries were developing. There was a need of space for development and also in need of a deep-water port on the bay to replace the existing inadequate natural harbor.

The mining industry was paved over, a new modern port was built, and the Carvonshire District was born.

The mines lay abandoned until, many years ago, long before my time, the upstart Jones Gang, a product of the Welsh community, deemed it their interest to put the below-ground network to beneficial use, that is, to facilitate their nefarious illegal activities.

This home-grown criminal element of Carvonshire put the mining skills of the Welsh immigrants to re-establish and repair the old mines. A whole new landscape under the streets came into being, a catacomb of sorts with secret entrances scattered about the city. To those with a villainous nature and a little creativity, there are obvious advantages to having access to this secret labyrinth that became known as the Underground.

The Welsh have dominated the rackets in this neck of the woods ever since.

Coppers in King City either don't know about the Underground or don't want to know. I learned about it several years ago through an incident involving Max. She needed a favor from the only honest cop in King City, me, the only cop not on her payroll. But that's a whole other story. In any case, that's why I know the locations of the secret entrances into the Underground.

"What you think all that shoot'en was about?" the trumpeter asked.

"Most likely, someone trying to bump off Max."

"Who?"

"Maxine Snowdon, the owner of the club."

"Why they after her?"

I looked at Big Agnes. "How's it this fool is still alive?" He was asking way too many questions.

"More than a couple of fellas have tried to beat some sense into him." Agnes flashed a gap-toothed smile. "It hasn't helped."

We walked on, easy now, passing several intersections with other tunnels. At each, I flipped on the lights in the one ahead of us and doused the one we came out of. On each corner at the intersection, there was a signpost of sorts, a white oak board nearly two feet high and a foot wide attached to a wall timber. Notches on the sides of the boards marked your location and what direction you were going if you could read the code. Even if the lights went out, a body could still find their way around, hopefully.

The last section of the labyrinth on my planned route led us to a steep iron staircase and an exit point. We were four blocks away from Lizzy's, reckoning by the streets above.

"This the way out?" the trumpeter asked.

"Yeah, it is."

"What's we wait'en for?"

"There's something I need from you before we hit the streets."

The musicians looked at each other, worried.

"I'm going to need your word that you will never tell anyone about the Underground." I waited.

"Sure, Detective, sure." Big Agnes piped up quick.

"What's if we don't?" The trumpeter had to ask.

"You don't make it out."

"You got it, sure thing." He was nodding vigorously.

I directed the two of them up the stairs. I gave Agness a hand up. "Wait at the door. Don't go out until I get up there. Hear me?"

"Got it, Sarge."

"Detective!" Jeez, does blowing long and hard on a trumpet cause brain damage?

I flipped the switch on the wall, and the tunnel went dark. I scaled the stairs and joined them in a dimly lit vestibule at ground level, an access point to the Underground located in the Lazarus Office Building. One small grimy window above the exit door allowed in a patch of light.

I pushed open the door that led to an alley a crack to take a look see. I poked my head out and glanced to both ends of the alleyway.

My vision was hampered by a thin blanket of fog, a mist that hung motionless in all directions. The springtime night air at street level was warm compared to our tour in the cool, dank Underground.

The coast was clear. "We're good to go."

The doorway we had passed through was a fake electrical panel decked out in danger signs meant to discourage the inquisitive. I pushed it back in place and set the latch, recessed in behind a skull and crossbones label.

I hustled my little troupe down the alley toward the west end and Third Ave.

We weren't far along, heading south on 3rd Ave when a police siren wailed. I stretched out my arm, halting our progress. I stepped out to the edge of the sidewalk and looked down the street at the approaching flashing lights.

Taking Agnes by the elbow, I scooted her into the next storefront alcove. The trumpeter was on our heels.

Walking the street with two colored folks in glad rags (*) might draw some unwanted attention. Especially since one of them was carrying a trumpet.

From our concealment, we watched two police cars whiz by, flashing and screeching.

As we moved back out on the sidewalk, "Shouldn't we have flagged em down?" the trumpeter questioned yet again.

"The first rule of King City," I said, "Don't trust the coppers."

The trumpeter widened his eyes and looked at Big Agnes. She, in turn, raised her eyebrows and squinted at me.

"Except for me, of course."

We strolled along the avenue like we belonged there up to the next corner. The fog was thickening up, rolling in off the bay, making us less visible.

At the end of the block, the newsstand that was manned by one of my boys was in view. The evening addition surely had already sold out, but I got lucky. He was hanging out with a couple of pals.

I brought two fingers to my lips and let go a shrill whistle.

The boy came alert, scanning for the call. His eyes landed on me, and I waved.

The little guy sprinted to our corner in record time.

"Have Jedd bring his taxi to Church and Broad," I instructed the lad.

"Yes sir, Danny." With a tip of his hat, the young'en rocketed away, heading to 4th Ave and Walnut, where Jedd kept his taxi parked.

"We only have to go a couple more blocks to meet up with my car. We'll get you out of here safe."

"Don't trust the cops, but trust the paper boys?" Agnes asked.

"Only if you're with me. They're solid, but they got their weaknesses. I try to keep em fed and in decent duds, but you never know. Poverty is a powerful motivator."

I motioned, and we started down the street.

"You just happen to know that a paperboy you could trust would be hanging round, waiting for instructions?" Agnes was walking alongside me.

"If not him, a block down, there's an establishment where some shoeshine boys hang out."

"So, you got what, a network of lackeys?" Agnes didn't sound too pleased with me.

"Not lackeys, Ma'am, associates."

"What's the difference?" Agnes asked.

"I like the sound of it better."

Twenty minutes and we strolled up to the corner of Church and Broad like we were going to church. Jedd's ten-cent box (*) was there waiting. I jumped ahead quick and opened the rear door for Agnes. The trumpeter sprang past me like a terrified cat and landed on the far side of the passenger seat. Big Agnes settled into her seat on the near side with a lot more grace.

"You own a taxi?" The trumpeter was pretty observant for a guy moving like a blue streak.

"No. I just got use of it when I need it." I had an arrangement with young Jedd, the owner of the taxi that put him and his ten-cent box at my beck and call. He kept the vehicle parked at Oswald's newsstand, two blocks from the station house, a real convenience for me.

I closed the door, stooped over, and rested my arm on the bottom of the open window, leaning my head in to speak to Agnes.

"Jedd here will take you to your hotel. He'll wait for you. Pack up quick. He'll take you to the bus station. I got a feeling that you're not safe in King City. You need to get out-of-town fast; all hell is gonna break loose."

"Does the boy's feet even reach the pedals?" The trumpeter was nodding at Jedd, a youthful-looking sixteen-year-old with freckles. His ginger hair poked out from under his tweed flat cap that dipped to one side.

"A gift horse, man, a gift horse." Jedd was shaking his head.

Agnes put her hand on my forearm like a hawk gripping a rabbit. "What about Slim and Billy?"

Slim was probably the oversized piano player, and Billy the unfortunate guy on the sax.

"I'll take care of them personally. Have them collected and transported to the undertaker on the colored side of town. He'll send you a telegram so you can make the arrangements." I waited. She released my arm. I had my connections in Henshaw, where the colored folk lived. Hell, I lived there myself.

"Thank you, Detective. I owe you."

"Sorry for your loss, Ma'am." She was right; she owed me big time.

I stood up, rapped my knuckles on the roof, and bounced back up on the curb. Jedd took off, the pedal to the metal.

As I watched, the taxi sped away up Broad Street. I could barely see the taillights in the fog. A couple of blocks and the cab jerked right and out of sight.

From my perch on the corner, I looked up and down the desolate, quiet street.

The head of the Jones Gang was dead. The glue that held Carvonshire together was gone. Organized crime wasn't organized anymore.

Yep, all hell was going to break loose.

EPISODE 2

THE SCENE OF THE CRIME

The bell hanging above the door jingled as I entered Kelly's Cafe. Sargent Sean O'Leary was already there, sitting at our usual table, always early, halfway through his first pastrami sandwich. We come here most every work day, Monday through Friday. Today, a Saturday, was an exception, being that we had a gangland massacre last night. Every copper in Carvonshire was on duty today.

The cafe is a good spot away from the station where we can talk business, not be overheard, and get the best grub in Carvonshire to boot. It's not like me and Sean are pals or anything; we got common interests. We look out for each other; work cases together.

Besides, Sean owed me. A while back, his womanizing got him in trouble when a dame didn't seem to understand that she was second fiddle. She had plans to wreck his marriage and his career. I intervened and got her to trade her vengeance for a bit part in a production at the Mercury Theater, a dream come true for her. I got connections in the theater business.

"Glad you could make it, O'Shea." Sean didn't look up from his plate.

"How's it shaken, O'Leary?"

"Not bad. Could use a little more mustard. You mind?"

I sauntered back over to the counter to retrieve the mustard jar and place my order with old Jen, the lunchtime waitress. My usual: macaroni and cheese, a small dish of rice pudding, and, of course, a cup of Joe.

I sat down across from Sean and slid the jar his way.

"Got a joke for ya, O'Shea."

"I heard it already."

"What do you call a guy who thinks a man can control his wife?"

"Don't know." Nothing will stop O'Leary's lame jokes; you just have to go along.

"A bachelor." Sean slapped a hand on the tabletop. "Like you, O'Shea. Ain't it about time you settled down and got hitched? Not getting any younger."

He was right about that; turned 32 last month. The years sneak up on you.

"That barmaid at the club, you know, the redhead. I think she's got eyes for you." That young doll is nice to look at. She wasn't the only reason I frequent the Griffin Street speakeasy, but she added to the charm of the place.

"I can only hope." Changing the subject, "Got any info on last night's shooting?"

"Not yet, but I'm work'en on it." Sean dabbed the corner of his mouth with his napkin. "I've only had the morning, for Christ's sake."

He pointed a finger at me. "Got a theory, though?"

Sean didn't come up with the best theories, but he had access to all the scuttlebutt at the station, which was sometimes helpful.

Having the reputation of being an honest cop, I didn't exactly fit in with the other not-so-honest boys in blue. But then, not taking money from the mob didn't mean a fella wasn't connected. There were rumors in the wind that I had the protection of Max Snowdon, which made the boys respectful. I didn't do anything to squash the rumor; it played to my advantage.

"My money is on Sleazy Sal," Sean said.

No one called Salvador that to his face, but you could smell him coming before catching sight of him. Apparently, he never got any instructions on personal hygiene.

Sleazy Sal or Little Billy, Maxine's lieutenants, were possible candidates for the shootout at Lizzy's. Play their cards right, and they could profit from Maxine's demise. They had motive, as we say in the police game.

"It's hard to believe that Sal or Little Billy could be that stupid. Max had everything set up real nice and smooth. One of those clowns might'a knocked her off and messed things up, but I wouldn't be putt'en any money on the locals just yet."

Maxine ran a tight ship: she put the 'organized' in organized crime. Whiskey, beer, and wine flowed into the speakeasies and clip joints real smooth. Dens of gambling and iniquity flourished. Violence was at a minimum. Bribes, flowing into the city council offices, judges' chambers, and police departments, greased the wheels of a well-organized city.

"You know something, O'Shea, don't you?" A finger wagged at me again.

I leaned in and lowered my voice to let Sean know we were talking in confidence here. Sean was the only man on the force I trusted. I got leverage on him, so I trust him. If I go down, he goes down.

"Between you and me?"

"Yeah, of course."

"I was there. I'm the guy who got the band out."

"No shit. How the hell did you manage that?"

"That's for me to know. But the thugs who busted in, They were likely out-a-town hires."

"What makes you say that?"

"It's the way the operation went down, just a feeling."

"Sometimes that works for ya," Sean smirked and shrugged.

Whoever they were, they were real keen that no one at Lizzy's survived, no witnesses. It was well known that Big Agnes and one of her band members had made it out. But they were tucked away safe in Chicago. For sure, no one else who saw me there was alive to tell the story. But then maybe one of the gunmen made me. I sure didn't recognize them, with the stocking masks and the chaos.

Sean reclined back in his chair. "I'll be damned, O'Shea. You should'a caught this case, not Foley. You got the inside line."

Detective Foley was the go-to guy when Donnelly, our illustrious police chief, wanted things to work out a certain way, to the Chief's advantage. That meant closing the case and putting someone in jail, not necessarily the guilty party.

Just then, Jen shuffled up to our table and plunked down my grub.

"Thanks, doll." I gave her a wink.

She ignored me but spoke to Sean. "Anything else I can get you, dear?"

"No thanks, Jen." Sean didn't look up.

As she walked away, the old waitress shot him a grand smile at the back of his head.

"We're going to keep my involvement under wraps. I don't want no target on my back."

"Gotcha."

"And to that end, I'm going to need a favor. I need you to cover for me."

"Sure thing, O'Shea."

"Dulley knows I planned on going to Lizzy's that night. I told him I changed my mind and spent the night with you at Griffin Street."

Fortunately for Dulley and his late-for-her own funeral wife, they didn't make it in time for the shooting.

"No sweat. I got you covered. Don't think you got to worry about Dulley. He's pretty much a dim bulb."

"True, but he shoots his yap off a lot."

Sean nodded and took another bite of his sandwich.

"I was think'en that you and I should go case out Lizzy's tonight, after hours, once Foley and his crew clear out."

"I'm with ya, Danny."

"Meet me on the corner of Cherry and 3rd at eight. Another thing Sean, see what you can dig up on the crime scene notes." O'Leary had connections with the station's secretary, more than connections, if you know what I mean.

Business taken care of, I turned back to my lunch. The coffee was cold, but there was no point in asking old Jen for a warm-up.

Ten o'clock on the dot, Sean and I walked up to Lizzy's main door. I took out my tools and picked the lock, the benefits of an ill-spent youth. I motioned to him to step to the side, just in case. He put his hand on his service revolver. I turned the doorknob and slipped inside, flicking the lights on. "All clear."

Sean followed me in, and we made our way to the bar. Directly in front of the bar, the first white outline of a victim was sketched out on the floor. "What's your notes say?"

Sean pulled out a patch of yellow steno pages from his breast pocket. "Male, took four bullets."

"Yeah, I remember an old guy on a barstool, nursing a beer."

"Says here, they found a female and two males behind the bar." Sean adjusted his reading glasses.

I put a foot on the bar rail and peered over at three more outlines. "One barmaid and the two bartenders. Makes sense."

We moved out into the center of the room amongst the turned-over tables and chairs.

"Six bodies, here in the middle of the room," Sean continued.

Six white silhouettes testified to the three unlucky couples, who had shown up early to get the best seats. They were the best seats until they weren't.

"I remember the three couples, probably my Ma's age."

Sean looked up at me over his glasses. "Says one of the dames was a barmaid."

"There were two barmaids, but I could have sworn there were three couples. Should be two barmaids and three women accounted for."

"Not like you to make a mistake." Sean pushed his spectacles back up on his forehead. "Always a first time, I guess."

The gunfire and bullets whizzing by my head might have clouded my memory.

"Did they identify all the victims?"

"Yeah, Doc Thomas was on the scene." Sean handed me the page with the list of the deceased.

I perused the list that our coroner had provided. I recognized the names of the bartenders, barmaids, and bouncers: I keep up to date and who's who in the Carvonshire rackets. The three male patrons were strangers. But the two dead women I knew to be members of Max's secrecy network of spies. They both worked as hostesses in a Welsh Town speakeasy.

I passed the page back to O'Leary.

"I was sitt'en there by the back door." I pointed off to my right.

"Good choice."

We walked to the back of the room and Max's office.

In front of the office door, two outlines showed where Max's bodyguards had fallen. That door and the walls were riddled with bullet holes.

"They found a revolver for each bodyguard next to the bodies."

I picked up one of the shell casings that littered the floor. "Looks like they got off quite a few rounds. Kept the shooters occupied while me and the band got out. Too bad I can't thank them for it."

The office door stood open to a ransacked mess; papers were strewn everywhere, chairs turned over, desk drawers lying on the floor. Inside, between the door and an enormous mahogany desk, two more silhouette outlines on the floor. Motioning to his right, "That would be Snowdon and her secretary. Says here, the secretary had a gun in her hand."

"She wasn't only a secretary; she doubled as a bodyguard."

A smaller mahogany desk off to our right was her normal habitat. Behind it, the door of a large floor safe hung slightly ajar. I stepped over the papers, journals, and notebooks that littered the floor and pulled the door full open to expose the empty safe.

"They must've had a can opener (*) with them. A robbery, you think?" Sean asked.

"Nah. I think the whole point was to take out Max."

"Might as well clean out all the moolah while they were at it then?"

"Could be."

The floor-to-ceiling bookshelves on the back wall behind the desk had been nearly emptied. Most of the books lay haphazardly across the floor. I moved in for a closer look. I ran my hands over and under the shelves, one by one.

"What are you doing?" Sean was asking.

I glanced back at him but didn't answer. I sat my butt down on the back edge of the desk, surveying the bookshelf and back wall.

"I know that look, O'Shea; you've got hold of a puzzle."

He was right about that. To the left of the shelving unit, the glass door of an oversized wall clock (mahogany like everything else in the room) hung open suspiciously. I reached in and fiddled around with anything I could get a hold of. The inside bottom panel had a gap at the back. My fingers slipped in easy. I pulled up on the little board; it was hinged. A subtle click came from the bookshelf. With my hands on the edge of the book unit, I tugged this way and that. With not much effort, the bookshelf shifted away to my right. It must have been mounted on a trolley system.

The opening revealed a closet about three feet deep with another wall-safe, same design, but much smaller and with its door wide open.

"Empty?" Sean was looking over my shoulder.

"Yep, cleaned out. Any mention of our boys finding this safe in the report?"

Sean took a moment to review his paperwork. "Nope, nothing."

Maxine was too smart to put all her eggs in one basket. There was probably something more important in the hidden wall safe than money. And I had an idea of what it might be. Max was a fan of using passwords for her nefarious activities. It was rumored that she kept them documented in a little red book.

I stepped back and slipped my hands into my pockets. "Odd that the thugs would put the shelves back in place after they cleaned out this safe."

Sean glanced up from his notes again and looked at the floor's white lines to our left. "It might have been personal with Max. She was shot in the face multiple times."

"Maybe. Let's check out the rest of the joint."

We turned and walked out of the office.

Sean read off his papers. "Two males in the back hallway and another two outside in the back alley, the band members."

"The two bouncers and the two band members."

"How'd the bouncers end up by the back door?"

"The way I remember it, and things were happening fast, the Torpedoes (*) came straight in the front door without any fuss. I'm think'en the bouncers got paid off to let them in and then got paid off again. No loose ends."

"Only the two musicians and you got out. Do you think they saw you?"

"They must've seen me, but the question is: Do they know me?"

"Not likely if they were out-of-town like you said. Do you still have that shamrock your granddad brought over from the old country?"

"Yeah, hope I haven't worn all the luck out of it already." I padded my back trouser pocket where I kept the leaf pressed in wax paper in my wallet.

"Good thing you don't always rely on luck."

"I can't believe I got the number of women patrons wrong."

"Maybe one got out, like you."

"Don't think so."

"Or she was in on it, and they let her go."

"Possible, but they didn't let the bouncers go." If it was an inside job, someone who worked for Max was a likely candidate. No way to trace her now; anyone who could have identified her was deceased.

Sean shuffled through his papers. "Not much to go on here. Just like Foley to keep things to a minimum."

Things weren't right, for sure; the crime scene was like a jigsaw puzzle with a few pieces missing.

"What else, O'Shea? I can see something is bothering you."

"That blood smear on the floor near the location of Max's body; anything in the report on that?" A trail of blood ran from the body out the doorway.

"Nothing."

"Figures," I said, "Looks like her body got moved. Why do that?"

Sean shrugged.

"And there's something else."

"There's always something else with you, O'Shea."

"Maxine's accountant, what about her? I didn't see her last night, but she's never a stone's throw from her meal ticket."

"Maybe she had the night off. Can't be do'en the books night and day."

"You sure are full of maybes, O'Leary." I was kidding; I don't mind, really. It's helpful to get all the dumb ideas out of the way early on. What Sean didn't know was that the accountant, Grace Snowdon, Max's niece, was also an assassin. And, that most evenings at Lizzy's, she added to Maxine's bodyguard contingent. All this I know because I am well-connected. It's best to keep tabs on the criminal element even if you don't intend to upset the apple cart.

Sean shrugged again. Shrugs and maybes, what more could you ask for in a crime-solving partner? Gave me room to do the real thinking.

Right then, the door swung open, and in burst Junior Detective Brady and Sergeant Murphy, shoulder to shoulder, closely followed by Detective Foley.

Brady and Murphy strode right up to us, a couple of paces away. They knew better than to step into Sean's personal space.

I was trying to stifle a grin; they looked like characters in a comic strip. Brady was five feet tall, and Murphy was five feet wide.

Sean quickly stuffed his papers into his breast pocket.

Foley stepped up alongside his two henchmen. "What the hell you do'en on my crime scene, O'Shea?"

Senior Detective Foley was tall, skinny, and good-looking, except for a scar that ran diagonally across his left cheek that glowed bright red when he was pissed off. He was pissed off.

"Helping out, sniff'en around, seeing if you boys missed anything."

"Fat chance." Murphy puffed out his chest. Despite most all cops in Carvonshire being Irish, the Sargent's brogue stood out, and not to the benefit of the race.

"What you doing out of the house, Murphy? Didn't recognize you, not sitting on your ass." I piped up; I couldn't help myself.

Murphy and Brady took a step forward. So did Sean. Sean could take both of them, no sweat, with one hand tied behind his back. So I hung back.

Foley raised both hands. "Easy boys. Let's not start a piss'en contest." His scar had faded.

I could tell by the look in Sean's eyes that he was disappointed. He was hoping for a thumping contest, where he did all the thumping.

Foley knew better than to put his boys up against Sean's six-foot-two, 280-pound frame.

All involved relaxed.

"You two need to vacate the premises," Foley nodded in the direction of the door.

"Yeah, go chase yourself," Brady spouted off. Not the most original wisecrack, but meant to impress his boss. Coming into the detective job via his connection as the

Chief's nephew, Brady was going to have to prove his worth. His round, boyish face with pimples was not going to be an asset in his chosen career.

"We were just trying to be helpful," I replied.

"I don't need no help from a junior detective like yourself." Foley shifted to a smile. "Maybe you should take a look at my sheet, the highest conviction rate in the department."

He added the junior to agitate me. I made senior detective four years ago; he just wouldn't acknowledge it. He was senior in years on the force, and he has connections with the brass. When Foley was on the case, someone was going to pay. Someone was going to jail, but not necessarily the someone who did the crime.

Foley had things worked out real smooth with our Chief of Police, the assistant DA, Llewellyn, and Judge Sanders. Foley got convictions, the Chief took credit, DA Llewellyn got reelected, and the judge got a 'tough on crime rep' and some cash. And as a side benefit, the public got its thirst for vengeance quenched. Sometimes, even the mark got something out of it, an early out-of-jail card, and yeah, sometimes some cash.

"We'll be on our way. Don't want to crimp the style of no *senior* detective." I put the emphasis on 'senior' as I slipped through between Murphy and Brady. Sean followed me, giving Brady a shoulder that bounced his Bowler hat off his head.

"Watch it," Brady called out, chasing the round hat as it rolled across the floor.

Sean was smiling as we walked out the door. "Gotta let the young pups know where they stand."

I was a little surprised that Foley got wind so quick that me and Sean were here at Lizzy's. Must've had a lookout posted who spotted the light.

We were down on the street in the calm of the night.

"We'll take this up again in the morning at the station." I slapped Sean on the back. "Thanks for your help."

"Sure thing, O'Shea."

We parted ways. Sean was on his way home to the old ball and chain, and me to my run-of-the-mill two-room apartment in Henshaw.

<hr>

"You got your teeth into this, don't you, O'Shea?" Sean said, "I can tell. You're too quiet."

"You can read me like a book, Sarge." I stared out over Sean's shoulder at my office windows, not really seeing anything, just the dark afternoon sky.

Had to admit, my office wasn't anything to write home about, but at least I wasn't parked at a desk in the squad room. This domain used to be a storage room. Not the best place for the claustrophobic. Only two narrow windows with frosted glass near the ceiling lit the room up. I always keep them open; no issue with bugs on the second floor. What this little den does provide is privacy, a spot where me and O'Leary can converse about our cases.

"Gonna be a tough case to crack. Tough one for Foley to pin on some patsy. Not too many out there willing to take the fall for 13 counts of capital murder," Sean said.

It had been a week since our visit to Lizzy's, and all we had was speculation, rumor, and some nagging pieces of evidence that didn't make sense. Me and Sean hadn't had much time to kick things around. Sean got tied up with another case, and I had been spending my time chasing down my informants and digging for dirt. Who did the hit and who ordered the hit was still a mystery.

"Some things add up, some don't." I put our problem on the table.

"Start with the stuff that adds up, O'Shea."

"Well, someone knew for sure Max would be at Lizzy's that night." For a crime boss, Max kept a low profile and rarely appeared in public. When she was at Lizzy's, she mostly stayed in her office and didn't venture out to the clip joint floor. The only flash she made was when she went out and about in her armored green Packard.

"So, it seems that the bouncers were in on it and tipped off the torpedoes," I added.

"What else?"

"The gunmen went right for the bodyguards at Max's office door before they turned their attention to cleaning up the rest of the clientèle."

"Lucky for you." Sean raised his eyebrows.

I patted my back pocket.

"Then they rewarded the bouncers for letting them in the door with a couple of slugs."

"Too bad."

"And for sure, they had a man or two in the alley to catch up any stragglers that might make it out the back door."

"Like the two musicians." Sean was nodding.

"Right." I swiveled back and forth in my chair.

"That it?"

"Yeah."

"Okay then, what don't make sense?" Sean was rolling up a cigarette on my desktop.

"The number of casualties doesn't line up with my recollection. There's the missing woman patron and Max's accountant." I was confounded, and I don't like confounded.

"You sure there were three couples, three men and three women?"

"I can count."

"But the accountant, you're just guessing that she was there."

"The odds are she was; she's always there." Sean didn't know what she was there for or why she was there. I do, but I don't share everything. I don't tell every story. For sure, not Grace's story.

I first became aware of Grace's activities years ago, just after Maxine took over as leader of the Jones Gang.

During that time, there had been a string of mysterious, unresolved deaths. I was a Junior Detective at the time. My pal, Senior Detective Foley, caught most of those cases.

All those particular deaths had a common denominator: that the deceased's sudden end of life benefited Maxine Snowdon. Most were rivals, gangsters trying to muscle in on Maxine's turf. Others were fellas that tried to cheat Max or crossed her in some way.

Max wasn't bashful about letting the story out that there was a strong possibility she may have been responsible for the demise of her enemies.

A rumor circulated, probably with Max's blessing, that she had a professional assassin on the payroll, which worked to her advantage, a deterrent for those who might be considering taking Max on. There was no future in crossing Maxine Snowdon.

Each killing had another common factor: panache.

On separate occasions, two perfectly able-bodied men apparently stumbled off the roof of the Kilmann building in broad daylight. And both, coincidently, had a red rose in their lapel.

Another fella was found in an alley near the Canal Street mule path, on his back, arms crossed, a red rose lying on his chest. Could have been mistaken for a fella taking a nap, except for the small caliber hole in his forehead.

One of my favorites was the guy found holding a suicide note crumpled up in his hand. A missive in which he confessed that he was a scum bag not fit to live, not written in his handwriting, and with a sketch of a rose in one corner.

There was another with a note. The fella who turned up sitting slumped over on a park bench. A letter was pinned to his chest, stating that he beat his wife and deserved what he got. He had multiple small caliber wounds in his face, all postmortem, the coroner declared, the actual cause of death unknown.

All the men were known thugs; their unsolved murders didn't draw much attention beyond their one-day mention in the newspapers.

I got caught up in one of the murders several years ago. It was not one of my favorites because I didn't solve it, which I now have come to believe was to my benefit.

The victim in this case was someone I had been investigating for six months. I felt that he was my man for several armed robberies of the local shops in town, in the last of which an elderly shopkeeper had been beaten to death. I just couldn't get the goods on the thug, not enough to convict, which became unnecessary when he turned up dead.

One evening, late under the street lights, on my way home, I was crossing the Canal Street bridge. Up ahead of me on the other side of the bridge was a man leaning over the railing, gazing down at the water. A drunk, I figured. I was almost past him when a shrill whistle pierced the cool air. I stopped, turned, and looked back. At the far end of the bridge, in shadow, was a tall, flashy-dressed woman holding a bouquet of flowers in one arm, totally out of place and time. I was stunned. She stretched out her arm, pointing to the man on the railing. I walked across the road to the fella and took a closer look. He was tied to the railing, a rope around his chest, and two others secured his hands to the handrail. Later, it was determined that the cause of death had been one bullet through the heart.

Getting my bearings, I whipped around, eye-balling the place the woman no longer inhabited. I rushed to the spot and looked in all directions, but the lamp light was poor. She could have gone any which way. It took a moment before I noticed the bouquet of red roses at my feet.

I didn't get a good look at the woman's face, only her figure and demeanor, which I thought I would recognize if I ever came across her again. Which I did the first time I saw Grace. Another time, I was taking in the jazz scene at Lizzy's. In the company of Maxine, she walked right past me, giving me a wink that chilled my spine.

I didn't think that encounter with Grace at the bridge was a coincidence; I don't believe in coincidence.

Oh yeah, and the common denominator was in place: my deceased suspect had been robbing businesses that were under Maxine's protection, another 'not a coincidence.'

A match flared as Sean lit up. "What about Johnny? He wasn't there. Maybe he was in on it too."

"I know the guy good: it's not likely. He usually doesn't come in till later anyway." Me and Johnny, Lizzy's manager, go way back. We played ball in the minor leagues when we were young. He wasn't the type to cross Max. I'd put money on it. But then, I have been wrong before when it comes to judging character. Who knows what may lead a man down a wayward path?

"That all you got?" Sean pulled an ashtray up close and tapped cigarette ash into it.

"No, the blood smear on the floor next to Max's body. Why would they take the time to move the body?"

"Got me."

"And why shoot Max in the face with a different gun after she was most already dead as a doornail?" The ballistics report showed that the slugs in the floor underneath Max's body were small caliber, unique rounds, not like anything else found in the joint. "And…"

"There's more?" Sean interrupted me.

"This wasn't just a hit to take out Snowdon. They took the trouble to bring along a can-opener (*) and risked taking the time to crack the safes. They were after something else. And why did the thugs bother sliding the fake bookcase back in place after they emptied the wall safe?"

"That's a decent list of things that don't smell right." Sean touched his nose.

"The big question is, though, who ordered the hit?"

"I'm still think'en Sleazy Sal or maybe Little Billy." Sean crushed out his cig and started rolling another. "That's the scuttlebutt around the station, too. Foley's got one of them down for it."

"If that's Foley's line, that's a good reason to doubt it." I rocked back in my chair and rested my hands behind my head so that I could have a good look at the swirls in the plaster ceiling. "Besides that, neither of those boys got the brains for this. I'm thinking some out-of-town action."

"Yeah, but neither one of those goons was at the scene that night. Could be they knew what was com'en."

"There'd be no reason for them to be there before things got lively, but that don't take them off the list, just at the bottom of the list."

"For a guy who don't frequent the place that much, you sure know a lot about what goes on Lizzy's."

"I got my connections. I stay up to date."

A good detective don't just wait on crime to happen; it's better to nip it in the bud. But to do that, you gotta see it coming. And to do that, you need to have connections, people who are willing to tell you stories. I know a lot of storytellers.

"What about the Italians?" Sean asked.

The Italians were known to operate outside their territory. Hell, they put out a contract on me one time. They came after me right here in Carvonshire.

Various criminal gangs had King City diced up real nice into territories. The Italians controlled the Hill Section, northwest of Carvonshire, and the King District, the downtown area which was due north of Carvonshire. Farther north, an area of town called the North End was populated by and controlled by various and relatively cooperative Slavic gangs. Last, but not least, east of Carvonshire was Henshaw, the colored part of town run by Big Anthony and his gang. All these areas matched up nicely with the Police Districts, ideal for organizing King City's corruption of payoffs and bribes.

Other ethnic groups had their particular place in the King City rackets. The English, in the criminal lottery, landed the most coveted spot, city politics.

And my clan, the Irish, did well, dominating the police department, the best job to have if you're of a criminal mind.

Not that King City was lawless, mind you, the criminal activities were, for the most part, organized, ran smooth, and didn't generally cause a ruckus.

But then, a few years back, the politicians decided to mess things up and make prohibition the law of the land. All for the sake of interfering with a man's need to wet his whistle.

"Got a serious question, O'Shea." Smoke escaped with Sean's words. "You think those torpedoes (*) saw you? Think they made you?"

That was a question I was trying not to think about.

"Things were happening so fast, and they were concentrating on getting to Max. And if I'm right that they're out-of-towners, it's not likely they made me."

"I hope you're right," Sean said, "But watch your back."

"Always do."

As Sean stood up, he pinched out his butt in the ashtray. "I got to get going; need to stop at Benson's and pick up the steaks. We got do'ens on tonight, her folks, for Friday night dinner."

"I'm going to hit Kelly's." My usual.

O'Leary, turning back, had his hand on the doorknob. "What's next, you think?"

It had been seven days since the massacre at Lizzy's. I figured it wouldn't be long before King City descended into mayhem and violence.

"Don't know, but it ain't gonna be good."

EPISODE 3

THE DOCKSIDE MASSACRE

Jen, not my favorite waitress, stood over me, face like a vulture looking for something dead. I swiveled on my stool and looked at the chalkboard hanging on the back wall, 'Kelly's Cafe's Friday Night Special' was the heading.

"I'll have the special." Sitting at the area of the counter that faced out gave me a good view of what might be coming down the street. I was expecting something; I just didn't know what or when.

Jen turned her head to Kelly at the grill and yelled, "One special." And then back at me. "And to drink?"

"Bottle of orange pop."

"You got it." She waltzed over to the end of the counter, planted herself on a stool, and took a drag on a butt that had been smoldering in the ashtray. She forgot my pop. Too much of a strain for the old broad, I guess.

Sometimes I envy Sean, having a wife to go home to and all, a family, supper on the table. But fortunately, I get over it quick. No sir, no dame is going to hog-tie Danny O'Shea. I'm a free man and intend to keep it that way. Don't get me wrong; I like the dolls; like them just fine. Just can't see any reason why I should limit myself to only one. There's a lot of Danny O'Shea to go around; why deprive the dames of King City?

I got my grub soon enough and my warm bottle of pop, eventually. The Friday evening crowd was filling up my favorite cafe. A second waitress was on duty, the one that hustles, but I always got stuck with Jen. The poor old woman sees no need to move beyond a snail's pace.

I had no plans to visit the clubs this Friday night. Not even Griffin Street. Didn't want to be out after dark. I had told Sean I was real sure the torpedoes at Lizzy's hadn't made me, but a little voice in my head wasn't buying it. No point taking any unnecessary risks in case someone was out there looking to put a slug in me.

This ain't no way to live, waiting for the hammer to fall. But I lived through it before, when the Italians put out a contract on my life. It was my fault, really. When I was young, a junior detective in my second year, I crossed a line I didn't know was there.

I was having a night for myself at the Canal Street clip joint, and this bozo got physical with one of the waitresses, slapped her across the face, and broke her jaw. What was I supposed to do, just sit there? I arrested the clown. He got two years in the slammer for assault and battery. Turns out, he was the son of Angelo the Suit, the crime boss from the

Hill Section. In my defense, the boy was out of his territory. He should have known better. Plus, that was a bad time in my life; drinking way too much and fighting came too easy.

In any case, Angelo didn't take kindly to my putting his boy in the slammer and decided that I was no longer required to walk this earth. I figured I'd be fine in the daylight hours. Taking out a copper in broad daylight just ain't done. But at night, things happen, and no one's the wiser. Gives a whole new meaning to fear of the dark.

To improve my odds of survival, I moved into the Henshaw section, the colored part of town west of Carvonshire, across the canal. I made arrangements with Big Anthony and his boys. They kept a lookout for me and sounded the alarm if any prominent white Italians came stumbling through the neighborhood. They would stand out like snow on a coal bank.

Big Anthony is the crime boss of the Henshaw District, a real complicated colored fella. His real name was William White, but he thought the moniker 'Big Anthony' had a tough guy ring to it. He got the name from a wanted poster hanging in the post office of an Italian mobster from Chicago. William didn't look like any Anthony I ever saw. And considering he was built like a mountain of muscle; Big Bill would have done just fine.

I spent a year hiding out nights in Henshaw before I got a reprieve. Maxine Snowdon negotiated with the Italians to get me off the hook. She didn't do it out of the kindness of her heart if she even had a heart. She let me know I owed her. And I owed her big time, not the way I like my arrangements. Owing a debt to Max was like having a millstone hanging over your head by a thread. I dreaded the day when Max would call in that marker. But with Max gone, that problem was gone with her.

But the memory of the night Max summoned me to her office to inform me that my debt had come due lingered like a bad dream.

There I was, standing in front of the door to Lizzy's, squirreling up the courage to knock.

It had been earlier in the day when I got a summons from Max to be at Lizzy's that same evening for a meeting.

Me and Sean were at Kelly's, a Monday at lunchtime, sitting at our usual table when the doorbell jingled. A thug in a black suit appeared in the doorway, scanning the place.

I nodded to Sean as my hand went for my pee shooter. Sean was twisting in his seat, going for his piece. The fella at the door spotted us and raised his hands out in front; one held a yellow envelope. Sean and I settled back in our chairs but kept a close eye on the guy, our hands not far from our weapons, as he edged his way across the room.

He didn't say a word as he dropped the note on our table right in front of me. He kept his eyes on us as he backed his way to the door. Only then did he turn and scoot away.

I went to the window. The thug was getting into the passenger seat of a green Packard.

The note was an invite from Max to meet at ten o'clock. On a Monday night, nothing is shaking at Lizzy's, or any clip joint for that matter. I wouldn't have any cover going in there alone.

But I had no alternative; I had to go. Even though I wasn't on Maxine Snowdon's payroll, I still had to live in Carvonshire, the emphasis on live.

A rap of my knuckles on the door, and the peep slot slid open. Eyeballs looked me up and down; the slot closed, and the door swung open.

"Big door, all the way back," the doorman growled.

I moved across the clip joint's floor, winding through the tables and chairs. It was eerily quiet, no music. It reminded me that I hadn't been to a venue in over two years to take in a jazz session.

In the center of the back wall was a larger-than-normal mahogany door with an ornate framework with scrolls and flowers. The fancy door was flanked by two burly bodyguards wearing oversized black suits. The hardware secured in their holsters bulged the finely tailored cloth. Why go to the trouble of covering up their weapons? They were so damn obvious.

I stopped at the door and waited. The thug on the left stretched out an arm and rapped on the door. Two loud knocks, not much of a secret code. A woman's voice called out, "Come in."

Neither henchman made a move, so I opened the door and stepped into Max's office.

Sitting behind an enormous mahogany desk, directly in front of me, was Maxine Snowdon, an average-looking middle-aged woman. Behind her, the entire wall was covered with bookshelves, almost entirely occupied by neatly organized books of various sizes and colored spines.

Off to my right, another but smaller mahogany desk was positioned in the corner. Both sides of that desk were flanked by low-level file cabinets with a pile of leger books on each. Between the piles, a woman with glasses and gray hair in a bun sat hunched over, scribbling on a notepad, paying me no mind. Behind her, the corner to the right was dominated by a hulking safe, five feet high and three feet wide, black with gold trim framing the door.

On my left, a dame decked out like a flapper with heavy makeup made her presence known. A shiver went up my spine. It took a second to place her; it was Grace Snowdon, Maxine's niece.

"Glad you could make it, Danny," Max called my attention back to her.

"Sure thing." It's not like I had a choice.

"You don't mind if I call you Danny, do you, Detective?"

"Not a problem." We had never met face-to-face before, might as well dispense with the formalities.

"I wasn't certain I'd see you tonight. You generally don't leave Henshaw at night. The word is you're more of a cautious chap."

"I try not to do anything foolish."

Grace chuckled.

"Good for you, Danny." Max stood up and came around in front of her desk. We were eye to eye for a moment. Then she sat back on her desktop, her hands resting on the edge at her sides. "To the point, Danny, I wanted to let you know personally that I got Angelo to lift the contract he has out on you. You're a free man, don't have to spend all your nights in Henshaw anymore. You can go out nights, take in the music scene. Jazz is your cup of tea, right?"

"Yeah, that's right." This was not what I was expecting. "I don't know what to say."

"How about, thank you?"

"Yeah, okay, thank you." I was standing there like a dope. "That it?"

"Hell no, Danny. Not by a long shot." Max smiled. "I'm going to need a favor."

"What is it?" I didn't really want the answer to that question.

Max straightened up and returned to her chair, putting distance between us and prolonging the agony.

"Nothing right now. Someday, Danny, someday. I'm sure that someday I will need a favor from you."

"Couldn't I just do something now and get it over with?"

A harsh chuckle erupted from Grace. She was grinning, but it sent no goodwill.

"I have no use for you right now, Danny. You were just an afterthought in my negotiations with Angelo. Just a tidbit I had him throw in."

Well, at least I knew where I stood. The only honest cop in Carvonshire that now owes Maxine Snowdon, the district crime boss, a favor. An insignificant, dispensable copper, but a free man, for the time being.

"I was wondering how you knew I was in trouble?" I now knew why she got me out of trouble.

Maxine didn't answer me except for a wink that said, "For me to know."

Secrets were the most valuable currency in King City. You just didn't give them away.

Feeling awkward, I asked, "You read all those books?"

"Yes, all of them."

"Why keep them if you already read them?"

"I may just want to read them again."

"Don't suppose I could borrow one sometime?" This was the dumbest line of questioning, but I couldn't help myself.

Max didn't answer but squirreled up her face and looked at Grace.

"Never mind, I'll hit the library." There was something about those bookshelves that didn't strike me as right and stirred my curiosity.

"Says a man who doesn't read books," Max said.

This dame knew way too much about me.

"Enough small talk." Max rolled her chair up to the desk and picked up a pen, turning her attention to the paperwork on the desktop. "Scram."

So, I did, quick as a bunny.

During my trip down memory lane, I had made short work of the special and decided to head home. With a wave, I got Kelly's attention at the grill. He nodded, not missing a beat as he spooned out plate after plate of Friday night specials. I laid down some jack (*) to cover the bill and a tip. At the door, I tipped my fedora to Jen, still sitting on her stool. Taking a heavy drag on her cig, she looked right at me but didn't see me.

Out on the sidewalk, I turned west and headed up Church Street toward home. I'd been walking this route night after night for seven years. Didn't see any reason to uproot myself from Henshaw, so I stayed put. I got my connections there now, and they've paid off too many times to count.

In addition, my second-floor two-room apartment overlooking the canal had grown on me despite the canal's aroma of sewage. Why move and have to educate a whole new batch of neighbors as to who I am and what I expect from them?

I cut over to Market Street and was almost to the canal bridge when I heard the station siren start to wind up, the all-call. Something big was happening! I did an about-face and started hoofing it toward the sound. Four blocks on, I was at the intersection of Market and Broad Street, looking north toward the station house. A couple of squad cars and a paddy wagon were heading my way.

After the cars zipped by, I stepped out into the street and flagged down the paddy wagon. The back door flew open, held for me by Dulley. Inside, I took a seat against the wall next to him.

"What's going on?" I asked as the vehicle jerked forward, bouncing Dulley against my shoulder.

"Some heavy action at the Jones Gang stash house. A shootout," Dulley countered.

On the other side of the van, across from me and Dulley, four patrolmen sat holding their rifles, looking like they were going to their own funerals, which just might be the case.

We rolled up on the corner of Bay and South Street, the location of the Jones Gang transfer house, the warehouse they used to store their moola, illegal libations, and other miscellaneous illicit gains.

The brakes gave up their screeching, and we stared at each other, waiting to see who was gonna go out the door first. I didn't hear any gunfire, so I figured, what the hell, out I went. I hustled around to the front of the wagon and got an eye full. There were bodies everywhere, scattered across the sidewalk, the loading dock, and the side alley of the South Street warehouse. Four squad cars were on the scene, lights flashing.

"What a mess." Dulley stood at my side.

"You got that right."

Foley and Brady were already there. Brady had his notebook out, penciling down whatever Foley was saying. That's all he was good for, taking notes. Can't expect much from the Chief's wife's nephew. Nepotism can move a man's career forward, but brains don't necessarily come with the package.

One meat wagon (*) was parked directly in front of the loading dock. Its crew was making their tour, checking bodies for signs of life.

I started my inspection of the massacre. Another meat wagon pulled up. I counted nine victims decked out in pin-striped suits and silk shirts. Three were still breathing but in real bad shape.

"O'Shea." Sean emerged from the loading dock doorway. He jumped down to ground level, real agile for a man his size. "Two more inside, dead."

"Jeez, Sean, two massacres in one week." With Maxine Snowdon in charge for the last ten years, we were accustomed to the general lack of extreme violence.

"I hope this ain't going to be the usual from now on." Sean shielded his eyes as a couple of flashbulbs popped.

The reporters were on the scene. There'd be no lack of grizzly pictures for the front page.

"Were you first on the scene?" I offered Sean a Sen-Sen from the pack I had pulled from my pocket. The licorice masks the smell of blood.

Sean held up his hand. "Yeah, but Foley and Brady were a close second."

"What's the story inside?" I nodded to the warehouse where Foley had just posted two of his men at the door.

"Lots of kegs of beer and wine barrels and a safe, most likely full of moola."

"Any witnesses?" I didn't hold out much hope for that.

"Yeah, one, Teddy," Sean replied.

"Did Foley get to him?"

"No, I steered him away to the side of the building. Gave him ten cents and sent him to Griffin's. Told him to go to the back door and ask for Joe."

"Good thinking. The last thing Teddy needs is to end up on a witness stand or going for a ride or both."

Teddy was a rummy who spent his time wandering around the docks. He had a screw loose: he's one of the few people who would run toward gunfire instead of away from it.

Joe, the Griffin Street speakeasy manager, would accommodate Teddy with a pint of panther piss (*). Tomorrow, Teddy probably wouldn't even remember that he was here tonight.

"Did he see anything?" I was hopeful.

"He didn't see the shooting. When I got here, he was going through pockets, checking for change. But he did get a look at some thugs that were still standing."

"Did he recognize any of them before they took off?"

"Yeah, Teddy said they were all locals, either Sal's or Billy's men. They were dragging the wounded into their cars when Teddy showed up."

All the bodies on the ground were locals, too. Sleazy Sal and Little Billy were among the dead, gone to meet their maker. Well, or more likely, the other fella.

As Sean and I came up Broad Street to the station, the press briefing was still going on. We had drug out our lunchtime trying to avoid the spectacle. On the station house steps, Foley, Brady, the Chief, and the Commissioner were holding court with a flock of reporters huddled in front of them on the sidewalk. Not your typical Monday; another weekend massacre to report on.

From our position at the south end of the station, I recognized the reporters from the local newspapers and radio stations, but there were also a lot of out-of-town folks.

One of them, a dame I'd never seen before, stood next to the King City Gazette crime reporter. She looked our way. It seemed like she was giving me the once-over. I didn't remember ever seeing her with the press and I would have remembered her.

"Let's go. I've seen enough of this," I declared.

Me and Sean moved on down the alley toward the station's side entrance.

Sean had his hand on the door handle when a woman's voice called out. "Hey, wait up. Just a minute." It was that female reporter, a real doll.

She hustled up to us. "You're Sergeant O'Leary, aren't you?" She stood right in front of Sean, ignoring me.

"Who's ask'en," Sean replied.

"Jane Dickerson, King City Gazette." She shifted her pen and pad to her left hand and held out the right.

Sean gave it a quick shake. "Miss."

"I'd like to ask you a few questions if you don't mind."

"That action is going on out front," I said, "And he does mind."

She looked at me like she just noticed I was there. "And who are you?"

"Detective Danny O'Shea."

"Oh." Her eyes flicked back to Sean. "I understand you were the first copper to arrive at the crime scene last Friday."

"Where'd you hear that," I asked before Sean had a chance to reply.

"I have my sources." I only got a quick flash of the eyes, not even a head turn. "Well, Sergeant?" She pressed Sean.

"Sorry, doll, we got police business to attend to," I announced.

I turned away, following Sean, who was already stepping through the doorway.

━━ ▰ ▰

"How'd you think that reporter found out I was first on the scene?" Sean was settling into his chair.

"Says she's got her sources." I closed my office door and took my seat on the other side of my desk from Sean.

"That don't make me feel any better." Sean pulled his cigarette papers and tobacco pouch from his breast pocket. "I don't like reporters knowing my business."

"People talk; can't be helped. Maybe she's got connections in the department." I rolled my chair back and put my feet up on my desk.

"Ah ha." Sean slapped both hands on the desktop, his face puzzled. "Strange for that dame to be at the press briefing."

"Whys that?"

"I just placed the name, Jane Dickerson. She's not a crime reporter; she writes for the society section in the Sunday edition of the Gazette."

"When did you start reading the King City socials, O'Leary?" I was busting on Sean, but I read them pages myself every Sunday, to tell the truth. I like to keep up to date on everything going on in King City.

Sean glared at me. "My wife reads em; she has to tell me all about it over Sunday dinner."

Then I had my own ah-ha moment. "I've seen her before. Thought she looked familiar. She was at Max's funeral." Me and Sean were settling in, sharing observations, examining the facts, working the case. "She wasn't with the reporters. That's what threw me off. She was with the mourners. Got out of a green Model A Duesenberg and joined the line putting flowers on the casket."

"You sure do keep track of the dames. O'Shea."

"I do keep track of the dolls. I'm surprised you didn't notice her."

"Not my cup of tea, not enough meat on her bones. A stiff wind would blow her away."

A smart-ass remark concerning Sean's relations with the dames came to mind, but razzing Sean about his indiscretions would cross the line. He sees his liaisons with his ladies as part of his police duties. He has his own network of informants. I've had those kinds of connections work out for myself as well.

"If she's dogging me, maybe she ain't buying Foley's line on what went down at the Dockside Massacre?" Sean posed.

The shootout had a name already, only three days, Friday to Monday, before it took its place in history, along with the Snowdon Massacre at Lizzy's.

"That may just be the case. That reporter don't strike me as no Dumb Dora (*)," I said, "She's got more gumption than your typical socialite."

Sean and I had a copy of Foley's report on the shootout. I dropped my feet to the floor and rolled my chair back to the desk. I picked up the papers off my desk and began thumbing through them.

It was nothing but malarkey. The only thing Foley got right was the body count, 11 dead. Surprised the guy could count that high. His story that the warehouse was empty, there was no booze, and the safe was empty was also complete bushwa (*).

"The idea that Sleazy Sal pulled off the hit on Max that night at Lizzy's is hooey." Sean took a long drag on his cig. "There's no way Sal's dying wish was to confess to the killing of Max Snowdon."

Also, in the report, Foley claimed to have gotten a confession on the Snowdon killings out of Sal right before he kicked off that night at the stash house.

"The autopsy report says Sal took four shots in the chest. Pretty talkative for a guy with that much lead in him," I added.

Sean smiled, pinching a cig in his lips, and lit up.

I flipped a page.

"So, the story Foley's telling goes like this." I nodded to Sean. "Maxine is murdered. Sal and Billy are the prime suspects. Sal confesses to bumping off Max. Sal and Billy kill each other off. Case closed, all tied up real neat and smooth just the way the Chief likes it."

"So, O'Shea, you're not buying it, and you got plans on figuring out what really happened at Lizzy's."

I got right into it. "For starters, we need to make a list of everyone who had motive. Those who wanted Max dead, who would benefit from her demise."

"That's going to be a hell of a list."

"Yeah, and we're gonna need another list—a list of thugs who could have pulled off a gutsy raid like that. It was carried out like a military operation. If we can identify them, they may lead us to the mastermind who organized the attack."

"At least that list won't be as long; not that many torpedoes in King City."

"My money's still on out-of-town thugs."

"That'll make things more difficult," Sean said.

"We should check in with our contacts. Let's eliminate all the local torpedoes; see if they have alibis."

"Gotcha."

"I think I'll start with the reporter, Jane Dickerson. She might have contacts outside of King City. I can probably coax some information out of her."

"She's too classy for you, O'Shea." A grin was forming on Sean's smart-ass face. "And she's got you by a couple of inches. But then, she's someone for you to look up to." Sean chuckled and slumped back in his chair.

"Right." I did my best not to let Sean know he could rile me. And even if those long gams (*) she swayed around on put her a head taller than me, I was all in.

"Should we be looking at Foley? Maybe he had something to do with the hit." Sean was serious again.

"Nah. He's dumb, but not that dumb. He had a good thing going with the payola, just like everyone else. He'd have to be a sap to upset the apple cart."

"Everybody's going to be looking to replace their missing scratch. There's gonna be a lot of action on the street." Sean blew a puff of smoke toward the ceiling.

Last Friday was the first in a long time that Dulley didn't have that extra pile of cash to divvy out. With the Jones Gang absent, the smooth operation that Maxine had going had come to a screeching halt. A whole new Carvonshire pecking order would have to be worked out. And that would take some time and some more bloodshed. What's left of Max's organization, the cops, and surely some out-of-town gangs would be making their move. We could only wait and see how it would all shake out. And, of course, keep our heads down.

"That's what worries me, lots of greedy people getting creative."

EPISODE 4

THE RESCUE

Another Friday, another lunch at Kelly's, and, of course, Sean couldn't contain himself.

"Got a joke for you, O'Shea."

"I heard it already."

"What's the main difference between an Irish wedding and an Irish funeral?"

"Got me."

"One less drunk at the party."

"Nice one."

All this week, since the shootings at the Bay Street warehouse, Sean and I had been shaking the trees, still looking for a line on the killing of Maxine Snowdon, to no avail.

I waved my hand at Jen, trying to get her attention. "How can she not see me? She's looking right at me."

"Jen. Get off your arse, the tab," Sean called out, not even looking back at the old broad.

"Coming, hon," Was her sweet-as-punch reply.

She took a long drag on her cig, stumped it out in the ashtray, and then slipped off her stool with the grace of a short-legged duck.

"Oh, I almost forgot." Sean reached into his breast pocket, placed a yellow envelope on the tabletop, and slid it my way. "Got this from a paperboy on my way to the station this morning."

Jen saddled up and laid the check on the table. "Here you go, Sergeant."

"Thanks," Sean replied.

I picked up and examined the envelope. Perfectly centered, in real neat handwriting, my name stood out bold in blue ink.

"How'd he come by it?"

"Said he found it tucked up in his stack of newspapers this morning." There were newsstands run by Old Lady Oswald all over the city, manned by young boys, selling the morning and evening additions of the King City Gazette.

"Which newsstand?"

"The one I pass on Adams and 4th Ave."

Robby works that stand, one of my boys, a little old at 14, to be a paperboy and only mostly trustworthy.

I slit the envelope open with my penknife and slipped out a yellow steno sheet. It was like the ones Sean gets from the station house secretary. I read the message, written out in precise handwriting in the same blue ink.

"What's it say?" Sean was stretching his neck to get a look.

"It's a tip-off. Says someone's going to try to kidnap that reporter from the Gazette, Jane Dickerson, the doll who was asking too many questions last week."

"How could I forget? That's the dame you haven't stopped talk'en about all week. Does it say when or where?"

"Yeah, tonight at the docks, at the union meeting."

"How about who's planning it?"

"Nope."

"What would a society reporter be doing at the docks covering a union meeting?"

"Beats me. But when she came looking for you, she was acting more like a crime reporter."

"Anything else?"

"That's it, but I'm thinking whoever sent this note is expecting me to interfere with the kidnapping." I tucked the note paper back into the envelope.

Jen strolled up to our table and topped off Sean's cup, not mine.

Sean waited a moment and turned to watch Jen walk back to her stool. "So, are you going to do some interfering?"

"I'm thinking we should. Better to prevent a kidnapping than to have to solve one." I leaned forward and took a quick look around. "We'll head over there tonight and catch the end of the meeting."

"Are you sure this note is legit? Could be we're walking into a trap. I'm think'en we should find out who sent the note before we go off half-cocked."

"How are you planning on doing that?" I asked.

"The way I see it, the truck driver who dropped off the papers could have planted the note. We should find him and have a word."

Sean's idea of having a word with a suspect usually involved a pummeling of some sort.

"Could have been someone at the newspaper plant, the guy who loaded the truck," I added.

"Yeah, we'll have a talk with him, too."

"Or maybe Robby ain't telling the truth." Robby was known for stretching a story beyond its limits.

"Right, him too." Sean was nodding in satisfaction.

"That's a lot of ground to cover before this evening."

"We got all afternoon."

I knew Sean figured that he could easily fit three drubbings into one afternoon.

One of my responsibilities during an interrogation was to hold Sean back. Hard to question a subject when they're prone on the ground unconscious. I wish he was still boxing in the police league: it helped him blow off steam. His wife put an end to it, he claimed. In his younger days, he had a shot at going pro in the heavyweight division, but he would've had to give up the police game. It was a business decision. He didn't want to give up a steady flow of cash for the sketchy future income of a boxer.

Sean took me to the gym once to learn the art of pugilism, but I didn't take to it. Punching people in the face hurt my knuckles. Where others are wanting to engage in fisticuffs, I prefer Little Betsy, my ever-handy solid oak nightstick. I brought her home from France. She was issued to me at Camp Changarnier during my short-lived stint in the military police.

"I'm thinking this note is legit, and I don't want to know who sent it."

I prefer anonymous help; that way, I don't owe anybody.

"You're thinking again, O'Shea. That don't always work out for you."

"I got a good feeling about this note." I held up the note and flipped it between my fingers. "Don't want to discourage the sender by ruffling their feathers."

"Thinking and feeling, Danny. You sure do know your police work."

"Have I ever steered us wrong?" My lame response to his smart-ass comment. "Don't answer that."

Sean no doubt had memorized a long list of steered-wrong episodes that he could readily recite.

"I'll find out what time the union meeting is, and we'll meet up at the station a little earlier so we can arrive sometime near the end of it."

"Doesn't look like we're gonna have any quiet Friday nights anymore. Ah, what the hell? At least I don't have to spend the evening with the in-laws." Sean slid our tab across the table in my direction. "Don't have the dough to buy steaks at Benson's anyway."

I could see his point; a lot of coppers were going to come up short on payday. That extra stack of cash on the side had evaporated.

"Let's bring Johnson with us; not sure how much muscle we'll run into," I added.

James Johnson was O'Leary's squad corporal, a handy guy to have in a fight, good with his hands. He had been a sharpshooter during the war, also handy. People say he's a bit off, but who ain't a little off? At least he's got an excuse, a shrapnel fragment in his head.

I took out my roll, laid down a few greenbacks, and we vacated the premises.

We rolled up in Jedd's taxi on First Ave, a block back from Bay Ave, where the union meeting was being held at a dock warehouse. Me, O'Leary, and Johnson piled out of the old cab. I asked Jedd to hang around in case we needed transportation later, but he was free to scram if he heard gunshots.

Back at the station, Johnson had been insisting on taking a squad car. He has a thing for sirens and flashing lights. Sean told him a taxi was the classier way to go, and Johnson bought it. He wanted to wear his cowboy hat; said he had to have it if there was going to be gunplay. It was everything Sean and I could do to talk him out of it. Johnson was a fan of Westerns. He's seen every Western flick that was ever made.

The three of us took a stroll around the block and popped out on Bay Ave. The sun had set, and it was closing in on dusk.

"I hope this damn fog doesn't get any worse," Sean said in a whisper.

Light waves of mist were rolling along the street, passing us by.

"This is good." I brought the boys to a halt at a corner with a clear view of the loading dock warehouse, where I expected the crowd to exit when the meeting ended. I checked my watch: half-past eight. That would be soon.

"Johnson, take a stroll down the street and then around the block, and report back what you see. Me and O'Leary will keep a lookout from here." We had a good bead on the warehouse doors and the two lookouts smoking cigs. We were all in civilian clothes, so we would blend in if spotted.

"You got it, O'Shea." Johnson touched his hat with a salute and took off.

In a shake of a lamb's tail, he was back and presented himself with another touch to his cap.

"Find anything interesting?" I asked.

"Sure did. See that black Cadillac down the way, past the warehouse on the opposite side of the street?"

"Yeah, got it."

"There's two goons inside. I recognized them, two of Little Billy's enforcers."

"Okay, let's wait and see how this plays out."

It wasn't long before the union meeting ended, and dock workers started pouring out of the warehouse doors. Near the end of the procession, the doll we met at the station with a notebook in her hand appeared. She was walking alongside the dock boss, George Goff, and a city slicker I didn't recognize, probably a union organizer from out of town.

The two men crossed the street, jumped into their cars, and took off. The reporter headed off in the opposite direction. She turned the corner and legged it out of our sight. The two goons jumped out of their vehicle and took out after her, looking like beer kegs on legs.

"Johnson, take care of the car, just in case. We'll follow the thugs."

"Gotcha." Another touch of his cap, and he was off at a jog.

By the time Sean and I got to the warehouse, the two goons had popped back from around the corner, half a block away. One of them pretty much had the doll tucked under one arm. She was bound and gagged but kicking and thrashing up a storm. They didn't notice us and made a beeline for the Cadillac. So did we.

By the time we got to the car, the thug in the driver's seat was cranking over the engine again and again, cussing a blue streak.

I knocked on the driver's window. I twirled my finger, and the window rolled down. Johnson popped out of the shadows in front of the car, holding up a nest of wires. Sean appeared at the passenger side.

"Evening boys. What's shaken?"

"Oh, it's you, O'Shea." The driver turned his face to me.

"I see you got a package in the back seat." Miss Dickerson was lying face down, hogtied. "What're your plans, fellas?"

"Things been a little slow. Needed to pick up a little jack."

"That package you got is going to bring all hell down on your heads. Not worth the trouble." My eyes scanned Johnson and O'Leary. "As you see, you already got some trouble."

The driver looked to the goon in the passenger seat, who nodded.

"Step out of the car, real slow, and put your hands on the hood." They both obliged.

As Johnson and Sean relieved them of their hardware, I slipped into the backseat and went to work untying Miss Dickerson. The work done, I backed out of the door. The doll followed, her notable legs coming out first.

On her feet, I guided her by the elbow down the sidewalk a few yards away from the car.

"You okay, miss?"

"Yes, fine, thank you. Thank you so much." She bent a bit forward, running her hands down, trying to straighten out her knee duster (*).

"Jane Dickerson, a reporter for the King City Gazette." She extended her hand.

I was looking into those gorgeous brown eyes.

I took up her hand. "Detective Danny O'Shea, King City Police." That came off really dumb. "We met last week at the station."

She smiled. "Oh yeah, sorry. Now, I remember."

"Danny, what do you want to do with these goons?" Sean had come up behind me.

"Put their hardware in the trunk and give them back the spark plug wires."

"What, you're not going to arrest them?" Miss Dickerson flared up.

"No, not today." I put my arm around those slender shoulders and directed her down Bay Ave. "Where's your car?"

"On Church Street." She was looking back over her shoulder at the Caddy. "You're going to let them go?"

"No harm, no foul."

She pushed me away. "No harm; they tried to kidnap me."

"Tried to." I spread my arms out, signaling her freedom. "Those boys were just a little misguided. There's been hard times in Carvonshire now that the Jones Gang is busted up."

"They can't just get off scot-free!" Our reporter was facing me, her brow in a bunch.

"You want me to arrest them? Put you and them on the front page of your daddy's newspaper?"

"You know who I am?"

"I got my connections. Dickerson, that's your mother's maiden name, right?"

Her actual name was Jane Henderson, daughter of Joseph Henderson, the owner of the King City Gazette.

Her brow relaxed and her lips pinched.

"Right. I see your point." Miss Dickerson folded her arms across her chest.

She must have been considering the ramifications of her father finding out she was here at the docks tonight.

After a moment, she huffed, turned, and stormed off down the street toward where her car was parked. I followed along after her like an obedient puppy. Nearing the car, she stooped over to pick up her pad and pencil that she had lost hold of when the thugs snatched her up. That alone was worth tonight's bother.

As she approached the car, I stepped up ahead and opened the driver's side door of the dark green Duesenberg. She slipped into the seat with the grace of a short stop shoveling up a grounder.

She glanced up at me. "I'm sorry for the way I behaved. It was silly of me to be angry with you."

"Don't sweat it." I pointed a finger at her. "But you need to be more careful. If you're going to be a crime reporter, you'll need to look out for yourself from now on."

"That seems to be your job, my guardian angel."

Her smile melted away any response I could have made.

"Thanks again." She pulled the door closed.

As the Duesenberg pulled out, O'Leary's hand fell on my shoulder. "Out of your league, O'Shea."

"Don't I know it?"

⸻

"O'Shea, there's a brunette on stilts (*) down at the desk ask'en for ya." Dulley looked like the cat that swallowed the canary.

"No kid'en." I turned back to my paperwork.

"No, O'Shea, I'm not josh'en ya."

"I think he's being straight," Sean put in. "Not your usual Monday afternoon, though."

I pushed back in my swivel chair, making its usual squeak, as I looked Dulley up and down. "All right, lead the way."

I followed him out of my office and down the stairs to the precinct lobby. He kept looking over his shoulder at me and smiling like a goofy clown.

In the lobby, on the bench to the left of the doorway, Miss Jane Dickerson was penning notes on a leather-bound pad.

"Miss Dickerson." I was standing in front of her.

"Detective." As she stood up, she laid her pad on the bench and extended her hand.

I took it up as gentle as a cat picking up a kitten by the scruff of the neck.

"How'd you find me?"

"You know, policemen, police station." She was eyeballing the station lobby.

I seemed to be getting dumber by the minute.

"I realized that I didn't thank you properly the other night. I wasn't myself."

"That's okay; it's my job. Besides, you were dealing with a difficult situation." Being kidnapped, a difficult situation.

"Anyway, here I am. Thank you for saving me from those hoodlums."

"You're welcome."

"I do have some questions, though. Do you mind?"

"Have at it." I motioned to the bench, and we sat beside each other.

"How did you find out about the kidnapping attempt? I assume you and your men didn't just happen to be hanging around the docks on a Friday night."

I hesitated; this kind of dame had a way about her; I was tempted to spill the beans. "I got a tip from a source."

"That's kind of vague, Detective."

"I like to keep my comments to reporters vague."

"Always?"

"Not always." I could see myself making all kinds of exceptions.

"Maybe we could get to know each other better, and we wouldn't have to be so… vague."

"How would we do that—get less vague?"

"A night out?" Her eyes seemed to flash. "Do you have any ideas?"

Boy, did I have ideas. "How about meeting me at the Griffin Street speakeasy for a drink Friday night?"

"A gentleman picks up his lady for a date."

"Want me to roll up your father's mansion in a squad car or a beat-up taxi?" I could have sprung for appropriate transportation, but I was thinking our relationship should be kept under wraps.

"No, on second thought, I'll meet you there." She stood up, picking up her notepad. "At nine?"

"Works for me."

Her hips propelled her to the station's double doors before I got to my feet. At the exit, without looking back, she raised her arm and twirled her pointing fingers. "Till tomorrow night, Detective."

"Till then." That's all I could come up with.

O'Leary, who had been leaning on the booking Sergeant's desk nearby, came up behind me. "I think that dame just landed herself an inside source in the police department."

"Don't you know it?"

I looked at my pocket watch again: a few minutes to nine. Should have just left it out on the table already. I'd been checking the time every five minutes since I arrived at Eight, but instead, I returned it to my breast pocket.

It was the same all week, time moving at a snail's pace. From Monday to Friday, only inched its way along.

Joe, the manager, got bothered when I showed up that early. I told him I was expecting a date. That's why I took a table up front. My usual spot at the Griffin Street speakeasy was near the back door.

The band was well into its first set, and I was on my third bourbon. I usually hold to a limit of two, but I was telling myself that tonight was a special night. I was starting to believe that all the smiles from the redheaded barmaid were only for me.

Smoke hung at the ceiling. People were getting chatty.

I noticed Miss Dickerson immediately when she waltzed in the main door, easy-peasy since I was checking the door every few seconds. I stood and waved her over. Should have gone to meet her, but I stood frozen like a statue.

"Glad you could make it, Miss Dickerson."

"My friends call me Jane."

"Jane, it is then. I'm Danny." Of course I am, jeez.

"What can I get you?" I raised my hand and motioned to the barmaid. The redhead was at our table in a flash.

"Gin Rickey, please."

"The lady will have a Gin Rickey."

"Sure, Danny, you got it." As the redhead sauntered away, she flipped a smile back at me over her shoulder.

"You come here often?"

"Yeah, every Friday, like clockwork, unless there's a better band somewhere. That happens occasionally."

Jane looked at the stage and nodded. "This band is the bees' knees."

"Yeah, they're local fellas from Henshaw. I introduced them to the manager." They were turning out some real smooth tunes.

"Very good of you. How do you know them?"

"They were playing at a little joint around the corner from my apartment. I was passing by and got an ear full."

Miss Dickerson looked puzzled.

"I live in the Henshaw District."

"Oh."

I was sure she was wondering why I lived in the colored section of town. She might not have thought it polite to ask, but she did anyway. She is a reporter, after all.

"Really. Sounds like a story there. Do you want to tell it?"

"Someday, maybe. As long as it don't end up in the papers."

"Oh, I can be discrete, Detective."

We both sat quiet for a moment, taking in the music and the alcohol. I was still nursing my third.

"Do you dance, Detective?"

"To jazz?" There were jazz styles folks liked to dance to, but not the ballad style we were taking in tonight.

"No silly, the Charleston, the Lindy, you know."

"Not on a regular basis." Actually, never, but I was thinking maybe I could learn.

"There's a dance hall uptown that brings in the big bands. We do all the latest dances. Since you visit other places occasionally, you should come sometime. It's the cat's meow."

"That sounds like a possibility." I was considering all kinds of possibilities.

The redheaded barmaid sauntered up to our table. "Can I get you another, Danny?" She flashed a wink and a smile my way. She wasn't helping my cause.

I looked to Miss Dickerson, and she nodded. "Yeah, both of us."

"A double, Danny?"

"No doll, a single." I needed to slow the flow of alcohol into my brain.

The joint erupted in applause. The band was taking a break. Jane and I joined in.

The place filled up with a mix of quiet chatter and rowdy outbursts. Dames were getting up in packs to go iron their shoelaces (*).

Jane held up her empty glass at eye level. "I don't mean to complain, but this Gin Rickey tastes a little off."

"That's because it's not exactly made to specs. Quality gin is hard to come by. It was undoubtedly cut with some bathtub gin."

Jane abruptly put down the glass. "Is it safe to drink?"

"Yeah, Joe knows the guy who makes it. He's local. You're okay."

"Good to know." Jane embraced the glass again. "Being a copper and all, you probably have the inside track on the bootlegging landscape."

"I got my connections."

"How does it all work, the bootlegging rackets?" Jane was rocking her drink, sloshing the alcohol around.

"I can give you the low-down, but none of it can appear in the papers. It would be a good idea if you stayed away from writing any stories about bootlegging. Got it?"

"Sure thing. I'm just interested in learning how things work here in King City."

I slid my chair around the side of the table to get closer to Jane and checked left and right to make sure our fellow patrons were out of earshot.

Leaning in close, I started my tale. "When Maxine was alive and in charge, she controlled the flow of booze coming into the Carvonshire port. Now, with her gone, that source of booze from the Rum Runners is cut off for the time being."

"All the booze? I thought that only rum came in from the sea. You know, from the Rum Runners."

"Rum Runners do bring in some rum that's produced in the Caribbean, but that's not all. The profitable booze is the imported liquors from Europe, like gin and bourbon."

I held up my glass. "Scotch, and the like. And some classy wines from France."

"Maxine had an arrangement with a woman from Nassau. She imported the booze from England, France, and other places and then arranged to have it shipped up to King City by Rum Runners. They anchor in the bay, a mile out, where small boats from the Carvonshire port go out to meet them and bring the booze to the docks.

But with Max gone, there's no one to provide protection for the shipments. It's a mess." My informants kept me up to date.

"So, King City is cut off. No quality alcohol is coming into the city?"

"Not through the port, anyway. There are a couple of cities up north where Rum Runners are still operating. Some booze is coming from there overland by truck. But that's expensive and a risky venture."

"How so?"

"Every time the product changes hands, the price goes up. Every gangster whose territory it goes through collects a tax. And, of course, the trucks are easy targets for high-jacking."

"How do you know all this?"

"That's a story for another day." I decided to change the subject; I didn't know this doll well enough to say anymore. I may have said too much already.

"So, how'd you finagle a reporter job at the King City Gazette?" I knew the answer to that already. I do my research, just wanted to hear what she would say about it.

"I talked my father into giving me the position of society reporter."

That was a lot more honest than I was expecting.

"You go by Dickerson, dodging the family name?"

"Yes. I'm trying to avoid the complications of being my father's daughter, so I use my mother's maiden name."

"How's that working for you?"

"Not as well as I would like. It's not much of a cover, obviously." She nodded at me.

"Yeah, but I'm a detective."

"True."

"What's your mother have to say about her daughter's employment in the newspaper game?"

"She passed when I was ten."

"Sorry to hear that."

"That's okay."

"How does your father feel about you working the crime beat? Venturing into a man's domain and covering things like the union activities at the docks."

"He doesn't know that I am. Actually, he forbade it. When he found out I was at the police station news conference, he laid down the law and told me to stick to the society pages."

"How are you managing to stay in the game without him finding out?"

"I have an arrangement with my editor." She gave me a stern look. "Not that kind of arrangement."

"I didn't say anything."

"You didn't have to; I know how you men think."

"That must be helpful for a reporter."

Jane flashed a 'Aren't you a smart-ass' look. Her voice fell to a whisper. "I plan on writing a story for the crime section on the Snowdon Massacre. I don't believe a word of Detective Foley's account. I'd like to know what you think about the hit at Lizzy's to take out Maxine Snowdon."

"I thought you already knew what men think?" Sitting here beating my gums to a reporter wasn't in my best interest, no matter how appealing that might be.

She gave me another 'Don't be a smart ass' look.

"I'd like to hear what you think first. You got a theory?" I hoped she had some dope I didn't and was willing to share.

"First off, I don't believe that Sleazy Sal was responsible for the murders, and I especially don't believe he confessed with his dying breath. It's nothing but baloney. Do you agree, Detective?"

"It's Danny. And yeah, I do." No harm offering an opinion.

"You do? I thought you'd hold up the official line."

"No, you didn't or wouldn't have asked."

"So, you don't believe that Sleazy Sal confessed?"

"What's the likelihood of my name appearing in the papers?"

"It won't. I protect my sources."

"O'Leary either?"

"No, of course not."

"Well, the idea that Sal did the hit and then confessed with his dying breath is about as likely as the Pope walking in here tonight."

"Do you have a theory about who is responsible?"

"Not yet. The problem is the motive ain't clear. Hard to see who had something to gain that was worth sending all of Carvonshire into chaos."

"Not somebody from her gang looking to move up?"

"I can't see any of them being that smart or that stupid. Another possibility is that it was personal, a grudge, or revenge. Have you seen the autopsy report?"

"No." Her first reluctant response.

"Four bullets to the face after she was dead."

"That does sound personal."

"Now, with Max gone, Carvonshire is going to get rough."

"I'm aware; I've had personal experience."

"Maybe you should think twice about getting yourself more involved in the crime beat.

"Because I'm a dame, right? You don't think I can hold my own, Detective?"

"It's Danny. And I'm just saying I would feel bad if something happened to you. The kind of stories you're taken an interest in could put you at risk." I knew I wasn't going to talk her out of anything. And didn't have much hope at this point of talking her into anything either.

"Very thoughtful, Detective. I can take care of myself."

"Oh." I tried not to smile.

"Well, usually, I can take care of myself. I'm going to be much more careful from now on. And just to be on the safe side, I plan on using a nom de plume, J.L. Gibson, for my byline, so no one will know that I'm the one writing articles for the crime beat section."

"Sounds like a solid plan."

"Thanks."

"Have you got anything that backs up your suspicions, a suspect, a line on the killers? Maybe your out-of-town contacts have a lead on the torpedoes?"

"No, I haven't unearthed anything as yet."

"You'll let me know if you do, right?" I was getting the picture now; this doll was a complete newbie, no sources, no contacts, just me, her inside man in the police department.

"Of course, Detective. Maybe we should work together on this Maxine Snowdon mystery. I have my sources, and you have your connections. We could share information and chase down leads. That way, you could keep an eye on me in case you're really worried."

That wouldn't be hard to do. "You might be on to something, kiddo."

"We could be like partners."

"Yeah, like partners." I liked the sound of that.

Jane raised her glass, and I responded with mine and a clink.

"It might not be a bad idea to shine a light on Foley's bushwa. It might shake something out of the trees. You could quote an unnamed source in the department and do some speculating in your article."

"I can do that."

We stayed until the end of the last set. I walked her to her car.

"Thanks for a great evening, Detective."

"It's Danny."

"The band was great. I loved their tunes."

"I hope to see you again soon, Miss Dickerson."

"I'll stay in touch, Detective."

It was a dangerous game the doll was entering into, and there was no way of talking her out of it. But with her and me on the same page, we might make some progress resolving the hit at Lizzy's. She might make a valuable connection. Besides, I should keep an eye on her: It's just the right thing to do.

EPISODE 5

IS NO ONE SAFE?

The station was buzzing: the word was spreading that the Commissioner was on his way.

Sean and I were hanging around the booking desk, trying to look nonchalant. Chief Donnelly was locked away in his office, waiting for the ax to fall.

In due time, the Commissioner arrived, busting through the main doors into the lobby with a rolled-up newspaper in his right hand, the Monday morning edition. Jane hadn't wasted any time getting her article about Snowdon Massare into the headlines.

Donnelly made a beeline to the Chief's office. Thrown open, the office door bounced back, almost coming off the hinges. Once inside, the Commissioner slammed the door behind him. The glass window in the door rattled but didn't break.

We had come down to the first floor hoping to listen in on the conversation between the Chief and Commissioner. We could have stayed on the second floor.

After a half-hour of shouting and cussing, the Commissioner had spent himself. The Chief's door swung open. The Commissioner, red as a beet, emerged, slamming the door again, rattling the window again. He stormed through the lobby and out to his waiting car.

One minute later, the Chief's door swung back open, and out came the Chief. He eyeballed the small crowd with the intent of cutting them dead. We all began to scatter. He strode away down the hall. Another door slammed, Foley's office this time, followed by another half an hour of shouting and cussing.

The show over; me and Sean retired to my office. Sean shook his head as he took his seat, looking like a schoolgirl about to break out in giggles. "Damn, that was great."

I had to agree. Jane's article in the crime beat section this morning had unleashed a hornets' nest. The article was full of well-written, convincing speculation that cast doubt on the official police theory on what happened at Lizzy's, the Snowdon Massacre. And to boot, no one knew who the new crime-beat reporter, J.L. Gibson, was and where he was getting his information.

"I told you this was going to work out. I think the doll has a future in crime reporting." I gave Sean a wink and a nod.

"It makes for grand entertainment, that's for sure. But is this new connection of yours going to pay off in the long run?"

"A crime scene reporter in our pocket; we're sitting pretty."

"Right, but who's in whose pocket? That ain't real clear to me."

*   *   *

"That was a clever way of sending a message, Detective." Jane was smiling at me from across the table, candlelight on her face.

I had had one of my paperboys deliver my note. He handed her a newspaper that had the note tucked inside. I told him to say, 'Danny O'Shea says you should see what's on page eight.' I had to admit, pretty clever. The note said I wanted to meet up and suggested my club, Griffin's.

Through a newsroom gopher, she sent a note back inviting me to join her at the Bentley, her father's private supper club. I'd never been to the joint, a swanky upper-class speakeasy in the King District. The King District wasn't my territory, but a good place to meet. The odds are nobody here would recognize me, especially dressed up in this spiffy suit I bought from a second-hand store so I'd fit in amongst the upper-class gents.

In addition to the monkey suit, Jane had created a cover story. For her nosy socialite friends, I was her out-of-town, distant cousin, Danny Witherspoon, visiting on business. I'd have to come up with an alias for Jane for our meetings at Griffin Street. So far, I was letting people think she was my uptown, well-to-do girlfriend.

"Next time you send a note, have your fella give it to one of my newspaper boys, and he can pass it on to me. It won't look good for me to be having regular correspondence coming from the King City Gazette." I was hoping for regular correspondence, though.

"As intriguing as sending a clandestine note is, I could just pick up the phone."

"Not a good idea. All the phone calls in and out of the precinct are monitored. The station switchboard operator writes down the juicy tidbits and delivers them to the Chief for his reading pleasure."

"That's terrible," Jane said, "You can't even use the phone in your own office."

Actually, it wasn't that much of a problem; me and Sean played it to our advantage. For one, we got to see the transcripts each week as well. Lois, our phone operator, was one of O'Leary's connections. Some women in King City will do anything for the guy; go figure. Secondly, sometimes we used the phone to plant information we wanted the Chief to hear, red herrings or diversions.

Changing the subject, "That was some article you wrote."

Jane was smiling ear to ear. "You liked it?"

"It was jake (*). It cast some genuine doubt on the official police line about what went down at the Snowdon Massacre. And it sure stirred up a hornet's nest at the station house this morning."

"That's what you wanted, right?"

"Yeah, it was entertaining as hell."

"I wasn't aiming for your personal entertainment."

"I wish you could have been there. The Commissioner kicked the Chief's ass; the Chief kicked Foley's ass. Couldn't have been better."

"Glad you enjoyed yourself."

"Bet that story sold some papers."

"Yes, my editor was thrilled with it."

"How are you doing keeping your identity secret?"

"My editor is telling everybody he's keeping the new reporter's identity a secret for the guy's safety."

"This must be a little confusing for you."

"What do you mean?"

"You got three identities to deal with. Jane Henderson, the newspaper mogul's daughter; Jane Dickerson, the society reporter; and J.L. Gibson, the crime beat reporter."

"I can keep more than one ball in the air at a time, Detective."

"It's Danny, and I bet you can."

A waiter with a white towel over his arm came to the table to take our order.

"Gin Ricky for me, please." Jane flashed those deep brown eyes at me.

I wanted to order something classy to impress, but instead, I said, "Two bourbons, straight." Old habits, they say. "And a Gin Ricky for the do…, lady."

I cast about the place, dimly lit by candles in glass vessels on red tablecloths and a scattering of wall sconces. Waiters hustled about with bottles of wine or platters balanced above their heads. Busy for a Monday night.

Lowering her voice a bit, "How did you come to be in your line of work, a snooper (*) in the police department?"

"My father was a copper, a detective."

"In the family, then. Was his father a copper, too?"

"No, he was a horse thief."

"Really?" Her face said she thought I was joshing.

"Yeah, he had a little ranch out west of here, a legit enterprise. But of course, he did a little rustling on the side to make ends meet."

"Your dad didn't go for that and switched sides?"

"Most of it was just being contrary. And he couldn't resist the lure of the city lights."

My dad didn't have much to do with me as a kid, but he sure came through getting me a spot on the force as a patrolman. I needed something solid to hold on to after I got back from the war. The job and Father Pat from St. Mary's got me through some tough times.

The waiter arrived and put our drinks on the table. "Are you ready to order?" He was looking at me. We hadn't even picked up the menus yet.

Jane piped up. "I'll have the filet mignon. You should try it, Danny. It's the house specialty."

I looked at the waiter. "The same."

The waiter spun away.

"So, Detective, how do you manage," Jane asked, "With that reputation of yours?" She placed her napkin in her lap just so.

"What do you mean?"

"Danny O'Shea, the only honest cop in King City, a city well known for its corrupt police department."

"Where did you get that on me?"

"I have my sources."

I nodded.

"You've even been promoted several times from patrolman to Junior Detective and then to Senior Detective. That's impressive for a guy who doesn't toe the party line. How's that happen?"

"I got my connections, doll."

"You've also made some amazing arrests. Cracked some tough cases."

"You know my history?" This dame does her homework.

"Stories, you know, in the newspaper?" She pointed to herself with a thumb.

"Yeah, right."

"You got promoted to Senior Detective right after you made that big bootlegging arrest back in '24'. It seems like a bootlegging bust in Carvonshire would get you bumped off rather than a promotion. Tell me about it."

That was the consensus at the time. The Chief gave me the bump, thinking I probably wouldn't live to pick up my first check. It remains a mystery to this day. People think I'm connected, but they don't know how. Works in my favor.

"Not much to tell. Me and O'Leary intercepted a truckload of high-end booze coming into the city."

"Over five grand worth, it said in the paper."

"Cases of fancy wine and barrels of German beer smuggled in from overseas; it adds up."

"You and Sergeant O'Leary seize a truck full of Maxine Snowdon's booze, five grand worth, and you get promoted instead of six feet under. I'm not getting it."

I wondered if we were at a point in our relationship where I could level with her about what really went down at that bootlegging bust.

"Well, sometimes things just work out in my favor; the luck of the Irish, they say."

"I guess I'm not going to hear the full story?"

I flashed my most charming smile. "Story for another day."

Right then, the waiter walked up with two plates of sizzling steak and laid them down in front of us.

As Jane cut into her steak, "You got anything cooking at the present?"

"Not this minute, but you'll be the first to know."

"I'm counting on that, Detective."

I was going to correct her and say, 'It's Danny,' but my yap was full of the best steak I'd ever tasted.

* * *

"You're early," I said. Sean always gets to Kelly's at lunchtime before me.

"Nah, you're late."

He was already chowing down on his first pastrami sandwich.

"Same old, same old. Why don't you branch out and try something else on the menu?"

Jen waddled up to our table. She was looking back at her perch at the counter. "What'll you have?"

"The usual," I said, although I really wasn't hungry. That steak at Bentley's last night was still a fond memory.

Sean rolled his eyes. "Got a joke for ya, O'Shea."

"I heard it already."

"Why did God invent whiskey?"

"Got me."

"To prevent the Irish from ruling the world!"

"Good one."

Jen was back sitting at the counter, dragging on a butt. She hadn't given Kelly my order.

"It's good that Kelly has great grub; the service here ain't up to par." I cocked my head in Jen's direction.

"Can't expect much when you hire your in-laws," Sean said.

Jen was Kelly's mother-in-law.

I pulled an envelope from my breast pocket and slid it across the table to Sean.

"I got another note this morning."

As he picked it up, "How'd you come by it this time?"

"Someone dropped it in my mail slot during the night."

"Got any idea who's sending them? Sean twirled the yellow envelope in his raised hand.

"I've got a hunch."

"Spill it."

"Grace Snowdon."

"The missing accountant?" Sean leaned back in his chair. "I figure she's long gone or six feet under. Anyway, how could an accountant get herself so connected?"

"I got a theory I'm working on."

"Okay, let's hear it already." Sean threw up his hands.

"The envelopes, the paper accountants use, the handwriting, they point to Grace."

"That's pretty flimsy." Sean was smirking and shaking his head. "Besides, it would be dumb on her part to be so obvious."

I wasn't thinking it was so much a clue, but more than that, a warning. If it was Grace sending the notes, it worried me. I knew what she was capable of.

"I've had my boys watching her apartment and her office for the last three weeks. She hasn't come up for air." Unknown to Sean, I had started the surveillance right after Max's funeral.

"Like I said, long gone." Sean shrugged his bulky shoulders.

"Nah, she was at Max's funeral."

"Oh yeah, I didn't spot her." Sean dabbed some mustard from his mouth.

"She was in disguise and hanging with her father."

"You sure it was her?" Sean asked.

"Yeah, I'm sure."

Grace was a master of disguise, but there was something sinister in the way she moved. My close encounters with Grace are not something a body will ever forget.

"Joe coming home for the funeral was a surprise," I added.

Grace's father, Joe Snowdon, had never approved of his sister Maxine's line of work. Max had taken up the reins of the family business from their father, the former head of the Jones Gang, after he got himself blown up.

"He left after a nasty family row, right?" Sean pinched out a butt in the ashtray, and the last smoke trail curled upward.

"Yeah, when he left, he even disowned Grace."

Joe had had it with his criminal family and moved away. Went down south somewhere and became a Baptist Minister.

"I could see his beef with Max, but why part ways with his own daughter?" A match flared to light Sean's next cig. "That goes against the teachings of the good book?"

"I figure he didn't like the line or work she was in."

"An accountant?"

"Working for Max Snowdon in any line would do it, I guess." If Sean had been aware of Grace's extracurricular activities, murder for hire and all, he'd have a better appreciation for her daddy's disapproval.

"You thinking that Grace might be trying to take over the family business, put the Jones Gang back on the map?" Sean asked.

"It's a possibility. She's got the connections." I took a sip of my cup of Joe that I had been neglecting.

I was starting to think Grace might have had something to do with there being a vacancy in the family business. It wouldn't make sense for Grace to knock off Maxine, but stranger things have happened.

Grace was a loner and not likely to have planned the messy event that took place that night at Lizzy's. Maybe she just took advantage of the situation somehow.

Sean and I had eliminated all of King City's torpedoes from our suspect list; they all had alibis, which left an out-of-town crew as the probable suspects. Finding the torpedoes and then them leading us to the mastermind was a dead end.

Sean put on his reading glasses and turned his attention to the note he had just pulled out of the envelope. His hands, both holding the note, dropped to the table. Looking over his glasses, "Jesus, Mother, and Joseph, says here someone's going to break Father Pat's legs. That's bold."

"Yeah, and out of line."

"It says it's going down tonight, but doesn't say where."

"My bet, the church, after dark."

Father Pat was the priest at St. Mary's, the Catholic church on the corner of Church Street and 4th Ave. The Father goes to McCarthy's drum (*), a few blocks down 4th Ave, every night just after dark. The McCarthy family are big donors at St. Mary's. Father Pat drinks for free. Helps ease up on the consumption of the sacramental wine.

"Who's after him, you think?" Sean asked.

The note didn't say.

"I'm pretty sure it's Leo the Greek."

Leonidas Dukas, a local Shylock (*), also known as Lazy Leo because he is hardly ever seen out of his office chair.

Father Pat likes to play the horses (boxing or any sports betting, really). Gets in over his head sometimes. The Father probably borrowed some jack from Leo to pay off his bookie, passing the buck down the road.

"Leo will be sending a message, a couple of goons to break Father Pat's legs."

Lazy Leo was of the same mindset on forgiveness as the church. If you want it, you got to pay for it.

"That takes some brass."

"We'll head over there this evening and stake out the rectory around dusk."

The Father can be counted on to stroll down to the speakeasy every day, like clockwork. That worked to Leo's advantage.

"Why couldn't they do the deed on a Friday night so I could avoid dinner with the in-laws? These days, always got to listen to them grousing about having to eat chuck roast instead of steak."

Sean was light on cash. I was going to have to do something about that before he did something about it, something stupid. Other coppers, some patrolmen, had taken up selling protection for the merchants on their beats to replace the payola they used to get from the Jones Gang.

"You can't expect hoodlums to schedule their crimes to accommodate your preferences. You think I should have a word with Leo?"

"Smart ass."

I waved my arm to get Kelly's attention and yelled, "The usual!"

I wanted to expedite my lunch; a scheme for this evening was starting to form in my mind; a little side action that I was seeing could be to my benefit.

Parked across the street from the church, Sean and I were playing the waiting game, a stakeout. Our car was a black Model T Ford I borrow from Owen O'Carroll, my barber, on occasions like this when we need to be inconspicuous. From the passenger seat, I had a better view than Sean, who sat behind the wheel.

Any minute now, Father Pat should emerge from the rectory adjacent to the church, built of the same red brick.

It was well after dusk. Wisps of fog from the bay swept along the street like ghosts looking for the church cemetery.

"What the hell," Sean was pointing to the corner up the street, "Who invited her?" He turned a scowl on me.

A green Model A Duesenberg had pulled up, parking on the same side as us, facing our way, a block away. Despite the rolling fog, I got a vague glimpse of Jane's face before the dash lights went out. She had gotten my invitation.

"We're going to get a collar tonight. No reason why we shouldn't get our names in the paper. She gets a story, and we take some hoodlums off the streets of King City."

"You might want to have a word with her, not to park her car under a streetlight. She might give up the whole shebang."

"She's new to the game. I'll have a talk with her."

Just then, the rectory door opened, and out came Father Pat. Passing in front of the church, he waltzed down the street, heading for McCarthy's speakeasy.

Right after, two thugs in black slipped out of a dark alley and fell in lockstep with the priest.

"You planning on letting them break the holy man's legs?" Sean's hand was on the door handle.

"Hold up a bit. We need to catch them in the act. Let them put their hands on the Father; then we got them for assault."

We eased out of the car and caught up real quick on the scene behind the thugs. One had the priest by the lapels of the coat. The Father was on his toes, backed up against a five-foot-high, black cast-iron fence at the sidewalk's edge. The other thug had a blackjack raised above his head, about to take a swing. Sean caught hold of the stick and wrenched it away. One punch and Sean's thug was down and out.

I brought Betsy down on the other hood's shoulder. Father Pat escaped his grasp and dropped back on his soles. The goon turned around just in time to see old Betsy coming round for a whack to the side of the head. He hit the sidewalk with a thud, laid out next to his pal.

Father Pat stepped up to me and Sean. "Danny O'Shea and Sean O'Leary, heavens abound. Praise be to God."

I was thinking that the priest's praise was misdirected. "All in the line of duty, Father."

"Sean, I will say the Mass for you and your family tomorrow morning." The Father was staring down at the goons lying flat on the sidewalk.

Sean and his wife are regulars at St. Mary's. She and her family are devout, as they say. Sean is more or less a tag-along.

"Thank you, Father," Sean said from his kneeling position. He was slapping the cuffs on one of the thugs, who he had rolled over on his stomach. Sean's guy was moaning, his face in a puddle of blood from a broken nose. Mine was still out cold.

Father Pat made the sign of the cross as he spoke to me. "And a special dispensation for you, Danny."

A little dispensation couldn't hurt. I probably don't have a lot of credits to my name in my heavenly account. I'm not devout or a regular.

"Who are these gentlemen, Danny?" Father Pat asked.

He probably knew, but was looking for confirmation. "A couple of goons, Leo sent to deliver a message, Father. "

At that moment, Jane rushed up, pad and pen in hand. "So, what's the story?"

"And who is this?" the Father was giving me a look of panic.

"Miss Dickerson, a reporter for the King City Gazette, Father."

Father Pat put his hand on my shoulder, turned me away, and whispered, "I can't help but wonder how this is all going to come out in the papers?"

"Not to worry, Father. She's all right. She's with me. I got you covered."

As I turned back, Jane wrinkled her brow and sent me daggers.

"I really appreciate this, Danny," the Father said.

"Does this mean we're even, Father?" I owed Father Pat. He saved me from myself after I came home from the war, a drunken, angry soldier. We spent a lot of time in his rectory office talking things through. I'd have been in a sorry condition if it weren't for Father Pat.

"You know that God and I don't keep score."

I knew that wasn't entirely true for Father Pat. He kept track of the score at ball games he had bets riding on.

"I thought that was the whole point of going to Mass. To get sins canceled out by indulgences, offerings, and prayers."

"A slight misinterpretation of the Gospel on the Church's part." Father Pat smiled at me and then looked at Jane and her notebook. "That's off the record, my dear."

"Of course, Reverend… I mean Father."

"Not a Catholic girl, I take it?"

"Presbyterian."

"You should stop by the rectory sometime for a little theological conversation. Maybe we could set you on the right path." Father Pat was smiling, as usual.

"I'll give it some thought." Jane was returning the smile.

I took Jane by the elbow and led her a few yards away for a private confab. "We need to get our story straight on what happened here."

"Since you knew about the time and place, those hoods were surely enforcers intent on sending Father Pat a message. We need to find out who sent them and why."

"No, it wasn't like that at all. It was a mugging. These goons thought Father Pat was carrying the Sunday offering with him and decided to relieve him of it." I didn't want these goons tied back to the Shylock and the Father's gambling debt. Later on, I'd have a private word with Leo to discuss his debt collection methods. What's acceptable and what ain't.

"At nine at night? That doesn't make sense."

"I'm just giving you the basics of the story, the possibilities. You'll need to fill in the blanks." I gave her a wink. "Get creative."

The doll looked at me blank for a long moment. Then she nodded, stepped away to get better situated under a streetlight, and started scribbling on her notepad.

I headed back to Sean and the Father.

"I'll call it in and get a paddy wagon sent over to pick up the goons," Sean said. He walked off to the end of the block to a police call box.

"Gotta go, Detective," Jane called out over her shoulder as she turned away. "I need to get this story in before the morning paper's deadline this evening." Jane hustled across the street to her car.

"You sure about this?" Father Pat's eyes were following her.

"Father, who can you trust if you can't trust Danny O'Shea?"

"I put my trust in God, and right now, he's telling me to trust you."

"I appreciate that you and God are putting your faith in me."

The Father laughed and slapped my shoulder.

"I miss seeing your face at Sunday Mass, Danny."

During the time Father Pat had been counseling me for my difficulties, I had been a regular at Sunday Mass for a while. I hung in there as long as I could, not wanting to hurt Father Pat's feelings.

"Got my fill of religion, Father. Not that I don't appreciate all you did for me."

"I know, my son. God loves you whether or not you attend Mass."

Jane's car pulled out and made a U-turn. She honked the horn. Sean was back at my side.

"Well, looks like you two have got things under control." The priest was making a study of the scene. "I have church business to attend to."

"Father, before you go."

"Yes," Father Pat said as he turned back to me.

"Do me a favor; the doll wasn't here tonight."

"Danny O'Shea, are you asking me to lie for you?"

"Of course not; suppose you could treat it like a confession, a secret?"

"Every place on earth is a potential confessional. Rest assured, Miss Dickerson's presence here tonight is between God and us." Father Pat winked.

With that, Father Pat was off, back on track, his original undertaking. Sean and I watched as he walked away, down the street, toward McCarthy's drum.

"Nothing can defer a man of God on a mission," Sean said. In this case, his mission was to meet his bookie and a bottle of red wine.

The McCarthy family, the glue that holds the St. Mary's Parish together, second in command to the Father, could be counted on to look out for him. Sean should have a word with the McCarthys about a little extra jack landing in the collection plate this Sunday in order to set Father Pat right with Leo.

Sean and I headed back to our car to wait for the paddy wagon.

"You sure the dame will get the story straight?" Sean was lighting up a cig.

"Yeah, she's a good egg," I said, "Tomorrow, you'll be the hero of the Parish. People will think they owe you and want to do things for you. It's like Jesus said, - You scratch my back, and I'll scratch yours."

Sean's head was turned toward me, his cig between his fingers hung in the air. "Jesus didn't say that."

"Well, he should have. He probably said - if you take care of the priests, good things will follow."

"Didn't say that either, the opposite, actually."

That was a surprise. Sean must be paying attention in church. I thought it was just an opportunity for a long nap.

"Well, I'm sure it will go a long way with Mary Claire and her family." Sean could use some extra points with his wife and her brood.

"Yeah, couldn't hurt." Sean took a drag and blew the smoke out the window. "Given any more thought on why you're getting these notes, and why?"

"Probably shouldn't look a gift horse in the mouth, but I can't help having my suspicions and hunches."

"Not ready to share?"

"No. Got to figure the motive and follow that. Still working on it."

These notes were little favors coming my way. I was thinking someone, maybe Grace, might show up someday, expecting a favor in return. Then again, it's not like I've been asking for them. Maybe it's me doing the favor. In any case, I don't like being the debtor.

A siren wailed, coming from behind us, the paddy wagon.

"Let's get this wrapped up."

"I'm with you, O'Shea."

We headed back to the scene of the crime to meet the coppers from the wagon.

The way things were going, ain't nobody gonna be safe in King City.

EPISODE 6

THE UNDERGROUND

"That article the newspaper dame wrote about us was swell; made us look like heroes." A mouth full of pastrami sandwich jumbled Sean's words. "Did you remember the pickles?"

Friday and another rainy day, the third in a row this week. We didn't want to walk in the downpour to Kelly's for lunch, so we hung back at my office.

"Yeah, right here." I reached into the bag of food I had delivered from Goldman's, the Jewish deli around the corner, and pulled out the pickles wrapped in wax paper.

Sean was referring to the article in the newspaper Jane had written about the attempted mugging of Father Pat and the thwarting thereof by two of King City's finest.

I decided to get right to it, the reason I sprung for lunch.

"I got some action going on tonight at the Pinnacle Club. A meeting with Vinny. And I want you there for backup."

"What's this meeting about?"

"Baseball and gambling."

"That's all? Why do you need me?"

"Because Vinny is going to find the conversation disagreeable."

"Of course he is. What time you thinking?" Sean knew not to press me for details. We worked on the 'the less you know, the better principle.'

Sean had a moonlighting job now on Friday night at Griffin Street. He was probably more worried about missing the extra cash tonight than what the meeting was about.

I had arranged with Joe, the manager of Griffin's, to take Sean on as private security. Sean was responsible for watching over the shipments of booze that were delivered to the speakeasy on Friday evenings. Some of the fellas bringing in the booze had been trying to raise the price on delivery. Sean put a stop to that. He hung around the rest of the night as a bouncer. Joe didn't really need another bouncer, but he took Sean on as a personal favor to me.

The job was meant to provide Sean with a cash stream to replace the payola he had gotten from the Jones Gang before it descended into disarray. It was supposed to have the side benefit of Sean avoiding Friday night supper with his in-laws, but Mary Claire moved the family mealtime to Sunday afternoon. And the jack was buying steaks at Benson's again.

"Not until twelve. I spoke with Joe; he won't short your pay."

Sean relaxed. "I thought you had a supper date tonight with that newspaper dame at the fancy Italian joint in the Market Place? You going to ditch her early?"

"No, I'm going to take her along."

"You're going to take a dame to a meeting with Vinny? A little risky, don't you think?"

He was right. Vinny wasn't the kind of guy you would introduce your doll to, let alone even have her in his vicinity.

Vinny was a promoter in the fight game and had several boxers in his stable. He was also a gambler, a gambler who didn't like to gamble, not if he could put the fix in on the bet. Fixing fights had recently expanded to fixing baseball games, which brought Vinny into my ballpark, so to speak.

"That's why I want you there for insurance." I pointed my finger at Sean's chest. "And for extra measure, you should bring Johnson along."

"You know he don't exactly blend in."

When in plain clothes, Johnson always wears his long-tailored coat like the cowboys in movies do in gunfights. Underneath, he has double-shoulder holsters for his two revolvers. The coat and the pistolas add to his persona — the copper not right in the head.

In an undercover operation, there's no concealing Johnson; he's always conspicuous. Better to put him on a roof with his sniper rifle.

"I don't care if he wears his cowboy hat. That's what I'm looking for: visible. I want Vinny to know he'll have more to deal with than just me if he gets it into his head to start trouble."

"Johnson ain't gonna check his revolvers at the door," Sean added. Standard practice at the Pinnacle.

"I'll have a word with the doorman; he won't give you any trouble." I looked out over Sean's shoulder at the darkened windows. I got up and turned on the lights that hung over my desk so I could see what I was eating.

"Does the dame know about this meeting?"

"Not yet, but she's got a big part to play in the scheme of things."

Sean sat back, shaking his head. "Why are you getting yourself involved with Vinny? It's best to steer clear of that guy. What's the deal? Did you get another note?"

A good point: Vinny was known for his less-than-peace-loving nature. He wanted his way, or else heads and limbs got busted; sometimes, fellas disappeared. That's why I set the meeting for the Pinnacle Club, an upscale spot where Vinny wasn't likely to start a rumpus.

"No, not this time. Johnny asked me to do him a favor. His son Gary got himself in some hot water with Vinny."

Me and Johnny Preece played ball together before the war when we were just lads, on the same team his kid is playing on now, the Kings, the local minor league team.

"What'd the kid do, throw a game?"

"Not yet, but that's what Vinny is looking for him to do. They're blackmailing him."

Gary Preece is the King's star starting pitcher. Doing real good for a 20-year-old in his second year. He could easily set his team up to lose.

"What do they have on him?"

"Vinny has some photos of him and a call girl from Sally's." Sally's was an uptown, classy creep joint (*) run by a madame named Pearl, if there is such a thing as a classy creep joint.

"Like what?"

"The pictures have him with the Dame on his arm coming out of a clip joint, him and her dancing at a club, and a couple of them in — let's say, in an embrace."

"So, he ain't the first young ballplayer with pockets full of jack to sow some wild oats, big deal."

Don't I know it? Me and Johnny painted the town red every Saturday night after the game. Raised hell, win or lose.

"Just because it's normal don't mean the ball club is going to accept it. They got expectations for their up-and-coming star. They been selling him as their upstanding, shining example for America's impressionable youth. You've seen the pictures in the papers, him signing autographs for the kids, showing them how to hold a bat."

"So the lad's between a rock and a hard place. Throw the game, or let them publish those incriminating photos. He's up shit's creek." Sean paused a moment. The thunder rumbled in the distance. "How about this? You get your newspaper girl to have a talk with daddy. The Gazette could refuse to publish the photos?"

"She might be able to pull that off, but one of the other rags would publish them. The story would get out."

King City had two other small-time newspapers. "And if she tried that, how would she explain her motives? It might blow her cover."

"But she's involved somehow? In a way that's not going to blow this sweet deal, you got going with her?"

"Yeah, that's right."

"So, with the dame's help, you think you got a way to save the kid's career?"

"Right again," I said, "It's looking good for him, a bright future. He has a shot at moving up to the majors."

I had a shot once, too, but the war put the kibosh to my plans. Could have been a short-stop in the big leagues.

"Had a shot, you mean. They got their hooks into him. If he starts throwing games, it's just a matter of time; career over." Sean clicked his tongue.

"You doubting my abilities?"

"No, no, not me. But couldn't we just let it slide and get in on the action? Place a bet or two."

"No, not this time. I got to take care of Johnny's kid."

"So, what can we do about it?"

"I got an angle."

"Of course you do. When does Danny O'Shea not have an angle?" Sean waited out another clap of thunder. Louder this time, it shook the building. "What kind of game you got going on? Give me the details."

"I got a way to take the heat off of Gary and put the skids to Councilman Ross."

"You ain't never forgot or forgave the councilman, I take it?"

"What goes around, comes around. Sometimes it just takes a while."

My Pa and Ross were friends as kids. But when Ross got elected to the city council, he got uppity and tried to get my Pa involved in some shady dealings. Pa refused, and Ross jammed him up with some false allegations of corruption. Pa lost his job. He drank himself to death. His career on the force was all he had.

"How's the dame fit in?"

"I'm going to get Ross, and she's going to get a good story."

***

"I've heard of this place, of course. But I've never been down here before." Jane took a sip of her red wine.

As promised, Jane and I were seated for supper at the Bella E Buona, here in the Market Place, the only Italian restaurant in Carvonshire. It has decent food, although expensive. Lusardi's in the Hill Section has the best Italian food in King City, but I don't go there anymore. Not sure if Angelo, the Hill Section crime boss, has forgiven me for putting his kid in the pen (*). Now that Max is gone, he might renege on the deal that canceled the contract Angelo had put out on me. She wouldn't be here to enforce it.

"This restaurant is in the place where the mule barn used to be." I rolled up some spaghetti with my fork and spoon. "The rest of the Market Place used to be storage areas for mining equipment, an area for staging coal cars, like that."

The Market Place was a small section of the abandoned coal mines that had been reclaimed for use by the public. More restaurants and all kinds of shops fit out the cavern that runs under Market Street from 4th to 7th Avenue, two levels below the surface. With its lampposts and hanging light fixtures, the concourse is accessed at each street corner by cast-iron staircases. Also, on each corner, large skylights are framed into old shafts used originally to let fresh air into the mines.

Kind of a unique venue for a date if you want to impress.

"A mule barn, underground, really?"

"Yeah, once a mule came down here to pull mine cars, it never saw the light of day again."

"That's awful."

I nodded and swirled the wine in my glass. I should have ordered bourbon, but I was trying to be classy. There was no way I was going to finish this swill.

"Me and Sean really appreciated that article you wrote about Father Pat. It was jake. Couldn't have been better if I wrote it myself."

"Glad you approve," Jane replied, "That means a lot to me." If sarcasm drips, this was a downpour.

"Sorry. I didn't mean no disrespect." Things were going great so far, a great meal with a beautiful doll, and I had to put my foot in my mouth. "You set up me and Sean real good. The Chief had to give us a commendation."

"Good for you."

"The best part was him choking on every word."

"Glad you enjoyed it," Jane said with a teasing smile.

"Sean is getting so many prayers and blessings from the parishioners at St. Mary's that he won't be spending any time in purgatory, going straight to heaven."

"How about you? Are you going straight to heaven?"

"Ah, not counting on it."

"Didn't you get enough prayers and blessings?"

"I got some, too, but looking out for Father Pat was good enough for me. I owe him, big time."

"You and Father Pat seem to have a close relationship."

"Yeah, we go back."

"Another story? Am I going to hear this one this time?"

"Why not?" I pushed the wine glass away and leaned back. "It was after the war. I wasn't right in the head. Father Pat and I spent some long evening hours talking. Talking through things." I wasn't sure why I was blurting out my personal history.

"So, he helped you through a tough time?"

"I couldn't sleep, nightmares. Started drinking heavy, trying to blank things out. Got in lots of fights. Made some bad choices."

"Good to hear that Father Pat was there to help you."

I pulled out my pocket watch for a quick check on the time: quarter to ten. I waved to the waiter to bring the bill.

"You keep looking at your watch. You got somewhere else you got to be?"

"No, doll, just thinking we should be heading over to the Pinnacle."

"But it's early; I wouldn't think the place would start hopping until late." Jane's glass clinked as she put it down on the table. "And the name's Jane, not doll."

"Right, sure, sorry." I insulted her twice in ten minutes, damn.

The waiter showed up with our bill. I pulled out a roll of jack and started laying down a pile of greenbacks.

I caught Jane's eye; she was looking a little bothered.

"You know that there's more to the Underground than just the Market Place?" I offered as a consolation, leaning forward again. "There's a secret Underground, a network of old tunnels, shafts, and rooms stretching out beneath all of Carvonshire," I whispered, drawing her in.

"Really?"

"When the Jones Gang was in business, they used them for various nefarious activities, bootlegging and the like."

"Go on, this is fascinating." Jane leaned in closer with a look that could pull confessions out of a serial killer.

"I can do better than that. I'll show you." I stood up, rounded the table, and put my hands on the back of her chair.

"You mean now?" Her face went into a pout. "I want to listen to music, maybe do some dancing. You promised we were going to the Pinnacle Club."

"We are. I never go back on my word." I gave her a wink. "But I know a shortcut."

"A shortcut? What's shorter than taking a taxi ten blocks?"

"It's more of a scenic route."

Jane shook her head and finally stood up. "Lay on Macduff."

"It's Danny." I assumed she was joshing me.

We left the restaurant and headed down the concourse.

"Over this way." I took the lead and motioned for Jane to follow me to the back of the house. We entered a darkened hallway with a sign over the entrance, "Maintenance Authorized Personnel Only."

She paused under the sign. "Are you sure you know where you're going?"

"Yeah, doll, follow me."

"Follow a man into a dark hallway. I think that is something 'dolls' are generally warned against."

I gave her my boy scout 'you can trust me' look and started into the shadowy, narrow corridor. We passed several doors on our right labeled as various supply closets, secured with padlocks hanging from hasps. At the darkened end of the hallway, a dingy red light enclosed in a cobwebbed wire cage hung over a doorway, barely lighting a sign: 'Electrical Room.'

The door was secured with an oversized padlock. I grabbed and twisted a hinge, which was actually a latch, and tugged the bulky metal door open a crack. The lock secured nothing; it was a prop.

I looked back over my shoulder to make sure no one was watching and then pulled the door wide open to reveal a staircase leading into a dark pit. At the edge of a metal grate platform, I toggled a wall switch that lit up the cavern below.

"We're going down there?" Jane eased over to the edge of the stair platform and peered down at the mineshaft floor two levels below.

"You're not up for a little adventure?"

"Out of my way, Detective." We bumped shoulders as Jane pushed ahead and down the steps.

She stopped at the bottom, looking back and forth into two dimly lit coal mine tunnels to her right and left.

"Mind if I lead, since you don't know where we're going?" I took the tunnel to the right. "This way."

We had gone the equivalent of six blocks before Jane broke the silence of our stroll through the black-walled, musty, damp burrow.

"What if we run into some of the hoodlums that frequent this place? I don't feel safe down here."

"There's nothing to worry about. Since the Jones Gang collapsed, there isn't much activity in the Underground anymore. Besides, the tunnel system is so complex that even if some unsavory characters were running around, we aren't likely to bump into them."

"That doesn't make me feel any better."

We turned a corner. I flipped on the tunnel lights ahead of us and flipped off those behind us.

"What is that noise?"

A rumbling mechanical drone was vibrating the walls.

"That's the water pumps. There's a mechanical room one level below us."

"The water pumps from the old mining operations? These mines haven't been active for over 50 years. Why are they still in use?"

"These tunnels are below sea level. If the pumps weren't working, this place would fill up with bay water pretty quick."

"Who keeps them running?"

"Well, Max does — did." I was wondering myself who was paying the electric bills these days.

"A mystery, Detective?"

"Yeah."

We walked another block in silence, except for the water dripping from the ceiling, which made little pinging noises in the puddles on the floor.

"Why is there more water dripping now?"

"We're only 100 yards from the bay." I pointed straight again into darkness: we had run out of the tunnel and stood under its last hanging bulb. "The water's surface is about 20 feet over our heads."

"What?" Jane was looking at the water running in the gutter along the wall. "This is not my idea of a fun date."

"Not to worry, remember the pumps? As long as they are running, we're golden." A date, she said. Prior, she had said the evening was just business, not an official date.

"Are we going to be *'somewhere'* soon?" Jane asked, "I'd rather be at the Pinnacle, dancing."

After a few steps into the darkness and another flip of a switch, a roughly ten-yard square, two-story room appeared. These transitions from darkness to the materialization of long tunnels or cave-like rooms must be jarring for Jane. It still unnerves me.

"Where are we?"

"About a block from the wharf, directly under the Jones Gang transfer house."

Jane shifted back, a little uneasy-like, taking in the scene. A ladder off to our left rose two stories to a trap door in the warehouse floor above. A rickety-looking elevator, just a six-foot square wooden platform, was attached to pulleys above by twisted cable. This man-elevator, operated by gears and a hand crank, was used to lower booze from the warehouse to this cavern room below.

"Don't worry, we're fine. Since Max's demise, along with Little Billy and Sleazy Sal, the stash house isn't in use anymore."

I moved past Jane and flipped another switch at the far wall. Another tunnel appeared, the narrowest yet, with a slight uphill grade. A row of lights, spaced far apart, hanging above a small gauge railway track, dwindled into the distance to a destination a good mile away.

"What went on here?"

"It was a really smooth operation Max had going. She used this tunnel to transfer the booze that the Rum Runners brought to the wharf across town to the Kilmann's building's basement."

"The Kilmann building? That's where the Pinnacle is, our destination for this evening."

"Right."

"If you're expecting me to walk down that tunnel to the Pinnacle from here, you're nuts." Jane crossed her arms. "That's no shortcut."

"Just hold on."

I proceeded to fill Jane in on the details of how the booze got delivered from the docks to the transfer house, a small warehouse on Bay Ave presently above our heads. Cases were lowered into this room via the elevator and loaded into a trolley wagon. A pump trolley handcar pulled the wagon along the tracks, through the tunnel to Canal Street, avoiding the risk of overland transport in trucks. The tunnel was the artery through which the high-quality spirits flowed into King City. From the Kilmann building on Canal Street, the booze was loaded into boats on the Henshaw Canal and delivered to various points around the city. All done at night, of course.

All the bootlegged booze coming in from the sea had to pass through Carvonshire. The other districts' crime bosses paid Max a tax to have their booze delivered safely. That gave the Jones Gang and the Welsh a leg up.

"And spirits come in from the Caribbean like you told me before?"

"Right, Max had contracts with persons in the Caribbean who shipped the booze with Rum Runners to King City."

Max had arrangements with an agent in Florida. She'd place orders through telegraph messages. She and the agent each had a secret cipher codebook they used to keep track of the orders and record the passwords (signs and countersigns) for the transfer of the goods from ship to boat. The same little book that was probably stolen from Max's wall safe the night of the massacre at Lizzy's.

"Is that the pump trolley?" Jane was pointing to the handcar setting in the tunnel mouth.

"Yeah, it is. Want to go for a ride?"

"So, that's the shortcut to the Pinnacle?"

"It is."

Jane stepped over to the trolley, gave it the once over, and looked back at me. "Sure thing, Detective."

I opened the door to a supply closet and took out a short broom and a rag.

"This contraption hasn't been used for a while; let me clean it up before you climb on board." It had been a month since Max's demise, and no booze from the Rum Runners had entered the city since.

It took a few minutes to sweep the platform and wipe off the bench seat where I planned on seating Jane.

"Cleaning supplies in a mine?" An eyebrow and one corner of Jane's mouth both turned up. "My mother used to say, 'Cleanliness is next to Godliness,' but I doubt that would motivate the gangsters that ran this place."

"Max had a staff of cleaning ladies that work in the Underground."

"To clean what?"

"There's lots of secret rooms scatted around the Underground. Some of them pretty swanky. Even a high-end speakeasy."

"Really?"

"Yeah. But the cleaning ladies had other duties besides keeping things neat and clean; they were part of Max's network of informants."

"Spies?"

"Right. That's how she kept tabs on the gang members, even down here, not the most trustworthy folks."

"Maxine Snowdon sure had things covered."

"There you go. Let me help you up." She took my held-out hand as she hopped up onto the trolley platform. "Have a seat. I'll do the pumping." I jumped up to the opposite side of the trolley and took hold of the pump handles.

"What, you expect me to sit here while you have all the fun? No way." Jane stood up tall, spread her feet, and took hold of the pump handles on her side.

It didn't take us long to put the machine in motion and gain speed.

"Yaaahooo!" Like a kid on an amusement ride, Jane was hooting and hollering, her voice in echos, bouncing off the shaft walls. The overhead lights whizzed by as we made short work of the one-mile tunnel.

"Slow'er down, we're coming to the end," I yelled over the din of the rail noise and Jane's hollering.

She eased up and then sat on the bench, looking over her shoulder as we coasted to a stop in a small, cavern-like opening. I hopped off the trolley.

Another flip of a light switch, and we were in an elevator lobby of sorts, below the Kilmann Building and the Canal Street clip joint, the Pinnacle.

I took Jane's hand again, helped her down from the trolley, and led her to the elevator door.

"Are we under the Kilmann building now?"

"Yeah, this elevator is our ticket up to the Pinnacle." I pulled out my pocket watch. Hanging on the chain was the special key used to call the elevator.

Just then, a voice called out from the mouth of another tunnel. "Who the hell are you? You don't belong down here."

The beam of a flashlight that had been on the floor was now flipping back and forth from my face to Jane's.

The light fell from our eyes, and three thugs with their heaters drawn emerged from the shadows.

"Hold it right there. Don't move," the one in front growled.

"We ain't mov'en; take it easy." I had my arms out in front of me, open palms out in full view. Jane had side-stepped toward me, her shoulder behind mine.

"You're that copper, O'Shea?"

"That's right." I knew these boys, too. They were some of Little Billy's thugs. Not good.

"He sure as hell don't belong down here." Another thug from the trio piped up.

"Maybe it's you guys that don't belong down here," I said. "What's the password?"

The one in front, Carlo, hesitated a moment. "The Great Gatsby. How about you?"

"F. Scott Fitzgerald." One of Max's favorite novels. The passwords changed every time Max came across a new novel she liked.

"Maybe he's legit; he knows the password," said the thug in the back.

"Yeah, we're under Max's protection." I knew that meant nothing the moment it came out of my mouth.

"That don't count for anything anymore," Carlo said, "I say we just take care of them right here and now." Carlo was a button man (*); he knew that end of the business. The other two didn't argue.

They had their peashooters trained on me. My piece was resting snug in my shoulder holster. I wouldn't have a chance to get a shot off. I was beginning to regret bringing Jane down here, showing off and all.

A loud clunk and rattle from my right; the elevator door opened. The thugs turned their attention and weapons in that direction.

"What's going on?" It was Harry Rosser, another one of Little Billy's stooges.

"We was just about to fit up this copper and dame with Chicago overcoats (*)." Carlo was looking at Harry, but his piece was still trained on me.

"Don't get in a lather, Carlo; he's alright. He gave ya the password, didn't he?"

"Yeah, but…"

"No buts about it. Danny O'Shea is a stand-up guy in my book." Harry gave me a nod and a wink.

"I don't know …" Carlo, the ugly thug, or should I say the ugliest thug, was still doing the talking.

"That's right; you don't know, but I do. Leave him about his business," Harry said as he turned away and started into the lighted tunnel Jane and I had come from, "We got our own business to attend to. Times a wast'en."

The two thugs in the back lowered their peashooters, shrugged, and walked away, following Harry. Carlo, after a moment of angry glare, did the same.

Harry and his gang climbed on board the trolley without even a thank you for us delivering it to them. A clank, the reverse level thrown, the trolley surged back into the tunnel, two of the goons pumping. The trolley quickly disappeared, the clickety-clack of wheels on rails fading into the distance.

"Close call," Jane whispered.

"Nah, I had it handled."

"Why did that hoodlum stand up for you?"

"He owes me."

"Is it a story I'm ever going to hear?"

"That's a story for another day."

"Oh, come on, Detective."

"Okay, sure, but not here, over drinks." Maybe it was the voice; maybe it was the eyes; maybe it wasn't possible to say no to this doll.

The elevator door had closed; the car had been called up above. I used my key to call it back.

A few minutes later, we stepped into the elevator and stood shoulder to shoulder. I punched the button for the penthouse; the door creaked closed.

Jane looked pretty calm for someone who probably never had a gun in her face, but she flinched when the elevator clattered into motion.

I generally avoid elevators myself; don't trust such noisy machinery. I take the stairs.

She had been right about the close call. I had been trying to play it cool, but didn't think Jane really bought it. It was a good thing Harry was in on what those thugs were planning. My guess was that Harry and Carlo were working on putting the trolley transport system back in business, which meant that booze from the Rum Runners would start flowing back into King City. A good thing, too; the city was getting mighty thirsty.

I had to wonder who was arranging the deliveries of booze from the Rum Runners and who was running the show. It wasn't Harry or Carlo; that kind of planning was above their pay grade. No, the remnants of Little Billy's gang had thrown in with someone with more weight, a big fish.

"What do you think those hoodlums were up to?"

"I think we stumbled onto the fresh start for the old bootlegging operation."

"Someone is bringing spirits from a Rum Runner through the port?"

The elevator bell dinged as we passed the ground floor.

"I'd bet on it."

"Could be a story there." Jane's eyebrows arched.

"You need to be careful who you write stories about. They may not take kindly to having their business operations interfered with. And you don't want to be the doll who cuts off a supply of booze to King City."

Another ding, second floor.

"But bootlegging is illegal, and someone should do something about it."

"Says the lady with wine stains on her blouse."

"Oh, no." Jane's eyes dropped as she pulled out her blouse.

"Just kidding," I said, "About the wine. But lay off the bootlegging story."

Ding, third floor.

I don't think she heard me or just wasn't paying attention.

The elevator car bounced, along with my stomach, and came to a stop with a clunk. Damn contraptions. The door creaked open, and we stepped out into the ten-foot square glass-walled penthouse lobby. Jane linked her arm in mine.

I breathed a sigh of relief. The encounter in the basement underground was a close call. And for that matter, here I was, taking her into another encounter that could just as well develop into another close call.

EPISODE 7

THE ROOFS

We moved through the elevator lobby's glass doors out onto the Kilmann building's roof into the unusually warm spring evening air. No need for topcoats.

From the southwest corner, in front of us, illuminated by street lights, lay an expanse of open roof, the south end of the building. A brick, three-foot-high, knee wall ran along all sides of the roof edges. There were brick posts at intervals, giving the look of a castle parapet.

To our left, the Pinnacle Club's penthouse occupied the entire north half of the building's roof. Its double doors were framed in closely spaced white light bulbs. To the left of the doors, an expansive glass atrium, the Pinnacle's dining room, was lit only by table lamps. Patrons inside, at the tables, were visible only as silhouettes. Waiters moved about like untethered shadows.

"Oh, my gosh!" Jane pulled on my sleeve and pointed to our right.

A couple dressed in their evening duds, walking toward us on the other side of the south knee wall, appeared to stroll along in thin air, three stories above the ground.

I led Jane to an opening in the knee wall. The couple were crossing over the skywalk that connects the Kilmann building to the Edison Apartment building.

As the couple, arm in arm, stepped onto the Kilmann roof, the gentleman touched his hat. I tipped my hat to them. The doll, a flapper, looked Jane up and down, winked, and smiled, which I assumed was an approving comment on Jane's dress and shawl. I sure approved of the dress. The way that garment fit, it was hard for me to take my eyes off her.

I provided an explanation. "It's a skywalk, a bridge, like several others, that connects the buildings in the Roofs district together."

We stood, staring out at the skywalk.

"Have you ever been up here before?"

"No, it's my first time. I've heard of it, of course." Jane paused. "To be honest, it's not considered a place where respectable folks go."

"Well, you're right about that. There's a lot of action up here. A lot of unsavory places; clip joints, speakeasies, gambling clubs, dance halls, creep joints, places the respectable wouldn't want it known they frequent."

"How do they get away with it?" Jane swept a hand out. "You know, all this corruption right out in the open. We don't have anything like it in the King District."

"You're right; where the other King City Districts pretty much kept their bootlegging and speakeasies under wraps, in Carvonshire, here on the Roofs, there's no holds barred. The local coppers don't bother; they're on the take. The only worry is the Federal Marshals, and those boys are few and far between. And when they do roll into town, the speakeasies get tipped off by the friendly Carvonshire constabulary."

Jane shook her head. "Unbelievable."

"Let me show you around." I laid my hand on hers that was gripping my arm.

I led Jane along the south side of the building on a boarded sidewalk a few inches above the gravel roof deck.

Jane was craning her neck, looking over the edge. "Oh, jeez."

"Perfectly safe," I said.

"I'm not sure if I agree with your concept of safe, Detective," Jane said. "What's at the other end of that skywalk?"

"The roof of the Edison Apartments and Carlo's, a clip joint."

"Carlo's, like the hoodlum in the basement?"

Not only was Carlo a torpedo (*) for the Jones Gang, he also owned a clip joint. He wasn't an assassin like Grace; there was nothing subtle about Carlo. He was the guy you sent when you wanted to send a message, a clear, ugly message. Max had always kept Carlo on a short leash. With her gone, the mutt was running loose.

"Yeah, same guy, he owns the place."

"What's it like? Have you ever been there?"

"Only on business. It's not a place to take a lady."

"I'll take that as a compliment." A corner of Jane's mouth turned up. "Judging from our encounter with Carlo in the basement, I understand your reasoning."

We continued along to the end of the south wall and turned left. We strolled along to another opening in the knee wall. Looking below, a cast-iron platform with decorative railings hung off the side of the building.

"Those stairs lead down to the El platform." I felt like a tour guide.

A stairway zig-zagged down two stories to one of Carvonshire's elevated train platforms. At that level, the rails, one and one-half stories above the street, ran along Canal Street and then looped around the rest of the district, following Market, Broad, and 2nd Ave. A train had just pulled in, and a small but boisterous crowd was exiting the doors.

With me leading the way, we did an about-face, stepped off the boardwalk, and strolled across the gravel roof to the west edge. There were no breaks in the knee wall. I encouraged Jane to look over.

She peered over the edge of the Kilmann building's roof. "I can't see a thing."

Not entirely true; in the fog, we could see the soft glowing circles of the street lights dotting the invisible alleyway three stories below.

"If it wasn't for the fog, you'd be looking at the Henshaw Canal and the mule paths on both sides. If you look to the south." I pointed that way. "You can just see the roof of my apartment building on the other side of the canal. See those four yellow lights just above the fog?"

"I see it. That's over in the Henshaw District, right? Are you ready to tell the story of why you live there?"

"Not today, doll. Maybe when we get to know each other better."

Doll slipped out again, but she let it rest.

"Well, I'm glad I live in the King District, where the sun shines."

"Look up." Despite the fog below, the sky was showing a first-rate panorama of stars.

"Nice." She spent a few moments craning her neck. "But I don't see how you can stand living in Carvonshire with foggy day after foggy day."

"It's not always foggy; just seems that way." It was true; when the fog rolled in off the bay, it sometimes overstayed its welcome. "You get used to it."

If the sky stayed clear, the fog would burn off tomorrow. I hoped so. I didn't want that damn fog to interfere with Jane's visits to Carvonshire.

I turned Jane around by the arm, and we headed back across the roof toward the Pinnacle.

"So, what do you think of the Roofs?"

She flashed a smile. "It's much more pleasant than the Underground."

Actually, our Underground experience was working out real well until we ran into those thugs at the elevator. I imagined Jane hadn't seen much of the world, at least not the same world I'd seen. Her father probably tried to keep a tight rein on her, but not too successfully as of late.

As we approached the doors of the Pinnacle, the doorman touched his hat as he opened the right-side door.

He was decked out in a spiffy double-breasted red uniform with two rows of brass buttons. Gold trim lined the collar and the sleeves. He wore a red captain's hat with a black band, also trimmed in gold. Always admired a man in uniform. I hated to give up my patrolman uniform when I became a detective.

I guided Jane through the doorway into the vestibule. She was smiling, taking the place in. Guess she was acclimating herself to the criminal element of King City.

The Pinnacle Club was a lot like the classy, upscale joints in the King district. The rest of the Carvonshire speakeasies couldn't be described as classy. Most are respectable, but some are dives, and some are downright dangerous, like Carlo's.

I chose the Pinnacle in a bid to impress Jane and, for the side benefit of it being the safest place, to have a meeting with Vinny.

Jane was looking the place over, pleased as punch, as I handed her shawl and my hat to the coat-check girl.

"Evening, Danny." Myrtle, a strawberry blonde, flashed me a smile and erased it when she turned her gaze to Jane.

Jane leaned in against my shoulder and whispered, "You sure are well known everywhere we go."

"That's the nature of my line of work."

Me and Myrtle were an item for a few long weekends. But when I found out she was one of Maxine's informants,

I put an end to it. I had to wonder how many of my liaisons over the years had been with women who belonged to Maxine's spy network. I was confident that I never spilled the beans on any police work. However, a little voice in the back of my head was wondering if that was a lie. Like Father Pat says, 'the worst lies you can tell are the ones you tell yourself.'

For the moment, the joint was quiet except for the murmur of the crowd. The band must have finished their first set and were on break. To our right, the bar was packed with couples perched on stools. Directly in front of us was the table seating area for the show, with a stage at the far end and a dance floor in between. Off to our left was the glass-enclosed atrium dining section we saw from outside.

As we walked toward the maître d stand, a waiter with a tray over his head busted through the kitchen door and headed for the tables.

"A table for two, Marvin," I said to the maître d as I pressed a fiver into his hand.

"Sure thing, Danny."

Jane twisted a bit to face me. "Do you know everyone in Carvonshire, Detective?"

"Only those worth knowing."

Marvin led us to a table near the dance floor. I pulled out a chair for Jane so she would face the stage and then took my seat, the one facing the bar and kitchen door.

The waiter was there in a jiff. "What are you and the lady having this evening, Danny?"

Jane looked up and rolled her eyes.

I looked at Jane, and she nodded. "A Gin Rickey for the lady and two shots of bourbon for me."

"Coming right up." The waiter was gone and back with our drinks in the shake of a lamb's tail.

A ripple of applause passed through the crowd. The band was coming back on stage. I pulled out my watch and glanced down, ten past eleven.

"Besides knowing a lot of people, you sure know a lot about the activities of the Jones Gang, Detective." Jane was looking coy. "I'm beginning to wonder about your reputation."

"What'd you mean?" I wasn't liking where the conversation was going.

"The only honest cop in King City?"

"I've never taken a dime from the Jones Gang, Maxine Snowdon, or any other thug!" That came out angry.

Jane didn't flinch. "It's just that things don't add up. Like that hood, Harry, we encountered in the Underground. You said he owed you a favor. How does a hoodlum owe a copper a favor? See my point?"

I nodded with a smile and took a sip of bourbon.

"And another thing, how is it that you know your way around the Underground so well?"

"Story for another day, doll."

"It's not doll." Jane was a bit ruffled.

I was going to have to remember not to say doll.

"If not that story, am I going to hear the story about why that hoodlum in the basement owed you?" Jane asked.

"As long as it doesn't end up in the papers." This doll was persistent. I figured I owed her something, considering she was being such a good sport about that close call.

"Surely, by now, you know you can trust me?"

I thought I saw her eyelashes flutter.

The band erupted with a real upbeat tune. People jumped out of their seats and headed for the dance floor. Jane's face brightened, and she started tapping her fingers on the table to the beat.

"Let me set the record straight on what went down between me and Harry." I placed my glass back on the table. "Harry got himself jammed up with some medical bills. His mom was in the hospital for a long time, and he was having trouble making ends meet. So, in order to fix that, he started adding twenty percent to the insurance premiums on the downtown merchants."

"Wait, Harry?"

"Harry Rosser, the guy in the basement who owes me a favor."

"He sells insurance?

"Yeah, but it wasn't right for him to just up the payments. Besides, Max would eventually find out, and then he'd be in real hot water. But desperation sometimes accounts for foolish courses of action."

"Hold on; what you're talking about is a protection racket."

"In a manner of speaking, it's insurance, a service. A small payment each month, so your business establishment is kept safe. So, a shopkeeper could go home at night and get a good night's sleep."

"Insurance?" Jane cocked her head with a smirk. "I'd call that extortion."

"Well, whatever you want to call it, increasing payments just wasn't right, and neither was Harry having to shoulder all those medical bills."

"So, you stepped in and fixed it?"

"Right."

"And how did you become aware of all this?"

"First off, a friend of mine owns Griffith's Radio Emporium over on 5th Ave. He was the one who told me about the jacked-up prices. So then, I went and had a conversation with Harry." I paused for another sip of bourbon.

"Go on."

I thought it best to end this conversation right there, but I continued. "I'm acquainted with this doctor over on Beech Street who'd got himself in a pickle. I arranged for his troubles to go away, and he arranged for Harry's medical bills at the hospital to go away, so Harry didn't have to charge extra on the merchant's premiums."

"So Harry owes you?"

"Big time." Not only did he get set to rights money-wise, but he also avoided the repercussions soon to be inflicted by Maxine Snowdon.

"What about the doctor? What did he get out of it?"

Again, a little voice was saying, 'knock off this conversation,' but, "The doctor, as well as his medical practice, had a little sideline, distributing opium."

"He was a dope dealer?"

"No, not like that. It was mostly an honest endeavor.

He started out just trying to help people relieve their pain, but things got out of hand when the son of some big-shot business tycoon from the King District turned into a dope fiend. The father wanted the dealer's head and accused the Doc."

"Wait, and how did you find all that out?" Jane shook her head. "Never mind, go on."

"The way things played out was—I had just arrested a fella for burglary (had him dead to rights), and he was going to the pen for sure. I convinced him to take the fall for selling the opium to the fat cat's son."

"Why would he do that?"

"He was the breadwinner, bread-taker, more like it, for his family, a big crowd, and they were going to be hurting with him in the slammer. So, the doctor agreed to arrange for the family to get a little stipend each month while their breadwinner was in the slammer. And he threw in free medical care for the lot." Turned out to be a bad move for Doc: the family was a nest of hypochondriacs.

"But the guy going to jail, wouldn't he get a longer sentence? That doesn't make sense. Why would he do that?"

"An arrangement was made with Judge Sanders; the fella just got the time for the robbery."

"And why would Judge Sanders do that?" Jane directed the flat of her hand toward me. "Never mind, I don't want to hear it."

"I wasn't going to tell you." The doctor had also made a contribution to one of the judge's favorite charities, the judge's tab at the Straight Eights gambling club.

"But how was the father convinced that the doctor wasn't involved?"

"The kid was not the most reliable source of information. I convinced him to tell his father he lied about the Doc. Besides, like most folks, his father didn't much care about who takes the fall for a crime, long as someone does."

"I have to admit; I'm a little confused."

"How so?"

"Well, some of what went on might be construed as illegal or at least unethical for a copper."

"Like what?"

"Like Harry collecting protection money from the merchants."

"Payment for a service, I don't see the problem. It was the extra 20 percent that crossed the line."

"What about the doctor influencing the hospital to cancel Harry's debt?"

"Necessary to right a wrong, the hospital gouging Harry with exorbitant bills."

"And the robber taking the fall for a crime he didn't commit?"

"Just some bartering to get the doc off the hook for something that wasn't his fault or intent."

"And bribing a judge, that for sure seems to fall into the illegal category?"

"Maybe, but it didn't cross the line, so not a problem."

"It didn't cross the line?"

"No, because it was the only way to set things right."

"Your logic is a little convoluted, Detective." Jane sat back and crossed her arms across her chest.

"Glad you see it my way. It's just a matter of one hand washing the other." I pointed to Jane's empty glass. "Another round?"

"Sure, why not? Maybe it will clear my head."

I raised my hand to signal to the waiter.

A little commotion at the main door caught my attention; It was Sean and Johnson. I looked at my watch: 11:30, right on time.

Johnson was standing tall up in the doorman's face.

Johnny Preece came running out of the kitchen door with a baseball bat in his hand. Since Lizzy's had shuttered, Johnny had moved from there and took over managing the Pinnacle.

After a few moments and a few waves of the bat, everybody calmed down. Reminded me of the old days, when we were on the field together. Johnny was a slugger.

Sean and Johnson walked over to the end of the bar closest to the kitchen door, where two fellas occupied the last two stools. One gent looked over his shoulder into Johnson's grinning face and then up to Sean, who was towering over him. He elbowed his buddy, and they skedaddled. Sean and Johnson took up the vacated seats.

Jane glanced back over her shoulder. "Everything okay?"

"Yeah, everything's jake."

"You sure seem fascinated with your watch. Do you have another date this evening to get to?"

"No, I don't have another date."

Jane went back to tapping her fingers, watching the band, and sipping her drink. I had expected her to be enthusiastic about the dancing, but either she was being kind to my two left feet, or she had another agenda.

"The Maxine Snowdon investigation. Have you made any progress?" Jane asked real quiet.

"That's slow going."

"Do you have any leads?"

"Nothing solid."

"What about possible suspects with motive? She must have had enemies."

"Does a dog have fleas?"

"That many?

"Too many to count."

"What about the hoodlums who attacked Lizzy's? Any idea who they are?"

"We've eliminated all the local torpedoes. Most of them aren't capable of pulling off a hit that sophisticated. It was carried out like a military operation. Plus, they all had alibis."

"Even that guy, Carlo? He seems like the type."

"Yeah. You're right. He was on the list, but he had a solid alibi." Me and Sean didn't question anyone directly so as not to tip our hand. We asked around discreetly.

"How about you? Have you gotten anything from your sources?"

"My sources? Oh no, not a peep; nothing."

Rather than dancing, Jane's agenda was, apparently, interrogation.

The waiter hustled up to our table and placed our drinks in front of us. I gave him a nod.

I had been keeping my eye on the kitchen door for a while. Johnny had just emerged and was scanning the place, looking for me. I caught his eye. He gave me a thumbs-up signal: the meeting was set. I nodded, and he ducked back through the kitchen door.

I finished up the last drops of bourbon from the second glass and put both hands on the table.

"Another round?" Jane asked.

"Not right now; I've got a meeting to attend to."

"What?" Jane put her glass on the table. "Now? Here?"

"Yeah, in the manager's office." I nodded at the kitchen door.

Jane glanced back over her shoulder for a moment.

"I need you to come with me; you got a part to play."

"What? What part? A meeting with whom?"

I filled Jane in on the predicament that Johnny's kid was in and who we were meeting with, the short version.

I provided the low down on Vinny, that he was less than an honorable fella. He could cross the line in a heartbeat. Just so she'd have an idea as to what she was getting into.

"Another great story, Detective." Jane was shaking her head.

I took that as a compliment.

"Tonight, we are going to get Gary out from under Vinny's thumb."

"But what is the plan, exactly? And how do I fit into all this?"

"First off, you should know you're going to get a scoop for your crime beat section out of it." I was setting the bait.

"Go on."

"I'm going to use you to threaten Vinny and get him to let up on Gary."

"Me, threaten a hoodlum? How am I supposed to do that?"

"You won't have to say anything; just play along. Maybe nod at the appropriate times."

"How am I going to play along if you haven't clued me in?"

"You sure ask a lot of questions."

Jane's face was somewhere between angry and confused.

I got up, rounded the table, pulled out her chair, and guided her away before she could say no.

As we walked toward the kitchen door, I signaled to Sean and Johnson at the bar. I wanted them in the room ahead of us, real handy.

Sean pushed through the manager's office door first, followed by Johnson and then me and Jane. The room was relatively small, not the ideal space for a gunfight. I was looking for any edge that would prevent Vinny from starting a ruckus.

Vinny was sitting behind the office desk. Two of his thugs with bulging jackets stood against the wall behind him. I pulled out a chair for Jane across from Vinny and took a seat next to her.

"How's it going, Vinny?" I asked.

"Not bad."

"Glad to hear it."

"Who's the dame?" He was looking Jane up and down. She squirmed in her seat.

"We'll get to that."

"What is it you want, O'Shea?" Vinny was leaning back, his arms at his side, making himself look wider than he already was. "I'm only here as a courtesy. I got better things to do."

So much for the small talk.

In my invitation for this meeting, I had implied that it would be in Vinny's best interest to attend lest he suffer some unnamed consequences. Not a threat, but close enough.

"It's about Gary Preece." Might as well get right into it. "I want you to lay off the kid."

"I figured as much. Johnny pulled you into this. But I ain't lay'en off nobody. Preece is my ticket to a sizable pile a scratch."

"Yeah, I understand that. But I'm here to warn you that the troubles coming your way might not be worth it."

"What troubles?" Vinny leaned forward. Both his punks shifted their weight. "You threatening me, O'Shea?"

Sean and Johnson straightened up, tense. Jane cleared her throat.

"Of course not, Vinny; I know better." I shook my head quick. "It has to do with that new crime-beat reporter, Gibson."

"What about him?" Vinny and his boys relaxed a bit.

"You seen the papers, writing articles about actual crimes, exposing actual criminals, and rooting out corruption. He's real keen on making a name for himself."

"What's that got to do with me?"

"I hear he intends to write a piece on the gambling rackets. He's looking into the fight game and the possibility that someone is putting in the fix on the fights." I let that sink in. "He's got sources that are pointing to you."

"What sources? Who are they?" Vinny huffed.

"That I wouldn't know. But I'm thinking that the baseball story might be something that he might be taking an interest in too."

"You should keep your mouth shut about my interests in baseball."

"Oh, for sure. I'm just looking out for you, letting you know."

"You got a line on this Gibson weasel? You know who he is and where I can find him?"

"I don't, but I got a connection at the Gazette."

"Who's that?"

I looked at Jane. "The doll here, she works with him. She's like a secretary, a gopher." I turned to Jane so only she could see my wink. She nodded with a little too much enthusiasm.

I continued with my line of bull. "Fortunately, Gibson doesn't really want to write stories about gambling. He thinks it's bad for business, King City business. And I would have to agree. There'd be an uproar. It would force the Commissioner's hand, the clamor for us to make arrests. A big hassle."

"Why's he chasing it, then?" Vinny asked.

"It's old man Henderson pushing it; he wants to sell newspapers. A good gambling scandal would do that. Plus, he's recently got religion and thinks gambling is a sin." Of course, Vinny knew nothing about Harold Henderson, the owner of the Gazette, which played to my advantage.

Vinny was looking interested. "You got an angle, O'Shea?"

"Gibson needs a story, something for the papers. Any good scandal will do."

"What you got in mind? You got something worked out?"

"That's why I called for this meeting. I need your help. If we were to provide an alternate juicy story, Gibson would drop the gambling piece. And since I'm helping you out here, it's only fair that you'd let Gary Preece off the hook like I asked."

"Why would I let go of the kid?"

"We wouldn't want that story in the papers either, a gangster leaning on an up-and-coming young baseball player. That story would sell a lot of papers. Even Gibson couldn't turn his back on that one. But I'm sure Jane here could convince him to drop it if I asked her to real nice."

Jane nodded her head, wearing a coquette version of a smile.

"I bet she could." Vinny was looking Jane up and down and grinning.

Vinny sat and stewed for a while.

Finally, "So, what's this other story you got in mind?"

"One of our illustrious city leaders, Councilman Ross, is known to spend a bit too much time in the creep joints (*). And it's rumored that he might also have a relationship with narcotics." Vinny would know, since he ran several such establishments.

"True."

"If someone were to pass on some of the details to the doll here, Gibson would have a juicy story. And he'd be inclined to let the gambling story go by the wayside."

Vinny gave us the silent treatment for a time. His hands, with interlocked fingers, rested on his belly as his gaze flipped around the room.

His glare on me again, "I could see that working out." Vinny wasn't happy, but resolved to the situation I had maneuvered him into. "If we serve up the Councilman, then you guarantee that the gambling story and the baseball story stay out of the papers?"

"Of course. And Gary Preece is off the hook?" I added.

More silence, then grudgingly, "Right."

"You got my word on the deal, Vinny." I didn't have much worth anything, but everyone knew my word was golden.

Me and Vinny locked eyes for a few long seconds, waiting for a blink. The place was starting to smell like the boy's locker room at the YMCA, nervous sweat all around.

I broke the silence. "We have an arrangement then?"

"Yeah."

I breathed a sigh of relief. Jane's body slumped slightly. Everybody relaxed. One of Vinny's thugs almost smiled.

"So, what I need is for you to have one of your boys drop off some notes with the dope on Ross tomorrow morning at the Carlson Hotel. Have him go around to the back entrance in the alley and ask for Johnson."

Vinny's face was screwed up in a grimace, but he nodded.

As I stood up, I glided Jane out of her chair. The four of us, me, Jane, Sean, and then Johnson, backed out the door. I kept my eye on Vinny and his boys the whole time. Sean and Johnson were surely doing the same.

Before Sean and Johnson headed back to the bar, I had a word with them. They would hang around a little longer until Johnny gave us the all-clear that Vinny and his thugs had left.

As I walked with Jane back to our table, I signaled the waiter for another round of drinks.

Jane slid into the chair I had pulled out for her. "My father is nothing like that. Where'd you get that story about him?"

That was the first thing she needed to ask?

"I didn't. Made it up on the fly." I gave her a wink. "Good story, don't you think?"

Jane screwed up her face; not her best look. "And why target this guy, Councilman Ross? Why are you setting him up to take a fall?"

"It's personal."

Jane waited a moment. "That's it, no details?"

"Let's just say I'm the kind of guy that holds a grudge." I took a few minutes to fill Jane in on some of my personal history—what happened between my Pa and Ross. I figured she'd need to know if she was gonna go along with this scheme.

"I didn't like the sound of the guy. I like him even less now."

"You're okay writing the story on him?" I asked.

"Sure thing."

"So tomorrow, you need to be at The Carlson Hotel by nine. Johnson will meet you in the lobby. He'll escort you to a back room to get the notes from Vinny's thug."

"You won't be there?"

"No, I got business to take care of Saturday morning." Actually, I don't like getting up early on Saturdays. "Don't worry; Johnson will take care of you." I had given Johnson his marching orders as soon as we left the meeting. He had gone home. Sean was still at the bar, chatting up a dame in a flashy red dress.

"Are you sure?"

"Not to worry, you'll be in good hands. Johnson punches above his weight."

Lickety-split, our waiter was delivering a fresh round. We both took a sip.

I pulled my chair up closer to Jane and turned a bit so I could see the dance floor and stage. No need to keep a close eye on the doorways anymore.

"So, you like the music?" I asked, looking over the rim of my glass of bourbon.

"Yes, they're doing a fine job." She relaxed some and placed a hand on her waist. "Not your cup of tea, is it—dance music?"

"Yeah, I prefer the ballad style, like the jazz Bix Beiderbecke lays down with his horn."

"Have you ever seen him in person?"

"Yeah, once. He came to town last summer."

"I saw Louis Armstrong perform once." Jane's eyes brightened.

"No kidding."

"When I graduated from college, my father took me on a trip to New Orleans as a graduation present."

"That's something."

"The only thing is, I didn't get to do any dancing. My father's a prude about the modern dances. It was all he could do to sit through one set."

"That's too bad."

"It wasn't a complete loss, though. I got to see a lot of historical sites, plantations, and the like. I even had a ride on a riverboat on the Mississippi."

"I bet that didn't compare to a night out dancing?"

"I've made up for it since. I can do all the modern dances, The Lindy, the Black Bottom, the Charleston; you name it."

I could name it, and I could picture her cutting a rug. I liked that picture. I was going to have to get over my fear of making a fool of myself on the dance floor.

"Since you were kind enough to take me out tonight for the music — and the adventures — I was wondering if you would like to go with me to a King's game next weekend. My father has a block of season tickets. A couple of seats are available. They're right behind home plate."

The Kings, the King City minor league team, usually have a home game every other Saturday afternoon.

"Sorry, I can't make it next Saturday, but thanks." I hated to turn her down, but I had too many people relying on me Saturday afternoons.

"That's alright: I just thought you would like to take in a game since you used to play ball yourself."

"You know about my short-lived baseball career?" Boy, this doll really did her homework.

"You were a star player in your day like Gary Preece is now, but a shortstop, right?"

"That's right."

"The way I understand it, you had an opportunity for a career in the major leagues. Why didn't you pursue it when you returned from the war?"

"I wasn't in the right state of mind to play ball when I came back."

Not being able to play ball was a hardship; I have to admit it. The alcohol, fights, and carousing were somehow more important than baseball at the time.

"Yes, I remember. You had some troubles that Father Pat helped you with."

"Yeah, he did."

We stumbled around in silence for a moment until I broke it.

"I do appreciate the offer about the game. I would go if it weren't for another commitment. I got goings-on at my apartment that I can't duck out of."

"That's okay; maybe another time?"

"You know, doll, there's no reason why you shouldn't come to my place next Saturday afternoon."

"I don't want to impose since you have company."

"Not a problem. I think you would enjoy it."

"You're not going to tell what the 'going-on' is?

"It'll be a surprise."

Jane's eyes flipped side to side as she bit her bottom lip.

"You want me to come to visit you in Henshaw?"

"That's right." I waited for the next question, but it didn't come, so I breached the subject. "You want to know why I live in the colored section of town?"

"Well, yes."

"Originally, for protection, now because I like it there." I gave Jane the lowdown on how I got myself in trouble with the Hill Section crime boss, Angelo the Suit. And then how Big Anthony, the crime boss of Henshaw, agreed to furnish a safe haven. I let her know that the contract on my life had been lifted years ago but left out the part about how Maxine Snowdon was involved.

"This crime boss from Henshaw who is doing you a favor; his name is Anthony?" Jane was puzzled. "An Italian gangster runs the rackets in Henshaw?"

"He's not Italian. His real name is William White, but he likes to go by Big Anthony. He picked up the name from a wanted poster of a Chicago mug. He only resembles the poster in the big part." Anthony was at least six-four and around 300 lbs.

"Gosh, that's an interesting story."

"I got a million of em."

"And I hope to hear them all, eventually."

"We'll need to spend a lot of time together for that."

"That's okay with me."

"So, how about Saturday then?"

"What is it, a poker game with your pals?" Jane said with a smirk.

"No, nothing like that. I wouldn't invite a doll to a poker game. What do you take me for?"

"What is it then? What have you got in mind?"

"Like I said, a surprise."

"More surprises?"

"I haven't steered you wrong so far, have I."

I got a 'you got to be kidding me' look.

"But isn't this another one of those things that young ladies are warned against — an invite to a gentleman's apartment?"

"Is that a no?"

"No, not a no. I'll be there." Jane narrowed her eyes and furrowed her brow. "But just how dangerous is this surprise going to be, anyway."

"Not at all doll, just a pleasant Saturday afternoon."

"The name is Jane." She wrinkled her brow again, only this time with piercing eyes.

"Right, sorry." Why can't I remember that?

EPISODE 8

PLAY BALL

As I entered Kelly's, I tipped my hat to old Jen. Passing by her perch on a counter stool, I said, "I'll have the rack of lamb and a side of caviar."

She took a drag on her cigarette, blew smoke in my direction from the corner of her mouth, and maintained that hollow stare out the window.

I shook my head and walked across the restaurant to my customary table that Sean already occupied. As I slid into the chair across from him, I called out to Kelly. "The usual."

"You got it, Danny," came the reply from behind the grill.

Sean glanced over his reading glasses and lowered the newspaper he was holding up in front of his chest. "That dame didn't waste any time. Did you read the story on Ross?"

"Several times. I was at Oswald's at dawn so I could get a copy as soon as it hit the streets." Jane's article was on the front page, better than I could have hoped for.

"Christ, O'Shea, that is an evil grin. You're giving me the creeps."

"I haven't enjoyed something so much since——I don't know——maybe Armistice Day."

"This connection you got with this newspaper reporter sure is a sweet deal. I got to hand it to you: I didn't see it coming." Sean took a sip from his cup of Joe. "You can have things set to rights without all the fuss of collecting evidence, arrests, and convictions. A well-placed piece in the paper, and you have your guy all tied up in a bow. Miss Dickerson makes out, too, of course. She gets some great press, sells a ton of papers, and a stellar reputation as the kick-ass crime reporter to boot."

"Yeah, a reputation she can't claim. All the credit goes to the mystery man, J.L. Gibson." I pointed a finger at Sean. "I'm glad you've finally seen the wisdom of engaging with Miss Dickerson."

"But the thing is, O'Shea, don't mess it up. Don't be sharing too much information. I know you think she's succumbed to your charms. Just remember that dames can't be trusted, especially a dame who's a newspaper reporter. Let her do the storytell'en; you keep a tight lip."

"You know me; always keep my cards close to my chest."

"Right," Sean said with a smirk and a headshake.

Truth be told, I may have spilled the beans a little, but there was no harm. I could trust Jane. Besides, she couldn't corroborate anything I'd told her: no one would talk. They owed me; she owed me; everything would be fine.

Sean folded up his paper and laid it on the table. "I got a joke for ya, O'Shea."

I looked to the heavens and rolled my eyes, but it didn't deter Sean.

"An Englishman, a Welshman, and an Irishman walk into a speakeasy. The man behind the bar says, 'What'll you have, gents?'. The Englishman says, 'I'll have a cup of tea and be toasting to a life of peace and tranquility.' The Welshman says, 'I'll be have'en the same.' And the Irishman says, 'I'll be have'en none of it.'"

Sean was beaming.

"Where do you get these jokes?"

"They just come to me. I'm thinking of go'en on stage. I figure I got prospects as a comic."

"I'm thinking you should give it a try." Not sure why I said that; my intent was a smart-ass remark.

"How'd the rest of Friday evening play out with your reporter?" Sean picked up the second half of his sandwich.

"A lot of stimulating conversation."

"No details?"

Sean knew I never provided details. I don't know why he always asked.

"And the doll in the red dress?" I didn't really want to know, but he expected me to ask.

"Couldn't swing the deal."

"That's too bad."

"What d'ya gonna do?"

As I slipped a yellow envelope out of my breast pocket, I waved it in the air.

"Another one?" Sean asked.

"Yep. It was dropped in my mail slot during the night."

"What are we in for now?" Sean took the note from my hand.

"It says that big Anthony's got a problem and needs our help."

Sean slipped the note from the envelope and peered at it through his reading glasses.

"Wish these notes would provide a little more detail."

I did, too. Anthony's got a problem; that was about it.

"The author of this note is expecting me to do something to help Anthony out of some jam."

"You should; you owe him."

"But if it was trouble I could help with, he should have come to me direct."

Sean just shrugged his massive shoulders. "I guess you'll have to arrange a meeting with Anthony to find out what's going on."

"Let's do some snooping around first. I don't want to go into a meeting knowing nothing. I'll ask around Henshaw, and you get the lowdown from our contacts at the places where Anthony delivers. Then we'll compare notes."

Anthony brought his moonshine to several distribution points in Carvonshire.

"I'll get right on it———after dessert." Sean waved his hand in the air. "Hey Jen, two rice puddings."

"You got it, deary." Jen jumped off her stool like a jackrabbit.

From my front porch, I saw Jedd's taxi round the corner and turn my way. I left my chair and headed to the sidewalk to meet it. I had sent Jedd to collect Jane. She was game to spend a Saturday afternoon at my apartment; go figure.

Jedd pulled the taxi up to the curb on my side of the street. Jane, in the back seat, waited for me to open the door.

Before she moved, she asked, "Is this okay?"

She'd probably been taking in all the colored folk sitting on their porches on both sides of the street. Some others were in chairs on the sidewalk right in front of my apartment.

"Sure. You're with me, doll." Doll slipped out of my mouth, but she didn't seem to notice. I took her arm as she rose up out of the cab.

I rested an arm on the taxi's roof and leaned in the passenger-side window to Jedd. "Thanks, pal."

He rolled his eyes. "Dames?" He drove off down the street.

I walked Jane up the sidewalk toward my apartment building. I was enjoying having this doll on my arm.

Her eyes scanned across the landscape. She was as nervous as a cat in a room full of rocking chairs. She wasn't enjoying herself, not yet. But I was sure she'd settle, given a bit of time.

We climbed the four steps up to the front porch of my apartment building. I introduced Jane to my neighbors, who were sitting in rocking chairs (Ed and Ethel, the elderly couple from the first floor, and Leroy, a middle-aged fella from the second floor who only ever nods). I occupy the third floor.

Jane's attention was drawn to the small folding table at the end of the stoop. "So, instead of going to the game, we're going to listen to it on the radio?"

"Every Saturday afternoon's home game." I stepped over and put my hand on my pride and joy. "This here is a Cosley Model X, and these babies are brand-new Motorola horns."

The radio and the two giant speakers took up the whole tabletop. A somewhat frayed extension cord draped out of my neighbor's first-floor window and ran across the porch, providing power for the contraption.

"I don't think my father has a setup as nice as this."

"They're the latest. Pete over at Griffith's keeps me up to date. Anytime something better comes out, he hauls it over and sets it up for me."

"The chap from Griffith's Radio Emporium, the one you helped with… his insurance premiums?"

"That's right."

"It was a great day when Mr. O'Shea moved in." Ed piped up.

"The way I remembers you say'en," Edith lowered her voice, "What the hell is Maybelle do'en rent'en an apartment to no Ofay (*)!"

Ed scowled at her.

Edith turned to Jane. "Our boy, Aaron, plays in the minors." Edith was beaming. She was practiced at ignoring Ed.

"Good for him," Jane said, "You must be proud."

"Couldn't be more pleased," Edith said.

Aaron played in the Negro league. There was a Negro's field at the west end of Henshaw, near the slaughterhouses.

Fortunately, today, a stiff breeze was coming off the bay from the east, pushing the stench away from our little get-together.

I checked my watch. "The game will be start'en soon. Let's have a seat." I motioned to the two empty folding chairs at the back wall of the porch.

Jane took up the one on the left. I shed my suit coat and hung it around the back of the other.

"That was a stellar article about Ross." I planted myself in a chair and leaned in. "Was that your first front-page byline?"

"Yes."

"Excellent writing."

"Thank you."

I suppose it was obvious that I knew nothing about writing, but I hoped she felt it was the thought that counted.

Off to my left, Maybelle, my landlady, and her two young boys were coming up the sidewalk, one in each hand. As they reached my place, both boys broke free from their mother's grasp and bolted to my porch.

"Hey, Danny." The two youngsters (probably six and eight years old) called out in unison as they came to a halt at the bottom of my steps.

Maybelle, who had hustled up behind them, grabbed them by the back of their collars. "It's Mister O'Shea. How many times I got to tell you?"

I got up from my chair and stood at the edge of the porch. "That's my fault, Maybelle; I told them it's okay."

"I'm trying to teach em manners, Danny."

"You're doing just fine. They're fine young lads, Maybelle."

"Thank you." Maybelle smiled and then released the boys.

"Dan… Mr. O'Shea, can we have some candy?" the oldest asked, eyeballing the dish of butterscotch candies sitting on the top step of the stoop.

"Sure thing, Malcolm, you boys help yourselves." Both rocketed to the bowl, and each tenderly selected two yellow-wrapped morsels.

"Thank you." Again, in unison, both boys called out louder than necessary. Malcolm gave me a wink his mother couldn't see.

"See Maybelle, proper gentlemen." I returned the wink.

"Uh-huh." Maybelle shook her head. It was then she turned her attention to Jane. "Hi-ya, Hon."

"Hello," Jane replied.

"Oh." I looked at Jane. "This here is Maybelle." I tilted my head toward Jane and looked to Maybelle. "And this is Jane."

"Nice to make your acquaintance, Maybelle."

"Same here." Maybelle was smiling like the Cheshire Cat.

Maybelle took hold of my shirt sleeve, pivoted me away from Jane, and whispered in my ear. "Looks like Danny O'Shea finally made it to the major leagues."

"Just the 'Luck of the Irish' Maybelle."

Maybelle gave Jane a wave, and the little troop returned to the sidewalk where Jimmy, the father, was setting up four lawn chairs.

I pulled out my pocket watch again. It was time for the pre-game program. I nodded to Ed, spry for his age, who jumped out of his chair and settled at the radio table. He turned on the radio and adjusted the tuner. The speakers belched out high-pitched squeaks and crackles before settling on the game announcer's voice.

A cheer rose up from the crowd out on the sidewalk as Ed turned up the volume.

"Pretty loud, huh?" I glanced at Jane as I settled back into my chair alongside her. "I needed something like this so everyone on the block could hear the game." I was speaking loud, right in her ear.

The announcer was going on with the roster introductions. From there, he spent a half-hour kicking round his predictions and dramatizing his analysis of the workings of baseball with his side-kick (a has-been ball player).

Jane held her own during the game, cheering and booing with the crowd. She even got into an argument with Ed about how important an Earned Run Average was as a measure of a pitcher's success. I was thinking Jane might have a future writing for the sports pages.

The game ended with a loss for the Kings, three runs to the opponent's six. The Kings were leaving the field, and the announcer was telling me what shaving lotion to use and what cigarettes to smoke.

After Ed turned off the radio, quite a few folks from the neighborhood came up to the stoop to say hi; others just waved; some stayed for a while to expound on their opinion of the game or share some gossip. I introduced Jane as the society section reporter. I passed out more butterscotch to the kids. The crowd scattered. Neighbors carried their chairs from the sidewalks to their homes.

Eventually, the street was empty, except for a group of boys inspired by the game, who were playing stickball. We sat on the porch for a long while conversing with Edith and Ed; old people have lots of stories to tell. Because Jane kept asking them questions, I got to hear several new ones, not just the same old repeats.

After the old-timers left to take their afternoon naps, Jane and I relaxed in our chairs, sipping from our glasses of lemonade. Edith had brought out an iced pitcher to share.

"If you don't have somewhere else to be, I was thinking we could have an early supper together?" I asked.

"Sure thing. I'd like that. What do you have in mind?"

"Down the street, on the corner, Jimmy's place."

"What's it like?"

"Good food, Jazz, and dancing."

"How could I say no to that?"

"Maybelle and her husband run the place. Do you like seafood?"

"Yes, I do."

"It's their specialty. You haven't had good gumbo until you've tasted Maybelle's."

"Had what?"

"You've never had gumbo? You're going to love it; it's loaded with shrimp."

"I'll give it a try." Jane looked a bit skeptical.

"Come on; let's take a stroll on down." Jane took my extended hand and eased out of her chair.

"Okay." Jane looked around as we walked out onto the sidewalk. "But how am I going to get home later?"

"Jedd will stop back in an hour or so around the time we finish eating. The music won't start up until around nine. If you want to stay for the music and dancing, I can have him come back later on."

"There'll be some time between supper and when the music starts. Do you have something planned for in between?" She gave me the side-eye.

"I do. After supper, I got a meeting with someone. He'll be at Jimmy's tonight."

"Of course you do. Another hoodlum?"

I just smiled and held out my arm. She slipped hers through my elbow.

"Unbelievable, Detective O'Shea, Unbelievable." Jane slowly shook her head. "Just a pleasant Saturday afternoon."

We walked down the street to the corner, to Jimmy's place.

From the outside, Jimmy's place wasn't much to look at. It occupied the first floor, the south side, of a two-story brick duplex. Jimmy's family lived on the other side. The onetime residence had been converted to accommodate Jimmy's and Maybelle's bar/restaurant establishment.

A hand-painted sign hung over a solid wooden door that was framed by a window on each side with brown curtains. The white woodwork around the door and windows could use a coat of paint.

Three young men were standing off to the right of the door, chatting up two attractive ladies who were pretending to have none of it.

"Who are we going to meet with?" Jane asked as we crossed the threshold.

I could feel the tension in Jane's hand tightening on my forearm. Couldn't blame her; she was out of her element. Over the last six years, I'd lived in Henshaw; I'd had time to season in. It was likely Jane felt as if she had entered a foreign land. We were like two bottles of beer in a wine cellar. Two lambs in a lion's den might come to mind, but only in the minds of the clueless. I was sure Jane wasn't one of those; reporters and detectives have in common the antidote for fear——curiosity.

"Big Anthony, himself."

"The crime boss of Henshaw?"

"The same."

Jimmy's crowd was sparse, mostly the early supper crowd occupying tables arranged in a row down the center of the long room. A few old men sat on stools at the bar. Curls of smoke rose up from their cigarettes. By nine tonight, the place would be packed and jump'en. Saturday was dance night.

I exchanged waves, nods, and greetings with our fellow patrons. I led Jane to a table at the back, the opposite end, away from the stage at the entrance.

From the kitchen door, Maybelle emerged in a stained white apron and waltzed over to our table. "Hello again, Hon."

She and Jane traded womanly smiles.

"Hello, Maybelle. This is a really nice place you have."

Maybelle tilted her head back with a quick chuckle. "It'll do."

"I'd like to introduce Jane to your world-famous gumbo. She's never had it before."

"My, my!" Maybelle placed her hands on her hips and turned full to Jane. "Child, you are in for a treat."

"That's what I hear." Jane nodded to me.

In two shakes of a lamb's tail, Maybelle was back carrying two steaming bowls of gumbo on a tin tray. "Hope you enjoy it."

"I'm sure I will," Jane replied.

Maybelle flashed a quick smile and headed back to the kitchen. The supper crowd was arriving in full force, filling up all the tables.

Jane looked into the bowl, stirring around the ingredients with her spoon. "What's all in here?"

"Shrimp, oysters, celery, peppers, onions…"

"And this?" She held up her spoon.

"Okra."

Jane's eyebrows arched. She took a sip of the broth. "Oh, my gosh." Her eyes brightened, and she brought her napkin to her mouth.

"Spicy?"

"I'll say." Jane blew out her breath.

"It's a Creole dish. Maybelle's from Louisiana." I lifted a spoonful to my mouth and blew on the stew. "Surprised you didn't have it on your trip to New Orleans?"

"My father's not a fan of trying anything new, especially in the food category."

"I sure wouldn't want to travel with your father." I ladled a big spoon full into my mouth.

"I don't plan on going traveling anywhere with him again."

"You're going to need something to wash that down." I went to the bar and came back with two glasses of water.

Jane took up her glass right away and downed half of it. "You sure have a lot of friends here in Henshaw."

"Yeah, that's true."

"What's this Anthony fella like?"

"I've only conversed with Anthony twice in the six years I've lived here."

"Why's that?"

"He's not a trusting soul when it comes to white folks."

"How did you get him to agree to let you live in Henshaw?"

"It's a long story."

"I got time." Jane was blowing on a spoonful of stew.

"I know this doll that works in the theater business that's good friends with Maybelle. Maybe you've heard of her, Francine Le Beau."

"I have, the French actress. I wrote a piece on her in the society section. She made quite a splash on the theater scene when she moved here from Paris."

Francine wasn't actually French; just said she was and spoke with a convincing accent. But she had spent time in Paris before and after the war. She had initially gone to Europe to make a name for herself on the stage. Rumor had it that during the war, she got caught up in the espionage business, working in Berlin for the French.

"Francine owed me a favor."

"Of course she did. Why did she owe you a favor?"

"Story for another day. Anyway, I asked her to intervene with Maybelle to get me fixed up in Henshaw."

"How did Maybelle manage that?"

"For one, she and her husband own the apartment building I live in. And for another, she's Big Anthony's sister."

"Okay, this is making sense so far." Jane took another sip from her water glass. "The seasoning in this stew is superb once you get past the hot."

"Told ya." I took a moment to fill my mouth with shrimp.

Jane dabbed her lips with her napkin. "So, Maybelle convinced her brother that it was a good idea to have a white copper living in his neighborhood. How'd that work?"

"It took a while, but he finally saw the value in having a Carvonshire copper in his debt."

"Makes perfect sense. So, you and Anthony still aren't friendly, even now?"

"The first time we met was right here when Maybelle introduced me. He plays cards in the back room on Saturday nights. He looked me up and down and only nodded."

"That was it?"

"Yep, the second time, we passed each other in the doorway." I motioned in the direction of the entrance to Jimmy's. "I was coming in; he was going out. I tipped my hat; he nodded again."

"A man of few words."

"Like I said, he has his issues with white folk."

"Why is that?"

"Anthony, Maybelle, and the rest of their family moved up here from Louisiana about ten years ago to escape the Ku Klux Klan. You heard of them?"

"Of course I have."

"Their father had a thriving bootlegging operation going just north of New Orleans. That's where Anthony learned the trade. The KKK, being righteous, upstanding, protestant types, frowned on the distribution of alcohol, especially by a black man turning a handsome profit doing it."

"What happened?" Jane leaned in.

"Their father and two of their brothers were murdered."

"That's terrible."

"Anthony and Maybelle, the oldest of the family, brought their mother and younger siblings up north, settling in King City, where Anthony set up a bootlegging operation in Henshaw."

"They seem to be doing well here." Jane glanced around.

"Yeah, Anthony got the colored farmers in the hill country to start producing corn liquor and then built up the distribution system to deliver it throughout King City. He had an arrangement with Max."

"I've heard some bad things about moonshine."

I took a quick survey of the place. No one seemed to have heard Jane. "Don't use that word around here. Anthony deals in high-quality corn liquor, not moonshine." I whispered.

"What's the difference?"

I shifted my chair closer to Jane. "Moonshine is the stuff the Italian mob brings in from the farmers in the flatlands. It ain't fit to drink. It probably starts out as a quality product, but the runners water it down, sometimes with anti-freeze."

"Jeez!"

"I'll say. I know of fellas going blind from drinking that stuff. The moonshine sells cheap. Anthony's high-quality corn liquor is worth the premium price."

"That's some story."

"Not for the papers." I shot a warning look.

"I know that. What do you take me for?"

I may have ruffled Jane's feathers, but I had to make sure.

Maybelle came over to the table, not brandishing her faithful smile for once.

"Is Bill ready to see us?" I asked before she had a chance to speak.

"Ready as he'll ever be." Maybelle nodded at the door that led to the back room. She hurried back to the bar, leaving Jane and me alone.

"Who's Bill?" Jane asked.

"That's Anthony's real name. William White, remember?"

"Oh, right." Jane looked over her shoulder toward the back-room door. "Another meeting with another hoodlum?"

"You're a crime-beat reporter, right?" I lifted my shoulders and eyebrows. "What more could you ask for? And if things go my way here, you'll get another great story, maybe front-page again." I winked.

Jane gave me the 'Okay, I'm game' look.

I knocked on the door and waited. Someone pulled the door open from inside. I went through the doorway first, not gentlemanly, but a wise precaution, I figured. Jane followed. A moment later, Maybelle was in the room, as a safeguard, I assumed. I appreciated that.

At the far end of a large round table that occupied the center of the room sat Big Anthony, holding a hand of cards. We had interrupted a poker game. Four other men sat around the table; two I recognized as Anthony's brothers. Each of the men, in turn, left their seats and took up positions against the wall, in slow-motion, surrounding Jane and me. No one said a word. We took up two of the vacated chairs.

Anthony squinted one eye and inspected Jane with the other.

I launched into my first actual conversation with Anthony. "This is Jane Dickerson. She writes for the society section in the Gazette."

Maybelle, who was standing behind Jane, said, "You know, she's the one who wrote that nice article in the papers about Francine. She's good, William."

A grumble came from his throat as Anthony laid his cards down on the table. Both eyes were now on me.

"I heard that you been having some problems?" I asked.

In addition to the note, our asking around had gotten us the information we required regarding the nature of Anthony's problem.

"What're ya talk'en bout?" Anthony's voice was higher pitched than I expected.

"A little birdie told me you been getting hit up for protection money by three different thugs. You're paying triple the fee on all the product you bring into Carvonshire."

In the past, on all the corn liquor Anthony bootlegged into the city, he had had to pay a tax only to Maxine Snowdon.

"Who's this birdie that's been singing?"

"That don't matter. What matters is that you didn't come to me about it. There's a chance I could set things straight for you."

"I can take care of my own business."

"I'm sure you can. But sometimes, it don't hurt to get a little help. Like you did for me years back." I was doing my best to ease into my proposition. Anthony was a proud man, not prone to admit to a problem, let alone be persuaded to take a helping hand, especially a white hand.

After a while, Anthony said. "So, you'd be paying me back a favor?"

"It's only right. I just need your okay to go ahead with the plan I got cooking that will set things straight."

Anthony took another long while before responding. He and Maybelle made eye contact. Some sibling conversation took place that wasn't visible. "Yeah, you got my okay."

That was our queue. Me and Jane made our exit.

Anthony didn't ask about my plan. Smart man; the less he knows, the better.

Maybelle escorted us to our table and sat down with us. She leaned back in her chair. "Best as could be expected. Thanks, Danny."

"My pleasure, Maybelle. But don't thank me yet. Me and Jane got some arranging to do."

"I'd bet money on you any day, Danny O'Shea."

I appreciated the confidence, but I was going to take another high-stakes meeting with more thugs to get the outcome I was looking for.

"These dancers are amazing." Jane was looking to the dance floor but addressing Maybelle.

The band had started up while we were in the meeting with Anthony.

"You like dancing, hon?"

"I certainly do."

"Then you came to the right place." Maybelle looked me up and down, grinning. "But you brung the wrong fella. He's a dead hoofer (*)."

"Maybe so." Jane was smiling at me.

"What dances you like doing, gal?"

"The Lindy, the Charleston. But what these folks are doing is over the top. Something like those dances, but …"

"But more? Where do you think those dances came from, hon? Us folk invented dancing——and jazz music."

"The place sure is hopping." Jane looked as if she was about to jump out of her seat.

Maybelle did jump out of hers, grabbed Jane by the hand, and led her to the dance floor. After a few introductions, Jane was gyrating away with the best of them. She only took occasional breaks for a drink and to tell me how much fun she was having repeatedly. She danced the night away, closing the place at four in the morning. I took her home in Jedd's taxi.

At the door of her father's mansion, Jane turned back to me after she had opened the door with her key. "I had a wonderful time, Detective. Thank you so much. I've never had so much fun dancing before. You should have given it a try." She was smiling, a smile a fella could fall into and get lost. "Jimmy's Place was the cat's meow."

"Glad you enjoyed yourself."

"So, what's our next move with Big Anthony's case?"

Not the question I was hoping for. "I'll have something set up by Monday morning. I'll let you know."

"Well, thanks again. Goodnight." She left me standing in the wake of the closing door.

I was sitting at a square banquet table that occupied the center of the storeroom. Jane was sitting next to me. She jumped at the chance for this Monday morning meeting with a couple more hoodlums.

"How is it that you have this storeroom available for your use?"

"It's payback from the manager here. I solved a hotel robbery here years ago."

"Isn't that what you do? Why would he think he owes you?"

"It's just that I saved his job and the hotel's reputation."

"And? Go on; tell the story."

I didn't hesitate telling this one. I was starting to worry about myself. "One weekend, some hotel guests got separated from their valuables by a jewelry thief. The burglar hit the rooms of four wealthy couples who were in town, throwing their money around. Needless to say, they were not happy and planned to go to the police. Henry Mills, the manager, called me in before they could make the formal complaint. As a favor to Henry, I convinced them to hold off. I promised to recover their jewelry within a week, and in return, they wouldn't file a complaint."

"How did you know you could do that?"

"I didn't. But I was young, cocky as hell."

"So, you got the valuables back to the guests in a week as promised?"

"That's right. And the story didn't hit the papers."

"How did you do it?"

"That's a story for another day."

Actually, it wasn't. I wouldn't ever tell that story to anyone, not Jane, not Sean, not anyone. I had promised Francine I'd take it to my grave, which was a strong possibility for me and Francine if the story ever got out.

It went down like this.

After I had committed to catching the thief at the hotel, I set up a trap for the following weekend.

I entered the hotel Friday evening with a doll on my arm, posing as my wife. She owed me a favor. We spent our time in the lobby and dining room pretending to be a wealthy couple from out-of-town rolling in dough. We were dressed up in glad rags I had borrowed from a pawn shop and behaving like obnoxious, boisterous high-rollers. I had the doll make a point of showing off her collection of pricey jewelry (not authentic, borrowed, but convincing looking from a distance) in an effort to attract the thief's attention.

On Saturday, we chatted up the desk clerk, the bellhops, the doorman, the waitresses, and the matri D, anyone who would listen. We let them know that we planned to be out painting the town that evening, out late, not to expect us back until the wee hours.

Around eight, we made a big to-do about of leaving for a night on the town. A short time later, using the back stairs, I snuck back to our room and hid in the closet.

Around eleven, I heard the lock being picked, and within moments, the dresser drawers getting ransacked. I popped out of the closet and caught Francine red-handed, dressed as a middle-aged maid. Francine is good with makeup and disguise.

I don't generally just haul a perpetrator off to the slammer. I like to listen to their story first; it can be educational and entertaining. Francine had a doozy.

She said that going to jail would be the least of her worries. She confided that she was the head of a secret spy network that she ran for Maxine Snowdon. Hotel robberies were just a sideline, a sideline that Maxine would not approve of.

Francine was responsible for coordinating the efforts of various agents, informants, and spies, only women——barmaids, waitresses, household staff, prostitutes, and others, everyone well placed to eavesdrop, seduce, or otherwise extract information from local gangsters, politicians, and businessmen. All these dames got a monthly stipend and also a bonus if they uncovered a juicy item.

I realized that arresting Francine would upset the apple cart and upset Maxine as well, putting me and Francine in the cross-hairs. Besides, I could see how having Francine in my debt could be useful in the future.

I arranged for the return of the jewelry and let Francine off the hook.

The hotel manager and guests were happy. I blamed the thefts on a maid who had skipped town.

After some knuckle rapping, Johnson, who was stationed at the door, pulled it open. The two thugs I had invited to the meeting strolled in, escorted by Sean, who had met them in the alley behind the hotel.

"I'll be out back." Sean left the room and headed back to his post at the back door to keep a lookout for any other thugs that might try to interrupt our Monday morning meeting.

"Who's the doll?" Dewi Lewis, the punk in the lead, asked.

"We'll get to that," I said, "Have a seat."

Dewi and his partner, Charlie Floyd, plopped into the chairs across from me and Jane. Both punks had been members of the Jones Gang before it fell apart when Max was killed. They had struck out on their own, each trying to take over and run a piece of Max's bootlegging operation.

"I see you brought the dummy with you." Charlie was looking back over his shoulder at Johnson, who had taken up a position right behind the thugs with his back to the door.

Johnson, arms crossed, had a sappy grin on his face.

"That's not how you should talk to a police officer." Jane leaned in toward Charlie.

"Scuse me, didn't mean anything by it." Charlie at least seemed to have some manners.

"Let's get down to business," I said.

"Yeah, what do you want with us; we ain't never done nothing to cross you, O'Shea," Dewi said.

"You two boys, along with Al Harris, have been leaning pretty heavy on Big Anthony."

The punks looked at each other and grinned.

"I'm asking you to ease up; you're taking too big a cut." I got right to the point.

"Why would we want to do that?" Dewi asked.

"Because I'm asking."

"What'd you care, anyway?" Charlie offered his two cents. "Why are you taking Big Anthony's side over ours, your own people?"

"Me and Anthony go way back."

"Don't see where you got any leverage on us, O'Shea," Dewi said.

"It's Detective O'Shea to you." I gripped the table edge with both hands: I was tired of being polite. "And I do have leverage. That's where the doll here comes in." I glanced at Jane. "She's Gibson's secretary. You've heard of him, the crime reporter for the King City Gazette."

"So?" Charlie was speaking through that stupid grin.

"If you don't play ball, your names are going to be in the papers along with your less-than-honest activities. Your rackets are going to take a hit."

"But we got coppers looking out for us," Dewi said, still with a smirk.

"Yeah, you got a few of the boys on the payroll, but you're not spreading around enough dough to provide iron-clad protection, not like Max used to." I decided to go for the 'no problem for me look". I leaned back and laced my fingers behind my head. "And besides, your coppers owe me a favor and could be convinced to take credit for putting you two in the slammer."

"You can't do this, O'Shea." Dewi wasn't grinning anymore, Charlie neither.

"I'm damn sure I can do it. Don't want to, but I got to see Anthony off the hook if you don't want to see yourselves in the papers or the slammer."

Both thugs sat there like deer with headlights in their eyes.

"This ain't right, O'Shea," Dewi said.

"It's Detective."

"What's stopping us from just taking you out?" Charlie leaned forward, staring out of his chair.

I stood up and put my hand on my pea shooter.

Dewi started to get up. Both punks were reaching inside their jackets.

In an instant, Johnson was behind them, grabbing the back of their collars, one in each hand. He yanked both men backward. Their chairs toppled over with thugs in them. They were lying on the backs, still in a sitting position, looking up into barrels of Johnson's two revolvers, one for both their faces.

Jane was out of her chair and backed up against the wall.

"I don't take kindly to threats. And Officer Johnson here don't either." Johnson flashed another sappy grin, upside down from their perspective this time. I reached inside their jackets and relieved the hoods of their hardware. Johnson took a step back and holstered his revolvers.

"Let's start over, boys." I motioned to the table and took my seat while Dewi and Charlie got themselves reestablished in their chairs. I looked at Jane, and she came back to her seat, although she was moving real reluctant like.

"First off, I don't plan on putting your names in the papers or your persons in the pen, that is, as long as you cooperate."

"What'd you got in mind?" Dewi was down in the mouth now.

"First, we're cutting Al Harris out of the picture. It's his name that's going to get splashed across the crime beat section."

Al Harris was one of the trio, including Dewi and Charlie, hitting up Big Anthony for protection money.

"You got the dirt on him?" Dewi asked.

"Not enough, but you fellas do. You're going to spill what you know to the doll here."

"Al ain't going to take kindly." Charlie was telling me something I already knew: Al Harris was a dangerous thug.

"Besides, we ain't no stool pigeons," Dewi said.

"That's right," Charlie added.

"Can't say the same for Harris, boys." I gave them a few moments to let that sink in.

"Remember that series of jewelry store robberies in the King District last year? Who do you think dropped the dime on those crooks?" They didn't answer. "Al Harris."

Al didn't believe in 'honor among thieves.' He'd double-crossed other members of the Jones Gang on more than one occasion. He had beat an extortion rap by peaching (*) on his buddies.

"How do you know?" Dewi asked.

"I know the coppers in the King District; we talk." The two thugs exchanged 'oh hell' looks.

"If we peach on Harris, what's in it for us besides not being in the papers?" Dewi asked.

"You both get to stay in business. I eyeballed each punk in turn. But you're going to reduce your cut to one-third of what you're taking now from Big Anthony."

"That's nuts!" Dewi said, "We only charged the same as Max did. And now you're saying he only has to pay two-thirds of the rate."

I was surprised Dewi got that figured so quick.

"It's only right Anthony pay the full amount," Charlie said.

"And it's only right that he gets what he's paying for, protection. Max provided that; you didn't."

"We should get fifty-fifty of the full till," Dewey said.

"Well, if you boys had figured this out on your own, you could have had a bigger cut. I'm doing you a favor here: letting you stay in business at all."

"What'd you want to know?" Dewi seemed resigned to the situation.

"You guys are going to add what they call background for the story, information on some of Al's illegal activities. We just need some details and names so that some nasty people know that Al Harris crossed them. Your names won't come into it; you guys are confidential informants."

After some hemming and hawing, the two thugs proceeded to spill their stories, the dirt on Al Harris.

Jane scribbled down her notes in what looked like the shorthand that stenographers use. She interrupted the two clowns at all the right times, questioning inconsistencies, and brought them back on topic when they wandered off.

I hardly had to say a word, only piped up when I knew they were leaving things out or outright lying.

About an hour later, the conversation came to a close. I was satisfied that we had enough dope on Al Harris to ruin him and sent the two thugs on their way.

"You wait here. I'll be right back." Jane looked up from her notes for a moment with a quick nod. She was deep in thought, flipping through her notebook.

I gave Johnson the punk's peashooters. We escorted the thugs out of the room and to the hotel's back alley.

"Get what you needed?" Sean was standing on the sidewalk by the taxi.

I nodded. "You bet."

At the curb, Jedd was leaning on the door of his ten-cent box. He would take the thugs back to their holes. Johnson deposited their hardware in the trunk, to be handed back to them at their destination by Jedd.

Jedd was a cool cucumber for a 16-year-old, ice in his veins. A kid from a sharecropper family, he came to the city to seek his fortune.

I first spotted him on the street near the Station House, panhandling. One day, I was in need of a runner, and my regular boys were nowhere to be found. I had a good feeling about the lad, so I trusted him to deliver a package across town and return an envelope of jack. It all went smooth.

I arranged for him to stay at the Radio Emporium. Pete lets him use a storage room. We tell Jedd he's the night security watchman. I try to help keep him in food and duds, but he does okay on his own; he has his own hustles. I had always been impressed with the lad's ambition. That's why I loaned him the money to buy the old Checker Model C from the junkyard. He's a decent mechanic: he got the old jalopy fixed up pretty nice, pretty quick.

I sent Sean and Johnson on their way to their regular duties.

Back in the storeroom, Jane was still focused on her notebook.

I sat down next to her. "For your story, leave out anything about Big Anthony and his bootlegging operation."

"I know that." Daggers flared from Jane's eyes. "I got plenty of other stuff to write about." She was flipping the pages of the notebook, stopping occasionally and making a mark here or there.

"Jedd should be back in an hour. If you want to wait, he can take you to your office."

"Okay." Jane closed the pad and laid it on the table. "I'm new to the police game, but it looks to me that with the earful we just got from those two hoodlums, you would have enough evidence on Harris to charge him with racketeering, bootlegging, and assault and make it stick."

"You're right about that."

"And with a little snooping, you could probably get a conviction on at least a couple of murder charges?"

"Right again."

"So?"

"Once your story hits the papers tomorrow morning, Al Harris is going to be in a real jam. Instead of going to all the trouble of gathering evidence, arresting him, and getting all tangled up in the judicial system, I prefer to let nature just take its course."

"You said you had solid information on the other two. They obviously believed you. Why not put their names in the paper or arrest them?"

"Dewi and Charlie provide a service as long as they charge a fair price. Taking them out would leave a vacuum. Hard to say what might fill it. It's like when you pull a thread on a piece of cloth; you can get some unraveling. If you pull too many threads at once, you can end up with a big hole, a mess to deal with."

Jane nodded and wrinkled her brow. I love when she does that.

"So, you're saying, 'Better the devil you know?'"

"Right." I thought my version was more interesting, but yeah.

"Besides," I added, "Wouldn't you rather have the scoop on Harris than just an arrest report to cover?"

"Absolutely, Detective." Jane picked up her notepad and gazed at it for a moment. "What is it you want from this story?"

"Al's name needs to appear along with a list of people he's double-crossed over the years, the rackets he's associated with, the murders he might be tied to."

"What do you think will happen to him?"

"He won't have any family or friends left to speak of. He's either going to have to leave town or stick around and deal with some real hard men who will come looking for him, wanting his hide." I was hoping Jane wasn't going to go soft on me, worrying about the health and welfare of Al Harris.

"Do you think the worst?"

"If he's smart, he'll vamoose quick like. But we'll see."

"I don't know what you got on the other two, but from what I got down here, Al Harris is one nasty customer." Jane touched the cover of her notebook.

"Yeah. Harris is a nasty customer; he crosses the line. Don't play by the rules."

"Whose rules?"

"Ah, mine. You know, what's reasonable."

"So, Detective, help me understand what's reasonable. I understand that Anthony helped you, and you feel obligated to help him. It's a matter of loyalty. But the others? You don't always go for an arrest. Some of these guys are hoods, for sure, criminals. They could be arrested, but you let them go about their business. Why some and not others?"

"That depends on their business and how they run it."

"So, some criminal activity is okay and some not? And you decide which is which?"

"It's like I said; It depends on whether they cross the line."

"You're evading my question, Detective."

That was my plan. "It's simple——No blood, no foul."

"Still evasive."

"Some crimes are criminal, some ain't." I usually do the questioning. Being on the other end of the stick was damned uncomfortable.

"How about an example then, as a way of explanation?" Jane leaned back in her chair. "As far as I can tell, you've only made that one bootlegging arrest in your career. So, in your book, bootlegging isn't criminal?"

"You been researching my arrest record." That made me feel important, but I wasn't sure it should. "How are you getting this information on me?"

She gave me her 'Are you kidding me' look. "The docket in the newspaper, you know, the list of all police activity in King City. I have access to all the old newspapers."

"You looked up all my arrest warrants?"

"That, and an old-timer who works in the record department and used to be the crime-beat reporter filled me in on your history."

"Sounds like you got a genuine interest in me."

"I want to know as much as possible about my sources."

"Sources? I thought we were partners?" Tension gripped my shoulders.

"Of course, you're right; we are. I didn't mean anything by it. I miss-spoke."

"Okay. We just need to keep things straight."

"But then, as partners, don't you think it's a good idea for us to get to know each other better?" Jane bit her lower lip for a moment. "I just want to know more about you."

I liked the way the conversation had just turned. "Sure, I'm okay with that."

"For starters, I've been waiting to hear the story about how you and Sergeant O'Leary got away with taking down a bootlegging operation of Maxine Snowdon."

She'd boxed me into a corner with an excellent line of questioning. I had to admire her methods.

There was a rap on the door. Jedd poked his head in but said nothing.

"Your rides here." I stood up and put my hand on the back of Jane's chair.

"What about the story you were about to tell me?"

"That's a story for another day."

"You say that a lot."

"Do I?" It seemed that I was just delaying the inevitable. Jane was going to pull all my stories out of me eventually, sins and all.

EPISODE 9

A NEW BIG FISH

"I been thinking." I was holding a pencil by the tip and tapping it on my desk.

"I know. You've been ignoring your paperwork and fidgeting in your seat for a good hour." Sean, lounging in a chair opposite me, came forward from a sprawled posture.

I'm not sure how Sean knew what I'd been doing; he'd been napping for about the same amount of time. Another dismal day, overcast, drizzling, and, of course, fog. A nap was a good way to spend a Wednesday afternoon at the office. But I was spending my time productively, puzzling on who killed Maxine and why.

"I got an idea about the Snowdon killing I want to look into."

"Spill it," Sean commanded.

"I've been putting two and two together."

"And getting four, I hope."

I ignored Sean's jab. "I think there's a new big fish looking to get involved in the King City rackets."

"How d'ya figure?"

"The rum that Joe has been buying lately is probably coming in through the port from a Rum Runner, not overland by truck." Sean had told me that one of Carlo Minx's boys had shown up at Griffin's a month back, offering some high-quality booze.

"What makes you say that?"

"I bumped into Carlo and his crew about two weeks ago. I'm pretty sure they were working on a plan to bring booze to Canal Street from the port." I figured that Carlo and Harry weren't just taking a stroll in the Underground the evening that Carlo had threatened Jane's and my life.

"So, Carlo's found himself a runner that's willing to risk deliveries to King City."

Without Maxine's protection, it was now a risky venture to transport booze through the port. The runner's ships could be attacked at sea, the transport boats hijacked on their way to port, or robbed while docked at the wharf.

"Yeah. But who made the connections in the Caribbean to run the booze up the coast, and who's protecting the shipments?" It was the main question on my mind.

"Carlo?"

"No, I think he's just a hired hand."

Sean's office chair squeaked as he shifted it toward the desk. "What does all this have to do with the Snowdon murder?"

"I think someone is making a play for Maxine's empire. It's likely someone took her out in order to put her organization up for grabs. And now they're recruiting locals to put it back together for their own benefit."

"Have you got any idea who that someone is?"

"I've got a list of suspects who fit the bill."

"Lay it out for me."

"First off, there's Mayor Hughes." The Mayor of King City was less than an honest individual.

"I could see him having something to gain."

"He does, but he doesn't have the brains for it or the ambition. Besides, Max paid him well. Anyway, he's at the bottom of my list."

Hughes was serving his third term, running for his fourth, the Welsh political establishment's golden boy.

"Who else?" Sean Asked.

"There's Roan Doyle. He has the brains. But that should mean he's smart enough to understand that taking Max out was a bad idea."

Roan Doyle was the president of the King City Workers Union, a blanket organization that included transit workers, sanitation workers, dock workers, and a few of the other smaller trades.

"You're right; he could have motive. But giving the fella credit for intelligence might be the wrong move."

I shrugged that comment off.

"Of course, Angelo the Suit is a possibility. He and Max had a profitable arrangement, splitting bootlegging profits. Maybe Angelo got greedy and set his sights on the whole pie. But now he's hurting like everyone else, with the flow of booze into King City curtailed. A possibility, but the odds are against it."

I continued up my list.

"And then there's Harold Patterson, a greedy, vicious bastard who has enough money to pay for a hit and then some. But his businesses are suffering due to the lawlessness in Carvonshire that was now spilling over into all of King City."

Patterson is a King City business tycoon, a banker, who has his fingers in all the pies.

"I don't see how striking every suspect off the list sheds any light on the case." Sean raised both hands and gave me the Italian salute.

"Ah, but it does. It points us toward a whole new angle: I'm thinking there's a new hood in town that ordered the attack at Lizzy's."

"Where does that leave us?"

"We need to broaden our horizons."

"Which means?"

"I got another angle."

"Of course you do."

"I want to have a conversation with Albert Jives."

Albert was known to be the best can-opener in King City. He's done jail time twice. Got a light sentence each time, probably on a count of bribes.

"Why? What's he got to do with anything?"

"The safes in Maxine's office. What do you think was in them that was so important that they took the time to take a crack at them?"

"Money." That's where Sean's mind always goes, the only motive.

"I think it was more than that."

"What?"

"I've got a theory, and I think Albert can set things straight for me."

"You think Albert was in the crew that night at Lizzy's? I thought you had it figured it was an out-of-town crew."

"I've been rethinking that. If the new big fish has recruited Carlo and Harry, maybe they weren't the first." I stood up and removed my jacket from the back of my chair. "We should pay Albert a visit."

"Now?"

"No time like the present."

Within an hour, we had Albert. We snatched him up as he came out of Tilly's Mercantile, a hardware store on 7th Avenue. Not that Albert had much interest in hardware; a bookie, Frank Price, operated out of a back room. Where you found a gambling racket, you found Albert. Price ran a sports betting operation in addition to a daily numbers game Albert couldn't resist, which made Albert predictable.

We escorted him along. Sean had him by one arm and me the other, all the way to the Carlson, where we settled ourselves in the storeroom for a little chat.

I pushed Albert down into a chair.

"We're here to talk about the hit at Lizzy's," I said as I pulled up a chair directly in front of him. I spun it around backward and straddled it, resting my elbows on the chair's back as I sat down. With his arms across his chest, Sean positioned himself against a wall a few feet away but in Albert's view.

"I thought that was all wrapped up; Sleazy Sal took the fall for that." Albert fidgeted in his seat.

"That's the official line. But what we're interested in right now is who cracked the safe in Maxine Snowdon's office."

"You can't be looking at me for that?" Albert looked back and forth between Sean and me.

"I understand you been throwing a lot of jack around lately."

One of my connections at the Straight Eight gambling club had let me know Albert had come into newfound money. For a can-opener like Albert, that could only mean one thing: he'd made a score.

"So, there's no law against a fella spending some of his jack."

"There might be a law against how he got it."

"It wasn't me, Danny. I swear on my mother's grave."

"It's Detective to you." I used my intimidating copper voice. "There are only a couple of fellas in King City with the skills to crack that safe——and Albert, you're known to be one of those fellas."

"You saying you got me connected to the job?" Worry crossed Albert's face.

"I may have a witness that places you in the alley right after the hit."

"No way, there weren't no one in the alley."

Albert looked at me, to Sean, then back to me. "I mean …"

Albert was great with his hands, a delicate touch, and the hearing of a hawk, but his mental faculties left something to be desired.

"I'm saying that everything so far is pointing to you, Albert."

Albert said nothing

"But the way I see it is, it's possible that the witness in the alley was wrong."

"Yeah, that's right," Albert piped up.

"Inviting you here was a courtesy rather than taking you to the station for an official interrogation. Fellas in that situation have been known to confess to crimes they didn't commit. And I wouldn't want that to happen to you."

Albert visibly gulped.

"We didn't want to play it that way." I glanced over at Sean, and so did Albert.

Sean's face showed his 'you don't want to be interrogated by me' look.

"I appreciate that, Danny."

"It's Detective." The guy had the attention span of a gnat.

"Look here, I'm not looking to jam up a small fry like you. I want the big fish, the thug who ordered the hit. So, in order to avoid an unpleasant ruckus at the station, you're going to fill me in about that night at Lizzy's."

"What is it you want to know?"

"First off, how'd you get the job offer?"

"A note delivered by a doll."

"Who was she?"

"Don't know, never saw her before."

"What'd she look like?"

"Foreign-looking, long black hair, dark skin. A real looker."

"Who was it that made this offer?"

"I don't know. But the note was signed——The Mayor."

"That's it, just the Mayor?" My first thought, could the note have come from Mayor Hughes?

"Yeah."

"What else?"

"She said I had two days to consider the offer. It was a sweet deal. She came back, and I said yes. I couldn't turn down that kind of moolah."

"You were willing to take the risk of crossing Maxine Snowdon? Are you nuts?"

"Like I said, that much jack; I couldn't turn it down. Anyway, Snowdon is gone, no sweat."

"What else do you know?"

"That's it. I didn't figure you'd have a problem with the job, Danny, a hood ripping off another hood."

"I have a problem with the eleven murder victims." I pointed a finger at Albert. "So far, you're the only punk we've connected to the homicides. You get my drift."

Albert gazed at the floor, looking for a crack to fall into.

He looked up. "But now you got a line on this guy, the Mayor, right? It's like I'm cooperating, right, Detective?"

"Who were the thugs you hooked up with?"

"I don't know. When I met them at Lizzy's, they were all wearing masks, stockings over their heads."

"But you could tell who they were. You worked with them before."

"No, I never seen them before, never worked with them before."

Like we thought, an out-of-town crew.

"What kind of payout did you get for this job?"

"A grand upfront and ten percent of what was in the safe."

"The money from both safes?"

"What d'ya mean both safes? There was only one."

"The floor safe, right side of the office?"

"Yeah."

That meant the thugs didn't find the small safe behind the bookcase. But someone had emptied it and left it open.

"Did they take anything out of the safe besides money?"

"No, but the head honcho was looking for something, and he was pissed that he didn't find it."

"Did he say what he was looking for?"

"No. He just threw the papers he pulled out of the safe on the floor and cursed a lot."

Max's codebook is probably what the thugs were really after.

"If this character, the Mayor, contacts you again, I want to be the first to know about it."

"You got it, Danny. Ah, I mean Detective."

Sean took a long stride in Albert's direction. "Scram."

Albert froze for a moment and then bounded out of his chair and out the door like a jackrabbit.

I got up, drug my chair back toward the table, and sat down, putting my feet up on another.

Sean pulled up the chair Albert had vacated across from mine, taking a seat. "Any idea who this goon is who calls himself the Mayor? You already ruled out Mayor Hughes as a suspect."

"Mayor Hughes, for sure, isn't our guy. This fella calling himself the Mayor must be the new out-of-town big fish."

Besides being lazy as hell, Theo Hughes had plenty of jack pouring into his pockets from city corruption rackets (bribes and graft).

"How about Roan Doyle? He's running for mayor. Maybe he's taking on the title a little early. Are you sure we should've ruled him out?"

"That's hard to swallow. He's got a lot on his plate already, union president and running for mayor." I put my hands behind my head. "And it's not his style——but he has the connections. We'll put him back on the list for now."

"We should put out the word that we're looking for the dope on a fella called the Mayor."

"Right, we need to start asking around, spread a wide net. See who else we can come up with that might fit the bill." My feet hit the ground, and I stood up. "Let's get to it."

I turned the corner onto Adams Street. Owen's red and white striped barber pole, hanging alongside the door of his shop, stuck out like a sore thumb. One of my boys had got word to me that Owen wanted to see me. Being it was a Thursday morning, it must be something that couldn't wait until tomorrow, Friday, the day I usually go to get my ears lowered. I was hoping he had a lead for me on the Mayor character. Sean and I had put out the word to our contacts to be on the lookout for any tidbit that might help identify the Mayor.

The screen door snapped shut behind me as I entered the barbershop. Both the guys, sitting against the wall waiting their turn, gave me a nod. The fella in the chair, his face and neck smothered in lather, didn't move; Owen's straight razor was at his throat.

"What'd you got for me, Owen?"

"Good morning, Detective." Owen stepped away from the barber chair and headed toward the back of the shop. He motioned with the razor for me to follow. "I'll be right with you, Jake." He looked back at the lathered face. "I got important business with the detective here."

"Take your time. I got all day," Jake said with a smart-ass edge.

Looking around for what I don't know, Owen leaned in and spoke in a hushed voice. "There's a new guy in town, been snooping, asking questions."

"Has he got a name?"

"He goes by Bob Paxton."

"What's he after?"

"He's ask'en about Maxine Snowdon and what rackets she was into. He was ask'en who her associates were and who worked for her. And he was making a list of the coppers who are on the take."

"That would be a long list."

"He asked about you, Danny, specifically. He's got it figured that you worked direct for Snowdon." Owen shifted uneasy.

"Me, really?"

"There are stories going around that you were connected with Snowdon."

"What did you tell him? Any of those stories?"

"No way, not me. I told him you were the only honest copper in King City."

"What did he say to that?"

Owen glanced at his shoes. "He laughed. Said he never met an honest cop."

I was thinking I would like to meet this fella.

"Is he spreading jack around?"

"Yeah, he's got a fist full."

"Did you share anything else with him?"

"Nothing, Danny. You know me."

I gave him a squint eye. "You sure?" Owen doubtless told him something; to be expected.

"Honest, Danny. You can trust me."

I did trust Owen. Obviously, every Friday, he had a razor at my throat.

"Yeah, I know. Just joshing with ya. What did you find out about him?" I could count on Owen doing some asking around.

"He's a private dick from the King District, new to King City. The word is he moved here from Brewster around a year ago."

Brewster is a smallish city with a port on the bay about 100 miles north of King City. A minor competitor for Carvonshire when it comes to bootlegging.

"Any connection to the Snowdon hit?" I was hopeful. It had been a while since the killings, over a month. No one was coming up with any dirt.

"No, nothing. I got my ear to the ground on that one. You can count on me, Detective."

"I know, Owen; I appreciate it."

"You thinking Paxton might be a torpedo or something?"

"Possible." I pulled a fiver out of my pocket and slipped it into Owen's hand, the one without the razor.

"I'm hearing about a new hood working the rackets in King City. He calls himself the Mayor. I want you to ask around and spread the word."

Owen was one of my best connections; you can count on barbershop conversation to be laced with gossip and tidbits of relevant information.

"You got it, Detective."

"I got a joke for ya, O'Shea."

I had just filled my mouth with grub and couldn't manage an objection.

"Why is prohibition so hard on the Irish?"

I shrugged.

"Sometimes they have to go for days trying to survive on only food and water."

I swallowed. "Good one. You know, O'Leary, you're the regular W. C. Fields of King City."

"Really? You think so?"

"Yeah."

Fields was Sean's favorite vaudeville performer. Several years back, while in New York for a boxing match, Sean had seen the comedian in Ziegfeld Follies. That's what kick-started Sean's desire to be on stage.

"Did I ever tell you that Field already has his epitaph written for his gravestone?"

"No."

"I'd rather be here than in Philadelphia." Sean slapped his knees and shook his head.

I took a break from my meal and surveyed Kelly's place, same old, same old, the usual Friday crowd. "We should branch out; try another place for lunch."

"We should?"

"Yeah, we should."

"Never gonna happen." Sean brought his napkin to his lips.

"I'm seeing some light shed on the Snowdon Massacre."

"That's good, cause I'm not. What'd you got cooking?"

"We had already ruled out the local torpedoes who were capable of carrying out the attack. Carlo, Al Harris, Sleazy Sal, Little Billy, and Angelo the Suit are all off the list.

"And Albert pretty much confirmed it Wednesday; it was an out-of-town crew of torpedoes that did the hit."

Sean was nodding and jawing on a mouth full of pastrami sandwich.

"But that leaves the question - who hired that crew?"

"Do you have some dope on that end?"

"Right now, we got a line on this Paxton fella, who only recently rolled into King City a year before the hit. Not likely a coincidence. And we got a foreign-looking doll delivering notes. We need to find out who she is.

"And we know this Mayor character is recruiting local talent, like Albert, Carlo Minx, and Harry Rosser that we know of."

"Albert was a help, but Carlo isn't ever going to talk to us." Sean took a sip of Joe.

"No need. I had a conversation with Harry. He confirmed that it's the Mayor they're working for. The Mayor is arranging shipments of rum into the port. Harry and Carlo are providing distribution throughout King City."

"Does Harry have any dope on the Mayor?"

"No, only Carlo has contact with him."

"So now what?"

"It's pretty clear that the Mayor organized and ordered the hit on Maxine. And it's possible that clown Paxton might be the Mayor. We need to find out more about him too."

Sean was nodding in agreement.

"One thing that bothers me, though, is that empty, small safe that those thugs didn't find. "

Sean paused, chewing for a moment. "Any thoughts on who emptied it or what they took?"

I did, but I wasn't ready to share it with Sean. I trusted the fella with my life, but there was no need to involve him at this point.

"I got some ideas I'm kicking around, but nothing solid."

Last night, I had gone to Lizzy's to test a theory. I came in from the Underground, so no one was the wiser. I nosed around the moving bookshelf and the small safe. Below the safe in the wainscoting, I found a removable panel that revealed a secret passageway. That passage led to the back hallway, which would have provided an escape route from Max's office to the Underground. I figured someone had used it that night. They probably followed the same path as me and the band, also finding their way into the basement and to safety.

And I figured that someone was Grace Snowdon. My theory was that she had opened the safe and taken out what the thugs had been looking for: Max's codebook, the cipher book, with all of Max's bootlegging secrets. With that book, a hoodlum with connections and smarts would be able to take up right where Max left off, running and profiting off the bootlegging operation at the Carvonshire port.

In addition, I had found bloodstains in the passageway. Grace may have been injured. Maybe Grace didn't make it. Maybe she hadn't had time to put the codebook info to play. Maybe the Mayor beat her to it; had his own connections.

Maybes and speculation didn't provide the solution for the Snowdon Massacre, but it was always part of the game.

Sean was waving to Jen and pointing to his empty coffee cup. "Have you talked with your lady reporter since your date Saturday?"

"No. I haven't heard from her all week."

"You set her up with three great crime-beat articles so far. Two made the front page. I thought she'd be dogging you for another big story."

"She must have something cooking."

"She sure made a splash this week with that front-page expose on Al Harris. Maybe she's taking time off to bask in the glory."

I doubted that. What was she up to? It was Friday already, and I was getting concerned. I should have reached out. But Sean and I had police work to take care of.

"We need to finish up here and get over to the Market Place."

There had been complaints about a pickpocket working the area. Not usually a big deal, but the Commissioner's brother-in-law had been separated from his wallet. The Commissioner wanted results and quick. He told the Chief to put his best man on the case. Generally speaking, pick-pocketing investigations are not in a detective's domain, but the Chief, who wanted the case solved, had to ask me to take charge. Every word stuck in his craw. I enjoyed every choking minute of it.

EPISODE 10

A NEAR MISS

In just an afternoon of snooping, Sean and I had pinched the Dip (*), who was working the Market Place, a local they call the Worm. I tried to convince him to give up his life of crime and go straight, but he just laughed in my face. So, instead, the clown is going to spend a year or two in the big house unless he has enough jack to bribe the judge.

And because of his stubborn attitude, I was stuck at the station, spending a late Friday evening filling out charging papers and a crime report. Sean had cut out early. He had gone home to catch supper before his night shift at Griffin's.

A light knuckle rap on my office door interrupted my focus on the paperwork.

"Come in."

The door opened partway; a young boy's face appeared. "Detective O'Shea?"

"Hey there, Donny. What's going on? Come on in."

Donny is one of my boys who keeps me informed on what's happening in Carvonshire. He works at Oswald's Newsstand just around the corner.

"A note for ya, sir." He hustled up to my desk, leaving the door ajar, and handed me a white envelope. I recognized Jane's handwriting right off.

As I laid it on the desktop, I reached into my change pocket and pulled out a nickel, which I flipped into the air. Donny's hand swooped out and snatched it.

"Thank you, sir," he said as he pocketed the coin. "Should I wait?"

"Yeah, hang on a minute."

I used my penknife to slit open the envelope and unfolded a note.

> *Dear Detective*
>
> *I know you don't approve of me snooping around the docks, but I have a line on a good story. A source, George Goff, says he knows who's bringing in the spirits from a rum runner. I have a meeting tonight with him at seven at the dock warehouse. I'll let you know what I find out and discuss it with you before publishing the story to get your take on it. You know me; I wouldn't do anything without your blessing.*
>
> *Jane*

"Jesus Christ," slipped out as I flipped my pocket watch open, six-thirty. "When did you get this?"

Donny's face turned pale. "Don't know exactly. Early this afternoon. I know it's late, but if I missed you here, I planned on running it over to Kelly's or your place to make sure you got it."

"What took you so long?"

"I was on my way over, honest. Some boys in an alley were playing stickball, and they needed another player, and they begged me to play and…"

"Okay, okay, I got the picture." Those were the days when all I had to think about was a stickball game instead of a doll that was hell-bent and getting herself in trouble.

Donny looked as if he was going to bolt. He took a step back, bumping the door. It swung closed; the latch clicked, trapping the lad facing an angry copper.

I held up my hands. "It's all right Donny; calm down. I need you to take a note to Sergeant O'Leary. He's home by now. You know where he lives?"

"Yes, Sir," Donny snapped. He was practically at attention.

I took a moment to scribble a message for Sean to meet me at the docks and bring Johnson along with his rifle. I folded the paper in half and handed it to Donny. "Right this minute, fast as you can. Got it?"

"Yes, Sir. You can count on me." He stood still, nodding like a chicken pecking corn.

"Go!" I yelled.

He spun himself around and collided with the door as he tried to open it. After a bit of struggle with the door, he was gone, and me right after him.

I raced down the stairs, through the station house, and out the side door. In the alley, I broke into a run. I was out on Fourth Ave in a heartbeat. A block away, I spotted Jedd's taxi parked on the corner. It was just dumb luck he wasn't out on a fare. He was leaning against his ten-cent box, taking a drag on a cig.

As I sprinted up, he straightened up and flicked the cig into the gutter. "What's up, Detective." His hand was on the door handle, ready to jump into the driver's seat.

I leaped over the hood and was in the passenger seat in a jiff. "Bay Ave, the union meeting warehouse. Step on it."

The gears clashed, and the taxi bolted forward out into the street.

I glanced at my watch: six forty-five. We couldn't get there in time to intercept her. Hopefully, they wouldn't just whisk her away but have a talk with her first, to find out what she knows, before… I didn't want to consider that. Instead, I spent the ride concentrating on the near collisions Jedd was avoiding by a hair's breadth.

Jedd had to go slow: the fog was rolling in thick off the bay. That and the overcast sky made the wharf dark and shadowy.

I had him stop a few blocks away from the warehouse. "You should take off. Things could get a little dicey."

"I'll wait right here, Detective."

"I'm going to post myself in the alleyway across from the warehouse. If you see Sergeant O'Leary, let him know where I am."

"You got it. I'll keep a sharp lookout for him."

It didn't take much stealth to sneak up to my hiding spot. The fog moving along the street like waves at the beach gave me cover.

Peering around the corner from across the street, I had a bead on two thugs standing guard on the loading dock, one on each side of the warehouse doors. Off to my left, a black car, with another punk behind the wheel, sat with its engine idling. I looked at my watch: seven twenty. There was nothing I could do but wait and hope: I couldn't just bust into the place by myself. I bided my time, stewing in my own juices for close to a half-hour.

"Danny." It was Sean's whispering voice; I knew it was, but my guts jumped up into my throat, anyway.

"Jeez, Sean." I looked over my shoulder into his face. "You sure do move quiet for a guy your size."

He shrugged. "What's the story, Danny? Your note was short on details."

"I didn't have the time to write you a novel."

"Fine, so tell me now."

"Is Johnson with you?"

"Yeah, he's on the roof right above our heads." Sean glanced skyward. "Somebody should do something about this fog. I hope Johnson's got a decent view of things."

Having Johnson on a rooftop with his Enfield P14 sniper rifle was like having a guardian angel. Somehow, he had managed to bring it home with him after the war. Probably, no one had the moxie to take it away from him.

"It comes and goes. Maybe we'll get lucky." I padded my back pocket, holding my wallet with my granddad's lucky shamrock tucked inside.

"Spill the story."

"Jane's been nosing round, trying to get a story on who's bringing in the booze from the Rum Runners. Goff arranged a meeting here tonight with a source that's supposed to give her the lowdown."

Nothing goes in or out of the Carvonshire port without George Goff, the union dock boss, knowing about it and him getting a cut of the action. He would have no interest in an article in the paper that would disrupt the flow of booze into King City.

"What? Is she nuts? She trusted Goff to set up a meeting?"

"Keep your voice down. Let's just say she's naïve; doesn't know her way around just yet."

"She might not have enough time left to get the lay of the land," Sean said, "How do you plan on getting her out of this mess?"

"I need a distraction."

"And that's me, I suppose?"

"Yeah. Go halfway up the block; get yourself some cover. I'll work my way up behind that car sitting out front. I figure that's the vehicle they plan on using to take her away."

"Sounds right."

"When they bring her out, wait until she's near the car, then give them something else to think about."

"Got it." Hunched over, moving behind a line of parked delivery trucks, Sean headed up and away on our side of the street.

I took off the other way, crossed the street, then worked my way back up the other side and crouched behind the parked car.

We didn't have to wait long before the warehouse doors flung open. Jane was escorted out, a goon on her left yanking on her arm, another on her right. She had a red rag stuffed in her mouth. The thugs turned and came down the loading dock steps, dragging Jane along the sidewalk to the waiting car. I recognized one of the thugs, Carlo Minx.

As planned, when the trio reached the car, gunfire erupted. "Pop, pop, pop." Sean shooting in the air.

Carlo and the other thug turned in the direction of the noise.

"Watch the dame," Carlo called out as he legged it back toward the warehouse. The two thugs on the dock had ducked in behind the doors and were returning fire into a fog bank in Sean's direction.

I sprung up from the back end of the car and brought Betsy down on the punk, who was twisting Jane's arm with more force than what was absolutely necessary. He folded up like a pretzel, collapsing to the sidewalk.

Now, I was pulling on Jane's arm myself, and she was pulling away from me.

"Jane, it's Danny." The fog wasn't that thick; we were face to face; she was just panicking.

"Oh my God," she blurted out after plucking the rag out of her mouth.

She relaxed and followed my lead as we headed down the sidewalk, away from the ruckus.

"Get the dame; she's gett'en away." Carlo was yelling from a distance.

I heard a car door open. The punk who had been behind the wheel was about to get into the fray.

"Pop, Pop." Shots rang out, and bullets whizzed over our heads as we ran down the street away from the car.

And then that distinctive pop-zing of several rounds of Johnson's sniper rifle split the air. He couldn't have been targeting anyone from the roof; he could probably only see shadows moving about. He wouldn't be able to tell Sean, Jane, or me from the thugs. The shots were just his way of putting the fear of God in Carlo's gang.

We crossed the street under the blanket of fog. I took Jane's hand and pulled her down low as we ducked behind a black Buick. More shots rang out, but no bullets whizzing by. The thugs were firing blind.

We were safe behind the Buick, shoulder to shoulder, our backs against the door, and our backsides rested on the running board.

"That was a close one." I released her hand.

Jane nodded.

"Ever been shot at before?"

She shook her head.

"Thank god for the fog," I whispered. If it weren't for the fog, we might not have dodged those bullets.

"Blessed fog," Came through Jane's ragged breaths.

"Blessed fog."

"All Clear!" Sean's booming voice broke the silence.

I got to my feet, took Jane's hands, and guided her up. We crossed the street to where Sean and Johnson were standing in front of the stash-house loading dock. Johnson had his rifle strung across his back by a shoulder strap.

"Did you get anybody?" I asked.

"No, they got away clean," Sean said, "Couldn't get a clear shot."

Jedd's taxi wheeled around the corner and came to a stop in front of us. He hopped out and bolted up to us. "Everyone okay?"

"Yeah, not a scratch." As I said that, I glanced back into Jane's pale, wide-eyed face.

"I'll be back in a minute," I said to Sean.

"Take your time; we got all night."

I took Jane's elbow and guided her into the back seat of the taxi. I hustled around to the other side and dropped into the seat alongside her.

"How are you doing?"

"Okay." Jane was wringing her hands.

"That's good," I said, "Tell me what happened in the warehouse." I wanted to get the story while it was still fresh in her mind. "Just start from the beginning."

Jane nodded slowly. "Two men met me at the door. They told me to go inside."

"Did you recognize either of them?"

"No, I never saw them before." Jane looked as if she had just flunked a test.

"That's okay, go on."

"I was expecting Goff, but he wasn't there. And there was another fellow that I didn't know. He was older, in his sixties probably, and had a bulbous red nose. One of the hoodlums at the door had called him Os."

"Oswald Nest, one of Carlo Minx's boys."

"He said we needed to get acquainted before Goff would show with his source. He asked me a bunch of questions and answered some of mine. I was even taking notes. Oh no." Jane glanced at her open palms in her lap and then at me. "My notebook. I dropped it in the warehouse when they grabbed me."

"Don't worry. I'll have the boys search for it. Sit tight; I'll be right back." I got out of the cab and hustled to the dock where my crew was waiting.

"Jane dropped her notebook inside. Would you two take a look-see?" I was speaking to Johnson and Jedd.

Johnson saluted and strode off. Jedd flashed a smirk and dropped his cig, stomping it out before he followed.

"You know, you're going to have to keep a better eye on that dame," Sean said.

"Right. I'll work on that." I shoved my hands into my pants pockets; it was cooling off.

I hung there with Sean as he lit up a cig and mixed smoke rings with the fog. I should be integrating the doll, but for some reason, I wasn't looking forward to it.

I glanced back at the cab. "I'm going to take her over to Griffin's. I'll see you over there later."

It was near the time Sean started his security shift at Griffin Street.

"Yeah, later." Sean nodded. He was looking over my shoulder at the transfer house.

Johnson and Jedd had just emerged. Jedd trotted up, holding the notebook over his head.

"Thanks, pal," I said as he handed it to me.

I addressed Johnson. "You're off duty for the rest of the night, soldier."

He flipped his hand to his cap in an off-handed salute and then marched off down the street. Sean looked at me, shrugged, and headed out after him, calling out, "Johnson, wait up."

"I'm going to need some more time with the doll," I said to Jedd.

He nodded, pulled a pack of cigs from his pocket, and sat down on the dock steps.

Back in the cab. "Go on with your story."

"I thought it was okay. That fella, Os, was answering my questions."

"They were playing the waiting game. Wanted to make sure you came alone. Did they ask if you had talked to the police or anyone else about your story?"

After a hesitation, "Yes."

"And you told them no?"

Jane's chin dropped. "I did." She started wringing her hands again. "That was a mistake, huh?"

"The first rule of King City: Honesty is the best policy, only when it plays to your advantage."

"Got it."

"What happened next?"

"After a half-hour or so, that hood we encountered in the Underground, Carlo Minx, came out of the back-room office. I knew I was in trouble then. He was probably in there the whole time, listening in on the conversation.

"He gave that fella, Os, heck for spilling so much information. But Os said it didn't matter since they were going to take me for a ride, anyway."

"The two men each took one of my arms and yanked me toward the door. I started to scream, but they stuck a rag in my mouth. They tried to shove me in the car. You know the rest."

I nodded.

"Do you think they were taking me to the swamps?"

I didn't answer; just held eye contact. It was rumored that the Black Water Swamp, south of Carvonshire, was the place where bodies went to disappear.

"What made you think you could get away with something like this?" I asked.

"I didn't think they would do anything to me. You know, I'm a reporter and all."

"And you thought that being the daughter of the owner of the King City Gazette would protect you?"

"Well, yes." Jane was staring at the floorboards.

"And the prospect of another big story in the papers may have clouded your judgment?"

She had likely gotten a big head over that front-page article last week, the Al Harris story, and then got greedy, looking for the next scoop. She'd have to rein in her ambition a bit. She'd learn.

Jane took a moment. "Probably true."

Her hands, lying in her lap, were clasped together tightly, but that didn't stop the trembling completely.

"Are you going to catch these hoodlums and arrest them?"

"Well, we could do that."

"What do you mean? You're not going to let them get away with trying to kill me, are you?"

"If I did arrest them, it would go like this. We pinch Carlo, Os, and the other thugs and charge them with assault and attempted kidnapping. I suspect that the jury would be inclined to take your side."

"Good, do it." Jane was still trembling but from anger instead of fear.

"During your testimony, you would have to explain why you were at the docks and who you were there to see."

"I could come up with a story about why I was there."

"And say Goff invited you?"

"I could name him. He set me up to be murdered." No more trembling; she was boiling mad.

"Since he never showed, it would be his word against yours. And being the union boss, he's got connections. With some union men on the jury, he might not get convicted."

"We could still get the other three."

"Maybe. I said the jury would be inclined to take your side. Carlo has been arrested a lot of times but never convicted. He has a way with juries. There's something about finding your pet dog mutilated on your front porch that calls for a not guilty verdict."

"Are you saying there's nothing we can do?"

"Not at the moment. Not using the judicial system."

A not-so-ladylike growl came out of Jane.

"Would you like to make these guys pay for what they did?"

"You bet."

"Getting even takes time. You need patience. You remember Councilman Ross?"

"Yes."

"It took me five years to work that out."

"I don't want to wait that long."

"It's possible we could speed up the process."

"What's stopping them from trying to take me out again in the meantime?" Jane's shoulders shuddered.

"For one, they know the police are involved now. Me, that is. It would be a big risk to come after you again. That provides you with a layer of protection."

"That's all it would take?"

"Yeah," I said, "It's not ironclad but likely to hold." I shrugged. "That's the nature of the game you're in now.

"It's your choice. I can arrest them tomorrow, or we can play the long game." I put my hand on her shoulder. "Think on it."

"Okay." Jane relaxed a bit, sinking back into the seat.

"Let's go over to Griffin's for a drink."

"We nearly got killed, and you want to go out for drinks?"

"Sure, can't think of a better time."

Jane didn't say anything for a long moment, just stared at me, unblinking.

"I'll be damned if you aren't right, Detective."

Nothing like a near-death experience to clear the cobwebs and set your priorities to right.

I poked my head out the window and called to Jedd.

"Where to, Danny?" Jedd asked as he dropped into the driver's seat.

"Griffin's."

"Of course." The lad touched his fingers to his cap.

We got to Griffin's in no time at all, but enough time for Jane to do some thinking on her near murder. She saw things my way. She opted for the long game instead of an arrest.

I waved to Joe as Jane and I passed the bar, heading for my usual table against the back wall.

Moments later, Joe approached with two shot glasses in his hand. "Heard what happened tonight; you two all right?" He glanced at each of us in turn.

Sean must have gotten here before us. He wasn't in sight; probably in the backroom tending to his Friday night business.

"Yeah, we came out of it all right. A close call, though."

Joe placed the shot glasses on the table, one in front of me and one in front of Jane. "On the house." He winked at Jane.

All my drinks were on the house: no copper in Carvonshire ever paid for a drink.

"What else can I get ya?" Joe was standing tall, hands-on-hips.

"Two bourbons." I looked at Jane. "Gin Rickey?"

With her wide eyes on Joe, "Make that two."

"You got it." Joe strode back to the bar.

"What's this?" Jane had her glass at eye level, examining the clear liquid.

"That's high-quality corn liquor."

"Anthony's?"

"Right."

Jane brought the shot glass to her lips and threw back her head, the liquor disappearing in one gulp.

"Ahhhhhh!" Jane choked out, followed by a few coughs and a very loud raspberry buzzing of her lips. She tried to speak, but nothing came out.

The people around us took notice. Two old men at the bar were looking our way, grinning.

"Another shot, Miss?" Joe called from behind the bar.

Jane pursed her lips and shook her head vigorously.

In a moment, Jane got her voice back. "Again, I have to thank you. You risked your life to save mine." Jane's eyes were tearing up. "I feel so stupid. Stupid, stupid."

"Don't be so hard on yourself. You're a rookie at this game."

"But you, Sergeant O'Leary, Officer Johnson, and that young boy, Jedd, all put your lives on the line to get me out of a jam I created. I'm so sorry." The faucets had turned on.

What to do with a crying dame? I really didn't know. Should I go over and put my arm around her shoulder, pat her back, say something soothing?

I handed her my handkerchief. She dabbed both eyes and blew her nose.

Joe was back, placed our drinks in front of us, and made a quick about-face.

I figured it best to continue with an interrogation.

"You arranged this meeting through Goff? He said he had a source that would fill you in on the bootlegging operation at the wharf?"

"I thought I could trust him. He seemed nice when I met him at the union meeting last month. I even wrote some articles that put the union in a good light. This is how he pays me back?"

"The first rule of King City - you can't count on the nice guys."

"Right." Jane leveled a smirk at me.

"If you had checked with me, I could've told you that the union leaders get a cut of the profits on all the booze that flows through the port. Some of the union dock hands have side jobs crewing the boats that bring the booze in from the Rum Runner's ships."

"Okay, I get the picture. I won't make a move from now on unless I check with you first." Her eyes were dried up and angry now.

I wished I could believe that, but I doubted that promise would hold.

"You mentioned that when you were in the warehouse, Os had spilled the beans. What did he tell you?"

Jane's eyes brightened up. She leaned forward.

"He said some things that didn't make any sense."

"Try me."

"When he was blabbing on, he said that the mayor was running the bootlegging operation at the wharf." Jane's face puzzled. "But Mayor Hughes, how could that be?"

"You're right; Mayor Hughes doesn't have the connections to run that kind of operation or the brains. But there's a new hoodlum in town that I got a line on who calls himself The Mayor."

"Who is he?"

"Don't know yet; still working on it."

"He also said that the booze shipments were coming in from St. Croix."

"Well, that's a whole new ball of wax. Remember when I told you that Max had arrangements with a dame out of Nassau to bring in high-quality booze?"

"Do you think someone has the same connection now?"

"Not likely; Nassau and St Croix are in the same neck of the woods, but I doubt Cleo would move her operation to another island."

"Cleo?"

"Gertrude (Cleo) Lythgoe, the source of top-shelf booze for the whole east coast. That's who Maxine was connected with, who she got her booze from."

"I've heard of her, The Queen of the Bahamas. I've read about her in the papers."

"Did you learn anything else?" I was thinking Jane's little adventure was paying off.

"No, that's about it," Jane replied, "You seem concerned. I didn't think you took bootlegging seriously."

"I like to know what's going on, who's pulling the strings, and what their intentions are. And, whoever he is, this Mayor fella, he threw in with Carlo Minx. Not a good sign."

Jane gazed into her Gin Ricky as she tilted the glass back and forth. She hadn't taken a sip of either of the two glasses in front of her.

As she looked up at me, "I don't get it."

"Get what?"

"I just ask around about bootlegging and almost get killed. You bust up a Maxine Snowdon operation, and nothing happens to you."

"You still got your teeth into my bootlegging arrest that hit the papers big time back in '24'?"

"Still waiting to hear that story, are you?"

"Yes, Detective, I am."

"Unlike your situation, it wasn't a problem for me because I was doing a favor for Max."

"The favor you owed her for getting Angelo to lift the contract killing he put out on you?"

"Right, I owed her for saving my life. That episode with the bootlegging arrest was a partial payback."

"Let me get this straight. Intercepting a shipment of extremely valuable spirits, dumping it in the streets, and sending one of her lieutenants to jail was doing Maxine Snowdon a favor?"

"Yeah." I figured that Jane was not going to let this go. And I was at the point where I felt I could trust her, so I decided to spill the story. Besides, I felt that a storytelling might provide a welcome distraction.

Jane tilted her head from side to side and raised her eyebrows.

"Okay, this is how it went down."

I got an invitation to meet with Max at her office. I figured this was the time my note was about to come due. Since I got the message, my mind had been twisting in the wind, conjuring all kinds of bad outcomes.

"Good to see you again, Danny." Max was sitting behind her desk; I was standing in front, the condemned man waiting for his sentence to be pronounced. "I need a favor."

I knew she was going to say it, but my insides chilled anyway.

"Someone's been intercepting my deliveries of wine before they reach Carvonshire. Three months in a row, my drivers have been hijacked on the outskirts of town. And I'm sure it's an inside job. I have a weasel in my organization." Max, always right to the point.

Max smuggled in high-priced wine from France to satisfy the upper crust of King City, a hundred dollars or more a bottle. It comes overland from Brewster. Two of her people, a hood and a dame, bring it in, driving a Cadillac, the cases of booze stashed in a concealed compartment.

"What do you want from me?" Max already had arrangements with the police to let the booze come in unhindered.

"I need someone to find out who's behind it, but I can't trust anyone in my organization."

"And that someone would be me?"

"That's right."

"You got it narrowed down any?"

"My bet is on Salvador, Billy, or Clarence." Her top three lieutenants.

"If you give me the delivery schedule for next month, I could take a squad of men and intercept the high-jacking."

"Too messy, and you might not get the top dog." Max waved a finger at me. "I would prefer that you find out who's running the operation and deal with them direct."

"You got some ideas on how to do this?"

"Yes." Max opened a desk drawer and brought out a folded, legal-sized piece of paper. "I plan to tell the boys that a shipment slipped through and that I have it stored in an Underground stash room."

She unfolded the paper and laid it out on the desktop. It was a map of the Underground. I wasn't familiar with the Underground at the time, but I had heard rumors about a secret network of old mine tunnels the Jones Gang had put to use for their criminal activities.

"You will only need to know one access point and how to get to the stash room. Take a good look." There were two Xs on the map and a dotted line between them. She gave me about 30 seconds, then flipped the map over.

She was expecting me to memorize the part of the map showing the two points I would need. Not a problem for me; I'm good with pictures and faces. Only got to see them once, and they're in the old noggin forever. I had the whole of the Underground map tucked away for future reference.

"You'll also need the password and the response." Max slid a small scrap of paper across the table in my direction. I took a quick glance, *The Sun Also Rises* by Ernest Hemingway. From the wall of books on the shelves behind her, I assumed Max was an avid reader. Since she doesn't socialize (in public anyway), that must be how she spends her time, along with running all the rackets in Carvonshire.

"So, you tip off the location to all three guys, and I go see who shows up?"

"You are as sharp as they say you are." You would expect a smile with that sarcasm, but nope.

"Then I could get creative and set something up to trap the rat. End of problem."

"Really sharp." Still no smile.

"What I'm thinking…"

"I don't need to know the details." Max raised her hand.

"These ain't details, but I hope you don't mind if the rat ends up in the slammer instead of six feet under."

"No problem."

"And if me and my boys end up with the collar and our pictures in the paper, no problem either?"

I already had the beginnings of a plan percolating.

"I expect you to get something out of it. It's only right."

"The favor; I don't suppose this makes us even?"

"It's a wash, Danny, I get something, you get something. We're a long way from even."

She was right; this little adventure was tit for tat, no reprieve for me. Saving some booze was not the same as saving my life.

A week later, I was in the Underground, heading for a blind date with a yet-to-be-named weasel. It turned out to be Clarence. He and one of his boys challenged me as they came upon the empty stash room. We exchanged passwords and introductions.

"What the hell are you do'en down here copper?" Clarence asked.

"Business for Max." The truth, really. "I just moved out a batch of fancy wine to the buyers. Got to make room for the next shipment."

"You mov'en the product for Max now?"

"Yeah, she was having trouble bringing in the product, so I stepped in, same setup, different timing, different routes."

"You know, I could be of some help if I was in on your plans," Clarance offered.

"I don't know; Max told me to keep a tight lip."

"I'm like her right-hand man; you can trust me, Detective."

"So, if I get in a jam, you'd be there to back me up?"

"For sure, Detective." Clarance was now all smiles. He slapped me on the shoulder.

"All right then, makes sense to me." I filled Clarence in on the shipment's route and schedule, the trap.

To set things up, first, we put a tail on Clarence. Johnson was the man for the job. He followed Clarence day and night. Johnson doesn't sleep anyway; the artillery roar from the war that's still booming in his head keeps him up. He found out where along the route Clarence planned to attack our car.

Next, we got ourselves a Caddy to make the fake run with the wine. We put a patrolman in to drive along with a girl from a local creep joint (*) that we had paid off.

On the scheduled evening, we had our decoy Caddy rolling along the road where Clarence and a pal lay in wait. Me and Sean were undercover, just outside their line of sight.

The two thugs ran out in front of our target vehicle, waving guns and shooting in the air. As planned, our patrolman pulled over and surrendered. Clarence thought he had it made until he opened the trunk and came face to face with Corporal Johnson with his two revolvers pointing at his mug. A moment later, me and Sean were pressing pee shooters in the theives' backs.

Since it wouldn't have been wise to give away Max's methods for bringing in the wine, we staged the arrest at the edge of town. The reporters were invited to the shindig, where we had a truck loaded with kegs of beer and fancy wine bottles filled with grape juice. Clarence and his pal were handcuffed and guarded by Johnson. I made a show of pouring grape juice into the gutter and smashing wine bottles.

Sean went to town busting up beer kegs with an ax. He was having a time of it. Sean likes nothing more than busting things up, except maybe busting up people. There were no beer kegs in the actual shipments, but we put a bunch of them on the truck, twenty-something full of stale beer. Thought it added to some theater of the event. We kept at it until the photographers had had enough. I was seeing blue spots for days.

Made a hell of a mess. The sanitation boys had their work cut out for them the next morning.

Our pictures appeared on the front page of the Gazette the next day. I got the collar for Clarance and his pal, along with a promotion to Senior Detective.

◼━ ▮▬ ▫▬

"That's pretty much it."

"You are something else." Jane was smiling and shaking her head. "That was a story worth waiting for."

I was wondering how many other stories I was just going to spill out.

"You implied that you did all that for Maxine Snowdon because you owed her a favor?"

"I did. You remember I told you that the contract Angelo the Suit had put on my head got lifted?"

"Yes. So, Maxine Snowdon arranged that? How?"

"I don't know what she did or what it cost her, but I owed her."

"That bit about memorizing the map, that's interesting. It must have come in handy over the years, that memory of yours, a real advantage in your line of work."

"I guess so."

"So, you're telling me if I let you look around my bedroom for just a minute—not that it's going to happen—

and then I moved my perfume bottle on my dressing table six inches, you would be able to tell about it when you got a second look?"

"Absolutely." I was picturing what Jane's bedroom might look like.

I caught a glimpse of activity at the bar. Jedd was there, speaking to Joe, who was pointing in my direction. Jedd hustled over to our table and handed me an envelope.

"An usher from the Mercury gave this to me and told me to get it to you right away." Jedd's face was flushed red.

'Detective O'Shea' was scrawled across the lavender envelope in classy handwriting, not like the tip-off notes I had received. It hadn't been sealed, so Jedd had probably read the contents on the way over. By the look in his eyes, it must be big news. I pulled out a note.

It was. I read it to Jane.

"There's been a murder at the Mercury. Roan Doyle was shot dead in his seat. The coppers are here. The shooter got away."

The Mercury Theater was Carvonshire's only upscale theater. The plays presented there were top-notch, as good as the playhouses

In the King District. So, I'm told.

I handed the note to Jane. "That's it, no signature." However, the source of this note was no mystery to me; the handwriting was definitely that of my connection in the theater world, Francine.

"I know Doyle; I met him at the union meeting last month."

Roan Doyle was president of the King City Workers Union and a mayoral candidate in the upcoming election.

Jane handed the note back. I slipped it into my breast pocket. My attention shifted back to the bar again, where Sean was standing, looking my way, motioning with his arm for us to get a move on. Jedd must have spilled the story to Joe, and Joe alerted Sean.

"I gotta go," I said as I stood up, "Jedd will be giving me a ride. But I'll have Joe arrange a ride home for you."

Jane was coming to her feet. "Oh, no. I'm going with you. But first, I need to get to the Gazette offices and round up a photographer."

"You're not thinking straight. You can't waltz into the crime scene at the Mercury as J.L. Gibson. You'll blow your cover."

Jane plopped back down in her seat. "I can't miss this."

"The way I see it, the Gazette has probably already sent a photographer."

"You're right. But I need a way to get the story directly from the crime scenes since I can't just show up."

"You go to your office and hang tight. I'll call you later with the details. You'll get a scoop for tomorrow's morning edition. Your photographer is only going to get some outside shots. I'll make sure you get a few of the police crime photos."

"I'll need them by four am."

"I can do that." Sean caught my eye. Both his hands were in the air over his head. "I gotta go."

"Thank you, Danny."

"No problem, Jane."

EPISODE 11

MURDER AT THE MERCURY

Jedd pulled up to the curb on the opposite side of the street of the Mercury Theater. The play of the evening on the marque, *Gang War by Willard Mack*, was outlined by glowing yellow bulbs. The theater side of the street was clogged with an array of cars, including several squad cars and a paddy wagon. A row of patrolmen stood guard on the sidewalk, keeping the reporters, photographers, and gawkers at bay.

Sean and I exited the cab and hoofed it across to the theater.

"Make sure there's someone posted at the back entrance, so none of these clowns try to sneak in." I nodded to the men of the press. "I'll meet you inside."

"Got it." Sean snagged a patrolman and headed around back.

As I entered the lobby, I spotted Jr. Detective Brady, notepad in hand, at the epicenter of a flock of agitated theatergoers. As the junior detective, he got saddled with desk duty on weekends and took the call that Friday evening.

"What are you doing here?" Brady's intent was to be a smart-ass, but he looked relieved to see me. "The Chief is probably going to give this case to Foley."

Brady, who was assigned to Foley, the precinct's other senior detective besides me, spent most of his time brown-nosing.

"Is Foley here?"

"No." A sheepish reply.

"Do you think he's going to show up anytime soon?"

Foley was undoubtedly at his club socializing and unlikely to make an appearance until sometime tomorrow, if at all. Brady knew this as well as I did.

Brady didn't answer.

"So, you want to handle this one yourself?" I turned toward the door. "I could leave."

"No. Don't do that." Panic crossed Brady's face.

"Okay then. Fill me in."

Brady, our boy wonder, had done a decent job so far. After he got the call, he mobilized a squad of men, got to the scene in good time, and secured the area. He had even started the interviews. I was impressed. I was going to have to rethink the derogatory names I'd been using and stop calling him wet around the ears.

By the time I got into the theater proper, Sean was already there, standing over a body laid out on its back between the stage and the first row of seats. It was Roan Doyle, alright, union president and mayoral candidate, now out of the race.

"We're going to have our hands full with this one," Sean said.

"Yeah."

By the looks of things, Doyle had been shot in the chest, possibly twice. Someone had pulled him from his first-row seat to the floor in an attempt at first aid. Hopeless, though, judging from the amount of blood.

"Brady is in the lobby interviewing what's left of the audience, about 30 of them. The manager said he had a full house tonight."

A full house at the Mercury Theater meant an audience of around 200 this evening to take in a murder mystery. But by the time the patrolmen had arrived, most had exited the premises soon after it became common knowledge that an actual murder had been committed.

"Any witnesses to the shooting?"

"According to Brady, most didn't even know there had been a shooting until well after the fact. The killer timed his shots to coincide with a scene on stage with some noisy gunplay. The real shots blended in with the cap guns. A few said they saw flashes of light coming from the curtain on the left side of the stage."

"Sounds like this might have been a well-orchestrated hit."

I wasn't sure if Sean meant that as a joke.

"The Doc's here." Sean had spotted Doc Thomas, the Carvonshire District Coroner, coming down the aisle.

"Good evening, Doc. Hope we didn't call you away from anything important," I said.

I meant that as a joke. The Doc had nothing that resembled a social life. He lived alone and spent most of his time in the morgue, in the bowels of the station house. Probably drank alone. No vices, except for the Cuban cigars.

"What have we got here, O'Shea?" Doc's cigar twitched as he spoke.

"A theater full of people and no witnesses," Sean said.

"They moved the body?" Doc didn't wait for an answer. He stepped over to the front-row seat, E12, which was soaked in blood. "Do they have pictures before he was moved?"

"No. Just after the fact," I said, "But we're pretty sure the shots came from the left side of the stage, from behind the curtain. There were three or four shots. A man sitting behind Doyle also took a slug in the shoulder. They took him to King City General."

Doc was looking back and forth from the stage to the seats. "From the blood spatters, that looks about right."

"We'll be wanting whatever you can get on ballistics," I stated the obvious.

"Right. If the slugs aren't still in Doyle, they might be lodged in one of the seats. I'll dig around a bit. After I get Mr. Doyle in the meat wagon, I'll head over to the hospital and check on that injured fella. If I don't find a slug in the seats or in Doyle, maybe he collected one for us."

"How about we meet back here tomorrow afternoon to go over things?" I said to Doc.

"Right." He opened his black bag and took out a knife and a screwdriver-looking tool. He turned away from us and got to work.

"The stage crew and the actors are being held by a couple of our guys backstage. They haven't been interviewed yet," I said to Sean, "Let's get to it."

"Hopefully, they'll have something for us."

Sean and I walked into the dressing room area, where two patrolmen had the stagehands and actors corralled, waiting their turn for interviews. I caught sight of Francine standing off in the back. The front of her dress and arms were sullied with blood. Me and Francine go way back; she was the likely candidate for the first aid attempt.

I told Sean to pick a dressing room for his interviews. I chose a room for myself and started with Francine. She was level-headed and probably had the most to offer.

It was well past midnight when we finished up the interviews and sent the witnesses home. All the coppers were gone. As Sean and I walked out together, we shared what we had learned. Most of the information concerning the sequence of events came from Francine. The rest of the witnesses offered bits and pieces that confirmed her account. But despite her cooperation, I had the sneaking suspicion she was holding something back. She wasn't quite her congenial self. But then, she just had a man die in her arms.

A picture of the evening came together. The shooter had things well planned out. He had stationed himself behind the curtain on the left side of the stage and timed the shot to occur with the fight scene in the third act, a scene complete with cap gun sound effects. When the unfortunate people in the second row behind Roan realized they had been splatted with blood, they started screaming bloody murder. The patrons seated on both sides of the victim soon caught on and joined the chorus of panic. Then the house lights came up, and everyone realized there had been a murder in the seats as well as on the stage. A fella in the third row to Roan's left also caught a slug. He was the guy on the way to the hospital.

Outside at the curb, Sean stopped to light a cig. We were in the dark except for the street lamp we were standing under; the marque lights were out. In the empty street, Jedd's ten-cent box sat right where we left it. Jedd was asleep with his head resting against the window.

"The shooter put some thought into this," I said.

"A hit by a torpedo, then?" Sean blew out a smoke ring and watched it drift away.

"I'd bet on it."

"Could be a connection to the mayor's race." Sean smiled. "It's too bad. They say Doyle had a shot at winning."

"Not funny, O'Leary."

Back at the Mercury Saturday afternoon, Sean and I strolled down the center aisle. Doc Thomas was already there, sitting in a front-row seat, his back to us, a cloud of cigar smoke hung over his head.

I stifled a yawn. I hadn't slept well last night; dead bodies still unnerve me. You never get used to it. Well, except for the Doc, he seems to have managed.

Earlier in the morning, I had met with the Chief. He officially assigned the Doyle case to me instead of Foley because, he said, I was the first senior detective on the scene. Claimed he was doing me a favor. What a joke. Foley wouldn't want any part of this mess. A high-profile murder investigation was going to require some actual police work.

As we approached, the Doc came to his feet. He extracted two cigars from his shirt pocket and waved them at us. "A Cuban?"

"Thanks, Doc." Sean took one.

"No thanks." I gave up that dirty habit years ago.

"Suit yourself," the Doc said as he returned the cigar to his pocket.

"What you got for us on the ballistics, Doc?"

"Doyle took two in the chest and one in the gut. I recovered two slugs, one out of Doyle and one out of a seat. The weapon was a small-caliber, 25 ACP, probably from a 1908 Vest Pocket."

"That's helpful." Sean puffed out cigar smoke with the words.

Should we get our hands on a suspected weapon, the Doc would be able to confirm it was the one used. He had a new-fangled comparison microscope. Fire a test bullet from the alleged gun and compare that with the recovered slugs. If the markings matched, we had our murder weapon.

"Our killer just got lucky taking out Doyle with that toy gun from that distance," I said.

The Colt Doc mentioned was small, great for concealment, but with limited range, not much more than the distance from the curtain to Doyle's seat. But our killer could have brought the peashooter into the theater in his shoe. No one would have noticed.

"He did put three slugs in Doyle, might have been a marksman," Sean said.

"A torpedo with a Colt, that's possible, I guess." I knew that Grace Snowdon, Max's assassin, carried a peashooter like that. But it wasn't Grace's style; she was more likely to be up close when she brought the hammer down on a mark. She wouldn't risk a shot from that distance, but you never know.

"Doc, what're the chances this could be the same weapon used on Maxine Snowdon?" A suspicion had entered my mind that Grace was the one who took out Maxine and now Doyle as well. I wasn't seeing the motive yet, but both murders looked like they had a gun in common.

"No, that was a tommy (*) for sure."

"But the way I remember it, she also took some slugs from a small caliber peashooter?"

"Oh yeah, you're right." The Doc's cigar slumped as he nodded. "I gotta be going. I have another body to look over back at the morgue."

The Doc snatched up his bag and was gone in a flash.

The Doc forgot a crime scene statistic; that was a first. And I hadn't heard anything about any other bodies falling of late.

"What's with him?" I asked Sean. "He didn't even answer my question."

"Got me." Sean was admiring his cigar, twisting it in his fingers.

I pulled out my pocket watch, eleven-fifteen. "Let's head over to Kelley's for lunch."

"On a Saturday?"

"This Saturday's a workday; why not?"

As we walked into Kelly's, I could see that our usual table was occupied, so we took a booth on the back wall.

A waitress started in our direction, but Kelly, who had seen us coming, waved her off. As he approached our table, he looked back at the waitress, pointing at the coffee urn on the counter and then holding up two fingers.

"What are you two doing here on a Saturday?"

"Working a case," I said.

"The Doyle murder?"

"That's right."

"Damn, that's going to be a big one. I was reading about it in the papers. That photo of Doyle made him look rather peaceful, except for the bullet holes and blood."

I nodded.

Kelly went on. "It said in the papers that the coppers had good leads on a suspect. What are you thinking? Mayor Hughes has the most to gain by taking out Doyle."

I had Jane put that in the article, hoping it would make the killer nervous and prone to make a mistake.

"Can't discuss police matters."

Kelly gave up his line of questioning. He had done it before in the past and got nowhere. "What'll you boys be have'en?"

Sean and I both said the usual.

"Sorry, we're out of pastrami, and I don't have any macaroni and cheese made up."

Sean and I didn't speak; we just stared at each other.

"How about the special? Meatloaf, mashed potatoes, and green beans," Kelly interjected into the silence.

"Alright," I said. Sean grunted.

Kelly left as the waitress scooted up with two cups of Joe. Vera was neatly printed on her homemade name tag. She asked if we wanted cream or sugar and then hustled off, returning in a jiff with a small pitcher of cream. Flashing a perky smile, our waitress asked if she could get us anything else. After Sean and I exchanged dumb looks, she was off to the grill and returned with our grub before I could get my coffee cup to my lips.

Again, she asked if we wanted anything else. After observing two head shakes, she was off to another table.

Jen must not work on Saturdays. I was missing the old battle-ax.

"I imagine she's expecting a big tip," I said.

"I got one for her." Sean was smiling. "Don't take any wooden nickels."

Sean's one-liners weren't working for him; he needed to stick to telling jokes.

"We could use a tip-off on the Doyle murder." Sean was dead serious now. "You didn't get one of those notes this time, did you?"

"No, no note this time. Whoever is sending them must not have had the dope on the shooting beforehand. Or they did, but had no intention of saving Doyle.

"We'll have to figure this one out on our own," I said.

Sean leaned in. "So, lay it on me; what are you thinking?"

"It's obvious that the killer knew the play, and that there was a scene with sound effects that would cover the report of his gunshots. And to his advantage, it took some time for the murder to be discovered, enough time for the shooter to get away unnoticed."

"That points to a bop (*). Someone who put in the effort."

"Someone who took the time to learn Doyle's habits. The manager told Brady that Doyle had attended all the shows for the last three weekends."

"A real fan of the theater, I guess." Sean was staring at the plate of special, befuddled.

"One other thing Brady got from the manager; Doyle always comes alone. Strange for a fella known to have a way with the ladies."

"So, what are you thinking on this one, for suspects and motives, O'Shea?" Sean was pushing his food around his plate with his fork.

"Like Kelly said, the person who would obviously benefit from the demise of Roan Doyle would be Mayor Hughes. Eliminating his only opponent in the mayoral contest this fall is surely to his benefit."

"Not something he could pull off himself, but he could have hired a torpedo. That fits."

"Right, but from what I heard, Doyle was not much of a threat, so far at least. He was down in the poles. Besides, if Hughes did feel threatened, our mayor could just put in a fix for the election. He had done it before. Knocking off Doyle probably wouldn't be worth the trouble or required."

"So, probably not Hughes?" Sean had dropped the fork and was sipping his coffee. "How about Patterson?"

Harold Patterson, King City's most successful business tycoon, was anti-union and fought the union's influence tooth and nail.

"Just because he hates the unions isn't enough of a motive. And besides, why now? Doyle has been a thorn in his side for years."

"Angelo then, how about him?"

"I don't see how he benefits from taking out Doyle." Angelo the Suit mostly minded his own business, running the crime syndicate in the Hill Section.

"How about the new thug in town, the Mayor fella?"

"We don't know enough about him to understand what his motives are, but it's a possibility. A union man, Doyle was likely involved in the bootlegging at the docks. And the Mayor recently just started bringing booze in at the port; it could be they had a falling out."

Sean had extracted the saucer from under his coffee cup and pushed it up against his plate. With his fork, he was banishing the green beans to the saucer.

"Those beans are good for you. They'll put hair on your chest."

"Oh yeah, but they're green." Mission accomplished; Sean banished the saucer to the far side of the table. "Except for Roan Doyle, this is the same list we laid out for the hit on Lizzy's, and the Mayor fella stands out in both cases."

"That has not escaped me."

"Assuming it was a torpedo, who have you got on that list?"

"With Al Harris gone, that leaves Carlo Minx, Grace Snowdon, Paxton, or someone from out-of-town, maybe one from the crew that hit Lizzy's."

"But Carlo was at the docks, taking potshots at us."

"Could have been one of his henchmen."

"It was a pretty clean hit. Carlo and his boys usually leave a mess."

"Still, he may have had a beef with Doyle. They're undoubtedly tied together with the bootlegging at the docks. Doyle might have asked for a bigger piece of the pie, and Carlo cut him out of the picture. Or maybe Carlo got his orders from the Mayor character."

"But hit Doyle and our Miss Dickerson on the same night. That's pushing it," Sean said.

"You got a point."

"You think Grace is still alive and working?"

I had made Sean aware of Grace's extracurricular activities as an assassin. I was getting a strong sense that she was still out there in the weeds. I figured it was best for him to know for his own safety.

"It's a possibility we got to keep on the table." Although, this wasn't really Grace's style. Her hits usually end up up close and personal. But the planning and the small caliber weapon pointed to her.

"How about some new freelancer? Could be one of the stagehands looking to pick up some extra cash. They could have had the Colt in their pocket the whole time. And they knew the play real good and could have found their way around the stage in the dark, easy."

Sean was full of ideas. This one didn't sound half bad.

"Another possibility. You interviewed the stagehands; any of them stand out in your mind?"

"I had them all down as saps, but I'll review my notes. I could bring them into the station and have a talk with them."

"Let's hold off on that." I didn't want a confession to the murder unless I was sure the fella offering the confession actually did it. "It would be good to know if any of them had a gambling habit or financial troubles. I'll have Brady look into it."

"Brady's going to do that for you?"

"Yeah, he owes me."

I waved at Vera and pointed to my coffee cup. In two shakes of a lamb's tail, our cups were refilled to the brim. My cup was full of Joe; my food was hot when it landed on the table. I wasn't used to this.

"Why do you have Paxton on your list? He just looks like another private snooper to me."

"I still think there's a possibility that he actually is the Mayor, running things from behind the curtain. He comes to town, and then we have two gangland massacres and an assassination. Hell of a coincidence. And besides that, I don't like him."

"You don't like him? You haven't even met him yet."

"I got a bad feeling about him."

Vera suddenly appeared with the check, asked if we wanted dessert, and proceeded to list a multitude of possibilities before either of us could answer. We declined, and she laid the bill on the table. She flashed the perky smile again and took off.

"Let's track down this Paxton fella and have a word with him."

"Because you don't like him?"

"Right."

It was first thing Monday morning, and I was sitting in one of the plush lobby chairs, facing the Carlson Hotel elevator door so I wouldn't miss the clown.

Sure enough, the elevator door opened, and out he steps, bigger than life. I have to say Owen was right; Paxton was a tall, handsome guy, sharp dresser. Nice set of threads; pinstripes looked good on him. The private dick game must be paying well.

I stepped in front of Paxton. "Yeah, fella, got a minute." I pulled my coat back, uncovering my badge.

He came to a stop. "What can I do for you?"

"I'm Detective Danny O'Shea, Carvonshire District. You're Bob Paxton, right?"

"That's right."

"I got a few questions for ya."

"I gotta be somewhere. Maybe another time." He tried to step around me.

"Make time." I stepped to the side, so he had a clear line of sight to the lobby door. In front of which, Sean stood, a mountain of blue with brass buttons.

"We could just charge you with something and take you down to the station."

"For what? I haven't done anything."

"It's not much of a ride to the station, and I'm a quick study. It wouldn't take me long to figure something up."

I didn't wait for more argument. I waved to Sean. "There's a back room here where we can have a private conversation." I turned; Paxton followed. Sean behind him.

In the storeroom, I pulled up a chair on one side of the table and pointed to one across from me. Paxton took it. Sean stood off against the wall, arms folded.

"I hear you been asking about me. Why not ask me direct?" I quizzed Paxton.

"I already know everything I need to know about you."

"I doubt that." I wasn't liking his cocky attitude. "What's your interest in Maxine Snowdon, and who worked for her?"

"I'm a private detective. My asking is private, none of your business."

"Who are you working for?"

"Again, private."

"What do you know about a hood who calls himself the Mayor?"

"Never heard of him."

"How about this? And I'm going to need an answer, or else you're going to be in a lot of hot water." I looked over at Sean, who lowered his arms and straightened up tall.

"Where were you last Friday evening?" I continued what was probably a useless line of questioning.

"The night that Doyle was murdered? I was right here in the lobby from seven o'clock till ten." Paxton had an annoying grin on his face.

"Just sitting in the lobby?"

"Yeah, you can check with the desk clerk on duty that night."

"I will. You make that a habit of sitting in the lobby nights?"

"I had a date with a doll for dinner here, but she stood me up."

"You waited three hours for a dame?"

"She was worth it, a real dish."

"What's her name so I can track her down?"

"That won't be too hard." Paxton twisted and draped an arm over the back of his chair. "She's the society reporter for the Gazette, Jane Dickerson." The corner of his mouth turned up in a smirk.

It was late afternoon, and I was sitting in the Carlson storeroom waiting for Jane. The smell of Paxton's cologne still lingered from my meeting with him this morning. As a matter of principle, you just can't trust a man who wears that much Bay Rum; they're trying to hide something.

After turning Paxton loose, Sean went to confirm his alibi with the desk clerk. And I hoofed it over to Oswald's newsstand to use the pay phone. I had questions for Jane. I left a message for her to meet me at the Carlson at four.

In the call, I used a code that Jane and I had worked out for secret phone communications. When I called her at the Gazette, I used different names, but always ones with my initials. The subject of the call I left with the operator was in code words for the place and time to meet (Griffin's, Bay Port Park, The Carlson, or the alleyway off Washington Ave near the Gazette, a good spot for a quick conversation).

In between time, I tracked Brady down and gave him the job of looking into the stagehands' financials. He was happy for the task; even thanked me. Assigned to work with Foley, he didn't get much action; mostly just sat around the station house on his dead ass (his words).

After a light rapping on the door, it opened, and Jane peeked in. She was a little early, wanting to talk about the Doyle murder for sure, looking for a follow-up story. King City was hungry for news on the killing.

"Danny, it's good to see you." Jane was through the door and closing it behind her.

"Good to see you, too." I was on my feet, pulling out a chair for her. "Another front-page splash for you. Your editor must be happy."

She took her seat, placing her handbag and notepad on the table.

"Yes, he is. Circulation has gone up twenty-two percent since J.L. Gibson started writing his column. Thanks for calling me with all the details and the photo. I owe you."

She certainly did.

"How are you doing with your list of suspects?" Jane continued.

"It's not a long list, but no one has risen to the top."

"I may have another one for you." Jane leaned in. "Have you considered Doyle's wife?"

"No." My detective sense peaked.

"Are you aware that Doyle and his wife were in the midst of a nasty divorce?"

"That either. They'd be Catholic, so technically, it would be an annulment."

Jane's eyebrows arched. "Anyway, he wasn't with his wife at the theater, I presume?"

"Right. He was alone," I said, "How do you know about this?"

"The society pages of the Gazette have a gossip column. I keep a look out for any tidbits I can gather up. To maintain my cover, I still have to write for the society section."

"What else did you gather up?"

"I heard his wife had taken the kids and moved back in with her family about two months ago. She found out he had a squeeze (*) on the side."

"How did you get this information?"

"He made a pass at me at the union meeting. I figured it wasn't a one-off, that there was something there. I asked around and found a fella who filled me in."

"What's the moll's (*) name?"

"I didn't get a name, but from what I heard, he was head over heels." Jane smiled and rolled her eyes.

"Why were you at that union meeting, anyway? You never told me."

"The union contacted me; they wanted to see some pro-union stories in the paper. Human interest stories for the society section. Stories about their families and the troubles they have."

"I don't remember seeing anything like that?"

"My editor wouldn't publish them. He said it wouldn't be in the best interest of the business community. If I wrote anything about the unions, he wanted the union painted as a nest of socialists and criminals."

"The paper wouldn't go for a pro-union slant on things, uh? No sense stirring up sympathies for the working man."

The Gazette was a mouthpiece for the King City business community.

I continued. "But then, the union bosses don't exactly have their noses clean either. They were in bed with Maxine Snowdon and her bootlegging operations."

"Despite that." Jane crossed and uncrossed her arms. "After a little investigating, I could see that the union families were getting a raw deal, and I wanted to tell their story."

"That's a shame—a waste of your time."

"Not completely; I gave the article to the Citizen's Voice. It might have got past you."

The Citizen's Voice is a small-time King City rag that favors the unions.

"That was generous of you."

"But Doyle's wife, she's a possible suspect, right?" Jane was obviously happy with herself, working the clues of a murder mystery.

"Yes, she is. A roaming husband and jealousy are strong motives. It's possible she hired a torpedo. One of the things we're looking into is a paid hit."

Her family might have connections with the mob, another avenue for Brady to take on.

"How about the Snowdon Massacre? Have you made any progress with that?"

"We've eliminated all the locals as suspects, which is how the police game works, the process of elimination. We figure it was an out-of-town crew that conducted the hit and an outsider that ordered it."

"Do you know who that someone is?"

"No, not exactly, but it's the fella that calls himself the Mayor."

"The same guy that's running the bootlegging at the port?"

"Likely, one and the same."

"So, you haven't identified him yet?"

"No, but I do have a suspect."

"Who's that?"

"There's a snooper (*) from the King District nosing around, asking questions about the Snowdon rackets. That's your neck of the woods. His name is Bob Paxton. you ever heard of him?" I studied Jane for her reaction.

I knew next to nothing about the fella, and that bothered me. I made it my business to keep tabs on the gumshoes (*) in King City. Some of them made for good connections; others I just needed to keep an eye on. Paxton was one of the latter.

"Yes, I have. And you think Bob might actually be the Mayor, the guy responsible for the hit on Lizzy's?"

"Bob? What do you know about Bob?"

I was wondering what she knew about—Bob.

"He's relatively new in town, about a year or so. He has a dandy office up on Second Avenue, near the hospital."

"You've been there, to his office?"

"No, no, that's just what I heard. He's done work for some of my father's friends."

"So, he's connected to the money men of King City. Have you had conversations with this fella?"

"Yes, I have. I thought he might be of use as a source. He's got connections, as you like to say."

"Connections, like what?"

"Well, for one, I heard that he has a well-heeled client that keeps him on retainer. I think that's how he manages the swanky office."

"When did you first meet him?" This was like pulling teeth.

"That night at the Union meeting. Paxton was there. He was talking with Roan Doyle about doing a job for him."

"And how would you know what they talked about?"

"I asked Paxton, after the meeting, outside on the dock."

"He just told you?"

"Yes, Detective. You'd be surprised what a fella will spill if a doll asks him in the right way."

I was picturing *the right way.*

"What did Doyle hire him to do?" I had that figured, but I wanted it confirmed.

"Doyle asked him to dig up information on Mayor Hughes. Stuff he could use in his campaign against Hughes, corruption, bribes, gambling, whatever."

"I suppose Paxton said he would share what he found out with you?"

"He did, yes."

"Why am I hearing about this clown just now, partner?"

"I didn't dream he could have had any connection to the Snowdon Massacre." Jane's voice kicked up an octave. "He didn't create the impression of a criminal mastermind or a killer."

"You may be right about the mastermind part, but I was thinking Paxton might be looking good for the Doyle murder." I was watching Jane's eyes. "But that's off the table now."

"Why is that?"

"I had a conversation with that clown, Paxton, this morning, right here." I taped a finger on the tabletop. "He claims he had a date with you the night of the murder?"

"It wasn't a date, per se, more of a meeting. He's a source." Jane tipped her head quick to the right with a shrug of the shoulders.

"He says you stood him up. That he waited for you at the Carlson all evening," I said, "While you were at the docks nearly getting yourself killed."

"When I got the call from Goff that afternoon, I sent Paxton a note, canceling."

"He didn't mention getting a note."

"But I sent it to the hotel with a gopher from the newsroom. Maybe he didn't get it somehow?"

"Either way, you gave him a rock-solid alibi for the Doyle murder and for your near murder. Of course, he could still be the one behind it all, the hit on Lizzy's and Doyle. If he's the Mayor, he could have orchestrated both. We know Carlo works for the Mayor, running the bootlegging at the port. And he could have hired a torpedo to take a shot at Doyle."

"But he was working for Doyle?"

"Loyalty is not a trademark for a private dick. If you're right and he's not the Mayor, could be one of Paxton's other clients wanted Doyle out of the picture, or it just suited him for some reason."

"Are you saying that he could have been involved in what happened to me at the docks?"

"Goff would have known about Paxton working for Doyle. Doyle probably knew about your meeting. Likely, Paxton did, too.

"Real convenient on Paxton's part to be sitting in a public hotel lobby sipping whiskey during a murder and an attempted murder. Who picked the time and place for your meeting?"

Jane's eyes widened. "He did."

Every morning this week, the Chief had called me to his office to demand, in no uncertain terms, results on the Doyle case, which occurred faithfully right after the Commissioner had called him, right after the city Mayor had called the Commissioner.

Sean and I had only seen each other in passing this week, no lolly-gagging at Kelly's for lunch. We were out every day and evening shaking the trees, looking for leads.

Friday afternoon now, we were in my office for the purpose of comparing notes and the lack of results.

Hands behind my head, I swiveled back and forth in my chair. Sean was stretched out in his chair on the opposite side of my desk.

"I got Brady's report on the stagehands. You were right;" I pointed a finger at Sean, "none of them fit the bill. Of the four of them, two of them have petty records; one lives with his mother and the other one's a choir boy. All dim bulbs. Nothing pointing to a gun for hire."

"Looks like we don't have any suspects for torpedoes. Pretty much exhausted all the possibilities." Sean was blowing smoke rings and watching them fade away at the ceiling. He was getting really good at it.

"A whole week since the murder, and we had nothing on the shooter and nothing pointing to who ordered the hit if that were the case."

I landed my feet on the floor and elbows on the desk.

"Have your contacts come up with anything

on Paxton?" I was hoping Sean had something on him, something that might confirm what I had found out.

Thanks to Jane and the desk clerk at the Carlson, Paxton has an alibi for the Doyle shooting, but I was still looking at him for some involvement in the hit on Maxine.

"He's been ask'en round about Snowdon's rackets, and who worked for her, that's it," Sean said, "Nobody has any dirt on him."

"My people are saying the same. Sounds like this is his first venture into Carvonshire. But I did get something on him."

"What's that?"

"Got another note." I pulled a yellow envelope out of my breast pocket and held it up.

"You been holding out on me, O'Shea? You been keeping it to yourself all day?"

"It's not relevant to the Doyle case."

"What's it say?" Sean asked.

I slipped the note out and read it out loud.

"Watch out for Paxton; he works for the Mayor, the man responsible for bootlegging at the port. The Mayor is trouble for King City."

"That's all it says?" Sean rose up from his slouch.

"Yeah, but another piece of the puzzle for what's going on in Carvonshire. We know this new Mayor thug is involved in the Snowdon hit, that he's responsible for the bootlegging at the port, and now that Paxton is connected to the Mayor." I handed the note to Sean. "That's something."

"Better than nowhere," Sean added with a look to the heavens.

"If Paxton isn't the Mayor but actually works for him, it makes sense that Paxton is nosing around for information about Maxine's rackets and who worked for her. He's looking for recruits for the Mayor's new mob. The Mayor is connected to the Snowdon killing for sure; Paxton may be as well."

"You're getting off track. We need to stay focused on the Doyle case. Paxton's not our guy for that. What we need is a little help from your note sender with the Doyle investigation."

"But there might be a connection between the two hits. Maybe this Mayor clown is involved in the Doyle murder as well."

"That's a big maybe." Sean pulled his reading glasses out of his breast pocket. "Who the hell is this new want-to-be crime boss, anyway? Calls himself the Mayor; that's an odd moniker."

"I don't know?" The words stuck in my throat. "The Mayor title could be his way of saying he plans to take charge of King City?"

I knew next to nothing about Paxton and nothing at all about this clown calling himself the Mayor.

"This note ain't all that helpful." Sean tucked his glasses away.

"It's something, though, a warning. The Mayor is trouble coming our way, and Paxton works for him."

"Okay, right? More trouble's coming, but what—when—and where?" Sean handed the note back to me. "Like I said, not all that helpful."

The back door of the Mercury Theater had been left ajar for me. I arrived a couple of hours after the evening's performance, one o'clock in the morning.

The lack of street lights in the alley behind the theater made my entrance less likely to be observed. I had gotten another note in Francine's handwriting, a request for a meeting this evening, one I had been expecting.

I serpentined my way through the twisting hallways of the back of the house to the dressing rooms. A sliver of light outlining a partially open dressing room door guided my way.

Francine, who had been peering into her mirror, swiveled around in her chair. "Ca fait longtemps mon ami. C'est bon de te voir."

Yeah, it had been a long time, but I doubted she was really that glad to see me. I had a tendency to only show up when I wanted a favor.

"Mind if we speak in English? My French is a little rusty."

To be honest, my French never was that good. I only had the basics I picked up during the war and the time I was briefly attached to the French Military Police.

"Anything for you, Danny, mon ami." Francine was seated at a makeup table in front of a mirror surrounded by light bulbs.

I stepped over to a chair on Francine's left, hung my hat on the corner of the back, and made myself comfortable.

"Nice to see you, Francine. It has been a while."

"Have you missed me?" Francine batted her eyelashes.

"Of course I have."

"Not enough to look me up?" The corners of her mouth drew down into a pout.

Francine was a perpetual flirt; she couldn't help herself. It served her well in her line of work, not just the theater game but in her other role as the leader of Maxine Snowdon's network of agents (spies and informants).

"I'm a busy fella. Police work keeps me occupied."

Over the years, Francine has helped me out with some of my investigations. At times, the ladies in her spy organization turned up information that was quite useful. But I never pressed her for it; that would have been crossing the line. In our agreement, she only sent cues my way if it didn't put her in harm's way with Max. Right now, with Max gone, I was considering asking her to do some snooping on the Mayor or that Paxton fella. But like Sean said, I needed to stay focused on the Doyle case.

"All work and no play, you know what they say, Danny."

"I assume you have information for me about Doyle?"

The night of the murder, Francine had provided the sequence of events and the basics of what had unfolded at the theater, but I figured she knew more.

"C'est exact."

I'm not sure why Francine always stays in character with the French accent and all. She was aware that I knew she grew up in Henshaw.

"Something that might point to a suspect, I hope."

"Oui. Are you aware of Monsieur Doyle's indiscretions and his marital problems?"

"Yes, I heard he was facing the prospects of a messy divorce."

"And do you know who he was dallying with?"

"I assumed it was more than one gal; it usually is."

"Au contraire. Monsieur Doyle's affections were rapt in the delight of just one woman, Evelyn Stone, the lead actress in the play that unfortunate evening."

"Interesting; what else you got?"

"Before Monsieur Doyle, Evelyn had another man enthralled in her charms. He was a childhood sweetheart who had recently resurfaced, a man of the lower classes, whom she cast to the curb in favor of the more suitable Monsieur Doyle."

More suitable, Doyle was a few notches up the food chain compared to the jilted working-class beau.

"What is the poor sap's name?"

Francine extracted a slip of paper from her cleavage. Her perfume swelled in my nostrils.

"Nom et adresse." After pressing the paper into my palm, her fingers faintly stroked my skin as she withdrew her hand.

I unfolded the note. The name wasn't familiar.

"Thanks. Would this fella be able to find his way around the stage area?"

"Oui, he was a frequent visitor before Monsieur Doyle took his place. He came to the rehearsals and all the performances, a lovesick puppy."

"Would he be familiar with the play, all the scenes, and the stage directions?"

"Qui, he would. The play has been in production for four months, very popular. He was here from the beginning."

"Access to the theater and the backstage area would not be a problem for him then?"

"Non, it would not."

"Thanks, Francine, you've been a big help." I gave her a wink. "But I'm thinking I may need another favor."

With Max gone, I was wondering if Francine had been able to hold the spy network together and if she was working for Grace now. But that was a question for another day.

"Another favor. Are we ever going to be even?" Francine's eyebrows raised in dramatic arks.

"With what I know about you and what you know about me, I feel like we are locked in a lifelong, mutually beneficial relationship. Which I appreciate, by the way." I added a gracious smile for effect.

"Umm, what is this favor?"

"It's still percolating. I'll be in touch." I lifted the note in the air before I tucked it into my breast pocket. "Thanks for this."

Francine cocked her head and sighed.

We both stood up. She approached and placed a kiss on each of my cheeks. I returned that favor.

"You're welcome, mon ami. Au revoir."

Jane had been avoiding me all week; I was sure she was embarrassed over the article in the Gazette covering the Doyle murder arrest. I had called her at the Gazette at least three times. She was always unavailable. Eventually, I sent a note asking her to meet at Griffin's Friday evening at ten. I got a message that she was coming.

I had arrived at nine and settled at my usual table to wait with two glasses of bourbon for company.

Last Monday evening, two days after my meeting with Francine, Sean and I had arrested Walter Short, the fella who landed the slugs in Roan Doyle.

We had confirmed that Short was staying in a flophouse in south Carvonshire at the address Francine provided. And what we needed to do was to put the squeeze on Short and find the weapon he used. A confession would, of course, be helpful. Francine did me the favor I'd been contemplating. With her help, we set a trap for Walter Short.

Francine contacted Walter and fed him the line that his actress ex-girlfriend wanted to see him so they could get back together. We booked a room at the Carlson for the meeting.

When the fella showed up, Francine was there to meet him. She told him that Miss Stone was going to be late. In the meantime, she manipulated him with conversation and vodka. Francine twisted the poor sap's brain around until he braggingly confessed to the murder, at which point I emerged from the wardrobe closet to make the arrest.

While Francine and I were occupied at the Carlson, Sean was at the flophouse searching Short's room for the Colt, which he found under a mattress.

I took Short back to the station, where I met Sean. Walter was so distraught when I explained that his ex-girlfriend never wanted to see him again that he couldn't wait to make a formal written confession. Doc Thomas confirmed the ballistics match between the slug he took out of Doyle and the weapon Sean recovered. A fingerprint match between our culprit and the prints on the Colt put the icing on the cake.

I contacted Jane as soon as I got to the station so she could send over a photographer. I provided her with the details of the pinch, except, of course, Francine's involvement. Working together, Jane and I created a more colorful and flattering narrative of the casework and the arrest.

From my position against the wall, I caught sight of Jane as soon as she came in the door. I got right up and greeted her as she reached the bar. We paused there long enough to get a Gin Ricky from the bartender. I dropped my usual nickel tip on the bar top.

Back at the table, the awkward small talk didn't last. Jane jumped headlong into her apologizing.

"I'm so sorry about the article in the paper. It wasn't me; it was my editor. He made changes to my draft. I didn't find out about it until it was already in print. I never dreamed he would do such a thing."

"Don't sweat it; I'm a big boy."

"I had the story laid out just the way we discussed. My editor changed it all around." Jeez, Jane was flustered.

He hadn't changed that much; just gave credit for the arrest to Chief Donnelly and briefly mentioned the Chief's thanks to the rest of the department for their support. And the editor also took the opportunity to highlight Doyle's infidelity, painting him as a shiftless union man.

"He got a little creative; so did we."

"Well, I told him; he better not try to pull something like that again, or else." Jane was nodding with a vengeance.

"Or else what?"

"I'd quit and go to work for another paper." Jane's head was rocking side to side.

"What'd he say to that?"

"That he would tell my father that I was J.L. Gibson." Her shoulders slumped.

"That would be big trouble, huh?"

"For sure. I don't know what my father would do if he found out, but it sure wouldn't be good."

I waited a bit. "Let's take a minute to think this through. What if your father did find out that you're J.L. Gibson? And suppose that he also was to learn through an anonymous source that it was all your editor's idea to assign you to the crime beat? And because of him, this editor of yours, you were put in danger, almost kidnapped, threatened by hoodlums, and shot at. How do you think your father would react to that?"

"Oh." Jane looked up from the drink she had been staring into. "I could threaten him too."

"Sauce for the goose is sauce for the gander.

"And you could also tell that punk editor that the copper he cut out of the article is mad as hell, that he's connected to the mob, and it's all you can do to stop him from contracting a hit."

"I thought you weren't mad?" Jane looked a little panicky.

"I'm not. It's just another line you can use if you need it." I took a sip of bourbon. "I'll have Johnson follow him around for a couple of days. There's nothing like looking over your shoulder and seeing Johnson eyeballing you to instill the fear of God."

"I like it. I like it a lot. I'll have a conversation with him tomorrow." An unnerving grin crossed her face. "Actually, I love it."

After a period of evil grinning and a few sips of her drink, Jane reached for her handbag.

"I wanted to show you this." Jane slipped out a sheet of paper. "I think I might have a way to get a lead on who's importing rum into the Carvonshire port."

It was a mimeograph of a newspaper clipping.

I read the title - 'Businessman, new to King City, related to Dutch Royalty entertains King City High Society on his yacht.'

"It's an article I wrote about a year ago for the society section. My father and I were invited to one of the parties Hans has on his yacht."

"Hans?"

"Yes. His full name is Baron Hansen Alexander Frederick Louis, but he goes by Hans for short."

I skimmed the article. "Says here he's related to Queen Wilhelmina of the Netherlands."

"Yes, a distant cousin or something. But he's not a snob about it or anything. He jokes about not getting his invitations to the royal affairs at the court. He's a real swell guy."

"You think he's connected with the Rum Runners bringing booze into the Carvonshire port?"

"Oh, no. But it dawned on me that Hans is from St. Croix. He might be able to provide a lead or know something about the bootlegging and who might be in on it. I could introduce you if you like if you think it's worth your time. I know you like to keep tabs on that kind of thing."

"What does this fella do for a living?"

"He imports sugar and bay rum from St. Croix. He's in business with several of my father's friends who run import businesses. They say he offers great prices, cuts out the middleman to reduce the cost."

Bay rum is a popular ingredient in cologne and aftershave. Rexall bottles the stuff as a medicinal that some dim-bulbs drink as a beverage (58 percent grain alcohol) to a detrimental toxic effect.

"You've been to a party on his yacht. Tell me about it." I was looking through the article and the list of guests. It was a who's-who of King City businessmen.

"They're the cat's meow. His yacht is anchored about a mile out in the bay. He charters small boats to shuttle his quests out to the yacht." Jane took a breath. "The food is great. They serve mostly seafood; oysters, a variety of fresh fish, and lobsters from Maine. The music is the best; he hires in the most amazing bands."

"Is he a teetotaler?"

"Oh no. He serves alcohol—rum, a red wine from Italy, and a Dutch dark beer, too bitter for my tastes. Hans insists everyone try it; it's his favorite."

"I assume he brings in help from the mainland for these events." I laid the sheet on the table.

"Yes, I think so. But he gives all the credit for the fabulous parties to the hostess. He introduces her as a business associate, but I think there's more to their relationship than that." Jane put up a hand to shield her mouth and lowered her voice. "I mean, there's an age difference. She's around thirty, and he's in his upper fifties. I'm not judging, mind you."

"Would you describe her as a looker, dark complexion, long black hair?"

"Well, yes. That fits Alina."

"How well do you know this doll?"

"She's very friendly. We've had some long conversations, girl talk."

"More than one conversation at a party?"

"Yes, she has an apartment in the King District. I've met with her a few times over the months for lunch. We get along fabulously."

I looked at Jane long and hard.

"What?" Jane's shoulders twitched, and she glanced from side to side.

"We have discovered a link between a woman who meets the description of your Alina and the Mayor and the hit at Lizzy's."

"That's hard to believe."

"Did it ever occur to you that this Hans character might be the Mayor?"

"Hans the Mayor? I thought you had Bob Paxton pegged as the Mayor?"

"Not anymore. He's not looking good for that," I said, "But think about it. This fella, Hans, couldn't he be a candidate? He could be the Mayor."

Jane's ability to converse stalled for a moment. "He just doesn't seem like the type. He's a refined gentleman. It couldn't be. He's so gracious and cordial. Everybody says he's a respectable businessman."

"A businessman, sure, selling imports on the cheap, a middleman not taking his cut." I caught the eye of the barmaid and pointed to our empty glasses. "Why would a businessman do that unless he's making his money some other way?"

"Like what?"

"There are lots of possibilities." I leaned back in my chair. "Like hiding bottles of rum in the sugar bags. Or maybe some of the barrels of Bay Rum are filled with actual rum instead." I have a vivid imagination when it comes to the criminal mind.

We halted our conversation while the barmaid laid down our drinks.

"Thank you," Jane said, flashing a weak smile. She chugged her Gin Ricky.

"This opens up a whole new can of worms." I downed a bourbon.

EPISODE 12

PRESCRIPTION FOR THEFT

Another Monday morning, I walked across the squad room, weaving through the desks and tables, right up to Brady's dingy little desk at the back wall. He was still looking at the papers on the desktop when I sauntered up, trying real hard to wish me away.

"What's shaken, Brady?" I leaned over and placed my hands on the desk's edge, putting us nose to nose. I was enjoying how much my presence was rattling him.

"Detective O'Shea," He pushed back in his chair, creating distance between us. "What do you want?"

Doing something for me was one of the last things on earth he wanted.

His boss, Foley, wasn't happy with Brady's and my collaboration on the Doyle murder case, now a week in the rearview mirror. It was common knowledge around the station house that Foley had given Brady hell, chewed him out, right here in the squad room.

"Let's you and me go for a little walk and have a chat." I took a step away and motioned to the doorway with a tilt of my head.

"Jeez, detective, I'd like to, but I got these reports I need to finish up for Detective Foley."

"A sharp fella like yourself won't need much time to fill in a report. Besides, we won't be gone long."

"I don't know?"

"It's just two coppers conducting police business. No sweat." We couldn't talk in the Station House; the walls had ears. "I'm guaranteeing the conversation will be beneficial for both of us."

Brady scanned the squad room. It was lunchtime, no one around. "Okay, Detective, I got time."

As we moved through the lobby, Brady sidestepped to the coat rack to grab his hat. It was a nice Bowler; it made him look taller.

Out on the street, I led the way. We walked up Broad and turned east on Dogwood, heading away from downtown. After several blocks, not speaking a word, we strode into a residential neighborhood with three-story tenement housing on both sides of the street. These red brick buildings, fronted on each level with wooden balconies reached by rickety-looking stairs, could easily disturb the claustrophobic.

We strode on a ways into the warren, under the ropes that hung over the roadway that dangled laundry (bed sheets, shirts, and undergarments). Women in aprons leaning on the railings called out to each other; others huddled on the street in gossip confabs.

I brought our march to a halt at the next corner and guided Brady into a deserted alleyway. The landscape didn't exude the most pleasant aromas but a mix of sewer and roasting meat. I would probably skip lunch today.

I broke the silence. "Okay, pal, what can you tell me about the Walgreens robbery?"

Brady and Foley had been first on the scene yesterday morning after the call came in that the Walgreens Drug Store had been broken into overnight. Some thugs had lifted all the prescription alcohol.

Considering the pull old man Walgreens had in the King City business community, this was going to be a high-profile case. Jane was going to be on it like fleas on a dog, looking for an exclusive. And I wouldn't mind getting in on the action, especially if I got an opportunity to poke Foley in the eye. Besides, I was wondering if this robbery might be connected to the Mayor character.

"If I tell you and it gets back to Foley." Brady was real twitchy.

"There's nothing to worry about." I rested my hand on Brady's shoulder. "This is how we are going to play it. You are going to spill the details about the robbery. When you get back, and Foley grills you about our conversation, you're going to say you told me nothing of value. And that you took the meeting to find out what I was after and what

I knew, real smart thinking on our part. What you found out was that I was looking for a way to screw up Foley's case and that you gave me some false tips to throw me off the track."

Brady chewed on that for a bit. "He'll buy that."

"Yeah, he's not the sharpest pencil in the box."

A faint smile crossed Brady's lips.

"So, what's the story on the robbery?"

The gist of Brady's report went like this. A couple of thugs had arrived sometime during the night and let themselves in by picking the lock on the alleyway door. They made their way through the store to the display lobby, where the guard was on patrol. They snuck up behind him, bashed him over the head, and left him unconscious on the floor. When Brady got there early the next morning, he found the guard sitting on the steps in front of the open main doorway. His head was wrapped in a rag to stop the bleeding by some good Samaritan. The prescription alcohol bottles had been lifted from the display cases in the lobby and the store room.

The robbery was mainly the drugstore manager's fault. When the Jones Gang was running the town, protection money was paid, so robberies like this wouldn't happen. With the Jones Gang out of the picture, the local patrolman on the beat stepped into the vacuum to collect the payola. The word was that the manager got greedy and stopped paying the patrolmen, who had no interest in protecting the store or catching the crooks.

"So, what's Foley's plan to wrap this one up? Has he got a pigeon willing to take the fall?

"No, he doesn't have the jack to pay someone off."

In the past, Foley had Jones Gang payoff cash to tempt some desperate fella into taking the fall for a crime they didn't commit. That money had dried up with Maxine's demise, and it was crimping Foley's style.

Brady continued. "He's looking for a way to frame someone for the robbery. He's got a fella in mind and is working on a way to plant some evidence on him."

"Do you know who or how?"

"Not yet."

"Keep an ear peeled. And get back to me on his progress."

"Sure thing, Detective."

"And when you finish that report, slip a copy into my desk, will ya?"

"Right."

"I owe you." I slapped Brady on the back. "Let's get out of here."

I got a nod and a smile.

We exited the alley and headed back toward the Station House.

Jane was chomping at the bit for the story of the robbery. She had sent two messages already today, one this morning and one at noon. She had the basics from the police report and had published it in this morning's Tuesday edition, but was hungry for a scoop.

I decided it was time she had the opportunity to do some snooping, and left a phone message for her to meet me at the corner of 3rd and Elm at four o'clock, a block south of the Walgreens store.

As I came around the corner off Spruce Street, I spotted Jane's unforgettable figure in the distance, a block away. She was early. We exchanged greetings and headed off for the Walgreens building.

At our destination, we turned into the alleyway and made our way to the back door of the drugstore.

"Are you sure we should be doing this?" Jane whispered from right behind my ear. "What if someone shows up?"

There was no need to whisper in the back alley. Besides, Walgreens, now a designated crime scene, would be closed for at least a couple more days.

I was leaning over, working with my tools to pick the lock.

"It's alright; we're just going to walk through a recreation of the crime." The lock clicked open. "According to the incident report, this is how the robbers got into the building sometime in the wee hours."

I swung the door open and ushered Jane into the back vestibule, ten feet square, and flipped on my flashlight.

"Why do we need these? It's broad daylight." Jane turned her flashlight on.

"To sweep the dark corners, looking for details." My beam was see-sawing back and forth across the floor.

"Got it." Jane followed suit.

"After the thugs picked the lock, they found their way through this hallway." I was moving on that path. "They came down this way."

We passed an office, the door standing open. I gave the room a quick look. Further on, we passed the storeroom's open doorway and ended up in the storefront display room.

Jane was following behind me, staying quiet.

"And here in the display room, according to the guard on duty, the robbers encountered him making his rounds and bashed him over the head." I leaned my backside against the display case and surveyed the area.

"The guard laid unconscious on the floor here until sometime around five in the morning when he came to and stumbled out the front door. A milkman caught sight of him and took it upon himself to go to a police call box. A washerwoman on her way to work stopped and wrapped up his head with some rags from the storeroom. She had left the scene before the patrolman or the ambulance arrived.

"So, partner, what do you think? Does this story hold water?"

Jane was scanning the floor with her flashlight. Not necessary, since plenty of light was streaming in through the picture windows on each side of the front double doors.

"Also, both the front doors were open, and the cloth on his head was soaked with blood." I was reading from the crime report.

Jane gave me a puzzled look.

"What's not there? I scanned a beam of light oscillating across the floor.

After a few moments, Jane's eyes lit up. "No blood."

"You would think a man with a bad head wound who laid on the floor for three or five hours would have left a substantial bloodstain."

"And if the woman had put the bandage on four hours after the wound occurred, there would only have been a little blood on it, if any," Jane said.

"Right." I motioned for Jane to follow me. "And did you flash your light around in the office as we walked past?"

"No."

"Come on."

Standing in the doorway, I flipped on the overhead lamp in the center of the office. "Tell me what you see."

"A small desk. Papers on the desktop in disarray. Some papers on the floor. The swivel chair flipped over, off to the side, away from the desk." Her light swept to a spot on the floor. "Is that blood?"

"That's my bet."

"So, the guard lied about what happened?"

"Right."

"Why?"

"Did you notice how the floorboards squeaked in the display room?"

"No." Jane's voice crest fell.

"There is no way the thugs snuck up on the guard in the front of the store. My bet is he was asleep in that chair with his feet up on the desk. This office is where he got his head bashed. And after they left, he bandaged up his head himself and waited for morning to go outside for help."

"He concocted a story to make himself look good." Jane flipped off her flashlight. "So, how does that help us?"

"It tells us that the guard might have information he's not sharing."

"And we should go have a talk with him." Jane was beaming.

"The hospital's not a far walk from here; he might still be there."

Jane led the way out the back door and down the street on our way to King City General.

I let Jane take the lead at the hospital. She found a talkative young nurse in a flash. The guard had been discharged hours ago with 15 stitches for a nasty gash on the side of his head.

We left the hospital with the fella's address in hand.

"What's next?" Jane asked.

"A taxi ride to the guard's place and some questioning."

"Right now?"

"No time like the present." I hailed the next taxi that pulled into the hospital driveway.

Jane practically bolted into the backseat ahead of me. Her enthusiasm for detective work made her like a kid in a candy store.

We arrived and exited the taxi on a street lined with two-story apartment buildings.

The guard lived on the second floor of a board-covered walk-up, accessed by stairs at the back of the building.

While we waited on the sloping porch, an orange tabby cat sauntered over and rubbed on my pant legs. It wasn't long before a gray-haired woman in a white apron answered our knocking.

She tried to shew us away, but after I flashed my badge, she led us through the apartment to the living room where her husband, our guard, was lying back in a lounge chair, his feet resting on an ottoman.

Jane and I pulled out a couple of straight-back wooden chairs from the kitchen table. The guard's wife perched on the arm of the sofa nearest her husband.

I introduced myself to the guard, Bill Jenkins, flashing my badge again. I introduced Jane as an associate.

"What is it you want with me? I gave my statement of what went down to the coppers already, some young pup named Brady."

"I'm aware, Bill, I read Detective Brady's report. But since then, some things have come to light. I got some questions of my own."

Bill looked at his wife. She was twisting the hem of her apron into a knot.

"We were at the Walgreens store this afternoon, and we found some particulars that don't seem to match up with the story you're tell'en."

"I ain't been saying nothing but the god's truth." Bill pushed himself upright and nodded aggressively.

"My husband is an honest man." The wife added as she looked back and forth from Jane to me, resting her focus on Jane.

Jane reached out and touched the back of Mrs. Jenkins' hand.

"I'm sure that's the case, Ma'am." I turned my attention to Bill. "But in some circumstances, speaking the truth isn't always our first impulse, especially when there's a family to think about." I glanced back at the wife.

"Bill, we're not looking to jam you up. Nothing you say is going past this room. We just need to know if you can provide any details that will help us find the thugs that robbed the store and bashed you in the head."

"You can trust Detective O'Shea; he's a man of his word." Jane was nodding to me. "He looks out for the common folk."

"Bill, think of it as doing me a personal favor. I'll be in your debt should you need a helping hand someday. Can't hurt to have a copper owing you a favor, right?"

Bill glanced at his wife, whose eyes said okay.

"We don't believe you were on your rounds when the thugs showed up. We figure you were in the office, asleep, not in the display area. That's how the robbers snuck up on you. Were you playing dead in the office that whole time they were robbing the place?"

Bill replied, "That's right."

"And after they finished looting the place, you bandaged yourself up and waited till they were gone before you showed yourself around dawn?"

"Yeah."

"Did you hear or see anything that would help identify the robbers?"

"They had Ruskie accents."

"Good, what else? Any detail you can think of."

"They were hauling all the booze out the front door and loading it into a car parked at the curb."

"Did you get a look at the car?"

"When I was sure they were finished in the storeroom, I crawled out behind the counter. I could see the car in the street. It was parked under a street light."

"And?"

"It was an older Tin Lizzy (*), a little beat up with a big dent in the passenger side door."

"That's great Bill, that's real helpful." I was trying to sound as encouraging as I could. "Anything else?"

Bill gave a onetime shake of the head. He looked pale and exhausted.

His wife leaned over to her husband and put a hand on his arm, but didn't say a word.

I stood up and looked to Jane, who followed suit.

Mrs. Jenkins bounced up and turned to us.

"Bill, things are going to be tough for a while with your injury and being out of work." I stood there, looking the guard in the eye. "But I'm serious about you reaching out if you need anything." I looked at Mrs. Jenkins and flashed a smile. I got one back. We took our exit.

Back on the curb in front of the Jenkins' apartment building, Jane and I entered into a confab.

"What do we do from here?" Jane asked.

"Russian-speaking thugs probably means the robbers are from the North End. I've got some contacts up that way. I'll reach out."

"What about me?" Jane asked.

"Just hold your water for now."

"But this is a fantastic story." Jane gave off the vibe of a shook-up pop bottle.

"Patience, you're going to get a great story out of this, not just yet."

"Really?"

"Have I ever steered you wrong?"

I asked Jane to meet me in City Park, on Walnut Street, several blocks from the Station House. I had picked out a bench on the park's west end by the kids' playground.

Spotting Jane coming down the street, I got up and waved my hat. She responded with a raised hand and an increase in gait.

From where we sat, we had a good view of the swings and sliding board. School was in session, so there were only a few moms with toddlers about. It was a sunny afternoon; the sun peaked through fast-moving patchy clouds. We're not used to that in Carvonshire, a little unnerving.

"Have you got a lead on the robbers?" Jane started.

She hadn't contacted me in the last two days since our interview with the guard. I was impressed by her patience.

"I sure have. One of my connections came through. She identified a couple of Russian fellas in her neighborhood that fit the bill.

"Sean and I are going up to the North End tonight to make the pinch."

"Can I come?"

"Absolutely not. The North End is a rough place, especially if you don't speak the language."

"What language is that, Russian?"

"Russian, Polish, Hungarian."

"You speak all those languages?"

"No, not really. I just understand the body language."

"Jeez, Danny, how do you know I don't speak those languages?"

"Do you?" I was thinking that could be real helpful.

"Well, no."

"Anyway, don't worry, you're going to get the story, all the details."

"All the details?"

"The relevant ones." I raised my hand to shield my eyes from the sudden reflection of the sun off the sliding board.

"Who is this connection of yours?" Jane shifted in her seat more in my direction.

"She's a young lady who goes by the name of Crystal. She lives in the Russian neighborhood." I removed my hat and placed it on the bench. It was getting warm. "And she owed me a favor."

"Of course she does." Jane's eyes glanced skyward. "A young lady? That sounds like a euphemism."

"A what?"

"How do you know her? What does she do?"

"Uh, she used to work in a creep joint on the Roofs." I hesitated. "She was a pro skirt (*), and she got herself in a jam."

"How did you meet this woman?" Jane's eyebrows arched. "In that line of work?"

"I didn't know her personally." I felt a need to explain. "I was acquainted with the madame of the joint she worked in."

"The madame? So, how did you know her?"

"That's another story." I felt like I was digging myself into a hole.

"I know, for another day. But the story about Crystal sounds like it could be interesting."

I figured Jane would dog me until I spilled the beans. Giving in, I twisted around to face her.

"Women in her profession hear things. Things they should ignore or at least keep to themselves. Crystal had a lapse in judgment and decided to use information a gangster had let drop to her advantage.

"One of her clients was a local bookmaker. He and some other fellas had put a fix in on a horse race. The favorite horse that drew in a lot of bets got drugged. So that a long shot nag would cross the line first, and the jockeys in the race got a payoff. The bookie and his pals bet on the nag, of course, but so did Crystal. She got greedy and put down a load of jack, which was way too obvious.

"When she tried to collect, the bookmaker took it as a personal affront and hired some thugs to put the hurt on her. Her madame contacted me. I convinced the fella that where there's no blood, there's no foul."

"How did you do that?"

"Crystal, of course, didn't get the payout, no harm there, just the bookie's bruised ego. And the bookie, it seems, was able to see the downside of the fixing scheme story getting out, especially since some higher-level gangsters took a bath on their bets. That's something a copper like myself could make happen."

"Interesting story." Jane's attention diverted momentarily to a woman passing by pushing a baby carriage. They exchanged smiles.

With eye contact again, "But back to the Walgreens robbery. How was this 'young lady' able to provide a lead on the robbers?"

"I had her keep a look out for that dented Model T and any Russian fellas that might be flashing cash or selling booze."

"And I guess in her line of work, that would be easy."

"Well, these days, she works as a seamstress, but the Russian quarter is a small place; everybody knows everybody's business."

"I guess she saw the error of her ways and changed careers?"

"She was aging out of the racquet at the time anyway. Tried for the easy money, but lost out on that bet."

I pulled out my pocket watch and flipped the lid open.

"You have to go, an appointment?"

"No, I got nothing going on until tonight. We'll land in the North End after dark. No sense alerting the local constabulary."

"You don't have a good relationship with the coppers in the North End. I'm surprised."

"Those boys are kind of a close-knit group. If I contacted them ahead of time, it's more likely than not the robbers are pals of theirs and would get the high sign."

"You sure I can't tag along?"

"No, is no on this one."

"Fine." Jane crossed her arms.

We sat on the bench in quiet for what seemed like a very long time.

Eventually, Jane broke the silence. She placed both hands on her knees and sat up straight. "I should get back to the office. I need to catch up on my articles for the silly society section."

We stood and said our goodbyes.

Sean, Johnson, and I rolled into the Russian Quarter in Jedd's taxi around ten. The neighborhood was dark; the North End powers-that-be didn't invest much in street lights. That suited us just fine; us Carvonshire boys tended to stand out in this neck of the woods.

I had made a trip up to this territory earlier this morning to check in with Crystal before my meeting with Jane.

Crystal gave me the address of two Russian thugs she thought might fit the bill for the Walgreens' Robbery. The fellas drove around in a dented Model T Ford and were just getting started in the bootlegging business, providing some high-quality booze.

I had scoped out their apartment. The Model T was parked out front. Around the back in the dumpster, I found a pile of empty pharmacy Rx bottles. Apparently, the thugs had the sense to transfer the booze to different containers before the sale. Probably even watered it down.

According to Crystal, the thugs frequented a speakeasy on Front Street, a few blocks from their place.

Their routine entailed a drinking binge every night that ended with them stumbling home about midnight.

We parked in an alleyway a block from the apartment. At the steps that lead up to the apartment porch, Sean and Johnson took up positions out of sight, one on each side. I wandered down the street towards the speakeasy, keeping an eye peeled for the Russians.

As expected, a little after twelve, the thugs came sauntering along the sidewalk in my direction, laughing and singing Russian folk songs. I ducked into the shadows to let them pass and then fell in behind them on the quiet at a distance. These fellas were so blattoed, I could have been leading a marching band and they wouldn't have noticed.

At the apartment building, as the thugs started up the steps, I called out, "у меня будет ДРУГОЙ" (*), the only Russian I know.

They pivoted around slowly with big ass smirks on their faces until I called out, not in Russian, "You're under arrest!"

They looked at each other, dumb-struck for a long moment. Apparently, they had a rudimentary command of the English language because their next move was to bolt, which was more of a stagger away. Immediately, Sean and Johnson did bolt out of the shadows. Both took a robber to the ground without much fuss, cuffed and quiet.

I walked down to the alley to retrieve Jedd and his taxi. We hadn't made a ruckus, but it was best to get out of town as soon as possible before we were discovered. Undoubtedly, these fellas would have some pals that might object to their arrest. And besides, the coppers from the North End district might not take kindly to our unannounced activities.

It took a little longer than expected to secure our cargo. The Russians were on the large side and didn't fit neatly in the taxi's trunk. We traveled back to Carvonshire with the trunk lid partially open, tied down, the thugs' legs hanging out.

The Station House was uncommonly crowded for a Friday afternoon. Foley had arranged a press conference for three o'clock. Coppers were hanging around rather than cutting out early, as usual.

While I had been doing actual detective work, Senior Detective Foley had been working hard at framing up an unfortunate low-level gangster for the Walgreens Robbery. Per Bailey's report to me, Foley had made the arrest and had the fella stashed in a holding cell in the back of the Station House. The bruised and battered thug had confessed. And Foley had found himself a witness who had overheard the suspect bragging about the robbery; a paid witness, you could call it.

Foley's plan for the afternoon was to parade his victim out for the press at three o'clock and announce the big bust, make a grand show of it.

Unbeknownst to Foley, I had Jane contact all the papers earlier this morning and say that the press conference had been moved up to two o'clock. I had also given her the low down on last night's bona fide arrest, the story for this evening's edition, the one I wanted in print, not the whole truth necessarily, but an exclusive for sure.

As expected, just before two, but not as Foley expected, crime reporters started gathering on the Station House steps, setting up tripods and cameras.

Foley got word about the commotion and was out front, perplexed, fuming, and directing a lot of "what the hell" comments at the reporters. The scar on Foley's cheek was beaming bright red.

A cadre of coppers poured out of the Station to check out the hubbub, myself included.

I stood with my back to the main doors, glancing now and then down Broad Street.

Right on schedule, two o'clock as planned, Sean and Johnson appeared, rounding the corner a block away, with the Russians in tow. The thieves, whose hands were cuffed behind their backs, stumbled ahead as Sean and Johnson gave encouraging shoves in the back to keep them moving in the right direction.

We hadn't taken the robbers to the Station House but had tucked them away overnight in the Carlson Hotel's storeroom, guarded by Johnson.

I pushed forward and went down to meet the entourage on the street, where I grabbed one of the Russians by the arm. As I pulled him up the steps, I put out my other arm, waving off the onslaught of questions from the press core.

"Not now, not now. This is police business," I called out as we approached the door.

"Detective O'Shea, isn't this the arrest that the press conference was called for?" a reporter close at hand asked.

"I don't know anything about a press conference," I spoke to the reporter but glanced at Foley.

"What's this about? What have you got going on?" another reporter shouted from the back of the crowd.

I was facing the throng now, my hand still gripping the Russian's arm. Johnson was on the other side, holding the left arm. Sean was next in line, constraining the other thief by the shoulders. We were all looking into the cameras when flashbulbs started popping.

"Police business." I was playing my part.

"Come on, Detective, spill it." An old newspaperman from the Citizen's Voice piped up.

I looked from side to side. "Alright, alright. I'm placing these fellas under arrest for the Walgreens' Robbery."

I was assaulted by a barrage of yelled-out questions that could not be distinguished. More flashbulbs popped; I was seeing stars and turned my head away. The Russians, with heads bowed, were trying to avoid the cameras, too. Only Johnson continued to stare right into the flashes.

"I gotta get these fellas processed. I'll be back out in a jiff with a detailed report for you boys." With that, I turned and guided my Russian through the Station House doors with the rest of my troupe in tow. Shouts from the press core assaulted my back.

My plan to parade the robbers into the station house and make a splash was a success. As a side benefit, the arrangement provided an embarrassment for Foley.

As promised, I was back out on the steps, spilling the particulars of the arrest. Johnson was with me, holding up a couple of Rx alcohol bottles, our evidence. Of course, I held back the exciting parts about the car chase, the fistfight, and the shots fired; I saved those details for Jane's exclusive.

EPISODE 13

THE ART OF RECOVERY

I was early, an hour before our two o'clock meeting. While I waited for Jane, I wandered around, getting the lay of the land.

I wasn't familiar with the Bay-Port Park; it's in the King District of King City, not my turf. As a kid, I didn't frequent the place either: the Irish weren't welcome here. The upper-crust English ruled the King District and built this park on the bay for their exclusive use.

From the hillock in the middle of the park, I looked out across the bay to the distant horizon where blue sky met blue water. To my left, a wharf extended out into the bay, providing shelter for the boatyard used by the wealthy of King City to anchor their yachts and sailboats.

The park, bordering the edge of the boatyard, was built on the remains of an old industrial area that served the old port's activities back in the day. This old port was replaced by the Carvonshire port, which is more modern, with deeper channels and sheltered from the prevailing westerly winds. That had given the Welsh and the Jones Gang a leg up when prohibition became the law of the land. All the bootlegged booze coming in from the sea had to pass through Carvonshire, where Maxine Snowdon guaranteed safe passage into the city with the payment of a reasonable tax.

I eventually settled myself on a lonely park bench on the north side near a small grove of trees, planted, I guess, to block the view of the remaining abandoned industrial buildings that still lurked at the northern edge of the park. The bench was a good choice for unobserved meetings.

From a distance off, Jane was easy to spot, tall, long-striding, and a natural sway. I stood up and waved my hat. She waved back. In a minute, she was at the bench with a demeanor that sounded an alarm in my male brain. I knew she had troubles, and I knew what that trouble was. The reports of the Henderson artwork heist traveled fast in police circles.

Two days ago, Monday, a collection of Jane's father's pricey art had been stolen. A van transporting the artwork from his mansion to a Merritt Gallery at the King City Municipal Museum had been ambushed. The goods were twelve highly valuable paintings meant to be on loan to the gallery for a year. A gang of armed thugs canceled the loan and made a withdrawal, killing two of the three guards and wounding the other. The driver escaped injury by hiding under the truck's seat.

"You heard?" Jane said as we settled on the bench next to me.

"Yeah, unfortunate. Tell me what's going on."

"A detective from the King District precinct, Joseph Bennington, is leading the investigation. Do you know him?"

"Yeah, I know Joe."

"What do you think of him?"

"He's a good egg, honest, mostly."

"Can we depend on him to solve this case and get the paintings back?"

"To be straight with you, Joe ain't the sharpest pencil in the box."

"I got that impression." Jane's eyebrows arched. "Could you do something to help out?"

"We don't, as a rule, cross over into each other's turf."

"Danny, since when do you play by the rules?"

She had a point there. Besides, the odds that I could turn down anything she asked was unlikely. Anyway, since I heard about the heist, I had given it some thought. I had a plausible theory, and a plan of action worked out in my mind. Just couldn't help myself.

So, I got right into it. "The crooks knew the date and time the artwork was being transported and the delivery truck's route. Someone passed that information on to them."

Jane interrupted me. "Detective Bennington said he thought it might be someone involved with the transport company. Maybe even one of the guards."

"The two dead ones or the wounded one?"

Jane just cocked her head and raised her eyebrows.

"Did your father share the van's schedule with the police beforehand?"

"Well, yes." Jane paused for a moment. "Are you saying that someone at the police department could have been in on the robbery?"

"It's a possibility, something to consider." I took off my hat and laid it on the bench. "Did Joe interview all your household staff?"

"Yes, he did, but I can't imagine that it was one of them."

"We can't rule them out just yet, either."

"Most of our staff has worked for us for years since I was a kid. They're loyal to my father, I'm sure."

"Does he pay them above the standard wage?"

After a hesitation. "I'm not sure what that would be."

"Are you or he acquainted with their families? Ever visited their homes?"

Jane's face was blank.

"How about Christmas bonuses?"

"Not sure." Jane glanced down and shrugged. "My father handles all that."

"I'll have to check them out."

"I can get a list of their names and set up interviews for you."

"Just the list; I'll handle the interviews."

"There might be another problem." Jane winced. "You're not going to like it."

"What's that?"

"My father hired Bob Paxton to help find the paintings."

"Your father reached out to Paxton because he didn't have confidence in the police?"

"No, Paxton just showed up at my father's office. He said he heard about the robbery, felt really bad, and wanted to help. He said something like that shouldn't happen in King City, and he didn't even need to be paid for his services."

"Why didn't you put a stop to it?"

"I didn't find out until after the fact." She slapped my shoulder with the back of her hand.

"Couldn't you have used your daughterly charms to persuade your father to dump the guy?"

Jane looked quizzical.

"You know, pout, cry, throw a tantrum or something."

A gasp of exasperation escaped from Jane. "I did tell my father that I was acquainted with someone who could help, that he didn't need Paxton."

"You didn't mention my name, did you?"

"Of course not; I told him I was friends with J.L. Gibson and that he had sources in the underworld that he could reach out to."

"That was creative." I had to give Jane credit. "The question that comes to mind, though, what's Paxton's motive for getting involved?"

"I'm guessing something sinister."

"My thoughts, too."

"Where do we go from here?" Jane asked.

"We've got some possibilities as to who could have tipped off the thieves. I will need to shake the trees to get a lead on what crew actually pulled off the heist."

"Do you think you can get the paintings back?" She reached out and touched the back of my hand.

"Sure, I'm going to get right on it."

"I really appreciate this, Danny. Those paintings mean a lot to me."

"I'm going to be working outside the normal law enforcement channels; there might be some strings attached. You good with that?"

"Anything. Anything to get the paintings back."

"They mean a lot more to you than just the money value, I take it?"

"Yes, they sure do." Tears swelled in her eyes.

It came to mind that Jane knew a lot about me and my history, but I knew next to nothing about hers, so I asked, "Tell me about it."

"Those paintings are very important to me. They were my mother's favorites. They were something to remember her by. It's like the art was a part of her." Jane paused, her eyes cast down. "It's hard to describe."

"I get the picture."

"When my mother was alive, the paintings were on display all around the house, in the library, the drawing room, the foyer, and the hallways. When she died, my father took them all down and put them in storage. I don't think he could stand seeing them every day, a reminder of my mother. He and she had had a wonderful time going on collecting trips."

"How's your father taking all this?"

"He's trying to hide it, but he's devastated. Yesterday, I overheard him in his study talking to himself, cursing. He'd been drinking, shouting that he should have kept the paintings in storage where they were safe. I heard something crash against the wall."

"What's the connection between your mother and these paintings?" My detective sense wanted to know more.

"When my mother came of age, her parents arranged for her to spend a year abroad in London, studying art. While there, she went on a school-sponsored trip to France that featured acclaimed art galleries and salons. At their stop in Paris, she visited a museum that displayed Impressionist work. She fell in love with the style. She skipped out on the tour and stayed in Paris. There were famous impressionists of the time in the Paris exhibits, Claude Monet, Paul Cézanne, Edgar Degas, and Mary Cassatt."

"When was this?"

"1899. She was 18 years old."

"Your ma sounds like a lady with spunk."

"She sure was." Jane's eyes were moist. "You spent some time in Paris after the war. Did you visit any museums? Was there any art style that you particularly liked?"

"After the fighting, I wasn't in the mood for museums. I spent most of my free time in cabarets and bars." I wanted to get back on topic. "So, these pictures that were stolen were by some of these famous fellas you mentioned? Pretty pricey then?"

"No, my father couldn't afford their work. My parents traveled around the States, collecting the artwork of American artists Edmund Greacen, Albert Henry Krehbiel, and Alden Weir. They did get a print by Mary Cassatt. She's American, but she lived in Paris as an expat. My mother met her at an exhibition there."

"I can see how they would be extra special."

Jane's eyes suddenly gave up the fight. She pulled a hankie from her purse to soak up the deluge.

It took a while before she could talk.

"The subjects of Cassatt's paintings were of women with children. Our print was of a mother holding her daughter." Tears streaked Jane's face.

"I'm going to get right on this." My eyes were tight. "I'll be in touch." I got up quick and left Jane just sitting there. At the edge of the park, I glanced back. She was still on the bench, staring out at the bay.

In my office very early Thursday morning, unusual for Sean and me, we traded pages of the crime report on Monday's robbery back and forth across my desk. It took a few minutes to digest the whole thing. The King District coppers had shared their incident report citywide.

The Commissioner had put all the cops in King City on alert. This was a high-profile case that the Commissioner wanted solved, and quick. When a member of the upper crust gets hurt, he gets involved and, in this case, along with the whole damned police force. Not the best idea, in my opinion; some coppers might be in bed with the thieves.

"Says here that the driver got a glimpse of the truck used in the attack. Couldn't identify it, though." Smoke was leaking out of Sean's nose.

"Hard to see anything when you're hiding under a seat."

A truck with the thugs aboard had cut off the transport van, coming to a stop right in front of it. Two henchmen jumped out with tommy guns. That's all the driver saw before he crawled out of harm's way.

"It was lucky the fella was on the small side. The engine block must have shielded him from the barrage of bullets."

He had stayed under the seat until he was sure the thugs were gone. He then ran to a call box to report the crime.

"Any word on the guard that's in the hospital?"

"Mildred says it's touch and go. He lost a lot of blood."

Mildred was a nurse at the hospital, one of Sean's contacts.

The transport van carried three guards. The one in the cab with the driver was found dead on the ground right next to the passenger side door. The two guards in the back of the van were found lying on the ground at the open back doors, one dead and one badly wounded.

"Looks like no one was supposed to survive to tell the tale." I placed the last page of the report on the pile on my desk.

"The driver said that the goons wore stockings over their heads as masks. That's the same M.O. as the crew that hit Lizzy's. Could they be one and the same?"

"Could be, but it's more likely this was a local operation. Someone had a connection that got the van's schedule and route. If we can find that fink, we'll get a line on the robbers."

"Who do you think looks good for it?"

"Someone at the trucking company or a copper in King District or a domestic at the Henderson mansion."

"Where do we start?"

"I want you to look into the employees at the trucking company, but discreetly. We don't want to rile up the King District boys. I'm going to have a meeting with Bennington to see what he knows that's not in the incident report. And then I'll take on the household staff."

"Got it."

I got to my feet and removed my coat from the back of my chair.

Sean stubbed out his cig in the ashtray and followed me out the door.

I had sent a message for Jane to meet early this morning, nine am, me at the corner of Washington and Second Ave, two blocks from the Gazette. I had a plan I wanted to put into effect over the weekend, and it required her buy-in.

From my position on the corner, I saw Jane come out of the lobby doors. I walked into an alley before she got to me. She followed me in.

"Danny, what have you got?"

"This evening, a middle-aged colored woman named Della Robinson is going to show up at your place to accept the maid's job you offered her."

"But we don't need another maid."

"Make up a story. You think your staff is overworked. She told you a sob story about being down on her luck. You felt sorry for her. The mansion needs a top-to-bottom cleaning. Something—get creative. Whatever you come up with, make sure she has access to your entire staff."

"So, she's going to be a kind of spy?"

"Something like that."

I had met with Francine again after her Thursday show last night. The theater had been cleared as a crime scene. Like they say, the show must go on. I imposed on her to spend a few days at the Henderson Mansion as a spy in disguise as a maid. If anyone could get a line on who in the Henderson household might have been in on the robbery, my money would be on Francine. I knew that Jane had interviewed Francine at one point for the papers, but Francine was as good with disguise and acting a part. I figured Jane wouldn't recognize Francine in character and let it slide.

"Have you got any leads?"

"Too early in the game. But I'll keep you posted."

We went our separate ways.

I'd never been in this hole-in-the-wall bar before; didn't even know it existed. It didn't rate as a speakeasy. It was just a one-room hangout for the locals, serving local beer and Big Anthony's high-quality corn liquor.

The bartender and his five patrons seated at the bar each gave me the once-over. A big crowd, I suspect, for a Monday night.

True to his word, Anthony had let the owner of the establishment know not to make waves when the white copper showed up in this colored establishment.

I had a lead on the robbery informant; Francine had come through. After spending the weekend at the Henderson mansion, she contacted me Sunday night with a line on who had tipped off the robbers. The household butler had a sideline going in the drug rackets, distributing cocaine and heroin for Carlo Minx. It was a sweet operation selling dope to the upper crust in the King District. It was just over a week since the robbery, and I was finally getting somewhere.

Francine also told me the butler spent his free time, late evenings, at this little bar on the north side of Henshaw. For the butler, it was only a short hop from the Henderson Mansion over the Broad Street bridge, spanning the King River to this little bar, his favorite hangout on Canal Street.

A tall, thin fella at the far end of the bar seemed to fit Francine's description of Henderson's butler.

He looked me up and down as I approached. "Can I buy you a drink, Darwin?"

"Who the hell are you?"

"Danny O'Shea, Carvonshire precinct." I pulled back my coat to show my badge.

"You ain't got no business in Henshaw."

"Anthony says I do. I got business with you, in fact. How about that drink?" I motioned to the bartender and pointed to Darwin's glass. I settled on a barstool next to the butler. "The same," I called out.

Out of habit, I took a sip from the shot glass the bartender had just placed in front of me. A mistake; moonshine was meant to get to the stomach as quickly as possible, bypassing the taste buds.

"I got a proposal for ya," I said after my throat cleared.

"And what's that?" The mention of Anthony's name had settled the fella.

I spent a few minutes with some preliminaries, explaining that I knew he was involved in the drug rackets with Carlo Minx. And that I had information that he was the one who tipped off Minx with the schedule for the delivery van loaded with art. Made sure he understood that he was an accessory to murder and I had a good case that I could make stick.

Darwin was twitching like a rabbit with a fox bearing down on him. He glanced from side to side, looking for an escape route. I was sure he was contemplating the consequences for a black fella accused of dope dealing in white King City.

"Now, just take it easy; I'm not looking to arrest you," I interjected quickly. "I'm after Minx for the heist and the murders. To get off the hook, you're going to help me nail him. The way this works is: you help me, and I help you."

I spent some time reassuring Darwin that there was a way out of the fix he was in. Not wanting him to bolt and leave town, I told him I had an arrangement with Big Anthony and that I could get him off the hook.

Actually, I had no such arrangement with Anthony. He's not a fan of drug dealers. He does his best to stomp out drug rackets when they emerge in Henshaw. By his way of thinking, moonshine was all a man needed to ease the burdens of life. I knew Darwin was also thinking about a stomping from Big Anthony.

I had felt it prudent to ask Big Anthony's permission to confront Darwin on Anthony's turf. Maybelle had set up a meeting, which Anthony agreed to, no problem. Apparently, we're pals now. Once I informed Anthony of Darwin's involvement in the drug rackets, he washed his hands of the fella. He said he didn't care if I dropped Darwin in the Henshaw Canal or the King River, my choice.

Of course, he didn't much care what white people did to themselves in the King District. But he was for sure concerned with the blowback his community might suffer from the conviction of a colored man selling drugs in the King District.

After a couple of more shots, Darwin eventually relaxed and came around to my way of thinking. He admitted to the drug dealing and the tipoff to Minx. Darwin had gotten a payoff for the information and the bonus of Carlo not fitting him for a Chicago overcoat (*).

His arrangement with Minx was a bargain with the devil, and from his perspective, another such bargain had to be made with me. I needed the location of the stolen art.

But all he could tell me was that the stash was being shipped by boat to an out-of-town buyer this coming Sunday, five days off.

That wasn't enough, I told him. But, if he could get lowdown on the painting's location and date and time of the shipment, I would make sure he avoided the slammer and didn't end up dead. Nothing was for sure in this game, but I said it for effect.

He agreed again, smart fella.

I gave him two days to meet his end of the bargain. We planned to meet again, here at the bar, on Wednesday at ten in the evening.

The waitress planted cups of coffee in front of Bennington and me. The diner, his choice, was a bit classier than Kelly's. But then, everything was in the King District compared to Carvonshire.

"I really don't have time for a cup of coffee, O'Shea. The Henderson art heist has got me tied up in knots." Joe took a sip from his cup. "If I didn't owe you one, I wouldn't be here."

"You're going to owe me another one. I got a lead on the heist. More than a lead, I know who was responsible. I know where the Henderson goods are stored and that it's going to be shipped out of King City this Sunday morning."

Joe choked and spit coffee on the counter. Looked like some came out of his nose too.

"Why the hell didn't you tell me that on the phone?"

"I didn't want it to be public knowledge. We got to keep this between you and me. I don't want the thugs tipped off."

"Smart think'en." Joe leaned in closer. "What have you got for me?"

I had met with Darwin last night, and he came through with the information I asked for. I filled Joe in on what I had learned; that Carlo Minx had the stash stored in an abandoned shoe factory in the old industrial complex just north of the King District wharf. And that the paintings were going out by boat to meet a ship in the bay and from there to an overseas buyer. I didn't tell him anything about Darwin, who I had instructed not to leave town until Minx had been arrested.

"Thanks, O'Shea." Bennington started to rise. "I'll take it from here."

"Not a good idea, Joe." I wagged my finger at him. "You should only involve the coppers you can trust, and that ain't a long list. We need to work this together, both of us combining resources. You and I playing our cards close to the vest is your best shot at closing this case."

Standing next to the counter, frozen, Joe looked to the door and then back at me before he settled back on his stool.

"Okay, Danny. What have you got in mind?"

<hr>

"This is mighty nice of you, O'Shea." I could feel the bite of the sarcasm as Sean took a bite of his sandwich.

I had an order of grub delivered to my office from the Jewish deli up the street, three pastrami sandwiches (two for Sean, one for me), a quart of potato salad, a side of coleslaw for Sean, and two of the biggest dill pickles they had.

"We haven't had a meal from Goldman's for a while. I know how much you like their sandwiches."

"Why do I feel like there's another shoe about to drop?" As an afterthought, Sean put down the sandwich, took up his napkin, and shook it open before he tucked it into the neck of his shirt.

"Can't a fella just do something nice for his partner?"

The station house was almost deserted; almost every copper was out looking under rocks and in the bushes for the stolen goods. Only Desk Sergeant Murphy and Dulley were downstairs manning the fort this Friday afternoon.

"Come clean already. What have you got us into this time?"

"It's off the book's action having to do with that art heist."

"How are we involved?"

"A raid in the King District to recover the paintings."

"Cross swords with the King District boys; I'm not sure if two pastrami sandwiches are going to cut it."

"Don't forget the potato salad and your favorite pickles. You can have mine."

Sean sighed and shook his head.

"Not to worry, Bennington is in on it. I met with him yesterday. The plan is to keep the raid a secret, just between him and us. We keep the brass out of it, too. Nobody in either precinct will know anything about it until it's over and done. He's going to recruit a few fellas he can trust, and we will do the same. I figure on our side, it's me, you, Johnson, and Brady."

"You think bringing that brat Brady into it is a good idea, considering his connections?"

Sean had a point; Brady was the nephew of the Chief's wife, and he reported to Foley.

"I got a good feeling about the kid. He's tired of sitting on his ass. He wants to get into the action."

"So, what's the deal then?"

I proceeded to give Sean the lowdown. We were going to hit Minx and his henchmen at the shoe factory Sunday morning at dawn as they were getting ready to transport the paintings to the wharf. I left out the details as to how I knew the score. Sean knew enough not to ask.

The King District boys and us had arrived at the abandoned shoe factory around four in the morning, just before dawn. We had met up at Joe's diner beforehand to discuss our plan. Joe drew up a sketch of the old industrial district on a napkin; he was familiar with the area. It was used by dope dealers and bootleggers.

The plan was to conduct a raid during the transfer of the paintings from the factory to their vehicle. Not just storm the place but wait for the thugs to come out in the open.

The shoe factory had a loading dock on the west side of the building on Chester Street. We decided that Bennington and his men would take up a position on the north end, and we would be stationed on the south, except for Johnson, who was positioned with his sniper rifle on the roof of an abandoned warehouse directly across the street.

Sean and I were sitting in Owen's Model T, Sean puffing away on his fourth cig of the morning. We had parked the car in an alley half a block from the shoe factory. In the early dawn light, I could see Brady now, hunched behind some old crates. I had stationed him at the end of the alley so he had a clear view of the loading dock to the north and the street to the south, the direction we expected the thug's vehicle to come from. Brady didn't balk at an assignment to spend hours in the dark and dank as our lookout. He was as happy as a pig in mud.

Bennington and one of his patrolmen were likewise camped out in an alley at the other end of the street. The other of his men were in hiding across the way from the loading dock in the same warehouse Johnson occupied. We had the shoe factory entrance tied up on three sides.

My eye caught a blur of movement as a vehicle passed by the alleyway. In a moment, Brady was at my window. "A delivery van, it just pulled up to the loading dock."

The three of us hustled up to the end of the alley and watched the goings-on at the dock from the concealment of the crates.

Two thugs and Carlo Minx popped out of the Lehigh Dairy Milk truck and made their way up the steps. The thugs stood on the edge of the dock, scanning the area, looking for trouble. Minx moved to the factory door and rapped on it with his knuckles. After a moment or two, the door swung open, and another thug emerged. After a brief conversation, Minx and the thug entered the building.

A while later, Minx appeared, followed by two men pushing handcarts, each holding a crate. The two men must have been stationed in the factory guarding the crated artwork.

I gave the word, and the three of us emerged from our hiding place. We marched up the street, bold as brass, weapons drawn. The thugs didn't spot us right away, but when they did, Sean let go a blast from his police whistle, alerting Bennington's crew to step out lively.

"Police. Give it up. You're surrounded!" I yelled.

We were ten yards from the dock. Carlo looked in our direction and then back the other way at Bennington's men closing in.

He started to raise his hands. A shot rang out, the distinctive pop-zing of a sniper round. Carlo staggered backward, bent over, struck in the stomach. He collided with the door. As Carlo straightened up, another shot, the slug hit his shoulder and spun him around. He fell, twisting in the air, landing on his back. For a long moment, no one moved. And then the thugs on the dock reached for their weapons. All hell broke loose.

The gunfight only lasted seconds before all four of Carlo's henchmen were down and dead. They didn't stand a chance. One of Joe's patrolmen had taken a bullet in the shoulder, possibly friendly fire.

Me and Sean started up the dock's steps. Two of Joe's men rushed to the wounded fella.

"What the hell is wrong with your man, taking out Minx?" Joe called out from the other side of the dock. "I heard he was off his rocker." Joe was looking across the street at the warehouse rooftop.

Just then, the pop and zip of another sniper round pierced the air. Everyone flinched. Carlo's arm, which he had raised in a call for help, fell limp. The round had struck him in the chest. I turned my attention to the rooftop.

Johnson was standing up behind a knee wall, his rifle pointed north, up the street. He fired a shot, another, and then a quick volley of four more.

We all jumped off the dock and took cover behind the truck.

Our heads were swiveling in every which way, scanning the roof level. We were not in a good position to see anything but in a good position as a target for the other sniper.

"All clear!" Johnson's voice rang out.

I jumped back up on the dock to get a better look around. Joe's boys had drug the wounded patrolman off the street into an alleyway. Johnson was no longer on the roof edge.

Sean was on his way to check on the wounded patrolman; he was a good man for first aid.

Bennington dispatched one of his men to look for a call box.

Brady started up the steps at the far end of the dock. As he reached the floor level, he got a good look at the mess. He turned around real quick, skipped back down the steps, and started puking his guts out.

Johnson emerged from a street-level door of the warehouse. I jogged across to meet him. He had seen the muzzle flash of the third shot, a sniper in a window of the next building over. He had unloaded his rifle, sending slugs through the window, meant to deter more shooting and on the off chance a slug might find his fellow marksman. We found our way through the building to the window the uninvited sniper had used. I collected three shell casings.

Back on the street, the sounds of sirens preceded the arrival of a meat wagon, a squad car, and two paddy wagons.

An hour passed before the newspaper reporters turned up on the scene. That gave Joe and me the time to get our story straight, how this raid would be reported in the press, and what we would tell the brass.

There would definitely be no mention of the second sniper. The case needed to be wrapped up nice and neat, no loose ends. Who had killed Carlo Minx was a whole nother matter, not for the public record, a problem to be worked out another day.

We agreed on our story - that I got a confidential tipoff from a person from Carvonshire, identity not to be disclosed. Of course, I did not share any information about Francine or Darwin, not even with Joe.

A joint venture between the King District and the Carvonshire precinct would normally have been coordinated with the chiefs of police. Our line was that I got the tipoff at the last minute, in the middle of the night, and didn't have time to rouse up men at the station house. I gathered up a few men and met Joe at his diner, where he happened to be socializing with a few of his boys. From there, the raid at the shoe factory was just made up on the fly.

This story was not at all plausible, but the brass would have to swallow it. The Henderson artwork was recovered, the crooks were dead, and the case was closed. All was well in King City.

Jane had arrived before me this time. She was sitting on the same park bench as last time, the remote one near the trees. Thursday afternoon after the Sunday raid, the Bay Port Park was practically deserted.

"Good afternoon, Jane." I startled her as I approached from behind the bench.

"Hi, Danny."

I sat down next to her and gazed out at the bay.

She turned her face to me. "I have to thank you for recovering my mother's paintings. I'm so grateful."

"All in a day's work."

"Gunfights shouldn't be in a day's work. I'm really glad you weren't hurt."

"Thanks for that."

"I'm sorry I had to write the article giving Detective Bennington most of the credit."

I wasn't able to provide Jane with any more information on the raid than what Joe provided to the other papers. No crime photos either since this case was being processed in the King District.

"That's the way the cookie crumbles sometimes."

Jane knew I was the one who solved the case, but she had none of the details.

"On the bright side, with Carlo Minx gone, we don't have to worry so much about your personal safety."

One photo on the front page of the Gazette was that of Carlo, flat on his back in a pool of blood.

"Yes. I'm grateful for that," Jane responded, "But seeing him dead was not as rewarding as I thought it would be."

"Killing never is. Even when it's the only apparent solution, it ain't pretty. It leaves a mark."

We sat in quiet for a while, digesting things before Jane broke the silence.

"You were right about having Corporal Johnson following my editor around for a couple of days. He's scared to death of me now. He's so deferential it's unnerving. He even gave me a raise in pay."

Giving the daughter of the newspaper's owner a raise did smack of desperation.

"That's good, but you can't be all stick. You need to have some carrot, too. Be on the lookout to do him a favor when you can."

"Why?" quizzical described Jane's face.

"So he knows what side of the bread the butter's on."

"What?"

"You want him in your debt, but not in a panic."

"Okay, what kind of favor?"

"Anything, get him tickets to a show. Help him out of a jam up, gambling debt, whatever comes up."

"He is a baseball fan. I could get him tickets, good seats."

"There you go."

A sea breeze picked up, rustling the leaves overhead. Jane turned her face to me with another point of concern.

"Our butler didn't come to work on Tuesday, which made me suspicious."

I interrupted. "Suspicious is good. You're learning."

Got some daggers; then Jane continued. "I found it hard to believe it was one of our people, but I think it's your influence that's turning me cynical."

"Let's just say more hard-boiled."

Jane cocked her head. "Sooo, I figured he might have been the one in on the robbery. I called Detective Bennington. He sent some men to the butler's apartment, but it was cleaned out. Bennington said he would conduct a search but thinks the butler probably skipped town."

"He's right; Darwin did skip. He's on his way down south to connect with his family."

I had met with the fella on Monday, got the address of where he was going, and sent him on his way.

"Wait." Jane's face was about as confused as I'd ever seen it. "How do you know him and where he went?"

"I arranged it. It's the least I could do for the fella."

"What? You arranged for the man who tipped off the robbers to escape?" Jane's tone was less than pleasant than at the start of our conversation.

"Right, I owed him a favor. He gave us the where and when the paintings were to be transferred from the docks to the boat."

"But he was in on the robbery; he should go to jail, not get away scot-free."

"There were extenuating circumstances. Darwin was in a bind with Carlo Minx. You know how that is. He didn't have much choice but to cooperate with Minx. Besides, he took a risk ratting on Carlo."

"Darwin has been with us for over five years. My father took a chance on him and gave him a good job as a stable hand. He worked his way up to the butler position. And this is how he pays us back? He did it for money, I assume?"

"For money, yes, and to save his neck. It was complicated."

"What do you mean?"

"Your butler was a drug runner for Carlo Minx."

"What? That's crazy. I don't believe it."

"Actually, he was the head of a distribution ring that operated in King District. His clients were members of the city's high society. Darwin had contacts in their households, a maid, a butler, a cook, or someone else in the domestic staff. Darwin picked up the drugs from Carlo, delivered them to his associates, and they, in turn, sold them to various members of the household.

"Basically, the high society types got their drugs delivered to their door, no need to slum around the low-class neighborhoods looking to score. A real smooth, lucrative racket."

"That's hard to believe."

"He might have been selling to someone in your house."

"There's only my father and me."

"Some people describe you as perky."

All I got was a dirty look.

"Your father is of the age of those who got addicted when the stuff was legal. In the old days, doctors prescribed the stuff hand over fist, plus you could buy cocaine and heroin over the counter. There was a real epidemic back then."

"My father does not do drugs!"

"In any case, I need a favor. I promised Darwin I would send him some cash."

"You did what? You promised a criminal money? A drug dealer, a thief who betrayed our trust."

"If you would wire him a grand, that would close the deal."

I extracted a folded piece of paper from my vest pocket and held it out.

"Danny O'Shea, are you hearing me? Are you out of your mind?"

"Not the first time I've been asked that."

"I can't do that."

"You got your pictures back. I told you there might be some strings."

Jane finally took the note from my hand, opened it, and read it. "Marion Blackburn, Safford Alabama. Who's this?"

"Darwin's sister. He's going down there to live with her family.

"Darwin, like most common folks, had money problems. He sent most of his pay home to support the family. But it wasn't enough. They're a big clan of sharecroppers that make their living picking cotton. They barely get by."

"Sorry to hear that."

"Besides that, they wanted to send the youngest girl to college in Selma, Darwin's niece."

"That's admirable."

"In order to raise the money for the tuition, Darwin got creative, running drugs for Carlo Minx. Apparently, it paid well.

"But that put him in a tough spot with some nasty characters. You see where this is going?"

"Yes, I got it."

"If I send this money, how can I be sure it will actually be put to good use?"

"No guarantees. But that's why we're sending it to his sister and not Darwin."

"What's to stop Darwin from going back to the drug rackets."

"I gave him a stern talking to. Suggested he find another line of work, something safer, maybe bootlegging." I waited for things to sink in. "So, we're good?"

"We're good?" Jane tucked the note into her purse.

That went a lot easier than I thought it would. Might as well let the other shoe drop.

"There's something I need to tell you about Minx's death. He wasn't killed by a copper's bullet. A sniper in a building across the street shot him during the raid."

"How's that possible?"

"Someone had the same information we had, the place the paintings were stored and the time they were to be shipped out."

"Do you think one of Detective Bennington's men tipped this someone off?"

"No, I think it was a coincidence." Something I usually put as much stock in as a benevolent God. "I think he was camped out there waiting for an opportunity to take out Minx."

"Any ideas on who the shooter was or who wanted Minx dead?"

"Could be the Barron ordered the hit."

"But Minx worked for the Barron."

"Maybe Carlo was getting too big for his britches. Could be the art heist was outside of his purview, not sanctioned by this boss. Just a theory; I got no evidence yet."

"Paxton was looking into the robbery. And he works for the Barron, right?"

"Right."

"Do you think the Barron sent him to kill Minx?"

"Could be. I know a gumshoe in Brewster, Paxton's neck of the woods. He owes me a favor. I'm going to have him look into Paxton's past."

"Could Paxton have been in the army, trained as a sniper?"

"Army, maybe; sniper, no. The shooter didn't have the confidence of a sharpshooter. It took three rounds to kill Carlo off, targeting the torso, not the head. And he wasn't that far off, only across the street."

"You could have been a target that day as well. Did you think of that?"

"The thought crossed my mind. After the fact."

We gazed out at the bay, the sun behind us casting simmers on the cresting waves.

"When I was getting started in the crime reporting, you tried to warn me off the crime beat."

"Yeah."

"Three months have gone by. And so far, I've been threatened by a gangster in the Underground, almost kidnapped, had a contract put out on my life, and shot at in the street. I didn't appreciate your warning at the time."

This is where I could have said, I told you so, but she'd done it for me.

"So far, we have dodged the bullet—for real." Jane's eyes cast to the sky. "If things get dicey, and we can't find a way out of it, maybe you and I could move to Paris."

"Why Paris?" That was the question that came out of my mouth?

"I told you about my trip to New Orleans with my father?"

"Yeah, I remember." I remember every word she ever uttered.

"I wanted to spend a year in Paris studying art. It was my dream. Actually, it was my mother's dream. I wanted to live it out for her. But my father wouldn't hear of it. He thought a trip down south was the next best thing." Jane huffed. "A consolation prize."

"Sure, a new life in Paris is a possibility. We'll keep it in mind."

I wasn't sure where to go next with this conversation. Apparently, Jane didn't either; we both sat silent, staring. At the end of the wharf, a sailboat was rounding the fishing pier that jutted out into the bay.

On the practical side of things, my French is rusty, but I do have some buddies from the French military police I could look up. And there's all those museums we could visit.

Practicality aside, I decided to put Jane's outburst down to her considerations of the Grim Reaper. Carlo's killing, her ma's death, her and my near misses of late.

But living in Paris with Jane that's a fantasy to keep me company during those lonely evenings in my apartment.

EPISODE 14

A PROPOSAL

From a street corner, a block away, I watched the line of cars drive up to the curb in front of the Henderson Mansion—Cadillacs, Packards, Chryslers, Duesenbergs, and even a Rolls. I had Jedd drop me off three blocks away, not wanting to pull up in his ten-cent box alongside those classy motor cars.

I waited until the line thinned out, wanting to be near the last one to enter the party, a Saturday night shindig I'd rather have avoided. But an invitation from Jane was an invitation from Jane, so there I was, biding my time, having an argument with myself about going in or not. I'd have preferred to spend my Saturday night at Griffin's. How mad could she be if I didn't show?

A black Packard pulled away, looking like it was the last in line. I squirreled up my courage and strolled up the sidewalk to the mansion's door. It opened as I raised my hand to knock.

"Good evening, sir, welcome," a butler in a monkey suit declared as he took a step back to let me pass into a grand foyer. "May I take your hat?"

I obliged. "When I get that hat back, I expect it to be in the same condition, Sam."

Samuel, hat in hand, stiffened. His eyebrows arched for a second. "You can count on me, Detective O'Shea." Not a bit of expression on his face, he turned away.

Samuel had a lot more class than Darwin, an easy sell as a replacement. I had arranged his interview for the job, but had never met him. A distant cousin of Francine's, she had asked that I recommend Sam for the Henderson butler position. Of course, I did; I owed her.

He had obviously made a positive impression on Jane and her father.

I suspected Sam was likely a welcome addition as an agent in Francine's secret network of spies. I had to wonder and worry about who was financing those agents these days. As far as I knew, this was the first male member accepted into Francine's network. It smacked of desperation.

Passing through the foyer, I walked down the wide, center hallway. A couple of Jane's mother's paintings hung on the walls, back where they belonged. Apparently, they were here to stay in the Henderson mansion. It wasn't likely old man Henderson would ever loan them out again.

From a room to my left, piano music and chatter floated out. Double doors to my right stood open, exposing a great room populated by King City's upper crust and a few coppers in whose honor this shindig had been arranged. Mr. Henderson had decided to express his gratitude to the police department for the recovery of his wife's artwork and to show off the paintings themselves.

Jane had lobbied to invite every copper who had participated in the raid (Brady, Sean, Johnson, and the patrolmen), but she was overruled. Just as well, they would have been out of their element, same as I was feeling. They each did get a check in the mail as a consolation prize. Jane's idea, no doubt.

Playing the part of an out-of-place statue of an ordinary police detective in my coat and tie, I scanned the room full of men in tuxes and women in gowns, dressed to the hilt. Off to my right, Joe Bennington was standing against the wall in conversation with a tall, blonde doll. This was his turf. Despite looking the handsome, confident police officer in his dress blues, I could sense his nerves showing even from the distance between us. To my left, our own Chief Donnelly was bending the ear of Chief Smith from the King Precinct. Each had a glass in hand, lemonade, not their usual. Even a power player like Henderson couldn't openly serve booze to his guests.

In a corner next to the bookshelves, our illustrious Police Commissioner and Harold Patterson had their heads together, like peas in a pod or, more likely, snakes in a pit.

I spotted Jane on the far side of the room. We made eye contact, and her hand raised in a delicate wave. She wiggled her way through the crowd to where I stood in the doorway.

"I'm glad that you made it, Detective O'Shea." She shook my hand. "I wasn't sure that you would show."

"Me, neither. Thanks for the invite, though."

Jane glanced around the room. "I want to introduce you to my father."

Still holding my hand, she led the way through the gathering until we were standing at her father's back. He was holding court with two of King City society's elite couples.

"Excuse me," Jane said as she punctured the circle. "I need to borrow my father for a moment."

"Forgive me. I'll be right back," Henderson said to his guests as he turned to face me. The men nodded and moved away with their gals.

"Daddy, I would like you to meet Detective Danny O'Shea from Carvonshire."

"It's a pleasure to meet you, Detective," he said as he shook my hand with a firm grip.

"Same here, sir."

"I'm glad you're here tonight. I wanted to thank you personally for the part you played in the return of our treasured paintings."

"You're welcome, sir."

"I understand you were the one who received a tip from an informant as to the location of the paintings?"

"That's right, sir."

"It must be helpful to have those kinds of connections in your line of work."

My eyes twitched in Jane's direction. I caught the slight head shake. She hadn't spilled the beans.

"Yes, just glad I could help out."

"How did you get to know my daughter?"

"Our paths have crossed on occasion."

Jane's shoulder touched mine as she stepped on my foot.

"Well, should that ever happen again, I would appreciate it if you would look out for her."

"Will do, sir."

"I need to make the rounds." Henderson looked over his shoulder as he turned away. "You enjoy yourself, Detective." Mr. Henderson weaved his way back into the throng.

Jane's old man was a mover and shaker in King City. To my way of understanding, he had inherited the Gazette from his father, who had died of a heart attack. Only 20 years old at the time, Henderson had turned the Gazette, a small-time rag, into a newspaper empire in short order. A man of considerable talent, apparently.

Looking over past Jane, her father had entered into a confab with our Chiefs of Police. He glanced back my way. Chief Donnelly eye-balled me for a moment.

"What's with the stomping on my foot?"

"My father doesn't know that we were previously acquainted."

"I think he did." I nodded in the direction of her father. "In any case, he does now."

Jane brought her attention from her father back to me. "Let me show you around."

She gave me a tour of the ground floor, starting with the ballroom and then on to the drawing-room, the library, and finally to her father's study, each room highlighting one or more of the recovered paintings. She presented each one with the enthusiasm and knowledge of a seasoned tour guide.

We lingered in the study, taking in the last but not least, the print by Mary Cassatt, named 'Young Mother Sewing.' It depicted a woman sitting in front of some windows with a young girl standing alongside, leaning on her mother's lap. It hung in a place of honor across from her father's desk. We stood quiet in front of the desk, admiring the picture. Jane took more time describing this one, along with the painting technique. All I knew was it was hard to take my eyes off it.

"I should get back to mingling with the other guests," Jane said.

She had spent as much time as she could that evening showing her appreciation to a copper that helped recover the precious artwork.

"Before I go, I need to tell you to expect a new crime-beat reporter from the Gazette. He's a cub reporter who works with J.L. Gibson, Herman Rinkley."

"Does he know who you are?"

"No, he reports to the editor, who passes the kid's items on to me. I set this up because I needed someone at the crime scenes and the police station, since Gibson can't go. It fits perfectly into the Gibson persona, secretive for his safety."

"Not too far from the truth. Good idea. I'll be on the look out for him."

"Well, I'm off." Jane lingered in the doorway. "I'm so grateful for the recovery of the paintings, Danny. Thank you." And she was gone.

I hung around for a few more minutes, taking in the Cassatt picture. After leaving the study, I moseyed down the hall, glancing in the ballroom on my way out. No one seemed to have moved. In the foyer, I thanked Samuel for returning my Fedora in mint condition.

❧

I was early for our nine o'clock meeting, a quarter of. I placed my two bourbons on the table and sat down to wait for Jane. But she was early too; she was coming in the door.

Jane stopped at the bar to collect her usual. But as she approached the table, I could see she had the Gin Ricky in one hand and a shot glass of high-quality corn liquor in the other. I guess I was having an influence on her.

"Did you put your drinks on my tab?" I joked as she settled into her chair.

"Coppers never pay for drinks in King City, and neither do reporters."

She had learned a thing or two.

"I hope you left a tip."

"Yes, a dime."

"You trying to make me look cheap?" A nickel was my usual.

Jane flashed a smirk.

"I got the impression from your message that you were anxious to see me," I said.

Her cryptic note I got at lunchtime asked for a meeting at Griffin's this evening, but offered no explanation.

"I am. I wanted to show you this." She extracted an envelope from her handbag and slid it across the table. "This note was delivered to the Gazette this morning."

I took up the envelope and slipped out an engraved placard. An invitation to join Baron Hansen Alexander Frederick Louis this Saturday evening for a festive gathering to be held on his yacht. That would be tomorrow, Saturday, exactly one week since the Henderson party.

"You got another invite; Hans must like you." I laid the note and placard in the middle of the table.

"I wasn't sure what to do. Should I go? Maybe I could learn something. Maybe something that ties him to the Mayor identity? But I'm not sure if it would be safe. If he is the Mayor, and he's connected to the hit on Maxine Snowdon and maybe Carlo Minx, I don't think I want to be out at sea with him. That's a pretty convenient place to dispose of a body." Jane paused to take a breath.

She was sounding cautious, a good thing.

I reached into my inside suit pocket, pulled out an identical envelope, and laid it next to hers.

"Looks like you'll have a copper as an escort."

"You received an invitation also?"

"Dropped off at the station house this morning."

Jane downed her shot. Her head and shoulders shook, and her face formed a grimace. "Should we go?"

"We should, but we'll need to take some precautions."

"What do you have in mind?"

"You'll need to ask around, make sure that people you know are going, your father's friends or your other social connections. I want to be in a big crowd, not a party for two."

"I can do that."

"And when we're on the boat, we stay on the top deck and away from the railings. No need to invite an accident."

Jane finished off her Gin Ricky, turned to the bar, waved to get the barmaid's attention, and pointed to her empty glass.

"Okay, I got it." She was a bit pale. "So, what's our plan when we get on board? How do we proceed with our investigation?"

"We'll just play it by ear."

"That's the plan?"

"Yeah, let things play out."

From our bench in the park, Jane and I sat watching King City's finest shuffle out onto the wharf and board the waiting launch boats. Each of the two boats could hold around 20 persons, but they were taking on ten or so at a time as the guests arrived. The launches were shuttling partygoers out to the horizon and presumably to the Mayor's yacht, which wasn't visible from shore.

We had been on the scene since dusk was settling in.

After the boats had made about six trips and it was approaching ten o'clock, I decided it was safe to take our turn. Only one other couple boarded the launch with us.

Our boat bounced out into the open water as we left the calm of the cove, where the fella at the helm hit the throttle, jerking our heads back. The speedboat moved quite lively across the waves. It was only a few minutes before the outline of a white yacht appeared on the horizon.

As we skipped along on the swells, I quizzed a crew member stationed at the back of the boat. He said that the crew of both boats were locals who were hired on when needed for parties. Apparently a sailor, he seemed to be impressed with the yacht, being it was 158 ft stern to bow, 422 tons, powered by a compound steam engine with a top speed of 16 knots.

He provided some useful information as well. He recalled having seen a man matching Bob Paxton's description visiting the yacht during the day, but not for the parties in the evenings.

As we approached the white yacht, outlined in lights, steadily grew in size. We could hear the melodies of a band playing dinner music.

The launch pulled up alongside the yacht. Two crewmen secured our position at the base of a gangway ladder that extended out from the hull. The other couple, moving ahead of us, made their way up the ladder to the yacht's midship deck.

"When we meet the clown, let's play our cards close to the vest. Let him do the talking. I don't want to share anything we know with him. Keep him guessing."

"Got it." Jane took the hand of one of the crew as he guided her up the ship's ladder.

At the top of the railing, we were greeted by Alina. In a long, colorful, flowing dress, with her dark hair and dark eyes, she was, as advertised, foreign and a looker.

"Welcome aboard, Jane. I'm so glad you could make it."

"Right." Jane's voice had a snippy edge.

"Lovely weather for a party at sea," Alina said.

"True." Short and not sweet. "Alina, this is Detective Danny O'Shea."

"I've been looking forward to meeting you, Detective. I've heard a lot about you."

"Same here, doll."

For a second, I glimpsed a crack in her charming persona.

"This way," Alina directed us away from the railing toward the yacht's cabin amidships.

At the doorway, a manservant in a white suit whisked away our overcoats.

Alina ushered us into the main cabin and up to the bar, where a waiter stationed there took our drink orders.

Alina excused herself to greet more guests, who were arriving on another launch boat that had just docked at the ladder.

From her unflappable demeanor, you would think that butter wouldn't melt in her mouth, but I was sure she was the mystery woman connected at some level to the Snowdon Massacre.

The waiter returned with my bourbon and Jane's Gin Ricky.

For once in my life, I wasn't sure what to do with the glass of bourbon in my hand. My stomach was reminding me why I had enlisted in the Army and not the Navy. The speedboat ride was fast and smooth; the yacht, on the other hand, pitched ever so slightly, not quite with the beat of the music.

Considering the condition of my stomach and the risk of being drugged or poisoned, I guided Jane over to a potted plant at the cabin's far doorway. Hopefully, the alcohol wouldn't kill it.

I scanned the cabin. The interior was finished in wood, with fancy light-grained paneled walls and a matching ceiling, probably teak. The deck flooring boards were lighter yet, but not as wide. The square windows on the aft and starboard sides were draped with pulled-back red curtains. Wall sconces in between provided the mood lighting. One built-in couch, upholstered in plush red velvet, spanned the width of the bow end of the room. Porthole windows rimmed in brass above the couch provided views of the bow deck.

We strolled out onto the deck. The music we had heard on the launch was coming from a band we couldn't see on the level above the main cabin.

The bow was an expansive open deck with polished wood plank flooring that reflected hazy images of the white light bulbs strung on cables hanging from the riggings on both sides, eight feet above our heads. Guests were standing around, wrapped in conversation. Others were seated in deck chairs lined up along the railings.

A fella in a white Panama suit and Panama hat was holding court at the center of a small group of revelers enthralled by his attention. He had the appearance of a refined gentleman, with graying hair and goatee; the Barron looked the part he was playing. He got a glimpse of us, excused himself, and headed our way.

"Welcome aboard." The Barron, the Mayor, Hans (whoever the hell he was) said as he approached. "It's a pleasure to see you again, Miss Dickerson."

"It's good to see you, Hans." It was a very convincing lie. There was hope for my partner.

"Danny, this is Hans." Jane provided the introductions. "Hans, this is Detective Danny O'Shea."

The Barron extended his hand. "I've been looking forward to meeting you. May I call you Danny?" He spoke with a European accent, not distinguishable.

"Suit yourself."

We shook hands, holding on for a few seconds, flexing our grips.

"I see your glasses are empty. Let me take care of that." He raised a hand to summon a waiter.

"No thanks," I said.

"Suit yourself, Danny." The Barron grinned. "Miss Dickerson?"

"No, thank you, Hans."

"Miss Dickerson, I want to express how gratified I was when I learned that your paintings were recovered. And Detective, congratulations on solving the case and taking out that gangster, Carlo Minx."

"Thank you. I appreciate your concern." Jane said.

"A day's work," I replied.

"I'm glad you both decided to accept my invitation. I wanted to speak to you in confidence." He took a step away. "We'll have more privacy in my stateroom. This way."

"No thanks," I stood like a statue.

The Barron stopped. A sharpness crossed his face. "I see. How about the stern deck? It's a quiet spot." His accent faded away for an instant. He swept out his hand, motioning back toward the back end of the boat.

I looked over my shoulder and along the railing to the back of the boat. "That'll be fine."

"Good then." Hans walked past us, heading down the alley between the cabin and the railing.

I didn't move. "He stays here." I was looking at the thug in the black suit with a prominent bulge below his left shoulder, who had been hovering a few yards away.

Hans held up his hand to the thug, who stopped in mid-stride.

The band music faded as we followed Hans to the far railing of the stern deck, the lapping of waves on the hull taking its place.

The Baron turned around to face us and leaned back on the brass rail. "So, Detective O'Shea, you don't trust me, but expect me to trust you?"

"That's right."

"A man who speaks his mind. I like that." Hans chuckled and shook his head. "I invited you both here to discuss a business proposition."

Jane and I exchanged a knowing glance.

"I've done my research on you two and believe you are both vested in what's best for King City. I admire your loyalty to our city. I am of the same mind and also want what is best for King city."

He paused for a reaction, but Jane and I remained silent.

"Imposing prohibition on a thirsty populace is an obviously foolish endeavor. I'm sure you would agree. But it has provided some lucrative business opportunities. To my understanding, Detective, you don't have any aversion to bootlegging operations. At least, that's the word on the street."

"I can find better things to do with my time than chasing down bootleggers."

"It's also said that you had an arrangement with Snowdon, although you weren't on her payroll like the rest of the police force."

He paused. I stayed quiet.

"In any case, I would like to have that same sort of relationship. I'd like you to ignore any bootlegging activities in King City with which I may be associated. I could offer you money, but I don't want to insult you."

"I appreciate that." I went for a snarky tone.

"I've never met a man that wasn't motivated by money." The Barron shook his head.

"They are rare ducks." Again, snarky.

"And Miss Dickerson, I was hoping for the same cooperation from you, that you wouldn't pursue any stories that would cast a negative light on my activities. Likewise, I doubt you could be influenced by an offer of financial reward."

"That is correct," Jane said.

"What I'm hoping for is that we can come to an agreement. An agreement that my business dealings are what's best for King City and that the two of you won't do anything to obstruct or frustrate my enterprises."

I felt an unspoken 'or else' in that statement.

"We could work together, as a team, to put King City back to rights. Fill the void, as they say, and put an end to the lawlessness. Like the robbery of your paintings, for example."

"We had things set to right before Maxine Snowdon was killed," I said.

"Yes, an unfortunate incident. But that's water under the bridge."

An unfortunate incident for Maxine but an opportunity for the Barron.

"Surely, you can see the benefit of having someone like me in charge of the bootlegging operations. For one thing, I have an aversion to violence. I am strictly a businessman willing to step in and provide for the libation needs of King City's citizens."

"And you have no interest in the other rackets? Say— Gambling, prostitution, protection, narcotics, loan sharking, robbery, and the like?"

"Of course not. I'm like you, Detective; I find criminality distasteful. I'm only interested in seeing to it that the good people of King City have the opportunity to partake of their preferred beverage, a privilege that the federal government has so unwisely taken away."

Jane and I turned to each other.

"I don't expect an answer this evening. Take a few days to think it over. I will be expecting a reply by—let's say—next Sunday."

I detected another 'or else' in his tone.

"Agreed," I said.

"I have other guests I must attend to. Enjoy the party." Hans moved away, down the side of the boat, leaving us standing alone on the stern deck.

"Why didn't you just say no to that hoodlum?" Jane asked.

"Because we need to think it over, and if we do say no, I would prefer that our feet were firmly on dry land when we did."

"Sensible," Jane looked over the railing into the dark sea.

"Since we're here and the night is young, let's do some digging around. Let's split up. You go mingle with the social set; see what you can shake loose. I'll go to the bar."

"Go to the bar?"

"Yes, bartenders can be a wealth of information."

"Okay."

I walked with Jane back to the cabin doorway, where we parted, her to the bow deck and me to the bar.

I picked out a barstool at the end, away from the crowd of serious drinkers. The bartender who presented himself was a different chap than the one who supplied our drinks the first time. He spoke with a Slav accent, Polish, I figured. He was probably from the North End, a King City district populated with various Slavic peoples, Poles, Czechs, Russians, etc.

"What are you having, sir?"

"A bourbon. Bring the bottle and two glasses."

"Right away." He moved to the center of the bar and returned with the items requested. He poured two shots.

"One's for you," I said, looking the fella in the eye.

He made a quick survey of the room and threw back a shot.

"You can leave the bottle." I slid a dime across the counter.

"You can't be too careful, Detective." He smiled and turned away in response to another patron's call for a dry martini.

I was right; this bartender knew who I was and likely his way around.

For the next couple of hours, Victor and I got to be real chummy. He spent all his free time at my end of the bar, drinking shots and scooping up the dimes that I was sliding across the bar top on a regular basis.

I encouraged him to spill his life story. He confirmed that he was Polish and did come from the North End, the district that boasted King City's industrial area, the rail yards, and the train station. At the same time, I quizzed him about the Baron and the Baron's activities.

It was near midnight when Jane popped into the room and plunked down on the stool next to me.

"Get anything good from your socialite friends?" I asked.

"Not really; all they wanted to do was gossip."

"Not a total waste; you still have to write for the society pages."

"I guess so."

Victor approached with another glass and poured a shot for Jane. She looked nervously into the liquid and then glanced in my direction.

"It's okay," I added with a nod.

Jane took up the drink as Victor moved away.

"Those people are so enthralled with the Barron. They think he's their long-lost uncle or something, a big deal, a man of royalty. If I hear someone say that Hans is such a sweetheart one more time, I'm going to spit."

I gave Jane a once over.

"What?" Her eyes went large.

"You know, you need to write an article about this grand party for the Sunday paper society page?"

"Hans is a gangster, possibly a murderer. I should write a nice story about him in the society section?"

"Right, to keep up appearances."

"Fine." Jane slowly rotated her glass back and forth.

"It's time for us to get going." I placed a fiver under the bottle and got up.

"Did you get anything of value?" Jane asked.

"Yeah, Victor, our bartender here, is a real talker and well-informed."

"Like what?"

Before I answered, I guided Jane out of the cabin to the side rail opening with the ladder. "Later, when our feet are on solid ground."

A steward stationed at the railing called out for our coats. After he helped Jane with hers, he leaned out and whistled. The three-man crew in the launch boat below came to life.

As we pulled away, I looked back and saw the Baron in his white suit, standing at the rail waving his Panama hat. I raised my hat in return, being the only polite thing to do.

After exiting the launch boat at the wharf, we walked from the park to Bentley's simply because it was close. Jane didn't speak all the way there, but I could tell she was itching to talk about the Barron's offer.

At the club, the tables were dimly lit with candles, and a music man was carving out some classy tunes on the grand piano. Pretty romantic under different circumstances.

As we made our way through the tables covered in red cloth, following the maitre d, I noticed we were getting eye-balled by other patrons. I didn't take the time to go home to change into my glad rags for this visit to Bentley's.

"You know, your story about me being your cousin from out of town isn't going to hold water," I said as we took our seats at the table.

"Maybe not, but I'm going to keep telling it. I'm a writer, a storyteller; it's what I do."

"Us being seen together too often by your socialite friends might just put you in the gossip column."

"I decide what goes in the social section, so not a problem."

A waitress sauntered up and took our drink order.

We sat quiet, staring past each other until she came back with our drinks. I didn't even thank her; just nodded.

Jane's eyes focused hard on me. "What do you think?"

"About what?" It was a smart-ass response, but I wasn't looking forward to hashing out the answer.

"Jeez, Danny. You know what? About the Barron's offer. We need to talk it out."

"Agreed." I offered.

Jane was slowly twisting her drink glass by the rim. "I have concerns and a load of questions."

"I do, too." I lifted my bourbon in her direction. "You start."

"You don't believe what he said, that he's only interested in bootlegging?" Jane asked.

"No way, he's the kind who wants it all, the whole ball of wax." I knew his type; I had recently got some dope on him from one of my connections. "That's probably why he calls himself the Mayor, a not-so-subtle reference to his plans for King City; he wants to be the mobster in charge."

"He sure is full of himself. I think he has a Napoleon complex, claiming to be royalty and all. He even wears lifts in his shoes to make himself look taller."

"He does?"

"I'm surprised you didn't notice, you being a detective and all."

Score one for Jane.

"He may have a complex, but what he's really got is a swelled head and a cold-blooded nature. Not a good combination."

"Thank you," Jane said to the waitress as she placed our drinks in front of us.

We sat in silence for a few moments.

Jane dove back in. "Why do you think he has such an interest in us? He seemed to have a particular desire to get us on board. No pun intended."

"He's done his homework. He knows I can cause him trouble, being the oddball copper that can't be bribed. And, of course, your articles in the paper have demonstrated your ability to take down hoodlums and scoundrels."

"Makes sense." Jane raised her Gin Ricky to her lips. "What did you find out from the bartender?"

I shared the skinny I had gotten from Victor.

Victor fancied himself as quite the ladies-man, to which he attributed much of his knowledge about the activities on the yacht. He figured he could sweet-talk just about any doll into spilling everything she knew.

According to Victor, the Baron only has a small permanent staff on board (a cook, two maids, and two stewards). The ship is manned by the captain and a crew of six sailors (25 when they went to sea).

For the evening parties, staged once a month or so, bartenders, waitresses, and additional cooks were hired on from the city.

The party guests were a who's who list of King City's finest. Regulars included Mayor Hughes, the police commissioner, our Chief Donnelly from Carvonshire, Harold Patterson, Chief Smith from the King District, Jane's father, and a host of other businessmen looking to hob-knob with the Baron. Roan Doyle also was, but no longer, a regular. Added to the mix were some of King's City's entertainers, like Evelyn Stone and other actors, musicians, and always the best bands. It all looked to be legit and normal socializing mixed with business, no thugs or known gangsters in attendance.

Victor told me that the Baron rarely leaves the yacht, only going ashore for absolutely essential business, probably for meetings with gangsters who weren't invited to the parties.

Having exhausted myself, "That's the story."

"All good to know," Jane said.

Since I was on a roll, I had more information to spill.

"Remember I told you I had a detective friend in Brewster look into Paxton?"

"Yes."

"I got word from him yesterday. He provided the dope on Paxton and some on the Barron as well."

"What's the story on Paxton? Does he look good for the murder of Carlo Minx?" Jane edged forward in her seat.

"During the war, Paxton came in late. He got through military training but didn't see any action at the front. He was a patrolman in the Brewster police for four years before he quit to take up as a private dick."

"So, no sniper experience or exceptional skills with a rifle?"

"No, but he was raised on a farm outside of Brewster. Farm boys usually know one end of a rifle from the other. Plus, as a boy, he was a member of the National Rifle Association youth program. They teach shooting based on scientific principles."

"Could he be good enough to be the shooter that killed Minx?"

"Yeah, he could."

"I wonder why he moved away from Brewster?" Jane was asking good questions.

"He may have been looking for a change of scenery. The word is Brewster's a pretty rough town these days. It wasn't too long ago his younger sister was killed. She was his only sibling and the only family left in Brewster."

"That's awful."

"There was a hit on the speakeasy where she was working as a barmaid. She was collateral damage in the gunfight."

Our waitress approached. "A refill?"

"For sure. Thanks, doll," I said as she scooped up our empty glasses.

"And the Barron, what did your pal say about him?" Jane asked.

"Says the Barron, who called himself the Mayor there too, has taken over all the rackets in Brewster."

"So he saw through the Barron's masquerade as the Mayor?"

"Yeah. Even though the Barron keeps a low profile, he has a reputation and history he can't escape. Seems that he's the reason Brewster is a lawless mess these days. His

MO is to come into town, get the businessmen on his side with lucrative legit deals so that when he does get into the rackets, they'll look the other way."

"He does seem to have the ability to charm his way into people's good graces." Jane's tone gave away her embarrassment.

"Once he's got his homework done and learns the lay of the land, he throws in with the most vicious thugs in town.

"He goes after it all, prostitution, the protection game, gambling; you name it. And he does it the hard way by starting a gang war." I took a sip of bourbon; I was going dry.

"So, he's not just interested in bootlegging like he said?"

"No, and after he's taken over all the rackets, he selects the most ruthless hoodlum in town and puts him in charge to run the mob in his stead. And in King City, that would have been Carlo Minx."

"If that's true, why would the Barron have had him killed at the shoe factory?" Jane's puzzled face was one of her most charming.

"I don't know. It opens a big hole in my theory. Could be another player involved. Complicates things.

"With what we know about the Mayor, it's not likely he would take out Minx over the robbery of a few paintings. He would probably be getting a cut of the profits.

"And if Minx was the guy in line to be the crime boss of all of King City, it's not likely Carlo would have done anything to put that at risk, like cross the Barron."

"And since Paxton works for the Barron, he's probably not the shooter." Jane was getting the hang of things.

"Right, we have no idea who took out Minx or why? There's a lot we don't know." I hated to admit it; not a good look for a detective.

Jane shook her head. A puff of air escaped those pretty lips.

"It would help if we had an inside source in Baron's orbit," I said, "You might be able to help with that."

"How?" Jane perked up.

"You were a little cool with that doll, Alina. In the future, you could patch it up with her."

"No way. She's a gangster and might be involved in multiple murders."

"Still, having a relationship with her could be helpful."

"I thought she and I were becoming friends, but she was just using me."

"You're going to have to get over your hurt feelings."

I got daggers in return for that comment, but I kept going.

"I learned from Victor, the bartender, that she doesn't live on the boat but has an apartment in the King District."

"I know." Jane's voice was rising. "I helped her find it."

"Sounds like the beginnings of a nice friendship."

More daggers.

"Look at it this way. Yeah, she used you. Now it's your turn." Jane's face softened.

"Just stay in contact with her. But only meet her in public places. Don't go off somewhere private."

"Oh, I've learned my lesson. I'm not going off by myself again."

"I hope so," I said, but couldn't hide the sarcasm.

Jane gave me the 'Oh yeah' face and turned back to the question at hand. "Well, anyway, we have bigger fish to fry. The Barron's offer."

"He's a big fish, alright. My gumshoe friend filled me in on the Barron's hijinks. Brewster wasn't the first city he took over. He did the same thing in Seabrook two years earlier. Looks like he's trying to set up a little racketeering empire along the bay coast, with King City next in his sights."

Brewster is about 100 miles north of King City, and Seabrook is nearly 80 miles north of Brewster, both with ports on the bay, both smaller than King City.

"So, the Barron has been busy the last few years, expanding his franchise in a southerly direction down the coast," Jane said.

"For sure. From what I was told, he got his start bootlegging in Maine, running booze up the Atlantic coast for at least 20 years from St. Croix in the Caribbean to St. Croix, Maine."

Prohibition in Maine has been in effect since 1856. A bit of a joke, mostly, but it created opportunities for gangsters like the Barron to enrich themselves.

"I need to tell my father what I know about the Barron so that he can cut his dealings with that gangster."

"Not a good idea."

"Why not?"

"For one, how are you going to explain how you came across this information about the Barron?"

"I could make up some story." Jane sounded cocky.

"That's your answer to everything; make up a story."

"Well, I…"

"Yes, I know. You're a storyteller; it's what you do."

Jane's grin was from ear to ear.

"There might not be any point in telling him anyway. Your father's no dim bulb; he probably already knows what kind of fella the Barron is."

Jane fidgeted but didn't say anything.

"Just keep a lid on it for now. Let's see how things play out." I meant it as more than a suggestion.

Jane nodded and took another sip of her drink.

"The Barron must be doing well, judging from the yacht and all the parties he throws," Jane said.

"He surely has a substantial cash stream at his disposal from the bootlegging operation in Maine and his cut of all the action in Brewster and Seabrook. He's going to be a formidable opponent to go up against."

"It sounds like you're thinking of rejecting his offer?"

"I'm thinking I don't like our options. Throw in with a weasel or take up a losing cause."

"Why a losing cause?"

"You and me going up against the Barron and the worst hoodlums in King City; not the odds I like to play."

"Surely we could enlist others that would stand up to the Barron?"

"That would be a tough sell, convincing people to risk their fortunes and their lives to take on a well-financed gang of ruthless thugs. Besides, signing up for the Barron's program is the path of least resistance."

"Boy, you sure are pessimistic."

"I like to think realistic, with a dash of commonsense."

Jane and I spent a few more hours at the Bentley,

beating a dead horse to death. Around three o'clock in the morning, we had exhausted ourselves and called it a night.

Jane was leaning back in her chair, eyes droopy. I stood up and downed the last sip of bourbon. "Come on, let's get out of here."

Jane pulled herself up, grabbing the table edge. I scouted to her side and took her arm by the elbow to steady her. As we made our way out and down to the street, we bumped and stumbled like a couple of drunks. But it wasn't just the alcohol; it was the exhausting debate and spit-balling, which, in the end, didn't get us any closer to the decision we needed to make.

At the curb, I hailed a cab, loaded Jane into the back seat, and gave the driver the address.

"See you," she said.

"See ya." We were too tired for a proper goodbye.

As I watched the tail lights fade in the fog, my mind started percolating on the variety of ways a fella could sink a yacht. Nothing to be proud of, I know, but I just couldn't help myself. I'm a creative kind of guy.

EPISODE 15

A ROCK AND A HARD PLACE

I had another yellow envelope with a note in my vest pocket, the same as the others I had received with tip-offs. This one, not a tip-ff, I wouldn't tell Sean about. I considered it, though. It might be good to have him along as backup or at least know where I was going. But I decided against it. No sense putting his life at risk as well as mine.

I got the note three days ago, the Tuesday after our meeting with the Barron and late-night confab at Bentley's. That gave me two days to stew in my own juices, contemplating the big question: Was I going to share the note with Jane or leave her out of it?

If I did include her, she would get pulled deeper into King City's seedy underbelly, a shady situation she would probably never escape. But then, there was no way for her to avoid what was coming down the pike. We already had to deal with a response to the Barron's ultimatum due this Sunday.

What's one more thorny issue to deal with this Sunday? The Lord's Day wasn't looking all that blessed.

If I didn't reveal this new invitation and she found out, she'd be mad as a wet hen and never forgive me. Besides, she got herself into this mess the day she started her clandestine career as a crime reporter. There was nothing I could do to save her now.

I had asked Jane for this meeting at the Carlson this Thursday afternoon to discuss the note even before I'd decided whether I was going to show it to her or not.

About the time I came to terms with the idea that I was going to share the note, there was a rap on the storeroom door. It opened, and Jane waltzed in.

"Hello, Jane." I stood up and pulled out a chair at the table for her.

"Danny, I'm glad you called. I wanted to talk to you about the Barron's offer. It's been on my mind all week; I can't think about anything else."

"I know what you mean."

"We can't just agree to the Barron's terms. It's just not right, but then what's his play?"

"Yeah, he's not going to take kindly to a snub."

"Maybe we could stay neutral, just stay out of things. His ambition to take over King City might not work out for him in the long run?"

"You're right; it's not set in stone that he will come out on top in the gang war he plans to start. We could sit on our hands and watch it play out."

"Jeez, Danny. It doesn't sound good when you put it that way."

"Well, anyway, I don't think sitting on the sidelines is an option now."

"How's that?"

I pulled out a yellow envelope from my vest pocket and held it up in my hand.

"I got this note yesterday. It concerns you."

"Where did you get it?"

"First, I need to tell you that I've been getting notes like this one off and on for the last couple of months."

"What are the notes about?"

"Up until this one, they were tip-offs, information I needed to act on."

"Like what?"

"One described Big Anthony's troubles. One let me know about the fix Father Pat was in. Another tipped me off to the kidnapping attempt on you. And one was a warning about the Mayor and Paxton."

Jane sat stewing on that for a moment.

"I'm familiar with the other incidents, but what about the Mayor and Paxton?"

"Remember I told you I got a tip from a source that made me think Paxton wasn't the Mayor?"

"Yes."

"A note was the source."

"What did it say?"

"Not much, just that Paxton worked for the Mayor and a warning about the both of them."

"And this latest note, it's not a tip-off?"

"No, it's another invitation." I handed the envelope to Jane.

"From the Barron?"

"No, another villain."

She pulled out the folded note and spread it out on the tabletop, smoothing the creases.

I watched her read it. I had it memorized; it was short and sweet.

Your attendance is required for a business meeting on Sunday, the 24th, at 10 a.m.

The coordinates for the meeting are shown below.

Bring Miss Dickerson with you.

It's time to square up some favors.

"What's this?" Jane was holding up the paper and pointing to the diagram at the bottom of the page.

"It's a map of the Underground. The lines mark out tunnels, the squares are rooms, and the letters and numbers are signpost markings. The X is where the meeting is."

"Who's sending these notes?"

"Like this one, they're never signed."

"So, you don't know who they're from?"

"But I do. Each note has the same style envelope, same steno-paper, and same handwriting."

"Quit being dramatic."

"Grace Snowdon."

A that-is-nonsense look crossed Jane's face. "Rumor has it she either left town or she's dead."

"I bought that at first, but I spotted her at Max's funeral, so I knew she was still walking the earth. Wasn't sure if she was still in town, so I did some snooping at her office. I found this type of paper and envelopes in her desk." I tapped the note on the table with a finger. "And comparing the notes with some of her correspondence, the handwriting matches."

Grace has an office on South Street, the second floor of an old mansion, a shabby-looking place. Grace's workspace is spartan, just a desk, a swivel chair, one two-drawer file cabinet and one uncomfortable straight-back chair. The joint did have a central staircase, a servant stairwell, and an exterior fire escape, three means of exit, essential and prudent in Grace's line of work.

"What does squaring up favors mean?"

"Since she helped me out by sending the tip-offs in the notes, she's likely expecting something in return."

"Why do you think she wants me at this meeting? What does she want from me?"

"A favor, I'm sure."

"A favor. For what? What did she ever do for me?"

"Saved you from a kidnapping."

"Oh," Jane said, "What kind of favor would an accountant for Maxine Snowdon want?"

Jane had the basic low-down on Grace, the accountant and niece of the Carvonshire crime boss.

"From her accountant persona, nothing. But as Maxine's right-hand woman and top-notch assassin, I suspect she wants to get the Jones Gang back together and take back control of the rackets in Carvonshire."

"Assassin? What?"

"I'm not sure which identity was the sideline, keeping the books or killing people."

"Wow! Do you think she is aware of the Barron's plans for King City?"

"For sure."

"That means she will have to go up against the Barron in that gang war you think is coming." Jane squirmed in her chair.

"Right."

"And from this note, by favors, she probably expects you and I to help with that?"

"That's my working theory. I suspect that Grace is low on cash and that doing favors for a copper is her new form of currency. It's not likely she could bankroll the payola it would take to pay off the entire Carvonshire police department like Maxine did."

"Are you going to this meeting?"

"I don't see that I have a choice. If I don't, Grace will see it as a double-cross. I don't want to be looking over my shoulder the rest of my life, which could be short, with Grace gunning for me."

"Jeez. I didn't ask for any favors. I don't want to go into the Underground to meet with an assassin."

"You don't have to go."

"I don't?"

"No, you could leave town. Lie low for a couple of years or until I send the all-clear signal. Grace is a dangerous woman, but she's in a dangerous game. Her life could come to an end anytime."

"A couple of years? No way."

"You could go to Paris and study art like you've dreamed about."

"What about you?"

"I can't leave King City now, not when things are about to get real interesting. I've got a part to play."

"And you think I don't have a part to play?" Jane was winding up. "Haven't you ever heard of the power of the pen?" Her eyes flashed from side to side. "Or—the pen is mightier than the sword?"

"I have, on both counts."

"We're partners, right?"

"Right."

"You think I'm the kind of gal who runs out on her partner?"

"No." I held up my hands in surrender. I knew my idea wasn't going to fly, but I had to run it past her.

"We're in this together. We both go, or we both stay. Right?"

"Right." At this point, she could have said anything, and she would have been right; the moon was made of cheese, for that matter.

<hr>

"How do you know where you're going? Shouldn't you be looking at the map?"

"I got it memorized." I whispered, "And hold it down, a voice carries down here. We don't want to be discovered."

I was leery of who might be roaming around down here these days. Maxine had a thorough understanding of the layout, which meant Grace did, as well. The thugs that had thrown in with the Baron's gang not so much, but they could try to work out the lay of the land.

We had come into the Underground from the Lazarus Building alley entry point on Third Ave, the same spot that me and the jazz band had used to escape the massacre that night at Lizzy's.

"Okay, fine." Jane exaggerated a whisper. "But it's so dark."

"Don't worry, I got the whole Underground committed to memory." I touched the side of my head with a finger. "Not just the map on the note.

"From that time ten years ago, when you got a glimpse of that map in Maxine's office? It's still in your memory?"

"Yeah, it is."

"Amazing!"

"And besides that, when I first moved to Henshaw, I used to spend my Sunday afternoons wandering around down here, exploring."

"That's kind of a creepy pastime."

"At the time, I had a contract on my head. I was safer down here than out on the streets."

"So, you're familiar with the location of our meeting?"

"Just the general area. Where the X is on our note, I don't remember anything there except a dilapidated mechanical room. But then, I'm sure there are some tunnels and rooms that are not on Max's map that I didn't discover when I was rambling around."

At the next corner, I stopped to run my hands along the edges of the wooden board attached to a support timber.

I knew my way around, but not in the dark. We were using flashlights. I didn't want to use the overhead lights and draw any unwanted attention.

"What are you doing?" Jane

"Checking the coordinates. These boards are signposts with notches on each side, letters on the left, and numbers on the right. It's how you find your way around down here."

"And you know the system how?"

"I'm a detective. Besides, it's just Morse code. All Boy Scouts learn Morse code."

"You were a boy scout?"

"Hell, no. I learned it in the army."

"Jeez, you're a smart ass."

I was doing my best to keep things light-hearted down here in the dark and dank Underground on our way to meet an assassin.

We continued through the mines. I stopped at junctions, checking the signposts, keeping my bearings.

We kept it quiet, listening to dripping water plunk in puddles and for any sound that might give away the presence of unwelcome company.

"Well, this is it." We had entered the old, dilapidated mechanical room I had predicted.

Our flashlight beams scanned the area, two levels high and ten yards square.

Between and around four decrepit, massive pumps that occupied the center of the room, each as large as a car, rusted pipes, and other miscellaneous debris littered the floor.

"Now what? I can't believe this is the meeting spot," Jane said.

I pulled the note out of my pocket and illuminated it with my flashlight. Jane came to my side and looked over my shoulder.

"According to the map, there should be a room opposite that wall." I flipped my light beam in that direction.

"There must be a secret passageway into that room." Jane's light danced on the far wall.

We headed over there, carefully stepping over twisted iron and rotted lumber. Half of the wall was rock; the other half was vertical wooden boards. I moved to the right to inspect the wooden section. The lumber appeared to be a more recent addition.

After a few moments of searching the wall with my light, "There's no doorway, secret or otherwise, that leads to the other side of this wall."

"Why wouldn't they provide a clue as to how to get in? Do we just wait here until someone shows up?"

Checking my pocket watch, we were right on time.

"It wouldn't be smart to put something like that in writing. Besides, they probably figured it shouldn't be a problem since I'm a detective."

"Well, Detective, get a move on. This place gives me the creeps."

With that encouragement from Jane, my next move was to investigate the wall off to our right. It was covered with rusted electrical panels and massive switches.

Jane followed close behind as I made my way in that direction.

The panels were connected to large diameter conduits running down from the ceiling that at one time brought power from the generators above.

I noticed a smaller conduit that looked out of place running down the left-hand corner. It appeared rusted up like the other conduits, but on closer examination, it was painted to look that way. The pipe continued from the wall along the floor. The conduit ended at a pile of old lumber on the other side of a pump. Two narrow boards lay on top, crossed like an X. The beam of my light reflected the shine of nail heads, new nail heads.

I pulled up on one of the boards with one hand. It didn't budge.

"Here, hold this." I handed my flashlight to Jane.

She trained both beams on the pile. I put my hands on both ends of the boards. The wooden pile rose up together on a hinge, a trapdoor.

"Very clever," Jane said.

She passed my light back, and we both peered into the hole, where a ladder led down about six feet to a tunnel floor.

"Here goes." I took the lead down the ladder. Jane came after me. We ended up in a very small tunnel. Not a great place to be if you're claustrophobic. I'm not, mostly.

"What's this?" Jane's light was trained on a six-inch diameter pipe extending from the tunnel's ceiling. It contained another square-looking pipe.

After a quick inspection, "It's a periscope. To check out the room above before you open the trap door."

"Grace is inventive."

"That was more likely Maxine's handiwork. Something she would have dreamed up."

We turned away from the ladder and shown our lights into the tunnel to where it ended at a small wooden door, not 20 feet away. We had to stoop over to travel the distance in the squat tunnel.

I rapped the end of my flashlight on the door. Best to announce ourselves, considering Grace's potential response.

As I moved through the doorway, I raised a hand to cover my eyes from the light. Jane's hand was on my shoulder. The room was actually dimly lit but a dramatic contrast to the mines.

Once my eyes adjusted, I was able to take in the surroundings. It was as if we had stepped out of the mines and into a fancy hotel lobby. Electric wall sconce lights illuminated the wooden wall paneling, a wood floor, and a plastered ceiling. A long table flanked by red cushioned chairs occupied the center of the room.

At the far side of the room, Grace Snowdon, big as life, sat behind an enormous mahogany desk, identical to the one in Max's office at Lizzy's. A bookshelf filled the wall behind her, again, like Max's office. Familiar steno paper and yellow envelopes were stacked in neat piles on the desktop.

Francine was there too, standing off to Grace's right.

"Right on time, Danny O'Shea, the only honest copper in King City." Hearing Grace say my name sent a chill up my spine.

"I told you he'd show. You owe me ten." Francine was smiling at Grace. Grace wasn't smiling; she must have just lost a bet. She rocked back in her chair.

"Good to see you, Grace." I didn't mean it. "I thought you might have been dead until I started getting those notes."

"The rumor of my demise was greatly exaggerated, but it was a useful rumor." Turning her attention to Jane, "I'm glad you chose to join us, Miss Dickerson."

"Yes, hello." Jane sounded uncommonly awkward.

"Francine, good to see you as well." I meant it this time.

"Bonjour mon ami," Francine replied. "Miss Dickerson, good to see you again. I haven't had the opportunity to thank you for that kind newspaper article you wrote about my acting career."

"My pleasure. Good to see you again." Jane probably meant that, too.

Grace abruptly stood up, quitting the formalities. She came around to the front of the desk and leaned her backside against the edge of the desktop. She nodded to Francine, who strode over to a door on the right side of the room. Francine touched the door with a light rap of the knuckles and stepped back.

Moments later, the door opened. A woman dressed in a black satin robe eased her way forward with halting steps. The robe hung open, exposing her right arm hanging in a sling. A black silk scarf wrapped around her head, all but covering a white bandage. The black attire contrasted with her pale, sunken face.

A few slow paces put her right in front of Jane. I wasn't sure if I could believe my eyes. She reached out and took up Jane's hand.

"You must be J. L Gibson. I have to say that I've thoroughly enjoyed every article you've written." She kept a grip on Jane's hand.

"Thank you," Jane said, as her eyes darted to me.

I cleared my throat. "Jane, meet Maxine Snowdon."

My brain went into overdrive, recalculating my theories and options.

"You look like you've seen a ghost, Danny." Max released Jane's hand and reached for mine.

"I wasn't expecting to see you again." I took up the offered hand. "You're a little worse for wear, Max."

"A hazard in my line of work, but I'm recovering."

Max smiled but choked on it.

"Let's all have a seat, shall we?" Maxine motioned to the long table. "We have a lot to discuss."

Francine pulled out a chair for Max at the head of the table. As the ghost settled into her seat, she winced in pain. Her wounds must have been severe. She didn't look good; she looked like death eating a soda cracker.

The rest of us settled in around the table, me and Jane on one side, Grace and Francine opposite us.

"Let me get right to the point. The favor you owe me, it's come due." Max was staring at me with sunken eyes. "Are you ready to deliver the goods? I'm expecting your cooperation."

"I'm a man of my word." Saying yes to a yet unknown favor is probably a bad idea in general, but it's seemed like the best move under the circumstances.

Max, speaking to Grace. "I told you we could count on our detective."

Grace just shrugged.

Max turned to Jane, "Miss Dickerson, I am also expecting cooperation from you."

"Well, that depends." Jane's frame straightened up to match the chair back. "What does this cooperation involve, exactly?"

Francine stiffened. One corner of Grace's mouth turned up. Maxine started to laugh, but broke into a coughing fit again. Francine started to rise, but Max held up a hand. We waited in silence until Max recovered.

"There is no *exactly* in my line of work, dear, or in life, for that matter. But what I'm asking for will be in the best interest of King City. You wouldn't want the city to slip further into violent chaos, would you?"

Her line of reasoning was sounding familiar.

"Of course not."

"And God forbid a gang war should break out. We want to avoid that and put King City back to rights. Merchants should be protected, and people should be able to go about their lives without fear of outbursts of random violence. Surely you agree?"

"Yes."

"Besides, my dear, we have been looking out for you, trying to keep you safe. And we will, by all means, continue to do so." Max's eyes darted to Grace and back. So did Jane's. "There's that to be considered."

I didn't like where this line of conversation was going, so I butted in. "I'm sure you could just give us a better idea of what you want from us?"

"What I'm proposing is the formation of a mutually beneficial alliance."

"That certainly sounds reasonable," I said, "But still a little light on the details."

"Let me lay it out for you then, what I expect from the two of you." Max adjusted her position with a grimace.

"I'm tired of living underground like a mole. I'm ready to make a move; take back what's mine. But I can't resurface just yet. It still plays to my advantage for people to think I'm dead.

"Since it can't get out that I'm alive, I will have agents carrying out my plans. And I'm also going to need friends on the surface acting in my best interest." Max eyeballed both of us. "For now, that means don't interfere or bring any unwanted attention to any of my operations."

The 'for now' did not escape my attention.

"Miss Dickerson, I want you to keep those activities and my state of health out of the papers.

"And Danny, I don't want any unnecessary police investigations into my bootlegging enterprise. Naturally, you're free to peruse lines of inquiry into the Barron's shenanigans. We'll be able to provide information you can use in that regard." Turning to Jane, "And you, my dear, can count on receiving tips regarding the Barron's illicit activities that are sure to result in some high-profile news stories."

"That does sound mutually beneficial." I exchanged glances with Jane.

Max must have picked up on the unease in my tone of voice.

"Don't worry, Detective; our relationship won't change anything; you'll still be the 'only honest copper in King City.'"

I nodded.

"And, of course, I would like assurance that both of you are on my side and haven't decided to join up with the Mayor."

"You might want to think twice before you throw in with his lot." Grace's tone was stone cold.

I was thinking twice, minutes ago, that my options were between the Barron and Grace, and now that they were between the Barron and Max. Dealing with Maxine was a lot more appealing than dealing with Grace, but still, we were caught in the middle.

"It's doubtful that Danny is even considering that offer, Grace." Max threw a subtle smile my way.

Max was probably aware of our meeting with the Barron. The staff he brought on board from King City that worked his parties probably had a few of Max's spies in the mix.

I decided to put in my two cents. "The Barron is going to be a real problem. He's got more than a foothold in King City already. The businessmen are in his camp, tied up with his lucrative legit deals. And the union is getting their cut of the bootlegging profits on booze coming through the port." The practicalities churning in my mind were flowing out of my mouth.

"I am aware. He followed the same playbook in Brewster and Seabrook." Max knew what I knew.

"From what I understand, He's got complete control of all the rackets in both cities. He installed a crime boss in each who reports to him. He can bring his resources from those cities to use against you." I was hoping to provide some useful dirt on the Barron and make some points.

"True. But I hope to undermine his grip up there. Some of the people under his thumb are unhappy with the current arrangement. He started out giving them a big cut. Lately, he's throttled back, leaving some disgruntled employees and politicians.

"His move into King City is spreading his resources thin. He doesn't have enough jack to grease the wheels properly here. He can't bribe all the necessary politicians or pay off enough of the coppers."

I knew that the more Max told me, the more information she provided, the more of my questions she answered, the deeper Jane and I would be drawn into her schemes. But I just couldn't help myself.

Max went on to describe her situation. Her cash reserves were running low. Francine's network of spies was only getting half their usual monthly stipend, loyal for now, but that might not last. And she needed payola for political bribes and to get the rank-and-file coppers back on her payroll.

To get the cash flowing again, her first step was to get back into bootlegging and reestablishing her connection with Cloe in Nassau. Apparently, her codebook had not fallen into nefarious hands. Grace had snatched it from the safe behind the bookshelves before she and Max made their escape from Lizzy's.

Obviously, Maxine wanted to put herself back on the throne and keep the Barron off it.

Maxine had disclosed a lot of sensitive information. She must have been desperate, assuming we were already on board and wouldn't spill the beans. In the event we did cross Max, there was Grace to deal with.

Max laid her palms on the table edge. "That's it in a nutshell, my plans and what I want from you. But of course, it's your decision." Max looked exhausted and frail, not the formidable crime boss she'd been three months ago.

Francine jumped up and helped Maxine from her chair. Taking Maxine's good arm, Francine escorted her back to her room.

Grace stood up. "Think hard, Detective."

We took that as our cue to leave.

After a long, silent walk through dark tunnels, we emerged from the Underground. I took a different route than the one we followed from the Lazarus building, just to be safe. We came out from the outside cellar entrance at Griffith's Radio Emporium in Welsh Town.

I raised my hand to cover my eyes to get a look around. The sun was shining, a rare event in Carvonshire. I slipped my watch out of my pocket, eleven-fifteen.

"How about I take you to lunch at my favorite cafe, Kelly's?"

"Aren't you worried about us being seen together in public?"

"We're living on the edge now, doll, no point holding back."

"You think we haven't been living on the edge so far, fella?" It was good to see Jane smile.

"A sharper edge."

"Sure then, let's go."

"It's over on Church Street, a ways. Do you mind if we walk? I could show you some of the sites on the way."

"I've already seen some memorable sites in Carvonshire."

"I'm talking above ground, not on a roof, during the daylight."

"Okay, then."

Jane slipped her arm around mine at my elbow. We set off on Oak Street, turning left at the corner onto Broad, heading south toward downtown Carvonshire.

The shops, storefronts, and department stores were shuttered on Sunday, courtesy of the blue laws installed by our religious-minded citizens. The legit businesses were required to observe a day of rest, the Sabbath, whereas speakeasies, clip joints, gambling dens, and creep joints were all open for business, having somehow received a dispensation.

I generally ain't a fan of religious rules and regs, but at least it gives some of the overworked common folk a day off.

Four blocks on, and we were approaching the station house. Dulley and a couple of patrolmen were standing on the steps having a smoke, shooting the breeze.

Coppers don't qualify for a Sunday off work. Actually, a Sunday shift was like a day off; not much action on the holy day. Robberies, assaults, and murders were far and few between. It seemed that the gangsters and thugs had a certain respect for the Lord's Day as well.

Dulley, a cigarette drooping from his lips, caught my eye.

"The top of the day to you, Dulley," I called out as we passed by.

"The rest of the day to yourself," he answered, the cig twitching with his words. His eyes were riveted on Jane.

"Officer," she said.

"Ma'am." Dulley touched his cap.

As we walked past them to the end of the block and around the corner onto Walnut Street, I could feel those boy's eyes on our backs.

We strolled on another block and came up on Oswald's newsstand. Two boys, Donny and Ralph, were manning the booth. Donny was on the sidewalk, waving the Sunday edition in the air, calling out to the folks passing by. Ralph, in the booth, was taking the money and making change.

When they spotted us, they both called out, "Morning, Danny." Their hands waving.

"Morning, boys." I returned the salute.

"Let's stop in here." I motioned to the storefront across the sidewalk from the newsstand. A dingy yellow sign with the word "Candy" in bold green letters hung over the doorway. The door was centered between two large display windows that displayed nothing. A closed-on Sunday sign was affixed to the door. I ignored it and pulled the screen door open for Jane to enter.

"Good morning, Mavis," I said to the heavyset woman behind the counter.

"I'll be dammed if it ain't Danny O'Shea. Don't usually see you out on Sunday."

"Just trying to shake things up a bit."

"Sure as hell you are." She was looking Jane up and down.

"Jane, this is Mavis," I said, "Mavis, this is Jane."

"Morning, Jane," The old woman said with a wink.

"It's a pleasure to meet you, Mavis."

"You come in to jaw, or can I get you somethin." Mavis snatched up a cig from an ashtray and took a drag.

"Give me a pack of Sen-Sens and fill a big bag."

Mavis plucked the Sen-Sens from a shelf behind her and laid them on the counter in front of me. With a flip of her wrist, she popped open a paper sack and moved along the counter, picking out penny candies, peppermints, dumdums, gumballs, sugar-daddies, and the like.

"Thanks, Mavis." I laid a greenback on the counter.

"You take it easy, Danny," Mavis replied, "You too, Jane."

"Goodbye, Mavis. Jane hadn't lost her smile since we emerged from the Underground.

With one hand, I pushed the screen door open to let Jane slip through.

"I didn't know you had such a sweet tooth." Jane nodded at the bag in my hand.

"I don't." I offered the bag to her. "Would you like some?"

"No thanks, a girl has to watch her figure."

"No need for that; you got lots of fellas doing that for you."

I think I caught a glimpse of a blush.

"What the heck." She fished around in the candy and extracted a peppermint.

Out on the sidewalk, I stepped over to Donny and handed him the bag. "Make sure these get passed around."

"Sure thing, Danny." He was eyeballing the contents.

"Mavis seems a little rough around the edges for someone selling candy to children," Jane said.

"Kids love going in there to pick up new cuss words."

Mavis had taken over the newsstand business a few years back after old man Oswald died of cancer. Mavis had a better rapport with the boys than he did. When she said jump, they asked how high.

We walked ahead to the corner, rounded the block back onto Broad Street, and continued south to the corner of Broad and Market. We paused.

"St. Mary's." I pointed. You could see the steeple and front facade of the church two blocks away on Church Street.

"We should go visit Father Pat sometime. He did invite me," Jane said.

"We should."

"We could go to Mass?"

"Maybe."

"It couldn't hurt." A flash of concern canceled Jane's smile for a moment.

I was feeling the same.

"True. It would put a smile on Father Pat's face to see the both of us sitting in a pew some Sunday morning." I glanced back from the church to Jane. "You're a Presbyterian, right?"

"Yes, but not a regular."

"We could go to one of those services too, you know, cover all the bases."

"That couldn't hurt either."

I turned Jane away from the view of St. Mary's. We strolled on along Market Street, taking in the Sunday afternoon atmosphere of Carvonshire's downtown.

Twenty minutes later, we were standing in front of Kelly's. Through the picture window, emblazoned with the words Kelly's Cafe in large black letters in an arc, I could see that it was pretty full, packed with folks that had come in after mass.

We waltzed on in. Jen was on duty, sitting on a corner stool, smoking, and reading the paper.

I cleared my throat. Jen looked up, glanced at me, and then her eyes went back to her paper. A moment later, her eyes popped back up with the look of a scared rabbit.

She practically jumped off her stool, started toward us, hesitated, and returned to the counter to put out her cig. She turned and hustled up to us so fast my hand reflexively went for my piece.

"Detective O'Shea, we don't usually see you in here on a Sunday. It's good to see you." Jen's hands were repeatedly stroking her apron, smoothing it out.

"Good to see you, Jen." I was pretty sure it was Jen. Maybe she had a twin, not the evil one.

"Do you want your usual table?" She was looking at the small table at the back wall near the kitchen door. "I can ask that couple to move."

"No, that's alright. We'd like something near the window."

"Of course. Just give me a minute to clear one off for you." Jen took off for a table right in front of the picture window. It was cluttered with dirty dishes. She was moving so fast to clear it that I thought I heard her joints creaking.

In a flash, she was motioning us over. I reached for the chair back to seat Jane.

Jane looked at Jen. "I need to powder my nose?"

"Right over there, hon." Jen, beaming, pointed to the ladies' room at the back.

I took a seat.

A few minutes later, Jane emerged and strode in my direction but was intercepted by Jen, who had just landed a creamer and sugar bowl on another table.

The two ladies entered into a confab, smiles, a grimace, looks my way, more smiling.

I twiddled my thumbs, waiting for quite a while.

Other patrons were calling for the old waitress, but she ignored them.

Back at our table, Jane took up the chair opposite me.

"I've never seen the old broad so cheerful or talkative. It's unnerving. I've never heard her issue a complete sentence."

"I guess I just have a way with people." Jane smoothed her napkin across her lap.

"What could you two have been talking about for so long? I asked.

"Just two ladies trading stories."

"Not about me, I hope?"

"In a way, yes. She told me that you reminded her of her late husband. Apparently, there is a striking resemblance."

"She's given me nothing but grief from the get-go. She must have really hated the fella."

"Yes and no."

"So, there's more to the story, spill it."

"In the beginning, their marriage was wonderful, full of joy. She said that when you and I walked in, arm-in-arm, it brought back the memories of the early days when she and her husband would go out together on dates around town."

"So, what went wrong?"

"A bad business decision, bankruptcy. He started hitting the bottle and eventually her as well."

"I'm getting the picture." And not a good picture. I was feeling a bit of sympathy; it explained why Jen was such a miserable piece of furniture.

Sean had shared some of Jen's history. He went way back with Kelly and his family. I believe he said that Jen's husband had died under suspicious circumstances; food poisoning was considered but never proven.

Just then, Jen was back in attendance. She took our order and hustled to deliver our coffee. I'm sure my mouth was hanging open.

With the coffee in place, Jen departed. Jane settled in, blowing on the steaming hot cup. "I have some questions, Danny."

"Go ahead, ask away."

"Maxine Snowdon was dead and buried. I don't understand how she could be alive."

"I got a theory about that." It was all coming clear in my mind. "The body at Lizzy's that was taken for Maxine was actually one of the patrons that evening. The shots in the face were, after the fact, to disguise the corpse. Three couples came in early that night, but only the bodies of two women were found. I was sure that Grace was also there in the office that night, and clearly, her body wasn't found either."

"Wait, how do you know so much about who was at Lizzy's that night?"

"Because I was there."

"You were at Lizzy's the night of the shooting?"

"Yeah, they had a great band there that night."

"And a massacre; how did you escape, and why is this the first I'm hearing of it?"

I figured I was in trouble with Jane, so I spilled the story, my night at Lizzy's, escaping with the band into the Underground. I described how I later found the secret passage in Max's office. At one point, I had assumed the blood trail in the passage might have come from Grace, but now I knew it was from Max.

"Jeez, partner, you've been holding out me." Jane was making a pout face.

"Over the past three months, I've been entertaining various theories on who organized the hit to kill Max. But up until this morning, I thought Max was dead, which took me down some blind alleys. With her alive, that changes everything; the pieces fit. Things make a lot more sense now."

"So, what's your current theory on what happened that night at Lizzy's?"

I started to speak but was interrupted by Jen, who hustled up to our table and laid down two plates in front of us, the special of the day, meatloaf, mashed potatoes with gravy, and green beans. Jane and I both offered a thank you.

"You got it, Danny. Can I get you anything else? Top off your coffee?"

"No thanks, we're good."

"If you need anything, just give the sign." Jen winked.

"Right."

After Jen had sauntered back to her perch at the counter, I started up again. "I figure that when the shooting erupted, Max was wounded by bullets coming through her office walls. Somehow, Grace managed to get herself and Max into the secret passageway behind the bookshelves. She must have waited it out while the thugs were ransacking the office. After the thugs left, Grace had time before the coppers arrived to stage the killing of Max by disguising the body of a deceased patron to look like Max. And then the pair of them managed to hobble their way down the stairwell and to a secret Underground entrance in the basement."

"That makes sense; it would be best for Maxine if she were thought to be dead and gone.

"But wouldn't the cops on the scene have figured out the body wasn't her?

"Foley was the copper in charge, a pretty dim bulb. Likely, all he was thinking about was the demise of his weekly payola rather than the demise of Maxine Snowdon. Besides, Maxine was a recluse, rarely appearing in public, not a recognizable character."

Maxine stayed in the shadows tending her criminal empire and reading her books.

"But the coroner surely would have known it wasn't her."

"I suspect that Doc Thomas was in on it; he faked the death certificate. He's likely been on Max's payroll for a long time anyway. He smokes some very expensive cigars. And I bet he's the one that tended to Max's wounds and has been doctoring her back to health."

"So, Grace and Maxine have been hiding in the Underground all this time."

"My theory that Grace might have killed Max in order to take over her organization was obviously wrong. Loyalty was apparently one of Grace's more endearing qualities." Probably the only one.

"All this time, it was Grace who was sending notes to you with the tips that helped point you in the right direction, except, of course, for Maxine's murder investigation."

"I think Max was the mastermind behind the notes."

"But why would a wounded gangster spend her time and effort helping us? It doesn't make sense."

"It makes sense to her. She apparently thinks that you and I are essential to her return to power."

"You think we are essential?"

"You are now an important and influential newspaper reporter who owes a debt to Max, a life debt."

"And you?"

"A well-placed copper in the Carvonshire precinct, who also owes a life debt to Max."

"Someone who pays his debts, who would never double-cross, the only honest cop in King City, Danny O'Shea." Jane had a fork in her hand that hadn't touched the food.

"Something like that."

"Maxine expects payback?"

"For sure."

"So, we were being set up so we would play a role in her plans to retake the rackets in Carvonshire?"

"Looks that way."

We fell silent, both spending the time pushing bits of meatloaf and beans around our plates. One of my grandmother's scoldings popped into my mind, 'Children in China are starving; clean your plate.' My stomach was suddenly occupied with feelings other than hunger. I just couldn't get myself to follow Grandma's edict.

As I pushed back from the table, I looked up from my plate and caught Jane's eye. "Let's get out of here and go for a walk."

"Sounds good." Jane was on her feet.

I tucked a fiver under my saucer.

From Kelly's, we headed north, up Canal Street. At the corner of Walnut Street, between two buildings, we could see the roof of my apartment building across the canal in Henshaw. We paused for a moment to recall Jane's visit and our meeting with Big Anthony.

Continuing in quiet, we wound our way through Carvonshire to the Broad Street bridge. From its height, looking back south into Carvonshire, we could see the facade of the station house where Jane and I first met. We talked and laughed about that encounter for a bit before crossing the bridge into the King District.

In no real hurry, we wandered along; Jane pointed out the sites and places she was familiar with, including Bentley's.

In time, we were at the entrance to the Bay-Port Park. I looked north to the old warehouse distinct, the location of the mysterious killing of Carlo Minx.

We made our way through the park, taking up a place on our bench by the trees overlooking the old wharf.

Yachts were motoring out along the jetty to the harbor mouth, unfurling their sales and catching the full force of the Bay's winds.

After a bit of time, we entered into the conversation we had been trying to avoid most of the day.

I pulled my pocket watch out; four-thirty, Sunday afternoon, was all but gone. "Looks like it's time to pick sides."

"Isn't there any other alternative than to choose between two gangsters?"

"Not unless you got some major connections and can get prohibition repealed."

Jane's shoulders slumped ever so slightly.

"The Barron has the cash flow on his side. Max is running out of money. Her bringing us into it is a desperate move." I glanced at Jane, who was poker still. "He's likely got most of the King City Police's upper brass on his payroll by now. And surely the King City businessmen won't want to interfere with his operations."

"This can't be just about calculus?"

"Just trying to be pragmatic."

"You owe Snowdon a favor. And I do, as well."

"There is that to consider."

"If we went with the Barron, I doubt you'd be able to keep your reputation intact as the only honest cop in King City."

"That's likely."

"Can we at least agree then that we're going to decline the Barron's offer?"

"I think that was a given from the get-go." Practicality aside, I just didn't like the clown. "There's no way we could throw in with the likes of him."

"I'm glad we're of the same mind," Jane said, "You had me worried for a moment."

We sat watching the sailboats slicing across the Bay for a while.

"Maxine and Grace Snowdon aren't a great option either," Jane added.

"Between a rock and a hard place, my Pa used to say."

"Better the devil you know, I've heard said." Jane caught my eye. "We don't actually have to join up with Snowdon's gang."

"For sure, we can play it by ear. Do our best to interfere with the Barron's agenda, but not take any orders for Max either."

We lapsed into our own thoughts.

"I guess it's time to send a message to the Barron declining his offer then?" Jane said.

"Yeah. I could arrange to have Francine deliver a note to Alina."

"I have another idea. I could write an article for the social pages about the party we attended on the Barron's yacht and include some subtle hints that the Barron might not be what he claims to be, that people who deal with him might be getting their hands dirty."

"Nothing concrete, just innuendo?"

"Right, gossip and rumor, that sort of thing."

"Bold." I stifled a chuckle. "That would tick him off." I was picturing the Barron's reaction as he read his morning paper, and I was enjoying it a lot.

"Glad you like it." Jane was beaming.

I stood up and took Jane's hands, pulling her up from the bench. "It's getting close to supper time." My appetite was back. "How about we go to Bentley's, with me as me, that is, not your cousin Danny Witherspoon. You can buy me one of those fabulous steaks."

"Sure thing."

We stood facing each other, still holding hands.

Jane spoke up. "What have we got ourselves into?"

"Whoever we'd picked, there was going to be a target on our backs," I squeezed her hands.

"You're sure about this?" Jane squeezed my hands back. "We're going to be okay?"

"Can't say. There's no guarantees in life."

"There is always Paris," Jane said.

"There's always Paris."

The End

GLOSSARY (*)

Bop - a hit (killing)

Bushwa - nonsense

Button man - hitman

Can opener - safe cracker

Chicago overcoats – coffins

Chopper squad: Men with machine guns

Clip joint - a high-priced nightclub where patrons are fleeced

Creep joint – a brothel

Dead Hoofer - a terrible dancer, someone with two left feet.

Dip - pickpocket

Drum - speakeasy

Dumb Dora - dumb woman

Gams - woman's legs

Glad rags - out-on-the-town clothes

Go iron their shoe laces - go to the restroom

Gumshoe - detective

Jack - money

Jake - great

Knee duster – skirt

Meat wagon - ambulance

Moll - girlfriend

Ofay - white person

Panther Piss - homemade whiskey

Peaching - snitching

Pen - penitentiary

Shylock - loan shark

Snooper – detective

Speakeasy - an illicit establishment that sells alcoholic beverages

Stilts - woman's legs

Squeeze - a female companion or girlfriend.

Ten-cent box - taxi cab

Tin Lizzy – Model T Ford

Tommy - machine gun

Torpedo – hitman

у меня будет ДРУГОЙ – I'll have another

ABOUT THE AUTHOR

Raymond G Dennis is a grandfather, writing stories for his grandchildren, great-grandchildren, and, if things go according to plan, maybe even great-great-grandchildren. His interest in genealogy led to research of family historical records, which provided basic data (dates of birth, marriage, death, etc.) about his ancestors but lacked the most hoped-for and interesting information - what those distant relatives thought, what interested them, what they believed, and what they valued.

So, to that end, hoping someday to be a subject of ancestral research by future relatives, Raymond has incorporated in his fantasy stories moral dilemmas, parables, and thoughts on the sciences of most interest - psychology, sociology, and neuroscience.